"Come here." Giancarlo's voice was a rasp, thick and hot, and it moved through her like joy.

Paige obeyed him, and this time she was happy to do it. She walked toward him, reveling in the way her blood pounded through her and her skin seemed to shrink a size, too tight across her bones. Because he could call this revenge. He could talk about hatred and penance. But it was still the same thick madness that felt like a rope around her neck. It was still the same inexorable pull.

It was still *them*.

He took her mouth like he was already deep inside her. Like he was thrusting hard and driving them both toward that glimmering edge. It was more than wild, more than carnal. He bent her back over her own arms, pressing her breasts into the flat planes of his chest, and he simply possessed her with a ruthless sort of fury that set every part of her aflame.

She thrilled to his boldness, his shocking mastery. The glorious taste of him she'd pined for all these years. The sheer *rightness*.

Paige kissed him back desperately, deeply, forgetting about the games they played. Forgetting about penance, about trust. Forgetting her betrayal and his fury. She didn't care what he wanted from her, or how he plan but this.

This.

USA TODAY bestselling author and RITA®-Award-nominated **Caitlin Crews** loves writing romance. She teaches her favourite romance novels in creative writing classes at places like UCLA Extension's prestigious Writers' Programme, where she can finally utilise the MA and PhD in English Literature she received from the University of York in England. She currently lives in California, with her very own hero and too many pets. Visit her at www.caitlincrews.com

Books by Caitlin Crews

Vows of Convenience

His for Revenge
His for a Price

Royal and Ruthless

A Royal Without Rules

Scandal in the Spotlight

No More Sweet Surrender
Heiress Behind the Headlines

Self-Made Millionaires

Katrakis's Last Mistress

Bride on Approval

Pure Princess, Bartered Bride

Undone by the Sultan's Touch
Not Just the Boss's Plaything
A Devil in Disguise
In Defiance of Duty
The Replacement Wife
Princess from the Past
Majesty, Mistress...Missing Heir

**Visit the author profile page at
www.millsandboon.co.uk for more titles**

AT THE COUNT'S BIDDING

BY
CAITLIN CREWS

MILLS & BOON

Published in Great Britain 2015
by Mills & Boon, an imprint of Harlequin (UK) Limited,
Eton House, 18-24 Paradise Road, Richmond, Surrey, TW9 1SR

© 2015 Caitlin Crews

ISBN: 978-0-263-25053-4

Printed and bound in Spain
by CPI, Barcelona

AT THE
COUNT'S BIDDING

CHAPTER ONE

"I MUST BE hallucinating. And may God have mercy on you if I am not."

Paige Fielding hadn't heard that voice in ten years. It wrapped around her even as it sliced through her, making the breezy Southern California afternoon fade away. Making the email she'd been writing disappear from her mind in full. Making her forget what year it was, what day it was. Rocketing her right back into the murky, painful past.

That voice. *His voice.*

Uncompromisingly male. As imperious as it was incredulous. The faint hint of sex and Italy in his voice even with all that temper besides, and it rolled over Paige like a flattening heat. It pressed into her from behind, making her want to squirm in her seat. Or simply melt where she sat. Or come apart—easily and instantly—the way she always had at the sound of it.

She swiveled around in her chair in instant, unconscious obedience, knowing exactly who she'd see in the archway that led into the sprawling Bel Air mansion high in the Hollywood Hills called La Bellissima in honor of its famous owner, the screen legend Violet Sutherlin. She knew who it was, and still, something like a premonition washed over her and made her skin prickle in the scant seconds before her gaze found him there in the arched, open door, scowling at her with what looked like a healthy mix of contempt and pure, electric hatred.

Giancarlo Alessi. The only man she'd ever loved with every inch of her doomed and naive heart, however little good that had done either one of them. The only man who'd made her scream and sob and beg for more, until she was hoarse and mute with longing. The only man who still haunted her, and who she suspected always would, despite everything.

Because he was also the only man she'd ever betrayed. Thoroughly. Indisputably. Her stomach twisted hard, reminding her of what she'd done with a sick lurch. As if she'd forgotten. As if she ever could.

She hadn't thought she'd had a choice. But she doubted he'd appreciate that any more now than he had then.

"I can explain," she said. Too quickly, too nervously. She didn't remember pushing back from the table where she'd been sitting, doing her work out in the pretty sunshine as was her custom during the lazy afternoons, but she was standing then, somehow, feeling as unsteady on her own legs as she had in the chair. As lost in his dark, furious gaze as she'd been ten years ago.

"You can explain to security," he grated at her, each word a crisp slap. She felt red and obvious. Marked. As if he could see straight through her to that squalid past of hers that had ruined them both. "I don't care what you're doing here, Nicola. I want you gone."

She winced at that name. That hated name she hadn't used since the day she'd lost him. Hearing it again, after all this time and in that voice of his was physically upsetting. Deeply repellant. Her stomach twisted again, harder, and then knotted.

"I don't—" Paige didn't know what to say, how to say

it. How to explain what had happened since that awful day ten years ago when she'd sold him out and destroyed them both. What was there to say? She'd never told him the whole truth, when she could have. She'd never been able to bear the thought of him knowing how polluted she was or the kind of place, the kind of people, she'd come from. And they'd fallen in love so fast, their physical connection a white-hot explosion that had consumed them for those two short months they'd been together—there hadn't seemed to be any time to get to know each other. Not really. "I don't go by Nicola anymore."

He froze solid in the doorway, a kind of furious astonishment rolling over him and then out from him like a thunderclap, deafening and wild, echoing inside of her like a shout.

It hurt. It all hurt.

"I never—" This was terrible. Worse than she'd imagined, and she'd imagined it often. She felt an awful heat at the back of her eyes and a warning sort of ache between her breasts, as if a sob was gathering force and threatening to spill over, and she knew better than to let it out. She knew he wouldn't react well. She was lucky he was speaking to her at all now instead of having Violet's security guards toss her bodily from the estate without so much as a word. But she kept talking anyway, as if that might help. "It's my middle name, actually. It was a— my name is Paige."

"Curiously, Paige is also the name of my mother's personal assistant."

But she could tell by the way his voice grew ominously quiet that he knew. That he wasn't confused or asking her to explain herself. That he'd figured it out the moment he'd seen her—that she'd been the name on all those emails from his mother over the past few years.

And she could also tell exactly how he felt about that revelation. It was written into every stiffly furious line of his athletic form.

"Who cannot be you." He shifted and her breath caught, as if the movement of his perfect body was a blow. "Assure me, please, that you are no more than an unpleasant apparition from the darkest hour of my past. That you have not insinuated yourself into my family. Do it now and I might let you walk out of here without calling the police."

Ten years ago she'd have thought he was bluffing. *That* Giancarlo would no more have called the police on her than he would have thrown himself off the nearest bridge. But this was a different man. *This* was the Giancarlo she'd made, and she had no one to blame for that but herself.

Well. Almost no one. But there was no point bringing *her* mother into this, Paige knew. It was his he was concerned about—and besides, Paige hadn't spoken to her own in a decade.

"Yes," she said, and she felt shaky and vulnerable, as if it had only just occurred to her that her presence here was questionable, at best. "I've been working for Violet for almost three years now, but Giancarlo, you have to believe that I never—"

"Stai zitto."

And Paige didn't have to speak Italian to understand that harsh command, or the way he slashed his hand through the air, gruffly ordering her silence. She obeyed. What else could she do? And she watched him warily as if, at any moment, he might bare his fangs and sink them in her neck.

She'd deserve that, too.

Paige had always known this day would come. That this quiet new life she'd crafted for herself almost by ac-

CAITLIN CREWS11

cident was built on the shakiest of foundations and that all
it would take was this man's reappearance to upend the
whole of it. Giancarlo was Violet's son, her only child.
The product of her fabled second marriage to an Italian
count that the entire world had viewed as its own, personal, real-life fairy tale. Had Paige imagined this would
end in any other manner? She'd been living on borrowed
time from the moment she'd taken that interview and answered all the questions Violet's managers had asked in
the way she'd known—thanks to her insider's take on
Violet's actual life away from the cameras, courtesy of
her brief, brilliant affair with Giancarlo all those years
ago—would get her the job.

Some people might view that harshly, she was aware.
Particularly Giancarlo himself. But she'd had good intentions. Surely that counted for something? *You know
perfectly well that it doesn't,* the harsh voice in her head
that was her last link to her mother grated at her. *You
know exactly what intentions are worth.*

And it had been so long. She'd started to believe that
this might never happen. That Giancarlo might stay in
Europe forever, hidden away in the hills of Tuscany building his überprivate luxury hotel and associated cottages
the way he had for the past decade, ever since she'd set
him up and those sordid, intimate photographs had been
splashed across every tabloid imaginable. She'd lulled
herself into a false sense of security.

Because he was here now, and nothing was safe any
longer, and yet all she wanted to do was lose herself in
looking at him. Reacquainting herself with him. Reminding herself what she'd given up. What she'd ruined.

She'd seen pictures of him all over this house in the
years she'd worked here. Always dark and forbiddingly
elegant in his particularly sleek way, it took no more

than a glance to understand Giancarlo was decidedly not
American. Even ten years ago and despite having spent so
much time in Los Angeles, he'd had that air. That *thing*
about him that whispered that he was the product of long
centuries of European blue bloods. It was something in
the way he held himself, distant and disapproving, the
hint of ancient places and old gods stamped into his aristocratic bones and lurking behind his cool dark gaze.

Paige had expected Giancarlo would still be attractive,
of course, should she ever encounter him again. What
she hadn't expected—or what she'd allowed herself to
forget—was that he was so *raw*. Seeing him was like a
hard, stunning blow to the side of her head, leaving her
ears ringing and her heart thumping erratically inside
her chest. As if he knew it, his head canted to one side
as he regarded her, as if daring her to keep talking when
he'd ordered her to stop.

But she couldn't seem to do anything but stare. As if
the past decade had been one long slide of gray and here
he was again, all of him in bold color and bright lights.
So glaring and hot she could hardly bear to look at him.
But she did. She couldn't help herself.

He stood as if he was used to accolades, or simply
commanding the full and rapt attention of every room
he entered. It was partly the clothes he wore, the fabrics
fitting him so perfectly, almost reverently, in a manner
Paige knew came only at astronomical expense. But it
was more than that. His body was lean and powerful,
a symphony of whipcord strength tightly leashed, the
crackle of his temper and that blazing sensuality that felt
like a touch from ten feet away, carnal and wild. Even
though she knew he'd never willingly touch her again.
He'd made that clear.

Giancarlo was still so beautiful, yes, but there was

something so *male* about him, so rampantly masculine, that it made Paige's throat go dry. It was worse now, ten years later. Much worse. He stood in the open doorway in a pair of dark trousers, boots, and the kind of jacket Paige associated with sexy Ducati motorcycles and mystical places a girl like her from a ramshackle desert town in Nowhere, Arizona, only fantasized about, like the Amalfi Coast. Yet somehow he looked as effortlessly refined as if he could walk straight into a black-tie gala as he was—or climb into a bed for a long, hot, blisteringly feral weekend of no-holds-barred sex.

But it did her no good to remember that kind of thing. For her body to ready itself for his possession as if it had been ten minutes since they'd last touched instead of ten years. As if it knew him, recognized him, wanted him—as deeply and irrevocably as she always had. As if *wanting him* was some kind of virus that had only ever been in remission, for which there was no cure.

The kind of virus that made her breasts heavy and her belly too taut and shivery at once. The kind of virus that made her wish she still danced the way she had in high school and those few years after, obsessively and constantly, as if that kind of extended, heedless movement might be the only way to survive it. *Him.* His marvelous mouth tightened as the silence dragged on and she sent up a prayer of thanks that he hadn't thought to remove his mirrored sunglasses yet. She didn't want to know what his dark gaze would feel like when she could actually see his eyes again. She didn't want to know what that would do to her now. She still remembered what it had been like that last time, that short and harsh conversation on the doorstep of her apartment building that final morning, where he'd confronted her with those pictures and had truly understood what she'd done to him. When he'd looked at her as if he'd only then, in that moment, seen her true face—and it had been evil.

Pull yourself together, she ordered herself fiercely. There was no going back. There were no do-overs. She knew that too well.

"I'm sorry," she managed to get out before he cut her off again. Before she melted into the tears she knew she'd cry later, in private. Before the loss and grief she'd pretended she was over for years now swamped her. "Giancarlo, I'm so sorry."

He went so rigid it was as if she'd slapped him, and yet she felt slapped. She hurt everywhere.

"I don't care why you're here." His voice was rough. A scrape that tore her open, ripping her right down her middle. "I don't care what game you're playing this time. You have five minutes to leave the premises."

But all Paige could hear was what swirled there beneath his words. Rage. Betrayal, as if it was new. Hot and furious, like a fire that still burned bright between them. And she was sick, she understood, because instead of being as frightened of that as she should have been, something in her rejoiced that he wasn't indifferent. After all this time.

"If you do not do this of your own accord," Giancarlo continued with a certain vicious deliberation, and she knew he *wanted* that to hurt her, "I will take great pleasure in dumping you on the other side of the gates myself."

"Giancarlo—" she began, trying to sound calm, though her hands nervously smoothed at the soft blouse and the pencil skirt she wore. And even though she couldn't see his eyes, she felt them there, tracing the curve of her hips and her legs beneath, as if she'd deliberately directed his gaze to parts of her body he'd once claimed he worshipped. Had she meant to do that? How could she not know?

But he interrupted her again.

"You may call me Count Alessi in the remaining four minutes before I kick you out of here," he told her harshly. "But if you know what's good for you, whatever name you're using and whatever con you're running today and have been running for years, I'd suggest you stay silent."

"I'm not running a con. I'm not—" Paige cut herself off, because this was all too complicated and she should have planned for this, shouldn't she? She should have figured out what to say to someone who had no reason on earth to listen to her. And who wouldn't believe a word she said even if he did. Why hadn't she prepared herself? "I know you don't want to hear a single thing I have to say, but none of this is what you think. It wasn't back then, either. Not really."

He seemed to *expand* then, like a great wave. As if the force of his temper soared out from him and crashed over the whole of the grand terrace, the sloping lawn, the canyons all around, the complicated mess of Los Angeles stretched out below. It crackled as it cascaded over her, making every hair on her body seem to stand on end. That mouth of his flattened and he swept his sunglasses from his face at last—which was not an improvement. Because his eyes were dark and hot and gleamed a commanding sort of gold, and as he fastened them on her he made no attempt at all to hide the blistering light of his fury.

It made her want to sit down, hard, before she fell. It made her worry her legs might give out. It made her want to cry the way she had ten years ago, so hard and so long she'd made herself sick, for all the good that had done. She felt dangerously, dizzyingly hollow.

"Enlighten me," he suggested, all silken threat and that humming sort of violence *right there* beneath his elegant surface. Or maybe not really *beneath* it, she thought, now that she could see his beautiful, terrible face in all its furious perfection. "Which part was not what I thought? The fact that you arranged to have photographs taken of us while we were having sex, though I am certain I told you how much I hated public exposure after a lifetime in the glare of my mother's spotlight? Or the fact that you sold those photos to the tabloids?" He took a step toward her; his hands were in fists at his side, and she didn't understand how she could simultaneously want to run for her life and run *toward* him. He was a suicide waiting to happen. She should know that better than anyone. "Or perhaps I am misunderstanding the fact that you have now infiltrated my mother's house to further prey on my family?" He shook his head. "What kind of monster *are* you?"

"Giancarlo—"

"I will tell you exactly what kind." His nostrils flared and she knew that look that flashed over his face then. She knew it far too well. It was stamped into her memories and it made her stomach heave with the same shame and regret. It made her flush with terrible heat. "You are a mercenary bitch and I believe I was perfectly clear about this ten years ago. I never, ever wanted to see your face again."

And Paige was running out of ways to rank which part of this was the worst part, but she couldn't argue. Not with any of what he'd said. Yet rather than making her shrink down and curl up into the fetal position right there on the terra-cotta pavers beneath their feet, the way she'd done the last time he'd looked at her like that and called her names she'd richly deserved, it made something else shiver into being inside her. Something that made her straighten instead of shrink. Something that gave her the strength to meet his terrible glare, to lift her chin despite all of that furious, condemning gold.

"I love her."

That hung there between them, stark and heavy. And, she realized belatedly, an echo of what she'd said ten years ago, when it had been much too late. When he'd believed her even less than he did now. When she'd known full well that saying it would only hurt him, and she'd done it anyway. *I'm so sorry, Giancarlo. I love you.*

"What did you say?" His voice was too quiet. So soft and deliberately menacing it made her shake inside, though she didn't give in to it. She forced her spine even straighter. "What did you *dare* say to me?"

"This has nothing to do with you." That was true, in its way. Paige wasn't a lunatic, no matter what he might think. She'd simply understood a long time ago that she'd lost him and it was irrevocable. She'd accepted it. This wasn't about getting him back. It was about paying a debt in the only way she could. "It never did have anything to do with you," she continued when she was certain the shaking inside her wouldn't bleed over into her voice. "Not the way you're thinking. Not really."

He shook his head slightly, as if he was reeling, and he muttered something in a stream of silken, shaken Italian that she shouldn't have felt like that, all over her skin. Because it wasn't a caress. It was its opposite.

"This is a nightmare." He returned his furious glare to her and it was harder. Fiercer. Gold fury and that darkness inside it. "But nightmares end. You keep on, all these years later. It was two short months and too many explicit pictures. I knew better than to trust a woman like you in the first place, but this ought to be behind me." His lips thinned. "Why won't you go away, Nicola?"

"Paige." She couldn't tolerate that name. Never again. It was the emblem of all the things she'd lost, all the terrible choices she'd been forced to make, all the sacrifices she'd made for someone so unworthy it made her mouth taste acrid now, like ash and regret. "I'd rather you call me nothing but *mercenary bitch* instead of that."

"I don't care what you call yourself." Not quite a shout. Not quite. But his voice thudded into her like a hail of bullets anyway, and she couldn't disguise the way she winced. "I want you gone. I want this poison of yours out of my life, away from my mother. It disgusts me that you've been here all this time without my knowing it. Like a malignant cancer hiding in plain sight."

And she should go. Paige knew she should. This was twisted and wrong and sick besides, no matter the purity of her intentions. All her rationalizations, all her excuses, what did any of them matter when she was standing here causing *more* pain to this man? He'd never deserved it. She really was a cancer, she thought. Her own mother had always thought so, too.

"I'm sorry," she said, yet again, and she heard the bleakness in her own voice that went far beyond an apology. And his dark, hot eyes were on hers. Demanding. Furious. Still broken, and she knew she'd done that. It stirred up sensations inside of her that felt too much like ghosts, an ache and a fire at once. But Paige held his gaze. "More than you'll ever know. But I can't leave Violet. I promised her."

Giancarlo's dark gaze blazed into a brilliant fury then, and it took every bit of backbone and bravado Paige had not to fall a step back when he advanced on her. Or to turn tail and start running the way she'd wanted to do since she'd heard his voice, down the expansive lawn, through the garden and out into the wild canyon below, as far as she could get from this man. She wanted to flee. She wanted to run and never stop running. The urge to do it beat in her blood.

But she hadn't done it ten years ago, when she should have, and from far scarier people than Giancarlo Alessi. She wouldn't do it now. No matter how hard her heart catapulted itself against her chest. No matter how great and painful the sobs she refused to let loose from inside.

"You seem to be under the impression I am playing a game with you," Giancarlo said softly, so very softly, the menace in it like his hand around her throat. What was the matter with her that the notion moved in her like a dark thrill instead of a threat? "I am not."

"I understand that this is difficult for you, and that it's unlikely you'll believe that was never my intention." Paige tried to sound conciliatory. She did. But she thought it came out sounding a whole lot more like panic, and panic was as useless as regret. She had no space for either. This was the life she'd made. This was what she'd sown. "But I'm afraid my loyalty is to your mother, not to you."

"I apologize." It was a snide snap, not an apology. "But the irony rendered me temporarily deaf. Did you—*you*— just utter the word *loyalty*?"

Paige gritted her teeth. She didn't bow her head. "You didn't hire me. She did."

"A point that will be moot if I kill you with my bare hands," he snarled at her, and she should have been afraid of him, but she wasn't. She had no doubt that he'd throw her off the estate, that if he could tear her to shreds with his words he would, and gladly, but he wouldn't hurt her. Not physically. Not Giancarlo.

Maybe that was the last remnant of the girl she'd been,

she thought then. That foolish, unbearably naive girl, who'd imagined that a bright and brand-new love could fix anything. That it was the only thing that mattered. She knew better now; she'd learned her lessons well and truly and in the harshest of ways, but she still believed Giancarlo was a good man. No matter what her betrayal had done to him.

"Yes," she said, and her voice was rough with all the emotion she knew she couldn't show him. He'd only hate her more. "But you won't."

"Please," he all but whispered, and she saw too much on his face then, the agony and the fury and the darkness between, "do not tell me you are so delusional as to imagine I wouldn't rip you apart if I could."

"Of course," she agreed, and it was hard to tell what hurt when everything did. When she was sure she would leave this encounter with visible bruises. "If you could. But that's not who you are."

"The man you thought you knew is dead, *Nicola*," he said, that hated name a deliberate blow, and Paige finally did step back then, it was so brutal. "He died ten years ago and there will be no breathing him back to life with your sad tales of loyalty and your pretty little lies. There will be no resurrection. I might look like the man you knew, for two profoundly stupid months a lifetime ago, but mark my words. He is gone as if he never was."

It shouldn't be so sad, when it was nothing more than a simple truth. Not a surprise. Not a slap, even, despite his harsh tone. There was absolutely no reason she should feel swollen anew with all that useless, unwieldy, impossible grief, as if it had never faded, never so much as shifted an inch, in all this time. As if it had only been waiting to flatten her all over again.

"I accept both responsibility and blame for what happened ten years ago," she said as matter-of-factly as she could, and he would never know how hard that was. How exposed she felt, how off balance. Just as he would never know that those two months she'd lost herself in him had been the best of her life, worth whatever had come after. Worth anything, even this. "I can't do anything else. But I promised Violet I wouldn't leave her. Punish me if you have to, Giancarlo. Don't punish her."

Giancarlo Alessi was a man made almost entirely of faults, a fact he was all too familiar with after the bleakness of the past decade and the price he'd paid for his own foolishness, but he loved his mother. His complicated, grandiose, larger-than-life idol of a mother, who he knew adored him in her own, particular way. It didn't matter how many times Violet had sold him out for her own purposes—to combat tales of her crumbling marriage, to give the tabloids something to talk about other than her romantic life, to serve this or that career purpose over the years.

He'd come to accept that having one's private moments exposed to the public was par for the course when one was related to a Hollywood star of Violet's magnitude—which was why he had vowed never, ever to have children that she could use for her own ends. No happy grandchildren to grace magazine articles about her *surprising depths*. No babies she could coo over in front of carefully selected cameras to shore up her image when necessary. He'd never condemn a child of his to that life, no matter how much he might love Violet himself. He'd pass on his Italian title to a distant cousin of his father's and let the sharp brutality of all that Hollywood attention end with him.

He forgave his mother. It was who she was. It was *this* woman he wanted to hurt, not Violet.

This woman who could call herself any name she wanted, but who was still Nicola to him. The architect of his downfall. The agent of his deepest shame.

The too-pretty dancer he'd lost his head over like a thousand shameful clichés, staining his ancient title, his relationship with his late father, and himself in the process. The grasping, conniving creature who had led him around by his groin and made him a stranger to himself in the process. The woman who had made him complicit in the very thing he hated above all others: his presence in the damned tabloids, his most private life on parade.

He'd yet to forgive himself. He'd never planned on forgiving her.

Standing here in this house he'd vowed he'd never enter again, the woman he'd been determined he'd cut from his memory if it killed him within his reach once more, he told himself the edgy thing that surged in him, making him feel something like drunk—dangerously unsteady, a little too close to dizzy—was a cold, clear, measured hatred. No more and no less than she deserved.

It had to be cold. Controlled. He wouldn't permit it to be anything else. He wouldn't let it run hot, burn within him the way loving her had, take charge of him and ruin him anew. He wasn't that trusting, gullible fool any longer, not as he'd been then—so sure he'd been the experienced one, the calloused and jaded one, that no one could take advantage of. She'd made certain he'd never be that idiot again.

He would save that kind of heated, brooding dislike for the sprawling, sunbaked city of Los Angeles itself. For California, brown and gold with only its manufactured, moneyed swaths of green as relief in another breathless summer. For the elegant monstrosity that was La Bellissima. For his heedless, callow twenties playing silly playboy games with films and a parade of famous and beautiful lovers, which *this woman* had brought to a screeching, excruciatingly public halt. For that dry blast of relentless heat on the wind, spiced with smoke from far-off brushfires and the hint of the Pacific Ocean that never cooled it, that made him feel too edgy, too undone. For his mother's recklessness in lovers and husbands and assistants, in all her personal relationships to the endless delight of the predatory press, a trait of hers Giancarlo had long despaired of and had shared but once.

Once.

Once had been enough.

He studied Nicola—*Paige*—as she stood there before him, gazing back at him from her liar's eyes that were neither blue nor green, that fall of thick, dark hair with a hint of auburn that she'd tamed into a side plait falling over one bare, exquisitely formed shoulder. Back then her hair had been redder, longer. Less ink, more fire, and he wished he found the darker shade unpleasant, unattractive. She was still as tall as he remembered but had gone skinny in that way they all did here, as if the denial of every pleasure in the world might bring them the fame they wanted more than anything. More than breath, more than food. Much, much more than love, as he knew all too well.

Don't even think that word, he snarled at himself.

She stiffened as he let his gaze roam all over her, so he kept doing it, telling himself he didn't care what this woman, whatever the hell she called herself now, thought or felt. Because she'd made it clear that the only things she'd ever seen when she'd looked at him—no matter how many times he'd made her scream his name, no matter how many ways they'd torn each other up and turned each other inside out, no matter how deeply he'd fallen for her or how enthusiastically he'd upended his life for her in those two months they'd spent almost entirely in his bed—were Violet's fame and a paycheck to match.

It wasn't only his heart she'd broken. She'd ground his pride, his belief that he could read anyone's intentions at a glance and keep himself safe from the kind of grasping predators who teemed over this city like ants, under her heel. She'd completely altered the way he'd seen himself, who he was, as surely as if she'd severed one of his limbs.

Yet she still held herself well, which irritated him. She still had that dancer's easy grace and the supple muscle tone to match. He took in her small, high breasts beneath that sleeveless white shirt with the draped neck, then the efficient pencil skirt that clung to the swell of her hips, and his hands remembered the lush feel of both. The slick perfection of her curves beneath his palms, always such a marvel of femininity in such a lean frame. The exquisite way she fit in his hands and tasted against his tongue. She'd left her legs bare, toned and pretty, and all he could think about was the way she'd wrapped them around his hips or draped them over his shoulders while he'd thrust hard and deep inside of her.

Stop, a voice inside him ordered, *or you will shame yourself anew.*

Her disguise—if that was what it was—did nothing to hide her particular, unusual beauty. She'd never looked like all the other girls who'd flocked around him back then. It was that fire in her that had called to him from that first, stunning clash of glances across the set of the music video where they'd met. She'd been a backup dancer in formfitting tights and a sport bra. He'd been the high-and-mighty pseudo director who shouldn't have noticed her with a band full of pop stars hanging on his every word. And yet that single look had singed him alive.

He could still feel the same bright flames, even though she'd darkened her hair and wore sensible, professional clothes today that covered her mouthwatering midriff and failed to outline every last line of her thighs. Like the efficient secretary to his mother that he knew she'd proved herself to be over these past years, for some reason—and Giancarlo refused to let himself think about that. About her motives and intentions. Why she'd spent so long playing this game and why she'd bothered to excel in her position here while doing it. Why he couldn't look at her without wanting her, even with all of this time between them. Even knowing exactly what she'd done.

"Is this where you tell me your sob story?" he asked coldly, taking a grim pleasure in the way she reacted to his voice. That little jump, as if she couldn't control this crazy thing between them any more than he could. "There's always one in these situations, is there not? So many reasons. So many excuses."

"I'm not sobbing." He couldn't read that lovely oval of a face, with cheekbones made for a man to cradle between his palms and that wide mouth that begged to be tasted. Plundered. "And I don't think I've made any excuses. I only apologized. It's not the same thing."

"No." He let his gaze move over her mouth. That damned mouth. He could still feel the slide of it against his, or wrapped hot and warm around his hardness, trailing fire and oblivion wherever she used it. *And nothing but lies when she spoke.* "I'll have to see what I can do about that."

She actually sighed, as if he tried her patience, and he didn't know whether he wanted to laugh or throttle her. He remembered that, too. From before. When she'd broken over his life like a hurricane and hadn't stopped tearing up the trees and rearranging the earth until she was gone the same way she'd come, leaving nothing but scandal and the debris of her lies in her wake.

And yet she was still so pretty. He found that made him angrier than the rest of it.

"Glaring ferociously at me isn't going to make me cry," she said, and he wanted to *see things* in those chameleon eyes of hers. He wanted something, anything, to get to her—but he knew better, didn't he? She hadn't simply destroyed him, this time. She'd targeted his mother and she'd done it right under his nose. How could he imagine she was anything but evil? "It only makes the moment that much more uncomfortable." She inclined her head slightly. "But if it makes you feel better, Giancarlo, you should go right ahead and try."

He did laugh then. A short, humorless little sound.

"I am marveling at the sight of you," he said, sounding cruel to his own ears, but she didn't so much as blink. "You deserve to look like the person you really are, not the person you pretended you were." He felt his mouth thin. "But I suppose this is Hollywood magic in action, no? The nastiest, most narcissistic things wrapped up tight in the prettiest packages. Of course you look as good as you did then." He laughed softly, wanting it to hurt. Wanting something he said or did to have *some* effect on her—which told him a bit more than he wanted to know about his unresolved feelings about this woman. "That's all you really have, is it not?"

CHAPTER TWO

GIANCARLO HAD FANCIED himself madly in love with her.

That was the thing he couldn't forgive, much less permit himself to forget, especially when she was *right here* before him once again. The scandal that had ruined his budding film career, that had cast that deep, dark shadow over what had been left of his intensely private, deeply proper father's life, that had made him question everything he'd thought he'd known about himself, that had made him finally leave this damned city and all its demons behind him within a day of the photos going live—that had been something a few shades worse than terrible and it remained a deep, indelible mark on Giancarlo's soul. But however he might have deplored it, he supposed he could have eventually understood a pampered, thoughtless young man's typical recklessness over a pretty girl. It was one of the oldest stories in the world.

It was his own parents' story, come to that.

It was the fact that he'd been so deceived that he'd wanted to *marry* this creature despite his lifelong aversion to the institution, make her his countess, bring her to his ancestral home in Italy—he, who had vowed he'd never marry after witnessing the fallout from his parents' tempestuous union—that made his blood boil even all these years later. He'd been plotting out weddings in his head while she'd been negotiating the price of his disgrace. The fury of it still made him feel much too close to wild.

She only inclined her head again, as if she was perfectly happy to accept any and all blame he heaped on her, and Giancarlo didn't understand why that made him even more enraged.

"Have you nothing to say?" he taunted her. "I don't believe it. You must have lost your touch in all these years, Nicola." He saw her jerk, as if she really did hate that name, and filed that away as ammunition. "I beg your pardon. *Paige*. You can call yourself whatever you want. You've obviously spent too much time with a lonely old woman if this is the best you can do."

"She *is* lonely," Paige agreed, and he thought that was temper that lit up her cheeks, staining them, though her voice was calm. "This was never meant to be a long-term situation, Giancarlo. I assumed you'd come home and recognize me within the month. Of course, that was three years ago."

It took him a moment to understand what it was he was feeling then, and he didn't like it when he did. *Shame.* Hot and new and unacceptable.

"The world will collide with the sun before I explain myself to you," he bit out. Like how he'd managed to let so much time slip by—always so busy, always a crisis on the estate in Italy, always *something*. How he'd avoided coming here and hurt his mother in the process. Those things might have been true—they were why he'd finally forced himself to come after an entire eighteen months without seeing Violet on one of her usual press junkets around the globe—but they certainly weren't *this* woman's business.

"I didn't ask you to explain anything." She lifted one

CAITLIN CREWS   29

shoulder, still both delicate and toned, he was annoyed
to notice, and then dropped it. "It's simply the truth."

"Please," he scoffed, and rubbed his hand over his
face to keep from reacting like the animal he seemed to
become in her presence. Ten years ago he'd thought that
compulsion—that need—was passion. Fate. He knew
better now. It was sheer, unadulterated madness. "Do not
use words you cannot possibly know the meaning of. It
only makes you look even more grasping and base than
we both know you are already."

She blinked, then squared her shoulders, her chin rising as she held his gaze. "Do I have time to get a list of
approved vocabulary words in what remains of my five
minutes? Before you have me thrown over Violet's walls
and onto the street?"

Giancarlo looked at her, the breeze playing in her inky
dark hair with its auburn accents, the sun shifting through
the vines that stretched lazily above them in a fragrant
canopy, and understood with a painful surge of clarity
that this was an opportunity. This woman had been like
a dark, grim shadow stretching over his life, but that was
over now. And he was so different from the man he'd
been when she'd sunk her claws in him that he might as
well have been a stranger.

She had never been the woman she'd convinced him
she was. Because *that* woman, he had loved. *That* woman
had been like a missing piece to his own soul that he'd
never known he lacked and yet had recognized instantly
the moment he'd seen her.

But that was nothing but a performance, a stern voice
whispered in his head.

And this was the second act.

"Does my mother know that you are the woman who
starred in all those photos a decade ago?" he asked,

sounding almost idle, though he felt anything but. He slid his hands into his pockets and regarded her closely, noting how pale she went, and how her lips pressed hard together.

"Of course not," she whispered, and there was a part of him that wondered why she wanted so badly to maintain his mother's good opinion. Why should that matter? But he reminded himself this was the way she played her games. She was good—so good—at pretending to care. It was just another lie and this time, he'd be damned if he believed any part of it.

"Then this is what will happen." He said it calmly. Quietly. Because the shock of seeing her had finally faded and now there was only this. His revenge, served nice and cold all these years later. "I wouldn't want to trouble my mother with the truth about her favorite assistant yet. I don't think she'd like it."

"She would hate it, and me," Nicola—*Paige* threw at him. "But it would also break her heart. If that's your goal here, it's certainly an easy way to achieve it."

"Am I the villain in this scenario?" He laughed again, but this time, he really was amused, and he saw a complex wash of emotion move over her face. He didn't want to know why. He knew exactly what he did want, he reminded himself. His own back, in a way best suited to please him, for a change. This was merely the dance necessary to get it. "You must have become even more delusional than your presence here already suggests."

"Giancarlo—"

"You will resign and leave of your own volition. Today. Now."

She lifted her hands, which he saw were in tight fists, then dropped them back to her sides, and he admired the act. It almost looked real. "I can't do that."

"You will." He decided he was enjoying himself. He couldn't remember the last time that had happened. "This isn't a debate, *Paige*."

Her pretty face twisted into a convincing rendition of misery. "I can't."

"Because you haven't managed to rewrite her will to leave it all to you yet?" he asked drily. "Or are you swapping out all the art on the walls for fakes? I thought the Rembrandt looked a bit odd in the front hall, but I imagined it was the light."

"Because whatever you might think about me, and I'm not saying I don't understand why you think it," she rasped, "I care about her. And I don't mean this to be insulting, Giancarlo, but I'm all she has." Her eyes widened at the dark look he leveled at her, and she hurried on. "You haven't visited her in years. She's surrounded by acolytes and users the moment she steps off this property. I'm the only person she trusts."

"Again, the irony is nearly edible." He shrugged. "And you are wasting your breath. You should thank me for my mercy in letting you call this a resignation. If I were less benevolent, I'd have you arrested."

She held his gaze for a moment too long. "Don't make me call your bluff," she said quietly. "I doubt very much you want the scandal."

"Don't make me call *your* bluff," he hurled back at her. "Do you think I haven't looked for the woman who ruined my life over the years? Hoping against hope she'd be locked up in prison where she belongs?" He smiled thinly when she stiffened. "Nicola Fielding fell off the face of the planet after those pictures went viral. That suggests to me that you aren't any more keen to have history reveal itself in the tabloids than I am." He lifted his brows. "Stalemate, *cara*. If I were you, I'd start packing."

She took a deep breath and then let it out, long and slow, and there was no reason that should have bothered him the way it did, sneaking under his skin and making him feel edgy and annoyed, as if it was tangling up his intentions or bending the present into the past.

"I genuinely love Violet," she said, her eyes big and pleading on his, and he ignored the *tangling* because he knew he had her. He could all but taste it. "This might have started as a misguided attempt to reach you after you disappeared, I'll admit, but it stopped being that a long time ago. I don't want to hurt her. Please. There must be a way we can work this out."

He let himself enjoy the moment. Savor it.

This wasn't temper, hot and wild, making him act out his passions in different ways, the line between it and grief too finely drawn to tell the difference. Too much time had passed. There was too much water under that particular bridge.

And she should never have come here. She should never have involved his mother. She should never have risked this.

"Giancarlo," she said, the way she'd said it that bright and terrible morning a decade ago when he'd finally understood the truth about her—and had seen it in full color pictures splashed across the entirety of the goddamned planet. When he'd showed up at the apartment she'd never let him enter and had that short, awful, final conversation on her doorstep. Before he'd walked away from her and Los Angeles and all the rest of these Hollywood machinations he hated so deeply. Five painful minutes to end an entire phase of his life and so many of his dreams. "Please."

He closed the distance between them with a single step, then reached over to pull on the end of that dark, glossy hair of hers, watching the auburn sheen in it glow and shift in the light. He felt more than heard her quick intake of breath and he wanted her in a thousand ways. That hadn't dimmed.

It was time to indulge himself. He was certain that whatever her angle was, her self-interest would win out over self-preservation. Which meant he could work out what remained of his issues in the best way imaginable. Whatever else she was, she was supple. *He had her.*

"Oh, we can work it out," he murmured, shifting so he could smell the lotion she used on her soft skin, a hint of eucalyptus and something far darker. *Victory,* he thought. His, this time. "It requires only that you get beneath me. And stay there until I'm done with you."

She went still for a hot, searing moment.

"What did you say?"

"You heard me."

Her changeable eyes were blue with distress then, and he might have loathed himself for that if he hadn't known what a liar she was. And what an actress she could be when it suited her. So he only tugged on her plait again and watched her tipped-up face closely as comprehension moved across it, that same electric heat he felt inside him on its heels.

That, Giancarlo told himself, was why he would win this game this time. Because she couldn't control the heat between them any more than he could. And he was no longer fool enough to imagine that meant a damned thing. He knew it was a game, this time.

"I want to make sure I'm understanding you." She swallowed, hard, and he was certain she'd understood him just fine. "You want me to sleep with you to keep my job."

He smiled, and watched goose bumps rise on her

smooth skin. "I do. Often and enthusiastically. Wherever and however I choose."

"You can't be serious."

"I assure you, I am. But by all means, test me. See what happens."

Her lips trembled slightly and he admired it. It looked so real. But he was close enough to see the hard, needy press of her nipples against the silk of her blouse, and he knew better. He knew she was as helpless before this *thing* between them as he was. Maybe she always had been. Maybe that was why it had all got so confused— she'd chosen him because he was Hollywood royalty by virtue of his parents and thus made a good mark, but then there'd been all of *this* to complicate things. But he didn't want to sympathize with her. Not even at such a remove.

"Giancarlo…" He didn't interrupt her but she didn't finish anyway, and her words trailed off into the afternoon breeze. He saw her eyes fill with a wet heat and he had to hand it to her, she was still too good at this. She made it so *believable*.

But he would never believe her again, no matter the provocation. No matter how many tears she shed, or *almost* shed. No matter how convincingly she could make her lips tremble. This was Hollywood.

This time, he wouldn't be taken by surprise. He knew it was all an act from the start.

"Your choices are diminishing by the minute," he told her softly. It was a warning. And one of the last he'd give her. "Now you have but two. Leave now, knowing I will tell my mother exactly why you've left and how you've spent these past years deceiving her. It might break her heart, but that will be one more black mark on your soul, not mine. And I'd be very surprised if she didn't find some way to make you pay for it herself. She didn't become who she is by accident, you must realize. She's a great deal tougher than she looks."

"I know she is." Her gaze still shimmered with that heat, but none of it spilled over—and he reminded himself that was *acting talent,* not force of will. "And what's the second choice?"

He shrugged. "Stay. And do exactly as I tell you."

"Sexually." She threw that at him, her voice unsteady but her gaze direct. "You mean do as you tell me *sexually.*"

If she thought her directness would shame him into altering his course here, she was far stupider than he remembered. Giancarlo smiled.

"I mean do as I tell you, full stop." He indulged himself then, and touched her. He traced the remarkable line of her jaw, letting the sharp delight of it charge through his bones, then held her chin there, right where he could stare her down with all the ruthlessness he carried within him. "You will work for me, *Paige.* On your back. On your knees. At your desk. Whatever I want, whenever I want, however I want."

He could feel her shaking and he exulted in it.

"Why?" she whispered. "This is *me,* remember? Why would you want to...?"

Again, she couldn't finish, and he took pleasure in these signs of her weakness. These cracks in her slick, pretty armor. Giancarlo leaned in close and brushed his mouth over hers, a little hint of what was to come. A little test.

It was just as he remembered it.

All that fire, arcing in him and in her, too, from the shocked sound she made. All that misery. Shame and fury and ten years of that terrible longing. He'd never quite got past it, and this was why. This thrumming, pounding excitement that had only ever happened here, with her. This unmatched hunger. This beautiful lie that would not wreck him this time. Not this time.

He needed to work it all out on that delectable body she'd wielded like a weapon, enslaving him and destroying him before she'd finally got around to killing him, too. He needed to make her pay the price for her betrayal in the most intimate way possible. He needed to work out his goddamned issues in the very place they'd started, and then, only then, would he finally be free of her. It had only been two months back then. It would have burned out on its own—he was sure of it, but they hadn't had time. He wanted time to glut himself, because only then would he get past this.

Giancarlo had to believe that.

"I know exactly who you are," he told her then, and he didn't pretend he wasn't enjoying this. That now that the shock had passed, he wasn't thrilled she'd proved herself as deceitful as he remembered. That he wasn't looking forward to this in a way he hoped scared her straight down into her bones—because it should. "It's long past time you paid for what you did to me, and believe me when I tell you I have a very, very detailed memory."

"You'll regret it." Her voice was like gauze and had as much effect.

"I've already regretted you for a decade, *cara,*" he growled. "What does it matter to me if I add a little more?"

He leaned in closer, felt her quiver against him and thrilled to it. To her, because he knew her true face this time. He knew *her.* There would be no losing himself. There would be no fanciful dreaming of marriage and happy-ever-afters in the Tuscan countryside, deep in all the sweet golden fields that were his heritage. There would only be penance. Hers. Hard, hot, bone-melting penance, until he was satisfied.

Which he anticipated might take some time.

"This doesn't make sense." Did she sound desperate or did he want her to? Giancarlo didn't care. "You hate me!"

"This isn't hate," he said, and his smile deepened. Darkened. "Let's be clear, shall we? This is revenge."

Paige thought he would leap on her the moment she agreed.

And of course she agreed, how could she do anything *but* agree when Violet Sutherlin had become the mother her own had been far too addicted and selfish and hateful to pretend to be? How could she walk away from that when Violet was therefore the only family she had left?

But Giancarlo had only smiled that hard, deeply disconcerting smile of his that had skittered over her skin like electricity.

Then he'd dropped his hand, stepped away from her and left her alone.

For days. Three days, in fact. Three long days and much longer nights.

Paige had to carry on as if everything was perfectly normal, doing her usual work for Violet and pretending to be as thrilled as the older woman was about the return of her prodigal son. She'd had to maintain her poise and professionalism, insofar as there *was* any professionalism in this particular sort of job that was as much about handling Violet's personal whims as anything else. She'd had to try not to give herself away every time she was in the same room with Giancarlo, when all she wanted to do was scream at him to end this tension—a tension *he* did not appear to feel, as he lounged about, swam laps in the pool and laughed with his mother.

And every night she locked herself into the little cottage down near the edge of the canyon that was her home on Violet's property and tortured herself until dawn.

It was as if her brain had recorded every single moment of every single encounter she'd ever had with Giancarlo and could play it all back in excruciating detail. Every touch. Every kiss. That slick, hard thrust of his possession. The sexy noise he'd made against her neck each time he'd come. The sobs echoing back from this or that wall that she knew were hers, while she writhed in mindless pleasure, his in every possible way.

By the morning of the fourth day she was a mess.

"Sleep well?" he asked in that taunting way of his, his dark brows rising high when he met her on the back steps on her way into the big house to start her day. Violet took her breakfast and the trades on a tray in her room each morning and she expected to see Paige there, too, before she was finished.

Giancarlo stood on the wide steps that led up to the terrace, not precisely blocking her way, but Paige didn't rate her chances for slipping past him, either. Had she not been lost in her own scorching world of regret and too many vivid memories as she'd walked up the hill from her cottage, she'd have seen him here, lying in wait. She'd have avoided him.

Would you? that sly voice inside her asked.

A smart woman would have left Los Angeles ten years ago, never to return to the scene of so much pain and betrayal and heartache. A smart woman certainly wouldn't have got herself tangled up with her ex-lover's mother, and even if she had, she would have rejected Giancarlo's devil's bargain outright. So Paige supposed that ship had sailed a long time ago.

"I slept like a baby," she replied, because her memories were her business.

"I take it you mean that in the literal sense," he said drily. "Up every two hours wailing down the walls and making life a misery, then?"

Paige gritted her teeth. He, of course, glowed with health and that irritating masculine vigor of his. He wore an athletic T-shirt in a technical fabric and a pair of running shorts, and was clearly headed out to get himself into even better shape on the surrounding trails that scored the mountains, if that were even possible. No wonder he maintained that lean, rangy body of his that appeared to scoff at the very notion of fat. She wished she could hate him. She wished that pounding thing in her chest, and much lower, was *hate*.

"I've never slept better in my life," she said staunchly.

Her mistake was that she'd drifted too close to him as she said it, as if he was a magnet and she was powerless to resist the pull. She remembered that, too. It had been like a tractor beam, that terrible compulsion. As if they were drawn together no matter what. Across the cavernous warehouse where she'd met him on that shoot. Across rooms, beds, showers. Wherever, whenever.

Ten years ago she'd thought that meant they were made for each other. She knew better now. Yet she still felt that draw.

Paige only flinched a little bit when he reached over and ran one of his elegant fingers in a soft crescent shape beneath her eye. It was such a gentle touch it made her head spin, especially when it was at such odds with that harsh look on his face, that ever-present gleam of furious gold in his gaze.

It took her one shaky breath, then another, to realize

he'd traced the dark circle beneath her eye. That it wasn't a caress at all.

It was an accusation.

"Liar," he murmured, as if he was reciting an old poem, and there was no reason it should feel like a sharp blade stuck hard beneath her ribs. "But I expect nothing else from you."

Bite your tongue, she ordered herself when she started to reply. Because she might have got herself into this mess, twice, but that didn't mean she had to make it worse. She poured her feelings into the way she looked at him, and one corner of that hard, uncompromising mouth of his kicked up. Resignation, she thought. If they'd been different people she might have called it a kind of rueful admiration.

But this was Giancarlo, who despised her.

"Be ready at eight," he told her gruffly.

"That could cover a multitude of sins." So much for her vow of silence. Paige smiled thinly when his brows edged higher. "Be ready for what?"

Giancarlo moved slightly then on the wide marble step, making her acutely aware of him. Of the width of his muscled shoulders, the long sweep of his chiseled torso. Of his strength, his heat. Reminding her how deadly he was, how skilled. How he'd been the only man she'd ever met, before or since, who had known exactly what buttons to push to turn her to jelly, and had. Again and again. He'd simply looked at her, everything else had disappeared and he'd known.

He still knew. She could see it in that heat that made his dark eyes gleam. She could feel it the way her body prickled with that same lick of fire, the way the worst of the flames tangled together deep in her belly.

She felt her breath desert her, and she thought she saw

the man she remembered in his dark gaze, the man as lost in this as she always had been, but it was gone almost at once as if it had never been. As if that had been nothing but wishful thinking on her part.

"Wear something I can get my hands under," he told her, and there was a cruel cast to his desperately sensual mouth then that should have made her want to cry—but that wasn't the sensation that tripped through her blood, making her feel dizzy with something she'd die before she'd call excitement.

And as if he knew that too, he smiled.

Then he left her there—trying to sort out all the conflicting sensations inside of her right there in the glare of another California summer morning, trying not to fall apart when she suspected that was what he wanted her to do—without a backward glance.

"I think he must be a terribly lonely man," Violet said.

They were sitting in one of the great legend's favorite rooms in this vast house, the sunny, book-lined and French-doored affair she called her office, located steps from her personal garden and festooned with her many awards.

Violet lounged back on the chaise she liked to sit on while tending to her empire—"because what, pray, is the point of being an international movie star if I can't conduct business on a chaise?" Violet had retorted when asked why by some interviewer or another during awards season some time back—with her eyes on the city that preened before her beneath the ever-blue California sky and sighed. She was no doubt perfectly aware of the way the gentle light caught the face she'd allowed age to encroach upon, if only slightly. She looked wise and gorgeous at once, her fine blond hair brushed back from her face and only hinting at her sixty-plus years, dressed in her preferred "at home" outfit of butter-soft jeans that had cost her a small fortune and a bespoke emerald-green blouse that played up the remarkable eyes only a keen observer would note were enhanced by cosmetics.

This was the star in her natural habitat.

Sitting in her usual place at the elegant French secretary on the far side of the room, her laptop open before her and all of Violet's cell phones in a row on the glossy wood surface in case any of them should ring, Paige frowned and named the very famous director they'd just been discussing.

"You think *he's* lonely?" she asked, startled.

Violet let out that trademark throaty laugh of hers that had been wowing audiences and bringing whole rooms to a standstill since she'd appeared in her first film in the seventies.

"No doubt he is," she said after a moment, "despite the parade of ever-younger starlets who he clearly doesn't realize make him look that much older and more decrepit, but I meant Giancarlo."

Of course she did.

"Is he?" Paige affected a vague tone. The sort of tone any employee would use when discussing the boss's son.

"He was a very lonely child," Violet said, in the same sort of curious, faraway voice she used when she was puzzling out a new character. "It is my single regret. His father and I loved each other wildly and often quite badly, and there was little room for anyone else."

Everyone knew the story, of course. The doomed love affair with its separations and heartbreaks. The tempestuous, often short-lived reunions. The fact they'd lived separately for years at a time with many rumored affairs, but had never divorced. Violet's bent head and flowing tears at the old count's funeral, her refusal to speak of him publicly afterward.

Possibly, Paige thought ruefully as she turned every last part of the story over in her head, she had studied that Hollywood fairy tale with a little more focus and attention than most.

"He doesn't seem particularly lonely," Paige said when she felt Violet's expectant gaze on her. She sat very still in her chair, aware that while a great movie star might *seem* to be too narcissistic to notice anyone but herself, the truth was that Violet was an excellent judge of character. She had to be, to inhabit so many. She read people the way others read street signs. Fidgeting would tell her much, much more than Paige wanted her to know. "He seems as if he's the sort of man who's used to being in complete and possibly ruthless control. Of everything."

The other woman's smile then seemed sad. "I agree. And I can't think of anything more lonely," she said softly. "Can you?"

And perhaps that conversation was how Paige found herself touching up what she could only call defensive eyeliner in the mirror in the small foyer of her cozy little cottage when she heard a heavy hand at her door at precisely eight o'clock that night.

She didn't bother to ask who it was. The cartwheels her stomach turned at the sound were identification enough.

Paige swung open the door and he was there, larger than life and infinitely more dangerous, looking aristocratic and lethal in one of the suits he favored that made him seem a far cry indeed from the more casual man she'd known before. *This* man looked as if he'd sooner spit nails than partake of the Californian pastime of surfing, much less lounge about like an affluent Malibu beach bum in torn jeans and no shirt. *This* man looked as forbidding and unreachable and haughtily blue-blooded as the Italian count he was.

Giancarlo stood on the path that led to her door and let his dark eyes sweep over her, from the high ponytail she'd fashioned to the heavy eye makeup she'd used because it was the only mask she thought he'd allow her to wear. His sensual mouth crooked slightly at that, as if he knew exactly what she'd been thinking when she'd lined her eyes so dramatically, and then moved lower. To the dress that hugged her breasts tight, with only delicate straps above, then cascaded all the way to the floor in a loose, flowing style that suggested the kind of casual elegance she'd imagined he'd require no matter where he planned to take her.

"Very good, *cara*," he said, and that wasn't quite *approval* she heard in his voice. It was much closer to *satisfaction,* and that distinction made her pulse short-circuit, then start to drum wildly. Erratically. "It appears you are capable of following simple instructions, when it suits you."

"Everyone can follow instructions when it suits them," she retorted despite the fact she'd spent hours cautioning herself not to engage with him, not to give him any further ammunition. Especially not when he called her that name—*cara*—he'd once told her he reserved for the many indistinguishable women who flung themselves at him. *Better that than "Nicola,"* she thought fiercely. "It's called survival."

"I can think of other things to call it," he murmured in that dark, silken way of his that hurt more for its insinuations than any directness would have. "But why start the night off with name-calling?" That crook of his mouth became harder, deadlier. "You'll need your strength, I suspect. Best to conserve it while you can."

He's only messing with you, she cautioned herself as she stepped through the door and delivered herself into his clutches, the way she'd promised him she would. *He wants to see if you'll really go through with this.*

So did she, she could admit, as she made a show of locking the front door, mostly to hide her nerves from that coolly assessing dark gaze of his. But it was done too fast, and then Giancarlo was urging her into a walk with that hand of his at the small of her back, and their history seemed particularly alive then in the velvety night that was still edged with deep blues as the summer evening took hold around them.

Everything felt perilous. Even her own breath.

He didn't speak. He handed her into the kind of low-slung sports car she should have expected he'd drive, and as he rounded the hood to lower himself into the driver's seat she could still feel his hand on that spot on her back, the heat of it pulsing into her skin like a brand, making the finest of tremors snake over her skin.

Paige didn't know what she expected as he got in and started to drive, guiding them out of Violet's high gates and higher into the hills. A restaurant so he could humiliate her in public? One of the dive motels that rented by the hour in the sketchier neighborhoods so he could treat her like the whore he believed she was? But it certainly wasn't the sharp turn he eventually took off the winding road that traced the top of the Santa Monica Mountains bisecting Los Angeles, bringing the powerful car to a stop in a shower of dirt right at the edge of a cliff. There was an old wooden railing, she noted in a sudden panic. But still.

"Get out," he said.

"I, uh, really don't want to," she said, and she heard the sheer terror in her own voice. He must have heard it too, because while his grim expression didn't alter, she thought she saw amusement in the dark eyes he fixed on her.

"I'm not going to throw you off the side of the mountain, however appealing the notion," he told her. "That would kill you almost instantly."

"It's the 'almost' part I'm worried about," she pointed out, sounding as nervous as she felt suddenly. "It encompasses a lot of screaming and sharp rocks."

"I want you to suffer, *Paige,*" he said softly, still with that emphasis on her name, as if it was another lie. "Remember that."

It told her all manner of things about herself she'd have preferred not knowing that she found that some kind of comfort. She could have walked away, ten years ago or three days ago, and she hadn't. He'd been the one to leave. He'd hurled his accusations at her, she'd told him she loved him and he'd walked away—from her and from his entire life here. This was the bed she'd made, wasn't it?

So she climbed from the car when he did, and then followed him over to that rail, wary and worried. Giancarlo didn't look at her. He stared out at the ferocious sparkle, the chaos of light that was this city. It was dark where they stood, no streetlamps to relieve the night sky and almost supernaturally quiet so high in the hills, but she could see the intent look on his face in the reflected sheen of the mad city below, and it made her shake down deep inside.

"Come here."

She didn't want to do that either, but she'd promised to obey him, so Paige trusted that this was about shaming her, not hurting her—at least not physically—and drifted closer. She shuddered when he looped an arm around her neck and pulled her hard against the rock-hard wall of his chest. The world seemed to spin and lights flashed, but that was only the beaming headlights of a passing car.

Giancarlo stroked his fingers down the side of her face, then traced the seam of her lips.

Everything was hot. Too hot. He was still as hard and male as she remembered, and his torso was like a brand beside her, the arm over her shoulders deliciously heavy, and she felt that same old fire explode inside of her again, as if this was new. As if this was the first time he'd touched her.

He didn't order her to open her mouth but she did anyway at the insistent movement, and then he thrust his thumb inside. It was hotter than it should have been, sexy and strange at once, and his dark eyes glittered as they met hers with all of Los Angeles at their feet.

"Remind me how exactly it was I lost my head over you," he told her, all that fury and vengeance in his voice, challenging her to defy him. "Use your tongue."

Paige didn't know what demon it was that rose in her then, some painful mixture of long lost hopes and current regrets, not to mention that anger she tried to hide because it was unlikely to help her here, but she did as she was told. She grabbed his invading hand with both of hers and she worshipped his thumb as if it were another part of his anatomy entirely, and she didn't break away from him while she did it.

She didn't know how long it went on.

His eyes were darker than the night around them, and the same hectic gold lit them, even as it burned within her. She felt molten and wild, reckless and lost, and none of that mattered, because she could taste *him*. He might hate her, he might want nothing more than to hurt her, but Paige had never thought she'd taste him again. She'd never dreamed this could happen.

She told herself it didn't matter, those things she felt deep inside her that she didn't want to acknowledge. Only that this was a gift. It didn't matter what else it was.

He pulled his thumb out then and shifted her so they were facing each other, and the space between them seemed dense. Electric.

"I'm glad to see you haven't lost your touch," he said, and though his tone was cruel his voice was rougher than it had been, and she told herself that meant something. It meant the same thing her breathlessness did, or that manic tightening deep in her belly, that restlessness she'd only ever felt with him and knew only he could cure.

He smiled, and it was so beautiful it made her throat feel tight, and she should have known better. Because he wasn't finished.

"Get on your knees, *Paige,*" he ordered her. "And do it right."

CHAPTER THREE

FOR A MOMENT Paige thought she really had pitched over the side of the hill, and this taut, terrible noise in her head was her own scream. But she blinked and she was still standing there before Giancarlo, he was still waiting and she didn't want him to repeat himself.

She could see from that faintly mocking lift to his dark brows and that twist to his lips that he knew full well she'd heard him.

"Not *here*, surely," she said, and her voice sounded thin and faraway.

"Where I want. How I want. Was I unclear?"

"But I—" She cleared her throat. "I mean, I don't—"

"You appear to be confused." His hands were still on her, and that didn't help. The offhanded sweep of his thumbs against the tender skin of her bare shoulders made her want to scream, but she didn't think she'd stop if she started. "*I* this, *I* that. This isn't about you. This is about me."

"Giancarlo."

"I told you what to do," he said coolly. "And what will happen if you don't."

She jerked back out of his grip, furious in a sudden jolt, and not only because she knew he could have held her there if he liked. But because he hated her and she hated that he did. Because he was back in her life but not really, not in the way she'd refused to admit to herself she'd wanted him to be.

God, in those first months, those first years, she'd expected him to appear, hadn't she? She'd expected him to seek her out once his initial anger passed, once the last of the scandal had died down. To continue that conversation they'd had outside her apartment the morning the pictures had run, so swift and terrible. Because they might have been together only a short time, but he'd known her better than anyone else ever had. *Or ever would.* Maybe not the details of her life, because she'd never wanted anyone to know those, but the truth of her heart. She'd been so sure that somehow, he'd understand that there had to have been extenuating circumstances....

But he'd never come.

So perhaps it was a very old grief that added to the fury and made her forget herself completely.

"Is this really what you want?" she demanded, forgetting to hold her tongue, the taste of his skin still a rich sort of wine in her mouth, making her feel something like drunk. "Is this what a decade did to you, Giancarlo?"

"This is what you did to me." He didn't use that name then, but she was sure they could both hear it, *Nicola* hanging in the air and weaving in and out of the scent of the night-blooming jasmine and rosemary all around them. "And this is exactly what I want."

"To force me. To make me do things I don't want to do. To—" She found she couldn't say it. Not to the man who was the reason she knew that love could be beautiful instead of dark and twisted and sick. Not to the man who had made her feel so alive, so powerful, so perfect beneath his touch. "There are words, you know. Terrible words."

"None of which apply." He thrust his hands in the pockets of that suit, and she wondered if he found it hard to keep them to himself. Was she as sick as he was if that made her feel better instead of worse? How could she tell anymore—what was the barometer? "You don't *have* to do anything. I have no desire to force you. Quite the opposite."

"You told me I had to do this—to—to—"

"Don't stutter like the vestal virgin we both know you are not," he said silkily, and she wondered if he'd forgotten that she'd been exactly that when she'd come to him ten years ago. If he thought that was another lie. "I told you that you had to obey me. In and out of bed."

"That I had to have sex with you *at your command* or leave," she gritted out.

He didn't quite shrug, or smile. "Yes."

"So then I do, in fact, have to do something. You *are* perfectly happy to use force."

"Not at all." He shrugged as if he didn't care what happened next, but there was a tension to those muscled shoulders, around his eyes, that told her otherwise. And it wasn't in the least bit comforting. "You're welcome to leave. To say no at any time and go about your life, such as it is, using whatever name appeals to you. I won't stop you."

It was as if her heart was in her mouth and she felt dizzy again, but she couldn't look away from that terrible face of his, so sensual and impassive and cruel.

"But if I do that, you'll tell Violet who I am. You'll tell her I…what? Stalked you? Deliberately hunted her down and befriended her to get to you?"

"I will." His face hardened and his voice did, too. "It has the added benefit of being the truth."

But Paige knew better, however little she could seem

to express it to him. She knew what had grown between her and Violet in these past years, and how deeply it would wound the other woman to learn that Paige was yet one more leech. One more user, trying to suck Violet dry for her own purposes. It made her feel sick to imagine it.

"That's no choice at all."

"It's a choice, *Paige*," he said with lethal bite. "You don't like it, perhaps, but that doesn't make it any less of a choice, which is a good deal more than you offered me."

"I can't hurt her. Don't you care about that? *Shouldn't* you?"

"There are consequences to the choices you make," he said with a certain ruthless patience. "Don't you understand yet? This is a lesson. It's not supposed to be fun." That smile of his was a sharp blade she was certain drew blood. "For you."

For a moment she thought she'd bolt, though it was a long walk to anywhere from high up on this hill. She didn't know how she kept herself still, how she stayed in one piece. She didn't know how she wasn't already in a thousand shattered bits all over this little pull out on the side of the deserted road, like a busted-out car window.

"Tell me, then," she managed after a moment, keeping her head high, though her eyes burned, "how does this lesson plan work, exactly? You say you don't want to force me, but you're okay with me forcing myself? When it's the last thing I want?"

"Is it?" He shook his head at her, that smile of his no less painful. "Surely you must realize how little patience I have for lies, *Paige*." He let out a small sound that was too lethal to be a laugh. "If I were to lift your dress and stroke my way inside your panties, what would I find? Disinterest?"

Damn him.

"That's not the point. That's biology, which isn't the same thing as will."

"Are you wet?"

It wasn't really a question, and her silence answered it anyway. Her bright red cheeks that she was sure were like a flare against the night. A beacon. Her shame and fury and agony, and none of that mattered because she was molten between her legs, too hot and too slippery, and he knew it.

He knew it by looking at her, and she didn't know which one of them she hated more then. Only that she was caught tight in the grip of this thing and she had no idea how either one of them could survive it. How anything could survive it.

"Please," she said. It was a whisper. She hardly knew she spoke.

And the worst part was that she had no idea what she was asking for.

"We'll get to the begging," he promised her.

Giancarlo looked as ruthless as she'd ever seen him then, and it only made that pulsing wet heat worse. It made her ache and hunger and *want*, and what the hell did that make her? *Exactly what he thinks you are already,* a voice inside her answered.

And he wasn't finished. "But first, I want you on your knees. Right here. Right now. Don't make me tell you again."

He didn't think she'd do it.

They stood together in the dark, close enough that any observer would think them lovers a scant inch away from a touch, and Giancarlo realized in a sudden flash that he didn't want her to do it—that there was a part of him that wanted her to refuse. To walk away from this thing before it consumed them both whole and then wrecked them all over again.

To stop him, because he didn't think he could—or would—stop himself.

Seeing her had taken the brakes off whatever passed for his self-control and he was careening down the side of a too-steep mountain now, heedless and reckless, and he didn't care what he destroyed on the way down. He didn't care about anything but exploring the phrase *a pound of flesh* in every possible way he could.

She didn't blink. He didn't think either one of them breathed. He saw her clench her hands into fists, saw her stiffen her spine. He wanted to stop her from running. From not running. From whatever was about to happen next in this too-close, too-dark night, where the only thing that moved was that long dress of hers, rippling slightly against the faint breeze from the far-off sea.

Then she moved, in a simple slide of pure grace that was worse, somehow, than all the rest. It reminded him of so many things. The supple strength and flexibility of her body, her lean curves, and all the ways he'd worshipped her back before he'd known who she really was. With his hands. His mouth. His whole body. She was his memory in lovely action, a stark and pretty slap across his face, and when she was finished she was settled there on her knees before him.

Just as he'd asked. *Demanded.*

Giancarlo stared down at her, willing back all of his self-righteous fury and the armor it provided, but it was hard to remember much of anything when she was staring up at him, her eyes wide and mysterious and her lips slightly parted, making the carnal way she'd taken his thumb inside her mouth seem to explode through him all over again.

Making him realize he was kidding himself if he thought he was in control of this.

As long as *she* didn't realize that, Giancarlo thought, he'd manage. So he waited, watching her as he did. The night seemed much darker than it was, heavy on all sides and far fewer stars above than in the skies over his home in Tuscany, and he *felt* the ragged breath she took. That same old destructive need for her poured through him, rocketing through his veins and into his sex, making him clench his jaw too tight to keep from acting on it.

He felt like granite—everywhere—when she tilted herself forward and propped herself against his thighs, her palms like fire, her mouth much too close to the part of him that burned the hottest for her.

"Your mother thinks you're lonely," she said.

It took him a moment to understand the words she spoke in that husky tone of voice, and when he did, something he didn't care to identify coursed through him. He told himself it was yet more anger. He had an endless well where this woman was concerned, surely.

Giancarlo reached down and took her jaw in his hand, tugging her face up so he could look down into it, and it was the hardest thing he'd done in a long, long time to keep himself in check. In control. To crush the roaring thing that wanted only to *take her, possess her* and force himself to *think*, instead.

"That's not going to work," he told her softly. He was so hard it very nearly hurt, but he stood there as if he could do this all night, and he felt the faintest shiver move through her, making it all worthwhile.

"What do you mean? That's what she said."

"It doesn't matter if she hauled out her photo albums and wept over pictures of me as a fat, drooling infant," he said mildly, though his hand was hard against her jaw and he could feel how much she wanted to yank herself back, away from him. He could feel the flat press of her hands on his thighs, and the heat there that neither one of them had ever been any good at harnessing. "You're not bringing it up now, on your knees in the dirt because I ordered it, because you have a sudden interest in my emotional well-being."

"I could be interested in nothing *but* your emotional well-being and you'd tell me I was only running a con," Nicola—*Paige* said, with more bravado than he might have displayed were he the one kneeling there in the dark. "I don't know why I bother to speak."

"In this case," he said silkily, moving his hand along the sweet line of her jaw, her cheek, cradling her head with a softness completely belied by the lash in his words, "it is because you hope to shame me into stopping this. Why else bring up my mother when you're about to take me into your mouth at last?"

Her mouth fell open slightly more, as if in stunned astonishment, and he laughed, though it wasn't a very nice sound.

"Fine," she said, though her voice sounded like a stranger's. "Whatever you want."

"That is the point I am trying to make to you, *Paige*," he bit out then, holding her immobile, so she had no choice but to gaze back at him, and he was a terrible man indeed, to revel in the temper he saw in her changeable eyes. "'Whatever I want' isn't an empty phrase. It could mean pleasuring me by the side of the road without any consultation whatsoever about your feelings on the subject. It is what *I* want. Are you beginning to understand me? How many object lessons do you think you will require before this sinks in?"

She said something in reply but the night stole her

words away, and she cleared her throat. She was trembling fully then, and he might have felt like the monster all that accusation in her gaze named him, but he could see the rest of it, too. The stain of color on her cheeks. That glassy heat in her eyes. And beneath the hand he still held to her face and against her neck, the wild drumming of her pulse, pounding out her arousal in an unmistakable beat.

He knew that rhythm better than he knew himself. He thought it might have been the only honest thing about her, then and now.

"How long?" she whispered.

"Until what?"

"Until this is done." She moistened her lips and he felt it like her wicked mouth, wet and soft and deep, and nearly groaned where he stood.

"Until I'm bored."

"A few hours, then," she said, with a remnant of her usual fire, and he smiled.

"I don't imagine you'll be that lucky." He traced a pattern from that stubborn chin of hers to the delicate shell of her ear, then back. "I've had a long time to think about all the ways I'd like to make you crawl. Then pay. Then crawl some more. There's no telling how long it could take."

"And yet when you had the chance, you talked to me for three seconds and then disappeared for a decade," she pointed out.

He felt that same wash of betrayal, that same kick in the gut he'd felt that long-ago day when he'd realized she'd used him the way his own mother always had—and it had been far more shattering, because Violet had only sold him out when he was clothed.

"I don't want to *talk* to you," he said, as harshly as he

could in that same soft voice. "I didn't then. I don't now. I thought I'd made that clear."

A car passed by on the winding mountain drive, the headlights dancing over them, and he saw something bleak in her eyes, across her lovely face. He told himself there was no echo at all inside him, no hollow thing in his chest.

"Then we'd better get started with the humiliation and sexual favors, hadn't we?" she said with a cheerfulness that was as pointed as it was feigned, and he felt her hands tighten against his thighs. She moved them up toward his belt and he didn't know he meant to stop her until he did.

He watched her face as he helped her rise to her feet, and he didn't let go of her arm when she was standing, the way he should have done.

"And here I thought we were right on target to get arrested for public indecency," she whispered, her voice still sharp but something raw in her chameleon gaze. "They could throw me in jail and charge me for solicitation and it would be like all your dreams come true in one evening."

"This is my dream," he growled at her, his hand wrapped tight around her arm and that fever in his blood. His revenge, he thought. At last. "It's not the act itself that matters, *cara*. That's a privilege you haven't earned. It's the surrender. It's all about the surrender." He laughed then, a dark sound he felt in every part of him, as if it was a part of the night and as dangerous, and then he let her go. It was harder than it should have been. "You'll learn."

It became clear to Paige in the week that followed that it wasn't Giancarlo's intention to *actually* make her have sex with him whenever and wherever he chose, no matter what provocative things he might say to the contrary.

That would have been easy, in its way. He was far more diabolical than that.

He wanted her in a constant state of panic, with no idea what he might do next. He wanted her to think of nothing at all but him and the little things he made her do to prove her obedience that were slowly driving her insane.

It's all about the surrender, he'd said. Her surrender. And she was learning what he'd meant.

One day—after nearly a week filled with anticipation and the faintest of touches, always in passing and always unexpected, all of which still felt like a metal collar around her neck that he tightened at will—he found her in Violet's expansive closet, putting together a selection of outfits with appropriate accessories for Violet to choose between for the event the star was scheduled to attend that evening.

"Pull up your skirt, take off your panties—if you are foolish enough to be wearing any—and hand them to me," Giancarlo said without preamble, making Paige jump and shiver into a bright red awareness of him, especially because her mind had been a long way away.

Ten years ago away, in fact, and treating her to a play-by-play, Technicolor and surround-sound replay of one of their more adventurous evenings in the Malibu house down on the beach she had no idea if he still owned.

"What?" she stammered out, but her body wasn't in any doubt about his instructions. Her breasts bloomed into an aching heaviness, making her bra feel too tight and too scratchy against her skin. Her stomach flipped over, and below, that shimmering heat became scalding.

And that was only at the sound of his voice. What would happen if he touched her this time?

"Is this your strategy, *cara*? To feign ignorance every time I speak to you?" He loomed in the doorway, looking untamed and edgy, furious and male. He'd forgone the exquisite suits and running apparel today and looked more like the Giancarlo she remembered in casual trousers and a top that was more like a devotional poem extolling the perfection of his torso than anything so prosaic as a *T-shirt*. "It's already tiresome."

She was standing too straight, too still, on the other side of the central island that housed Violet's extensive jewelry collection, entirely too aware that she resembled a deer stuck fast in the glare of oncoming headlights. But she couldn't seem to move.

Anything besides her mouth, that was. "I did try to warn you that this would get boring."

Giancarlo's mouth crooked slightly and made hers water. His eyes were so dark the gold in them felt as much like a caress as a warning, and she was terribly afraid she could no longer tell the difference.

"Show me that you know how to follow directions." He folded his arms over that chest of his and propped a shoulder against the doorjamb, but Paige wasn't the least bit fooled. He looked about as casual and relaxed as a predator three seconds before launching an attack. "And I'd think twice before making me wait, if I were you."

"It's all the threats," she grated at him. "They make me dizzy with fear. It's hard to hear the instructions over all the heart palpitations."

"I'm certain that's true." That crook in his mouth deepened. She was fascinated. "But I think we both know it isn't fear."

Paige couldn't really argue with that, and she certainly didn't want him to wander any closer and prove his point—did she? She glanced down at her outfit, the short, flirty little skirt with nothing on beneath it, and realized that she'd obeyed him without thinking about it when she'd dressed this morning. *Make sure that I have access to you, should I desire it,* he'd told her two nights ago, a harsh whisper in the hallway outside Violet's office. She'd obeyed him and in so doing, she'd revealed herself completely.

When she raised her gaze to his again, he was smiling, a fierce satisfaction in his dark gold eyes and stamped across that impossibly elegant face of his. He jerked his chin at her, wordlessly ordering her to show him, and her hands moved convulsively, as if her body wanted nothing more than to prove itself to him. To prove *herself* trustworthy again, to jump through any hoop he set before her—

But that wasn't where this was headed. This wasn't a love story. No matter how many memories she used to torture herself into imagining otherwise.

"Come over here and find out for yourself, if you want to know," she heard herself say. Suicidally.

Giancarlo only shook his head at her, as if saddened. "You seem to miss the point. Again. This is not a game that lovers play, *cara.* This is not some delightful entertainment en route to a blissful afternoon in bed. This is—"

"Penance," she finished for him, with far more bitterness than she should have allowed him to hear. "Punishment. I know."

"Then stop stalling. Show me."

Paige could see he meant it.

She told herself it didn't matter. That he'd seen all of her before, and in a far more intimate setting than this. That more than that, he'd had his mouth and his hands on every single inch of her skin, in ways so devastating and intense that she could still feel it ten years later. So what did it matter now? He was all the way across the room and he *wanted* her to balk. To hate him. That was why he was doing this, she was sure.

So instead, she laughed, like the carefree girl she'd never been. Paige stepped out from behind the center island so there could be no accusations of hiding. She watched his hard, hard face and then, slowly, she reached down and pulled her skirt up to her hips.

"Satisfied?" she asked when she was fully bared to his view—because she was.

She'd been so lost in her guilt, her shame, her own anger at everything that had happened and Giancarlo too, that she'd forgotten one very important fact about this thing between them that Giancarlo had been using to such great effect.

It ran both ways.

He stared at her—too hard and too long—and she saw the faintest hint of color high on those gorgeous cheeks of his. And that hectic glitter in his dark eyes that she recognized. Oh yes, she recognized it. She remembered it.

She knew as much about him as he did about her, after all. She knew every inch of *his* body. She knew his arousal when she saw it. She knew he'd be so hard he ached and that his control would be stretched to the breaking point. The chemistry between them wasn't only his to exploit.

She stood there with her skirt at her waist, supposedly debasing herself before the only man she'd ever loved, and Paige felt better than she had in years. Powerful. *Right*, somehow.

"Looked your fill?" she asked sweetly when the silence stretched on, taut and nearly humming. He swallowed as if it hurt him, and she felt like a goddess as he dragged his gaze back to hers.

"Come here." His voice was a rasp, thick and hot, and it moved in her like joy.

She obeyed him and this time, she was happy to do it. She walked toward him, reveling in the way her blood pounded through her and her skin seemed to shrink a size, too tight across her bones. Because he could call this revenge. He could talk about hatred and penance. But it was still the same thick madness that felt like a rope around her neck. It was still the same inexorable pull.

It was still *them*.

Paige stopped in front of him and let out a surprised breath when he moved, reaching down to gather her wrists in his big hands and then pull them behind her, securing them in one of his at the small of her back. Her skirt fell back into place against the sensitized skin of her thighs, her back arched almost of its own accord, and Giancarlo stared down at her, a hard wildness blazing from his eyes.

Paige remembered that, too.

She didn't know what he looked for, much less what he saw. He stared at her for a moment that dragged out to forever and she felt it like panic beneath the surface of her skin. Like an itch.

And then he jerked her close, her hands still held immobile behind her back, and slammed his mouth to hers.

It wasn't a brush of his mouth, a tease, like before. It wasn't an introduction.

He took her mouth as if he was already deep inside of her. As if he was thrusting hard and driving them both toward that glimmering edge. It was more than wild, more than carnal. He bent her back over her own arms, pressing her breasts into the flat planes of his chest, and he simply possessed her with a ruthless sort of fury that set every part of her aflame.

She thrilled to his boldness, his shocking mastery. The glorious taste of him she'd pined for all these years. The sheer *rightness*.

Paige kissed him back desperately, deeply, forgetting about the games they played. Forgetting about penance, about trust. Forgetting her betrayal and his fury. She didn't care what he wanted from her, or how he planned to hurt her, or anything at all but this.

This.

There was too much noise in her head and too much heat inside of her and she actually moaned in disappointment when he pulled back, holding her away from him with that iron strength of his that reminded her how gentle he was with it. How truly demanding, because he knew—as he'd always known—exactly what she wanted. How far away from *force* all of this really was.

"You kiss like a whore," he said, and she could see it was meant to be an insult, but it came out sounding somehow reverent, instead.

She laughed. "Have you kissed many whores, then? You, the exalted Count Alessi, who could surely have any proper woman he wished?"

"Just the one."

She should be wounded by that, Paige thought as she studied him. She should feel slapped down, put in her place, but she didn't. She cocked her head to one side and saw the fever in his dark gaze, and she knew that whatever power he had over her, she had it over him, too. And more, he was as aware of that as she was.

"Then how would you know?" she asked him, her voice like a stranger's, breathy and inviting. Nothing like hurt at all. "Maybe the whore is you."

"Watch your mouth." But he'd moved closer again, his shoulders filling her vision, her need expanding to swallow the whole world. Or maybe it was his need. Both of theirs, twined together and too big to fit beneath the sky.

"Make me," she dared him, and he muttered something in Italian.

And then he did.

He let go of her hands to take her face between his hard palms, holding her where he wanted her as he plundered her mouth. As he took and took and then took even more, as if there was no end and no beginning and only the madness of their mouths, slick and hot and perfect. The fire between them danced high and roared louder, and he didn't stop her when Paige melted against him. When she wound her arms around his neck and clung to him, kissing him back as if this was the reunion she'd always dreamed of. As if this was a solution, not another one of his clever little power games.

And she didn't know when it changed. When it stopped being about fury and started to taste like heat. When it started to feel like the people they'd been long ago, before everything had gone so wrong.

He felt it, too. She felt him stiffen, and then he thrust her aside.

And for a long moment they only stared at each other, both of them breathing too fast, too hard. Paige tried to step back and her legs wobbled, and Giancarlo scowled at her even as his hand shot out to steady her.

"Thank you," she said, because she couldn't help herself. Her mouth felt marked, soft and plundered, and Giancarlo was looking at her as if she was a ghost. "That certainly taught me my place. All that punitive kissing."

She didn't know what moved across his face then, but it scraped at her. It hurt far worse than any of his words had. She had to bite her own tongue to keep from making the small sound of pain that welled up in her at the sight of it.

"It will," he promised her, a bleakness in his voice that settled in her bones like a winter chill. Like the fate she'd been running from since the day she'd met him, loath as she was to admit it. "I can promise you that. Sooner or later, it will."

Kissing her had been a terrible mistake.

Giancarlo ran until he thought his lungs might burst and his legs might collapse beneath him, and it was useless. The Southern California sun was unforgiving, the blue sky harsh and high and cloudless, and he couldn't get her taste out of his mouth. He couldn't get the feel of her out of his skin.

It was exactly as it had been a decade ago, all over again, except this time he couldn't pretend he'd been blindsided. This time, he'd walked right into it. He'd been the one to kiss her.

He cursed himself in two languages and at last he stopped running, bending over to prop his hands on his knees and stare down the side of the mountain toward his mother's estate and the sprawl of the city below it in the shimmering heat of high summer. It was too hot here. It was too familiar.

Too dangerous.

It was much too tempting to simply forget himself, to pick up where he'd left off with her. With the woman who was no longer Nicola. As if she hadn't engineered his ruin, deliberately, ten years ago. As if she hadn't then tricked her way to her place at his mother's side with a new name and God only knew what agenda.

As if, were he to bury himself in her body the way he wanted to do more than was wise and more than he cared to admit to himself, she might transform into the woman she'd already proved she wasn't in the most spectacular way imaginable.

He was already slipping back into those old habits he'd thought he'd eradicated. The work he'd left in Italy was piling up high, and yet here he was, running off steam in the Bel Air hills the way he'd done when he was a sixteen-year-old. She was the first thing he thought of when he woke. She was what he dreamed about. She was taking over his life as surely as she ever had, very much as if this was *her* revenge, not his.

He was an addict. There was no other explanation for the state he was in, hard and ready and yearning, and he didn't want that. He wanted her humbled, brought low, destroyed. He wanted her to feel how he'd felt when he'd woken that terrible morning to find his naked body splashed everywhere for the entire world to pick over, parse, comment upon, like every other time his private life been exploited for Violet's gain—but much worse, because he hadn't seen the betrayal coming. He hadn't thought to brace himself for impact.

He wanted this to hurt.

Giancarlo straightened and shoved his hair back from his forehead, the past seeming to press against him too tightly. He remembered it all too well. Not just the affair with Nicola—*Paige,* he reminded himself darkly—in all its blistering, sensual perfection, as if their bodies had been created purely to drive each other wild. But the parts of that affair he'd preferred to pretend he didn't remember, all these years later. Like the way he'd always found himself smiling when they'd spoken on the phone, wide and hopeful and giddy, as if she was sunshine in a bottle and only his. Or the way his heart had always thudded hard when she'd entered a room, in the moment before she'd seen him and had treated him to that dazzling smile of hers that had blotted out the rest of the world. The way she'd held his hand as if that connection alone would save them both from darkness, or dragons, or something far worse.

Oh yes, he remembered.

And he remembered the aftermath, too. After the pictures ran in all those papers. After those final, horrible moments with this woman he had loved so deeply and known not at all. After he'd done the best he could to clear his head and then made his way back to Italy. To face, at last, his elderly father.

His father, who had felt denim was for commoners and had thought the only thing more tawdry than Europe's aristocracy was the British royals, with their divorces and dirty laundry and *jeans.* His father, Count Alessi, who could have taught propriety and manners to whole nunneries and probably had, in his day. His father, who had been as gentle and nobly well-meaning as he was blue-blooded. Truly the last of his kind.

"It is not your fault," he'd told Giancarlo that first night in the wake of the scandal. He'd hugged his errant son and greeted him warmly, his body so frail it had moved in Giancarlo like a winter wind, a herald of the coming season he hadn't wanted to face. Not then. Not yet. "When I married your mother I knew precisely who she was, Giancarlo. It was foolish to imagine she and I could raise a son untainted by that world. It was only a matter of time before something like this happened."

Perhaps his father's disappointment in him had cut all the deeper because it had been so matter-of-fact. Untouched by any hint of anger or vanity or sadness. There was nothing to fight against, and Giancarlo had understood that there had been no one to blame but himself for his poor judgment. His father might have been antiquated, a relic of another time, but he'd instilled his values in his only son and heir.

Strive to do good no matter what, he'd told Giancarlo again and again. *Never make a spectacle of oneself. And avoid the base and the dishonorable, lest one become the same by association.*

Giancarlo had failed on all counts. It was why he knew that the vows he'd made when he was younger were solid. Right. No marriage, because how could he ever be certain that someone wanted *him*? And no heirs of his own, because he'd never, ever, subject a child to the things he'd survived. He might not be able to save himself from his own father's disappointment, he might find his life trotted out into public every time his mother starred in something new and needed to remind the world of her once upon an Italian count fairy-tale marriage, but it would end with him.

Damn Nicola—*Paige*—for making him think otherwise, even if it had only been for two mostly naked months a lifetime ago.

It was that, he thought as he broke into a run again, his pace harder and faster than before as he hurtled down the hill, that he found the most difficult to get past. He hated that she had betrayed him, yes. But far worse was this *thing* in him, dark and brooding, that yearned only for her surrender no matter how painful, and that he very much feared made him no different than she was.

He thought he hated that most of all.

CHAPTER FOUR

AFTER A LONG shower and the application of his own hand to the part of him that least listened to reason, Giancarlo prowled through the house, his fury at a dull simmer. An improvement, he was aware.

La Bellissima was the same as it ever was, as it had been throughout his life, he thought as he moved quietly through its hushed halls, gleaming with Violet's wealth and consequence in all its details. The glorious art she'd collected from all over the planet. The specially sourced artisan touches here and there that gave little hints of the true Violet Sutherlin, who had been born under another name and raised in bohemian Berkeley, California. Old Hollywood glamor mixed with contemporary charm, the house managed to feel light and airy rather than overfed, somehow, on its own affluence.

Much like Violet herself, all these years after her pouty, sex kitten beginnings in the mid-seventies. He should know, having been trotted out at key moments during her transition from kitten to lion of the industry, as a kind of proof, perhaps, that Violet could do more than wear a bikini.

There was the time she'd released a selection of cards he'd written her as a small child, filled with declarations of love that the other kids at school had teased him about all the way up until his high school graduation. There was the time she'd spent five minutes of her appearance in a famous actor's studio interview telling a long, involved anecdote about catching him and his first girlfriend in bed that had humiliated fourteen-year-old Giancarlo and made his then-girlfriend's parents remove her to a far-off boarding school. He knew every inch of this house and none of it had ever been his; none of it had ever been safe. He was as much a prop as any of the other things Violet surrounded herself with—only unlike the vases, he loved her despite knowing how easily and unrepentantly she'd use him.

He followed the bright hall toward Violet's quarters, knowing how much she liked to spend her days in the office there with its views of the city she'd conquered. He had memories of catapulting himself down this same hallway as a child, careening off the walls and coming to a skidding halt in that room, only to climb up on the chaise and lie at his mother's feet as she'd run her lines and practiced her voices, her various accents, the postures that made her body into someone else's. He'd found her fascinating, back then. He supposed he still did, and Giancarlo couldn't remember, then, at what age he'd realized that Violet was better admired than depended upon. That her love was a distantly beautiful thing, better experienced as a fan than a family member. The first time she'd released a photo of him he'd found embarrassing? Or the tenth, with as little remorse?

He only knew they'd both been far happier once he'd accepted it.

Giancarlo paused in the doorway, hearing his mother's famous laugh before he saw her. She wasn't in her usual place today, reclining on her chaise like the Empress of Hollywood. She was standing at the French doors instead,

bathed in soft light from the summer day beyond with
a mobile phone in her hand, and even though there was
no denying her celebrated beauty, his gaze went straight
to the other woman in the room as if Violet wasn't there
at all.

Paige sat at the fussy little desk in the corner, typing
something as a male voice responded to whatever Violet
had said from her mobile phone, obviously on speaker.
Paige was frowning down at her laptop as her fingers
flew over the keys, and when Violet turned toward her
to roll her eyes at her assistant, Giancarlo could see the
face Paige made in immediate response.

Sympathetic. Fully on Violet's side. Staunch and true,
he'd have said, if he didn't know better.

He'd seen that expression before. *That* was the woman
he'd loved in all the passionate fury of those two months
of madness. Stalwart. Loyal. Not in any way the kind of
woman who would sell a man out and print it all up in
the tabloids. He'd have sworn on that. He'd have gam-
bled everything.

Giancarlo still couldn't believe how wrong he'd been.

His stomach twisted, and it took everything he had
not to make a noise, not to bellow out his fury at all of
this—but mostly at himself.

Because he wanted to believe, still. Despite everything. He wanted there to be an explanation for what had
happened ten years ago. He wanted Paige—and when
had he started thinking about her by that name, without stumbling over it at all?—to be who she appeared
to be. Dedicated to his mother. Deeply sorry for what
had gone before, and with some *reason* for what she'd
done. And not the kind of self-serving reason Violet
always had…

He wanted her back.

And that was when Giancarlo woke up with a jolt and recognized the danger he was in. History could not repeat itself. Not with her. Not ever.

"Darling," Violet said when she ended her call, turning from the window and smiling at him. "Don't lurk in the hallway. It was only my agent. A whinier, more demanding fool I have yet to meet, and yet I'm fairly certain he's the best there is."

But what Giancarlo noticed was the way Paige straightened in her chair, her eyes wide and blue when they flew to him, then quickly shuttered when she looked back to her keyboard.

He could think of a greater fool than his mother's parasitical agent. It was something about finding himself back in Los Angeles, he thought as he fought back his own temper, as well as seeing Paige again. It would have been different if he'd encountered her in some other city. Somewhere that held no trace of who they'd been together. But here, their history curled around everything, like a thick, encroaching smog, and made it impossible to inhale without confronting it every time.

With every goddamned breath.

"I must return to Italy," he said shortly. Almost as if he wasn't certain he'd say it at all if he didn't say it quickly and that, of course, made him despise himself all the more.

"You can't leave," Violet said at once. Giancarlo noticed Paige seemed to type even more furiously and failed to raise her head at all. "You've only just arrived."

"I came because it had been an unconscionably long time, Mother," he said softly. "It was never my intention to stay away so long. But I have a solution."

"You are moving back to Los Angeles," Violet said, a curve to her mouth that suggested she didn't believe it even as she said it. "I'm delighted. That Malibu house is far too nice to waste on all those renters."

"Not at all." He wanted to study Paige instead of his mother but he didn't dare. Still, he was as aware of her as if she was triple her own size. As if she loomed there in his peripheral vision, a great dark cloud, consuming everything. "You must come to Italy. Bring your assistant. Stay for the rest of the summer."

Violet looked startled for a moment, but then in the next her face smoothed out, and he recognized the mask she wore then. As impenetrable as it was graceful. A vision of loveliness that showed only what she wanted seen, and nothing else. Violet Sutherlin, the star. Giancarlo didn't know what it said about him that he found this version of her easier to handle than the one who pretended motherhood was her primary concern.

"Darling, you know my feelings about Italy," she murmured, and a stranger might have believed her wry, easy tone. "I love it with all my heart. But I'm afraid I buried that heart with your father."

"Not that Italy," he said. He smiled, though he understood he was speaking as much to the silent woman in the corner of his eye as to his mother. "My Italy."

"Do you have your own?" Violet asked. She laughed again. "You have been busy indeed."

"I've completely transformed the estate," Giancarlo said quietly. "I know we've discussed all these changes over the years, but I'd like you to see them for yourself. I think Father would be proud."

"I know he would," Violet said with a glimmer of something raw in her gaze and the sound of it in her voice, and Giancarlo knew he had her. Paige knew it too, he could tell. He felt more than saw her stiffen at her desk, and it took everything he had to keep the triumph from his voice, the sheer victory from his face. "Of course, Giancarlo. I'd love to see Tuscany again."

He only let himself look at Paige again when he was certain he had himself under complete control. *Like iron,* he thought fiercely. Like the old houses he'd rebuilt on the ancestral estate in Tuscany, stone by ancient stone, forcing his will and vision onto every acre.

He would take her away from Los Angeles, where history seemed to infuse every moment between them with meaning he didn't want. He didn't know why he hadn't thought of this sooner.

In the far reaches of Tuscany, as remote as it was possible to get in one of the most famous and beloved regions of the world, she would be entirely dependent on him. Violet could relax in the hands of his world-class staff, her every need anticipated and met, and he would have all the time in the world to vanquish this demon from his past, for good. All the time he needed to truly make her pay.

Because that was what he wanted, he reminded himself. To make her pay. Everything else was memory and fantasy and better suited to a long night's dream than reality.

"Wonderful." Giancarlo tried not to gloat, and knew he failed when Paige frowned. And it was still a victory. It was still a plan. And it would work, he was sure of it. Because it had to. "We leave tonight."

Paige had dreamed of Italy her whole life.

When she was a child, she'd sneaked library books into her mother's bleak trailer in the blistering heat of the rocky Arizona desert. She'd waited for Arleen to pass out before she'd lost herself in them, and she'd dreamed. Fierce dreams of cypress trees in stern columns marching across a deep green undulation of ancient fields. Monuments to long lost gods and civilizations gone centuries before her birth, red-roofed towns clustered on gentle hills beneath a soft, Italian sun.

Then she'd met Giancarlo, who carried the lilt of Italy in every word he spoke, and her dreams had taken on a more specific shape. Even back then, when he'd wanted to play around in Hollywood more than he'd wanted to tend to his heritage, he'd spoken of the thousands of rural acres that his father had only just started to reclaim from the encroaching wilderness of a generation or two of neglect. They were his birthright and in those giddy days ten years ago she'd dared to imagine that she was, too.

And now she was finally here, and it turned out it was extraordinarily painful to visit a place that she'd once imagined might be her home and now knew never, ever would be. More than painful—but she told herself it was the jet lag that made her ache like that. Nothing a good night's sleep on solid ground wouldn't cure.

Even if it was *this* solid ground.

The vast estate sprawled across a part of Tuscany that had been in the Alessi family in one form or another since the Middle Ages. It was dotted with old farmhouses Giancarlo had spent the past decade painstakingly renovating for a very special class of clientele: people as wealthy as his mother and as allergic to invasions of their privacy as his father had been. As Paige supposed he must be himself now, after his too-public shaming at her own hands.

Here at Castello Alessi and all across its hilly lands, thick with olive groves and vineyards, lavender bushes and timeless forests of oak trees—according to the splashy website Paige had accessed a hundred times before and once again from the plane when she'd accepted she was really, truly coming here at last—such privacy-minded people could relax, secure in the knowledge that the "cottages" they'd paid dearly either to rent or to buy outright and fashion to their liking were as private and remote as it was possible to get while still enjoying world-class service akin to that of the finest hotels, thanks to Giancarlo's private, around-the-clock staff.

But none of that applied to Paige, she was well aware.

They'd landed on a private airstrip in a nearby valley after flying all night. It had been a bright, somehow distinctly Italian summer morning, filled with yellow flowers and too-blue skies, and a waiting driver had whisked them off to the estate some forty minutes away. It was a long, gorgeous drive, winding in and around the hills of Tuscany that looked exactly as Paige had imagined them while also being somehow so much *more* than she'd anticipated. Violet had been installed in the lavishly remodeled *castello* itself, arrayed around a welcoming stone courtyard with heart-stopping views and her own private spa with waiting staff to pamper her at once, as if she was truly the High Queen of Italy.

Paige, on the other hand, Giancarlo ushered into a Jeep and then personally drove far out into the heart of the property, until all she could see in all directions was the gently rolling countryside and one lone house at the top of the nearest hill. All of it so gorgeous and yet so *familiar*, as if she'd been here before and recognized it like a homecoming, and yet, she was forced to keep telling herself, none of this was hers. Not the perfect sky, the charming lane, the pretty little houses on this or that ridge. *Not hers.* The man beside her least of all.

"Are you deliberately stranding me out here as some kind of punishment?" she asked him, when it became clear that a smaller cottage down in the valley beneath that lone house was where he was headed. She was doing her best not to look at him, braced beside her in the smaller-by-the-moment front of his Jeep as they bumped along the lazy dirt road that meandered toward the little stone house, because she was afraid it might make all these raw emotions inside of her spill over into tears. Or worse. "Don't you think that looks a little bit strange?"

"My mother will be waited on hand and foot in the *castello*," he said, his gruff voice either impatient or triumphant, and Paige couldn't tell which. She wasn't sure she wanted to know. "And if by some chance she needs you while undergoing a battalion of spa treatments, never fear, the Wi-Fi is excellent. I trust she can manage to send out an email should she require your presence."

"So the answer is yes," Paige said stiffly as he pulled up in front of the cottage. He turned the key in the ignition and the sudden quiet seemed to pour in through the open windows, as terrifying as it was sweet. "This is a punishment."

"Yes," he said in that low way of his that wrapped around her and made her yearn, then made her question her own sanity. "I am punishing you with Tuscany. It is a fate worse than death, obviously. Just look around."

She didn't want to look around, for a thousand complicated reasons and none she'd dare admit. It made her feel scraped to the bone and weak. So very weak. So she looked at him instead, which wasn't really any better.

"You think I don't know why you brought me here, but of course I do." She laughed, though it was a hollow little sound and seemed to make that scraped sensation expand inside of her. "You're making sure I have nowhere to run. I think that counts as the most basic of torture methods, doesn't it?"

"Correction." He aimed a smile at her that didn't quite

reach the storm in his eyes, but made her feel edgy all the same. "I don't care if you know. It isn't the same thing."

Paige pushed her way out of the Jeep, not surprised when he climbed out himself. Was this all a prologue to another one of these scenes with him—as damaging as it was irresistible? She tucked her hands into the pockets of the jeans she'd worn on the long flight and wished she felt like herself. *It's only jet lag,* she assured herself. Or so she hoped. *You've read about jet lag. Everyone says it passes or no one would ever go anywhere, would they?* But she didn't feel particularly tired. She felt stripped to the bone instead. Flayed wide-open.

And the way he looked at her didn't help.

"How long?" she asked, her voice not quite sounding like her own. "How long do you think you can keep me here?"

Giancarlo pulled her bags from the back and carried them to the door of the cottage, shouldering it open and disappearing inside. But Paige stayed where she was, next to the Jeep with her eyes on the rolling green horizon. The sweet blue of the summer sky was packed with fluffy white clouds that looked as if they were made of meringue and were far more beautiful than all of her dreams put together, and she tried her best not to cry, because this was a prison—she knew it was—and yet she couldn't escape the notion that it was *home.*

"I'll keep you as long as I like," he said from the doorway, his voice another rolling thing through the morning's stillness, like a dark shadow beneath all that shine. "This is about my satisfaction, *cara.* Not your feelings. Or it wouldn't be torture, would it? It would be a holiday."

"By your account, I imagine I don't have any feelings anyway, isn't that right?" She hadn't meant to say that, and certainly not in that challenging tone. She scowled at the stunning view, and reminded herself that she'd never really had a home and never would. Longing for a place like this was nothing more than masochistic, no matter how familiar it felt. "I'm nothing but a mercenary bitch who set out to destroy you once and is now, what? A delusional stalker who has insinuated herself into the middle of your family? For my own nefarious purposes, none of which have been in evidence at all over the past three years?"

"I find *parasite* covers all the bases." Giancarlo drawled that out, and it was worse, somehow, here in the midst of so much prettiness. Like a creeping black thing in the center of all that green, worse than a mere shadow. "No need to succumb to theatrics when you can merely call it what it is."

She shook her head, that same old anguish moving inside of her, making her shake deep in her gut, making her wish for things she knew better than to want. A home, at last. Love to fill it. A place to belong and a person to share it with—

Paige had always *known better.* Dreams were one thing. They were harmless. No one could have survived the hard, barren place where she'd grown up, first her embittered mother's teenage mistake and then her meal ticket, without a few dreams to keep them going. Much less what had happened ten years ago. What her mother had become. What Paige had nearly had to do in a vain attempt to save her.

But *wishes* were nothing but borrowed trouble. And she supposed, looking back, that had been the issue from the start—being with Giancarlo had made her imagine she could dare to want things she knew, *she knew,* could never be hers. Never.

You won't make that mistake again in a hurry, her mother's caustic voice jeered at her.

Paige risked a look at Giancarlo then, despairing at the way her heart squeezed tight at the sight of him the way it always had, at that dark look on his face that was half hunger and half dislike, at the way she had always loved him and understood she always would, and to what end? He would have his revenge and she would endure it and somehow, somehow, she would survive him, too.

It hurts a little bit more today than it usually does because you're here and you're tired, she tried to tell herself. *But you're fine. You're always fine. Or you will be.*

"I know you don't want to believe me," she said, because she had always been such an idiot where this man was concerned. She had never had the slightest idea how to protect herself. Giancarlo had been the kind of man who had blistering affairs the way other people had dinner plans, but *she* had fallen head over heels in love with him at first glance and destroyed them both in the process. And now she wanted, so desperately, for him to *see* her, just for a moment. The real her. "But I would do anything for your mother. For a hundred different reasons. Chief among them that she's been better to me than my own mother ever was."

"And here I thought you emerged fully grown from a bed of lies," he said silkily. He paused, his dark eyes on her, as if recognizing how rare it was that Paige mentioned her own mother—but she watched him shrug it off instead of pursuing it and told herself it was for the best. "I was avoiding the city my mother lived in all these years and the kind of people who lived in it, not my mother. A crucial distinction, because believe me, *Paige*, I would also do anything for my mother. And I will."

There was a threat in the last three words. A promise. And there was no particular reason it should thud into her so hard, as if it might have taken her from her feet if she hadn't already been braced against all of this. The pretty place, the sense of homecoming, the knowledge he was even more lost to her when he stood in front of her than he had been in all their years apart.

"I loved my mother, too, Giancarlo," Paige said, and she understood it was that scraped raw feeling that made her say such a thing. Giancarlo would never understand the kind of broken, terrible excuse for love that was the only kind Paige had ever known, before him. The sharp, scarring toll it exacted. How it festered inside and taught a person how to see the world only through the lens of it, no matter how blurred or cracked or deeply twisted. "And that never got me anything but bruises and a broken heart." And then had taken the only things that had ever mattered to her. She swallowed. "I know the difference."

He moved out of the doorway of the cottage then, closing the distance between them with a few sure steps, and Paige couldn't tell if that was worse or better. Everything seemed too mixed up and impossible and somehow *right*, too; the gentle green trees and the soft, lavender-scented breeze, and his dark gold eyes in the center of the world, making her heart beat loud and slow inside her chest.

Stop it, she ordered herself. *This is not your home. Neither is he.*

"Is this an appeal to my better nature?" Giancarlo asked softly. Dangerously. "I keep telling you, that man is dead. Killed by your own hand. Surely you must realize this by now."

"I know." She tilted up her chin and hoped he couldn't see how lost she felt. How utterly out of place. How hideously dislocated if it seemed that *he* was the only steady thing here, this man who detested her. "And here I am. Isolated and at your beck and call. Just think of all the ways you can make me pay for your untimely death."

She couldn't read the shadow that moved over his face then. His hand moved as if it was outside his control and he ran the backs of his fingers over the line of her jaw, softly, so softly, and yet she knew better than to mistake his gentleness for kindness. She knew better than to trust her body's interpretations of things when it came to this man and the things he could do to it with so seemingly careless a touch.

The truth was in that fierce look in his eyes, that flat line of his delectable mouth. The painful truth that nothing she said could change, or would.

He wanted to hurt her. He wanted all of this to *hurt*.

"Believe me," he said quietly. Thickly, as if that scraped raw thing was in him, too. "I have thought of little else."

Paige thought he might kiss her then, and that masochist in her *yearned* for it, no matter what came after. No matter how he made her pay for wanting him, which she knew he would. She swayed forward and lifted her mouth toward his and for a moment his attention seemed to drift toward her lips—

But then he muttered one of those curses that sounded almost pretty because it was in Italian. And he stepped back, staring at her as if she was a ghost. A demon, more like. Sent to destroy him when it was clear to her that if there was going to be any destruction here, it would be at his hands.

It was going to be her in pieces, not him. And Paige didn't understand why she didn't care about that the way she should. When he looked at her, she didn't care about anything but him and all these terrible, pointless wishes that had wrecked her once already. She should have learned her lesson a long time ago. She'd thought she had.

"I suggest you rest," he said in a clipped tone, stalking back toward the driver's side of the Jeep. "Dinner will be served at sunset and you'll wake up starving sometime before then. That's always the way with international flights."

As if he knew she'd never left the country before, when she'd thought she'd hidden it well today. His knowing anyway seemed too intimate, somehow. The sort of detail a lover might know, or perhaps a friend, and he was neither. She told herself she was being ridiculous, but it was hard to keep looking at him when she felt there had to be far too much written across her face then. Too much of that Arizona white trash dust, showing him all the things about her she'd gone to such lengths to keep him from ever knowing.

"At the *castello*?" she asked, after the moment stretched on too long and his expression had begun to edge into impatience as he stood there, the Jeep in between them and his hand on the driver's door. "That seems like a bit of a walk. It was a twenty-minute drive, at least."

"At the house on the hill," he said, and jerked his head toward the farmhouse that squatted at the top of the nearest swell of pretty green, looking sturdy and complacent in the sunlight, all light stones and an impressive loggia. "Right there. Unless that's too much of a hike for you these days, now that you live on a Bel Air estate and are neck deep in opulence day and night. None of it earned. Or yours."

Paige ignored the slap. "That really all depends on who lives there," she replied, and it was remarkably hard to make her voice sound anything approximating *light*.

"A troll? The Italian bogeyman? The big, bad wolf with his terrible fangs?"

His mouth moved into that crooked thing that made her stomach flip over and her heart ache. More. Again. *Always*.

"That would be me," he said softly, and she thought he took a certain pleasure in it. "So that's all of the above, I'd think. For your sins."

A long nap and a very hot shower after she woke made Paige feel like a new person. Or herself again, at last. She had been too weary and inexplicably sad to explore the cottage when Giancarlo had driven away, so she did it now, with the whisper-soft robe she'd found in the master bathroom wrapped around her and her feet bare against the reclaimed stone floors, her wet hair feeling indulgent against her shoulders as she moved through the charming space.

It was a two-story affair in what had looked from the outside like a very old stone outbuilding. Inside, it was filled with the early-evening light thanks to the tall windows everywhere, the exposed beams high above, and the fact the interior was wholly open to best take advantage of what would otherwise have felt like a small space. Stairs led from the stone ground floor to the loft above, which featured a large, extraordinarily comfortable bed in the airy room nestled in the eaves, a small sitting area with a balcony beyond, and the luxurious master bath Paige had just enjoyed.

The main floor was divided into an efficient, cheerful kitchen with a happily stocked refrigerator, a cozy sitting area with deep sofas arranged around a wide stone fireplace, a small dining area that led out to a patio that spanned the length of the cottage and led into a small, well-tended garden. And everywhere she looked, behind everything and hovering near and far and more beautiful by the moment, the Tuscan view.

Home, she thought, despite herself.

Evening had crept in with long, deep shadows that settled in the valley and made art out of the soft green trees, the cypress sentries and the rounded hills on all sides. The road that had felt torturously remote when Giancarlo had driven her here looked like something from one of her beloved old books now, winding off into the distance or off into dreams. Paige stood there in the window until the air cooled around her, and realized only when she started back up the stairs that she hadn't breathed like that—deeply and fully, all the way down to her feet, the way she had when she'd danced—in a very long time.

Almost as if she was comfortable here. As if she belonged. She'd felt that way in only one other place in her whole life, and had been as wrong. Giancarlo's Malibu home, all wood and glass, angled to best let the sea in, had only been a pretty house. This was a pretty place.

And when you leave here, she told herself harshly, *you will never come back. The same as that house in Malibu. Everyone feels at home in affluent places. That's what they're built to do.*

Paige dressed slowly and carefully, her nerves prickling into a new awareness as she rifled through her suitcase. Should she wear the sort of thing she would wear if this was a vacation in Italy she happened to be taking by herself? Or should she wear something she suspected Giancarlo would prefer, so he could better enact his revenge? On the one hand, jeans and a slouchy sweatshirt, all comfort and very little style. On the other, a flirty little dress he could *get his hands under,* like before. She didn't have the slightest idea which way to go.

"What do *you* want?" she asked her sleepy-eyed reflection in the bathroom mirror, her voice throaty from all that sleep.

But that was the trouble. She still wanted the same things she'd always wanted. She could admit that, here and now, with Giancarlo's Italy pressing in on her from all sides. The difference was that this time, she knew better than to imagine she'd get it.

Paige dried her hair slowly, her mind oddly empty even as the rest of her felt tight with all the things she didn't want to think about directly. Taut and on edge. She pulled on a pair of soft white trousers and a loose sort of tunic on top, a compromise between the jeans she'd have preferred and what she assumed Giancarlo would likely want to see her wear, given the circumstances.

"What he'd really like is me, as naked as the day I was born and crawling up that hillside on my hands and knees," she muttered out loud and then laughed at the image, the sound creaky and strange in the quiet of the cottage. She kept laughing until a wet heat pricked at the back of her eyes and she had to pull in a ragged breath to keep the tears from pouring over. Then another.

Paige frowned as she slipped her feet into a pair of thonged flat sandals. When was the last time she'd laughed like that? About anything?

What a sad creature you've become, she scolded herself as she dug out her smartphone from her bag and scrolled through her messages. But the truth was, she had always been a fairly sad thing, when she looked back at the progression of her life. Sad and studious or determined and stubborn, from the start. It had been the only way to survive the chaos that had been her mother. There had only been one two-month stretch of laughter in her life, gleaming and overflowing and dizzy with joy, and she'd ruined it ten years ago.

"My goodness," Violet said in her grand way when she picked up her private line, after Paige apologized for disappearing and then sleeping for hours, "this is *Italia,* Paige. One must soak in *la dolce vita*, especially when jet-lagged. I plan to spend the night in my lovely little castle, getting fat on all the *marvelous* local cuisine! I suggest you do the same."

And Paige would have loved to do the same, she thought when she finally stepped out of her cottage into the cool evening, the Tuscan sky turning to gold above her. But she had a date with her sins instead.

Sins that felt like wishes granted, and what was wrong with her that she didn't want to tell the difference between the two?

She took her time and yet the walk was still too short. Much too short.

And Giancarlo waited there at the crest of the hill, his eyes as hard as his body appeared loose and relaxed, in linen trousers and the sort of camel-colored sport coat that made her think of his aristocratic roots and her lack of them. And Paige was suddenly as wide-awake as if she'd drowned herself in a vat of espresso.

He looked like something more than a man as he waited there, at first a shadow next to the bold upright thrust of a thick cypress tree, then, as she drew closer, very distinctly himself. He'd clearly watched her come all the way up the side of his hill, and she wasn't sure if she'd seen him from afar without realizing it or if it was that odd magnetic pull inside of her that had done it, pointing her toward him as unerringly as if she'd been headed straight to him all along.

Home, that thing in her whispered, and she didn't have

the strength to pretend she didn't feel it when she did. Not tonight.

She stopped when she was still some distance away and looked back the way she'd come, unable to keep the small sigh of pleasure from escaping her lips. There was the hint of mist in the valley the lower the sun inched toward the hills, adding an elegant sort of haunting to the shadows that danced between them, and far off in the distance the *castello* stood tall and proud, lights blazing against the coming night. It was so quiet and perfect and deeply satisfying in a way Paige hadn't known anything could be. Gooseflesh prickled up and down her arms and she felt it all like a heavy sob in her chest, rolling through her, threatening her very foundations.

Or maybe that was him. Maybe it had always been him.

"It's gorgeous here," she said, which felt deeply inadequate. "It doesn't seem real."

"My father believed that the land is our bones," Giancarlo said. "Protect it, and we strengthen ourselves. Conserve it and care for it, and we become greater in its glory. Sometimes I think he was a madman, a farmer hiding in an aristocrat's body." His gaze moved over her face, then beyond her, toward the setting sun. "And then another sunset reminds me that he was right. Beauty is always worth it. It feeds the soul."

"He sounds like some kind of poet."

"Not my father. Poets and artists were to be championed, as one must always support art and culture for the same reason one tends the land, but Alessis had a higher calling." He shook his head. "Endless debt and responsibility, apparently. I might have been better off as an artist, come to that."

"If I had a home like this, I don't think I'd mind doing

whatever it took to keep it," Paige said then. She remembered herself. "I don't think anyone would."

She thought Giancarlo smiled, though his face was obscured in the falling dark and then she knew she must have imagined it, because this wasn't that kind of evening no matter how lovely it was. He wasn't that kind of man. Not anymore. Not for her.

"Come," he said. He reached out his hand and held it there in the last gasp of golden light, and Paige knew, somehow, that everything would be divided into before and after she took it. The world. Her life. This *thing* that was still between them. And that precarious, wildly beating creature inside her chest that was the battered ruins of her heart.

His mouth crooked slightly as the moment stretched out. She made no move; she was frozen into place and wasn't sure she could do anything about it, but he didn't drop his hand.

"Did you make me dinner?" she asked, her voice shockingly light when there was nothing but heaviness and their history and her treacherous heart inside of her, and she thought neither one of them was fooled. "Because food poisoning really would be a punishment, all joking aside."

"I am Italian," he said, with a note of amused outrage in his voice, which reminded her too strongly of all that laughter they'd shared a lifetime ago. As if the only things that had mattered in the whole world had been there in his smile. She'd thought so then. She thought maybe she still did, for all the good that would do her here. "Of course I can cook." He paused, as if noticing how friendly he sounded and remembering how inappropriate that was tonight. As if he, too, was finding it hard to recall the battle lines he'd drawn. "But even if I couldn't, the estate has a fleet of chefs on call. Meals are always gourmet here, no matter who prepares them."

"Careful," she said softly, more to her memories and her silly heart than the man who stood there before her, still reaching out to her, still her greatest temptation made flesh. Still the perfect embodiment of all the things she'd always wanted and couldn't have. "I might forget to be suitably intimidated and start enjoying myself. And then what would happen?"

He definitely smiled that time, and Paige felt it like a deep, golden fire, lighting her up from the inside out. Making her shiver.

"Surrender takes many forms," he replied into the indigo twilight that cloaked them both, now that the sun had finally sunk beneath the furthest hill. "I want yours every way I can get it."

"I can surrender to *la dolce vita*," she said, as airily as possible, as if her tone of voice might make it so. "I understand that's the point of Italy."

He still stood there, his hand out, as if he could stand like that forever. "That's as good a place to start as any."

And there was no real decision, in the end. There had been so many choices along the way, hadn't there? Paige could have got a different job three years ago. She could have left Violet's house and employ the moment Giancarlo had appeared, or anytime since. She could have declined the offer of that "date" that night, she could have stayed standing up instead of sinking to her knees by the side of that road, she could have shown him nothing in Violet's closet that day but her back as she walked away from him. She could have refused to board his plane, refused to leave her cottage tonight, locked herself inside rather than climb this hill to stand before him like this.

He hadn't *happened* to her, like the weather. She'd

chosen this, every step of the way, and even here, even stranded in the countryside with this man who thought so ill of her, she felt more at home than she had in years. Maybe ever. She supposed that meant she'd made her decision a long time ago.

So Paige reached out her hand and slid it into his. She let the heat of him wash through her at that faintly rough touch, his palm warm and strong and perfect, and told herself it didn't matter what happened next.

That she'd surrendered herself to Giancarlo a long time ago, whether he understood that or not.

CHAPTER FIVE

"If this is your revenge," Paige said, a current of laughter in her voice though her expression was mild, "I think I should confess to you that it tastes a whole lot like red wine."

He should do something about that, Giancarlo thought, watching her move through the refurbished ground floor of his renovated house. She was still so graceful, so light on her feet. Like poetry in motion, and he'd never been able to reconcile how she could flow like that and have turned out so rotten within. He'd never understood it.

It doesn't matter what you understand, he snapped at himself. *Only what you do to make this* thing *for her go away—*

But something had happened out there as the sun set. Something had shifted inside him, though he couldn't quite identify it. He wasn't certain he'd want to name it if he could.

"It may prove to be a long night, *cara,*" he told her darkly, pouring himself a glass of the wine they made here from Alessi grapes. "This is merely the beginning."

"The civilized version of revenge, then," she murmured, almost as if to herself, running her fingers along the length of the reclaimed wood table that marked his dining area in the great, open space he'd done himself.

In soothing yet bright colors and historically contextual pieces, all of which dimmed next to that effortless, off-handed beauty of hers. "I'll keep that in mind."

This didn't feel like revenge. This felt like a memory. Giancarlo didn't want to think too closely about that, but the truth of it slapped at him all the same. It could have been any one of the long, lush evenings they'd shared in Malibu a decade back that still shimmered in his recollection, as if the two of them had been lit from within. It shimmered in him now, too. Again. As if this was the culmination of all the dreams he'd lied and told himself he'd never had, in all those years since he'd left Los Angeles and started bringing the estate back to life.

There was too much history between them, too much that had gone wrong to ever fix, and yet he still caught himself watching her as if this was a new beginning. But then, he had always been such a damned fool where this woman was concerned, hadn't he?

Earlier he'd stood in the courtyard of the *castello* with Violet, toasting her first night back in Italy since his father's funeral eight years ago, and he'd felt a sense of deep rightness. Of homecoming, long overdue. These hills held his happiest childhood memories, after all. When his parents had both been alive, and in those early years, so much in love it had colored the air around them.

"You've done a marvelous thing here, darling," Violet had said, smiling as much at him as at the achingly perfect view.

"I remember the days when we couldn't drive out the gates in Bel Air without having to fight our way through packs of photographers," he'd said, gazing out at the slumbering hills, all of them his now, his birthright and his future. His responsibility. And not a single paparazzo in a thousand miles or more. No lies. No stories. Only the enduring beauty of the earth. "Just to get to school in the morning."

"The tabloids giveth and the tabloids taketh away," Violet had said drily, looking as chic and elegant as ever though she wore her version of lounge wear and what was, for her, a practically cosmetic-free face. "It's never been particularly easy to navigate, I grant you, but there did used to be a line. Or perhaps I'm kidding myself."

"I want this place to be a refuge," he'd told her then. "It's nearly fifteen miles to the nearest main road. Everything is private. It's the perfect retreat for people who can't hide anywhere else."

Violet had tasted her wine and she'd taken her time looking at him again, and he'd still been unsure if she was pausing for dramatic effect or if that was simply how she processed emotion. She was still a mystery to him and he'd long since accepted she always would be. Or anyway, he'd been telling himself he'd accepted it. It might even have been true.

"Yes," she'd said, "and it's very beautiful. It's always been beautiful. I imagine I could live here quite happily and transform myself into one of those portly, Italy-maddened expatriates who are forever writing those merry little Tuscan memoirs and waxing rhapsodic about the *light*." Her brows had lifted. "But which one of us is it that feels they need a hiding place, Giancarlo? Is that meant to be you or me?"

"Never fear, Mother," he'd replied evenly. "I have no intention of having children of my own. I won't have any cause to hide away, the better to protect them from prying eyes and a judgmental world. Perhaps I, too, will flourish in the heat of so many spotlights."

She'd only smiled, enigmatic as ever, seemingly not in the least bit chastised by what he'd said. Had he expected otherwise? "Privacy can be overrated, my darling boy. Particularly when it better resembles a jail."

And now he stood in the cheerful lounge of the house he'd taken apart and put back together with his own two hands, and watched the woman he'd once loved more than any other walk through the monument—he wouldn't call it a *jail*—he'd built to his own unhappiness, his lonely, broken, betrayed heart.

How had he failed to realize, until this moment, that he'd built it for her? That he'd been hiding here these past ten years—deliberately keeping himself some kind of hermit, tucked away on this property and in this very cottage? That it was as much his refuge *for* her as it was *from* her?

That notion made something like a storm howl in him, deep and long. And as if she could read his mind, Paige turned, a small smile on that distracting mouth of hers.

"I always liked your films," she said, her voice the perfect complement to the carefully decorated great room, the furnishings a mix of masculine ease and his Italian heritage, as if he'd planned for her to stand there in its center and make it all work. "I suppose it shouldn't surprise me that that kind of attention to detail should spill over into all the things you do."

"My films were laughable vanity projects at best," he told her, that storm in his voice and clawing at the walls of his chest. "I should never have taken myself seriously, much less allowed anyone else to do the same. It's an embarrassment."

Paige wrinkled her nose and he thought that might kill him, because finding her *adorable* was far more dangerous than simply wanting her. One was about sex, which was simple. The other had consequences. Terrible consequences he refused to pay.

"I liked them."

"Shall we talk about the things you like?" Giancarlo asked, and he sounded overbearingly brooding to his own ears. As if he was performing a role because he thought the moment needed a villain, not because he truly wanted to put her back in her place. "Your interest in photography and amateur porn, for instance?"

Some revenge, he thought darkly. *Next you'll try to cuddle her to death with your words.*

But she only smiled in that enigmatic way of hers, and moved closer to one of the paintings on the wall, her hands cupped around her glass of wine and that inky black hair of hers falling in abandon down her back, and it wasn't cuddling he thought about as he watched her move. Then bite her lower lip as she peered up at the painting. It wasn't *cuddling* that made his blood heat and his mouth dry.

"I don't understand why I'm here," Paige said, so softly that it took him a moment to realize she'd spoken. She swiveled back to look at him, framed there like a snapshot, the woman who had destroyed him before the great, bright canvas that stretched high behind her, all shapes and emotion and a swirl of color, that he hadn't understood until tonight had reminded him of her.

Giancarlo told himself it was a sour realization, but his sex felt heavy and the air between them tasted thick. Like desire. Like need.

Like fate.

"It seems as if you've achieved what you set out to do," she continued as if she couldn't feel the thickness, though he knew, somehow, that she could. "You've separated me from Violet without seeming to do so deliberately, which I'm assuming was your purpose from the start. But why bring me all the way here? Why not leave me in California and spirit Violet away? And having made me come all the way here," Paige continued, something he couldn't identify making her eyes gleam green in the mellow light, "why not simply leave me to rot in my little cottage? It's pretty as prison cells go, I grant you. Very pretty. It might take me weeks to realize I'm well and truly trapped there."

He let his gaze roam over her the way his hands itched to do. "You've forgotten the most important part."

"The sex, yes," Paige supplied, and she didn't sound particularly cowed by the idea, or even as outraged as she'd been back in Los Angeles. Her tone was bland. Perhaps too bland. "On command."

"I was going to say obedience," he said, and he didn't feel as if he was playing a game any longer. He was too busy letting his eyes trace over her curves, letting his hands relish the tactile memory of her face between them as if she'd burned her way into his flesh. He could still taste her, damn it. And he wanted more.

"Obedience," she repeated, as if testing each syllable of the word as she said it. "Does that include feeding me a gourmet dinner in this perfect little mansion only a *count* would call a cottage? Are you entirely sure you know what *obedience* involves?"

Giancarlo smiled, or anyway, his mouth moved. "That's the point. It involves whatever I say it involves."

He took a sip of his wine as he walked over to the open glass doors that led out to the loggia, nodding for her to join him outside. Stiffly, carefully—as if she was more shaken by their encounter than she appeared, and God help him, he wanted that to be true—she did.

Because the truth was so pathetic, wasn't it? He still so badly wanted her to be real. To have meant some part of the things that had happened between them. All these years later, he still wanted that. Giancarlo despaired of himself.

A table waited out in the soft night air, bright with candles and laden with local produce and delicacies prepared on-site, while a rolling cart sat next to it with even more tempting dishes beneath silver covers. It was achingly romantic, precisely as he'd ordered. The hills and valleys of the estate rolled out beneath the stars, with lights winking here and there in the distance, making their isolation high up on this terrace at a remove from all the world seem profound.

That, too, was the point.

He moved to pull her chair out for her like the parody of the perfect gentleman he had never quite been and waited as she settled in, taking a moment to inhale her scent. Tonight she smelled of the high-end bath products he had his staff stock in the cottages, vanilla and apricots, and that hint of pure woman beneath.

"This house was a ruin when I started working on it," he told her, still standing behind her, because he didn't know what his face might show and he didn't want her to see it. To see *him*. He succumbed to a whim and ran his fingers through her hair, reveling in the heavy weight of the dark strands even as he remembered all the other times she'd wrapped him in the heat and sweetness of it. When she'd crawled over him in that wide bed in Malibu and let her hair slip and tumble all over his skin as she tortured him with that sweet mouth of hers, driving them both wild. Giancarlo hardened, remembering it, and her hair was thick silk in his hands. "It sits on its original foundation, but everything else is changed. Perhaps the walls still stand, but everything inside is new, reclaimed, or altered entirely. It might look the same from a distance, but it isn't."

"I appreciate the metaphor," Paige said, with a certain grittiness to her voice that he suspected meant her teeth were clenched. He smiled.

"Then I hope you'll appreciate this, too," he said as he rounded the table and sat down across from her, stretching out his legs before him as he did. "This is the Italian countryside and everything you can see in every direction is mine. You could scream for days and no one would hear you. You could try to escape and, unless you've taken up marathon running in your spare time, you'd run out of energy long before you found the road. You claimed to be obedient in Los Angeles because it suited you. You wanted your job more than you minded the loss of your self-respect, such as it is. Here?" He shrugged as he topped up their wineglasses with a bottle crafted from grapes he'd grown himself and then sat back, watching her closely, as she visibly fought not to react to his cool tone, his calmly belligerent words. "You have no other choice."

"That's not at all creepy," Paige said, though he could have sworn that gleam of green in her chameleon gaze was amusement, however beleaguered. "I'm definitely the terrifying stalker in this scenario, not you."

Giancarlo laughed. "Not that I would care if it really was creepy, but I don't think you really think so, do you? Shall we put it to the test?"

He wanted her to push him, he understood. He wanted to see for himself. He wanted to peel those crisp white trousers from her slim hips and lick his way into her wetness and heat and know it was all for him, the way he'd once believed it was. The way he'd once believed *she* was.

Soon, he assured himself as his body reacted to that image with predictable enthusiasm. *Soon enough.*

"Again," Paige said tightly, taking a healthy gulp of

her wine, "it seems to me that there are more effective forms of payback than a romantic dinner for two, served beneath the starry night sky on what might be the most intimate terrace on the entire planet." She looked out at the view as the heavens sparkled back at her, as if they were performing for her pleasure. "I suspect you might be doing it wrong."

"Ah, Paige," Giancarlo said softly. "You lack imagination." Her eyes swung back to his and he smiled again, wider, pleased when that seemed to alarm her. "The romantic setting will only make it more poignant, will it not, when I order you to strip and sit there naked as we eat. Or when I demand that you please me with your mouth while I soak in the view. Or when I bend you over the serving table and make you scream out my name until I'm done." He let his smile deepen as her eyes went very green, and very round. "The more civilized the setting, the more debauched the act," he said mildly. "I find there is very little more effective."

She looked stunned, and then something like wistful, and he almost broke and hauled her into his arms—but somehow, *somehow*, he reined himself in. *Just a little bit longer,* he promised himself. She blinked, then coughed, and then she folded her hands together in her lap with such precision that Giancarlo knew she was torturing *herself* with all those images he'd put in her head.

Va bene.

"You say that as if this isn't the first time you've done this." Her voice was his own little victory, so raspy was it then, with that stunned heat in her gaze and that band of color high on her cheeks. "Do you spend a lot of time enacting complicated revenge fantasies, Giancarlo? Is that another one of your heretofore hidden talents—like architecture and interior design, apparently?"

"I went to architecture school after university," he said, and something about the fact she didn't know that bothered him. Had he never told her his own story? Had he been as guilty of wearing a false persona ten years ago as she had been? Had it simply been the rush, the need that had kept them in bed and focused on other things? Had it been by her design—or had it been his own selfishness at play? He shoved that disconcerting thought aside. "But when I was finished, I decided I wanted to leverage my position as Violet's son, instead. That didn't work out very well for either one of us, did it?" He reached over and removed the silver cover from the plate of antipasti in front of her, then from his own, and smiled at her when she looked confused. "The *salsicce di cinghiale* is particularly good," he told her. "And you should be certain to eat well. We have a very long night ahead of us."

He expected her to do as she was told. It took a moment or two for him to realize that she hadn't moved. That she appeared to have frozen solid where she sat and was staring at him with a stricken sort of expression on her face.

Giancarlo lifted a brow. "Was I unclear?"

"I appreciate all the tension and drama," Paige said after a moment. "I don't think I realized how very much you take after your mother until now. That's a compliment," she added in a hurry when he frowned at her. "But I'll pass."

"That is not an option you have." He shrugged. "You persist in thinking what you want comes into play here. It doesn't."

"What will you do?" she asked softly, so softly it took a moment for him to hear the challenge beneath the words, and then to see it there in her chameleon eyes.

"Make me scream for people who won't hear me? Make me walk for days in search of a road that's still hours from anywhere? Force me to stay in that gorgeous little cottage down the hill like a bird in a cage?"

"Or, alternatively, merely call my mother and tell her exactly who you are," he suggested. "A fate you felt was worse than death and far more terrible than anything I might do a week ago."

But tonight she only shook her head and she didn't avert her gaze, reminding him of that moment in his mother's closet across the world. Reminding him he'd never controlled this woman, not even when she'd agreed to let him.

"I think if you were going to do that, Giancarlo, you would have. You wouldn't have dragged me across the planet and then presented me with wine and a four-course meal."

He laughed, a smoky little sound against the night. It did nothing to ease the mounting tension. "Do you really want to test that theory?"

She leaned forward, holding his gaze, and his laughter dried up as if it had never been. He was aware of everything at once. The stars above them, the faint breeze that teased him with the intoxicating scent of her. The rich food before them, the dancing candlelight. The way she sat now, the wide neck of her brightly patterned tunic falling open as she leaned toward him, hinting at the soft curves beneath.

And all that fire, as bright as it had ever been, burning them both where they sat.

Her gaze was like a touch on his, and he felt it everywhere. "I have a different theory."

"I'm all ears, of course. Every inmate is innocent, every killer was merely misunderstood, every con man an

artist in his soul, et cetera. Tell me your sob story, *cara*."
He felt his mouth crook. "I knew you would, sooner or
later."

But Paige only smiled, and her eyes were so green tonight they rivaled his own lush fields. It moved in him
like summer, an exultation of all that boundless heat that
spiked the air between them.

"You don't want revenge. Not really. You want sex."

Her smile deepened when he only stared back at her,
that mouth of hers still an utter distraction, still his undoing. Her gaze proud and unwavering and he had no
defense against that, either.

"You don't want to admit it, given what happened the
last time we had sex, but look where we are." She lifted
a shoulder, somehow encompassing the whole of the estate in that simple little gesture. "You've made sure there
couldn't possibly be a camera here. You've cut us off
from the rest of the world. And you're calling it *revenge*
because you're furious that you still want me."

"Or because *wanting* you is only part of it," he replied,
stiffer than he should have sounded, because it was that
or let loose the wild thing in him that wanted nothing but
her however he could have her. That didn't give a toss
about the rest of it as long as he got his hands on her one
more time. Just one more time. "And not mutually exclusive with revenge, I assure you."

Her smile seemed to pierce straight through him
then, heat and fire and danger, and it sank straight to
his sex.

Making him nothing at all but that wildness within.

"Call it whatever you want," she suggested in that
rough voice of hers that hinted at her own dark excitement, that called to him like a song the way it always had.
That sang in him still, no matter how he tried to deny it.

"Call it *hate sex*. I don't care, Giancarlo." She shrugged. "Whatever it is, whatever you need to call it to feel better about it, I want it, too."

"I beg your pardon?" Giancarlo's voice was a rough whisper that somehow sounded in Paige like a bellow.

It was the wine, Paige told herself as she stared back at him, her own words seeming to cavort between them on the heavily laden tabletop, making it impossible to see or hear much of anything else. Of course it was the wine—though she'd only had a few sips—and the lingering jet lag besides, though she didn't feel anything like tired at the moment.

Nothing else could possibly have made her say such things, she was sure, much less throw down the gauntlet to a battle she very much feared might be the end of her.

She opened her mouth to take it back, to laugh and claim she'd been kidding, to break the strange, taut spell that stretched between them and wrapped them tight together, caught somewhere in that arrested expression that transformed his beautiful face. But Giancarlo lifted an aristocratic hand that stopped her as surely as if he'd placed it over her mouth, and she knew she really shouldn't have shivered in a rush of dark delight at the very image.

"I find I'm not as trusting as I used to be," he told her, though *untrusting* wasn't how she would have described the wolfish look in his dark eyes then. "It is a personality flaw, I am sure. But I'm afraid you'll have to offer proof."

She was watching his mouth as if it was a show, which was only part of the reason Paige didn't understand what he'd said. She blinked. "Proof?"

"That this is not another one of your dirty little games

that will end up painting the front page of every godforsaken gossip rag in existence." He lounged back in his chair, but his eyes were hot, and she had the notion that he was coiled to strike. "You understand my reticence, I'm sure."

"And I'd offer you my word," she said, not sure how she kept her tone so light, as if *dirty little games* hadn't pricked at her and hurt while it did, because he had no idea what kind of dirt she'd been drowning in back then, "but somehow, I'm betting that won't be enough for you."

"Sadly, no," he agreed. He sounded anything but sad. "Though it pains me to cast such aspersions on your character, even if only by insinuation."

"Oh, that's what that look on your face is." Her tone was arch and if she hadn't known better, if she hadn't known it was impossible, she might have thought she was enjoying herself here. "It looks a bit more like glee than pain from this side of the table, I should tell you."

Giancarlo smiled, dark and intent. "I can't imagine why."

The night air seemed to shimmer in the space between them, in the flickering light of the candles and in the velvety dark that surrounded the table like an embrace. He settled even farther back in his chair and stretched his legs out again, like an indolent god awaiting a sacrifice, and Paige knew she should put a stop to this before it got out of control—but she didn't. The truth was she didn't want to stop it. She didn't want to do anything but this.

"Strip." It was a hoarse command, rich and dark, like the finest chocolate poured over her skin, and she should have been outraged by his arrogance. Instead, she wanted to bathe in it. In him.

Wasn't that always what she'd wanted?

She didn't pretend she hadn't heard him or that she didn't understand. "Here?"

"Right here." His dark gaze burned, gold and onyx, daring her. "Unless there is some new reason you refuse to obey me this time?"

"You mean, besides the fact that we're sitting outside? Where anyone could see us engaged in all manner of shocking acts? I thought you had a horror of public displays of anything."

"How shocking could a simple strip show be?" he asked, and there was something else in his gaze then, sharp and hard. "It has slipped your mind, perhaps, that the entire world has already seen us having sex. I doubt anything we do could possibly shock them now. Unless you've learned new tricks since I last saw you?"

"Nothing but the same old tricks here," she said, keeping her tone the same as it was, as if that slap of history hadn't made her feel dizzy at all. It was too bad nothing seemed to keep her from wanting him. She was that masochistic. "I'm sorry to disappoint you. Should I keep my clothes on?"

Paige saw that flash of fury in his gaze once more, but it melted into molten heat in the space of a heartbeat, as if they were both masochists here. Somehow, that made her feel better.

"No," he said in a low voice. "You most certainly should not."

"Then it seems I have no choice but to obey you, as promised," she said quietly. "Despite your poor, apparently unshockable neighbors and the things they might see."

"The closest resident aside from my mother is over forty miles away tonight," Giancarlo said, as if impatient. But she could see the fire in his gaze. She could practically taste his need. "Your modesty is safe enough, such as it is. What other excuses do you have?" He let out a bark of something not quite laughter. "We might as well address them all now and be done with them."

"What happens after I strip for you?" Paige asked, almost idly, but she was already pushing her chair back with a too-loud scrape against the stones, then rising to her feet. "This is daring, indeed, to get me naked and then leave me standing here all alone. Is that the plan? It's something of a waste, I'd think."

"First we'll worry about whatever cameras you might have secreted on that body of yours," he told her, and if she hadn't known him she might have thought him cold. Unmoved by all of this. But that wild, uninhibited lover she'd known lurked there in the sensual curve of his lips, that gleaming thing deep in his gaze. Giancarlo might hate her, but he wanted her as much as she did him. And Paige clung to that, perhaps harder than she should have. She clung to it as if it was everything and opted not to listen to the alarms that rang out in her at the thought. "Then we'll worry about what to do with that body."

"Whatever you say, Count Alessi," she murmured, which was as close to obedient as she'd ever come. She saw a certain appreciation for that—or for her wry tone, more like—in his dark eyes, but then it was time to dance.

Because that was what this was. Paige didn't pretend otherwise. The only music was his breath and hers, the only audience the primeval explosion of stars above them. She hadn't danced in years. Ten years, in fact. But she could feel him in her feet, in her hips. In the glorious stretch of her arms over her head. Her pulse and her breath. She could feel him everywhere, better than any sound track with her own hopeful heartbeat like the kick of drums, and she danced.

She poured herself into each undulation of her hips, each exultant reach of her hands. She'd kicked off her shoes when she'd stood and she curled her toes down hard into the smooth stones beneath her, feeling what was left of the day's heat against her soles and that wildfire that only arced higher between the two of them as she moved. She tried her best to catch the sensation in the movement of her hips, her legs, her torso. She took her time peeling off her trousers, managing to kick them aside with a flourish, and then she moved closer to him as she rid herself of her shirt, as if his intent expression beckoned her to him.

She took her time with her bra, offering her breasts to him when she finally dropped it at her side, and she smiled at the way he moved in his chair, his gaze a wild touch on her skin, so fierce it made her nipples pull taut. And she wasn't done. She kept up the dance, the ecstatic dance, and she made it her apology, her regret. She told him all about her love and her silly, shattered hopes with every move she made, and when she stepped out of her panties she didn't know which one of them was breathing more heavily.

Paige only knew that he was standing, too. And that she was naked before him and she still wasn't done.

Naked in the Tuscan night, she danced for all those dreams she'd let carry her away as a girl. For the dream she'd destroyed with a single phone call and a cashed check ten years ago, and none of it worth the sacrifice, in the end. It was like skinny-dipping, warm and cool at once, the summer air a sensual caress against her flesh. She danced for the joy she'd only ever felt in this man's presence, the laughter she still missed, the love she'd squandered for good reasons that seemed nothing but sad in retrospect.

She danced and she danced, and she might have danced all night, but Giancarlo swept her into his arms instead, high against his chest, and that was like a much better dance. Hotter and more intense, and then his mouth came down on hers, claiming her and destroying her that easily.

He came down hard on top of her and she loved it. That lean, hard body of his crushing her with his delicious weight, his narrow hips keeping her legs apart, and it took her a moment to realize that he'd moved them over to one of the sun chaises that sat around the gleaming, sleek pool that jutted out from the loggia toward the vineyards. And that he'd lost his jacket in the move.

And he looked as gorgeously undone as she felt, and very nearly as wild.

"Giancarlo," she whispered, the dance still running madly in her veins, almost as addictive as he was. "Don't stop."

"I give the orders, not you," he growled, but his lips were curved when they took hers all over again.

And then everything slowed down. Turned to honey, thick and sweet.

Giancarlo feasted on her as if she were the gourmet meal his chefs had prepared for him, and beneath his talented mouth she felt almost that cherished, that perfect. She wanted his naked skin pressed to hers more than she could remember wanting anything else, ever, but he kept her too busy to peel his shirt back from his strong shoulders.

He kissed her until her head spun, and then he followed the line of her neck, tasting her and muttering dark things in Italian that she told herself she was happy she didn't understand.

Even if they moved in her like music, dark and compelling, sex and magic and *Giancarlo*, at long last.

He found her breasts and pulled one of the proud nipples deep into his hot mouth, and she didn't care what he *said.* Or in what language. She arched into him, mindless and needy, and he punished and praised her with his lips, his tongue, the scrape of his teeth. He played with her until she begged him to stop and then he only laughed and kept going, sending a catapult of pure wildfire straight down into her core.

She thought for a panicky, wondrous second that he might throw her straight over the edge with only this—

But he stopped, as diabolical as ever, raising his dark head to take in the flushed heat on her face and all down her neck. Her sensual distress. Her driving need.

"This punishment appears to be far more effective than you imagined it would be, *cara,*" he murmured, his voice another sensual shiver against her sensitive skin, with its echoes of the playfully wicked lover she'd met so long ago. "It's almost as if you forgot what I can do to you."

"Thank you for the harsh lesson, Count Alessi," she whispered, not trying too hard to keep her tone anything approaching respectful when she was this close to the edge. "May I have another?"

He laughed, and she did too, and she didn't know if she'd been kidding or if she'd meant it when he returned his attention to her body, shifting to crawl down farther. If these were harsh lessons indeed, or gifts. He left a shimmering trail of fire from her breasts to her belly, and when he paused there, his breath fanning out over the hungriest part of her, Paige realized she was breathing as heavily as if she was running a race. The marathon he'd mentioned earlier, God help her.

"You'd better hold on," he warned her, dark and stirring and *right there* against her sex. "I'm going to stop when I'm done, not when you are."

And then he simply bent his head and licked his way into her.

Paige ignited.

She went from the mere sensation of burning straight into open flame. She couldn't seem to catch her breath. She arched against the exquisite torment of his wickedly clever mouth, or she tried to escape it, and either way, it didn't matter. He gripped her hips in his strong hands and he tasted her molten heat as if it was his own greatest pleasure, and before she knew it she was bucking against him, her hands buried deep in his thick, dark hair.

Calling out his name like a prayer into the night.

And he was as good as his word. He didn't stop. He didn't wait for her to come back down, to come back to herself. He simply kept on tasting her, settling in and taking his time, laughing against her tender flesh when she begged him to stop, laughing more when she begged him to keep on going.

The fire poured back into her, hotter and higher than before, and then he plunged two fingers deep inside of her and threw her over the side of the world. Again.

This time, when she shuddered her way back to earth, Giancarlo had moved off her to stand beside her, his hard hands impatient as he pulled her to her feet. It took her a moment to realize he'd finally stripped but she had no time to appreciate it, because he was lying back on the chaise and pulling her down to sit astride him.

"I want to watch," he told her, his voice dark and nearly grim with need, and it lit that flame inside of her all over again.

And then he simply curled his strong hands around her hips the way he had a thousand times before, the way she'd never dreamed he would again, and thrust home.

CHAPTER SIX

HE WAS INSIDE her again. At last.

Finally.

Giancarlo thought the sensation—far better than all his pale memories across these long years, far better than his own damned hand had ever been—might make him become a religious man.

She was so damned hot, molten and sweet and slick and *his,* and she still held him so tightly, so snugly, it was nearly his undoing. Her hair was that deep black ink with hints of fire and it tumbled all around her in a seductive tousle, falling to those breasts of hers, still high and pert, the tips already tight again and begging for his mouth.

Paige looked soft and stunned, exactly how he liked her best, exactly how he remembered her, and then she made everything better by reaching out to prop her hands against his chest. The shift in position made her sink down even farther on him, making them both groan.

He let his hands travel back to cup the twin globes of her delectable bottom, and tested the depth of her, the friction. God help him, but she was perfect. She had always been perfect. The perfect fit. The perfect fire.

Perfect for him.

Giancarlo had somehow forgotten that, in all the long years since he'd last been inside her. He'd convinced himself he'd exaggerated this as some kind of excuse for his own idiocy—that she'd been nothing more than a pretty girl with a dancer's body and all the rest had been a kind of madness that would make no sense if revisited.

But this was no exaggeration. This was pure, hot, bliss. This was that same true perfection he remembered, at last.

Paige looked down at him, her gaze unreadable. Bright and something like awed. And then she started to move.

He had watched her dance ten years ago, and he had wanted her desperately. He'd watched her dance tonight, that astonishing performance for him alone, equal parts sensual and inviting, and he'd thought he might die if he didn't find a way inside her. But nothing compared to *this* dance. Nothing came close.

She braced herself against him, her hands splayed wide over his pectoral muscles, while her hips set a lazy, shattering, insistent rhythm against his. And Giancarlo was lost.

He forgot about revenge. He forgot about their past. Her deceit, his foolish belief in her. All the terrible lies. The damned pictures themselves, grainy and humiliating. He lost his plans in the slide of her body against his, the sleek thrill that built in him with every rocking motion she made. Every life-altering stroke of the hardest part of him so deep, so very deep, in all of her soft heat.

"Make me come," he ordered her, in a stranger's deep growl. He saw her skin prickle at the sound of it, saw the way she pulled her lower lip between her teeth as if she was fighting back the same wave of sensation he was. "Make it good."

Not that it could be anything but good. Not that it ever had been. This was a magical thing, this wild, hot fire that was only theirs. He could feel it every time he sank within her. He knew it every time he pulled back. He felt it in the sure pace she set with her hips, the tight hold of her flesh against his. He wanted it to go on forever, the way he'd thought it would when he'd met her that first time.

The way it should have, that little voice that was still in love with her, that had never been anything but in love with her, whispered deep inside him.

But she was following his orders and this was no time for regrets. She moved against him, lush and lovely, her hips a sinuous dance, a well-cast spell of longing and lust and too many other things he refused to name. He'd thought he'd lost her forever and yet she was here, moving above him, her lovely body on display because he'd wanted it, holding him so deep inside her he couldn't tell where he ended and she began. He didn't want to know.

"Your wish is my command, my count," she teased him, her voice a husky little dream, and then she did something complicated with her hips and the world turned to flames all around them.

When he finally exploded, a bright rush of fire turned some kind of comet, rocketing over the edge of the night, he heard her call out his name.

And then follow him into bliss.

Giancarlo did not welcome reality when it reasserted itself.

Paige lay slumped over him, her face buried in his neck, while he was still deep inside of her. He opted not to think about how easy it was to hold her, or how she still seemed to have been crafted especially to fit in his arms, exactly this way. It took him much longer than it should have to get his breathing under control again. He held her the way a lover might, the way he always had before, and stared out over the top of her head at the faint lights on distant hills and the smear of starlight above.

He wished he didn't care about the past. More than that, he wished he could trust her the way he had once. He wished so many things, and yet all of the stars were fixed tonight, staring down at him from their cold positions, and he knew better.

Paige was an accident waiting to happen. He'd been caught up in that accident once—he wouldn't subject himself to it again. Even he wasn't foolish enough to walk into the same trap twice. No matter that it felt like glory made flesh to touch her again, like coming home after too long away.

He would learn to live without that, too. He had before.

She shifted against him, and he felt the brush of her lips over his skin and told himself it was calculated. That everything about her was calculated. There was no use remembering the afternoons they'd spent curled around each other in his huge bed surrounded by the Malibu sea. When she'd tasted him everywhere with her eyes closed, as if she couldn't help herself, as if her affection was as elemental as the ocean beyond his windows or the sky above and she had no choice but to sink into it with all of her senses.

That had been an act. This was an act. He needed to remember it.

But that didn't mean he couldn't enjoy the show.

"You've obviously been practicing," he said, to be horrible. To remind them both that this was here and now, not ten years back. "Quite a lot, I'd say, were I to hazard a guess."

He felt her tense against him, but almost thought he'd imagined it when she sat up a moment later, displaying her typical offhanded grace. And then she smiled slightly as she looked down at him.

"I was about to compliment you on the same thing," she said, a brittle sort of mischief and something else lighting up her gaze. "You must have slept with a thousand women to do that so well! My congratulations. Especially as I would have said there weren't ten women you could sleep with in a hundred miles, much less a thousand. The privileges of wealth, I presume?"

"You're hilarious." But he couldn't help the crook of his mouth. "I have them flown in from Rome, of course."

"Of course." She wrinkled her nose at him, and it was as dangerous as it had been earlier. It made him want things he knew he couldn't have. He couldn't have them, and more to the point, she couldn't give them. Hadn't he learned anything? "You realize, Giancarlo, that people might get the wrong idea. They might begin to think you're a playboy whore."

"They won't."

"Because you tell them so?" She shook her head, her expression serious though her mysterious eyes laughed at him. "I think that tactic only works with me. And not very well."

"Because," he said, his hands moving to her bottom again, then higher along the tempting indentation in her lovely back to tug her down to him, "a man is only a playboy whore when he appears to be having too much of a certain kind of uncontrolled fun in public. I can do all the same things in private and it doesn't count. Didn't you know?"

Her attention dropped to his mouth and he wanted it there. He was already hardening within her again and she shifted restlessly against him as if she encouraged it, making the fire inside him leap to new life that easily.

"It all counts," she breathed. "Or none of it does."

"Then I suppose that makes us all whores, doesn't

it?" he asked. He indulged himself and sank his hands deep into her hair, holding her head fast, as he tested the depth of her again and found her hotter around him. Wetter. Better, somehow, than before. That quickly, he was like steel. "But let's be clear. How many lovers have you taken in the last ten years?"

"Less than your thousand," she said, her voice a thin little thing, as her hips met his greedily. Deliciously. He grunted, and then pulled out to flip them around, coming down over her again and drawing her legs around his waist. He teased her heat with the tip of his hardness, and he didn't know what it was that drove him then, but he didn't let her pull him into her.

"How many?" he asked. He had no idea why he cared. He didn't care. He'd imagined it a thousand times and it scraped at him and it changed nothing either way. But he couldn't seem to stop. "Tell me."

Her eyes moved to his, then away, and they looked blue in the shadows. "What does it matter? Whatever number I pick, you'll think the worst of me."

"I already think the worst of you," he said, the way he might have crooned love words a lifetime ago, and he couldn't have said what he wanted here. To hurt her? Or himself? To make this all worse? Or was this simply his way of reminding them both who they were? "Why don't you try the truth?"

"None," she said, and there was an odd expression on her face as she said it. He might have called it vulnerable, were she someone else. "I told you there were no new tricks."

It took another beat for him to process that, and then something roared in him, a primal force that was like some kind of howl, and he thought he shook though he knew he held himself perfectly still.

"Is that a joke?" But he was whispering. He barely knew his own voice.

Her wide mouth twisted and her gaze was dark with something he didn't want to understand. Something that couldn't possibly be real.

"Yes," she said, her voice broken and fierce at once. "Ha ha, what a joke. I meant ten. Twenty. How many lovers do you imagine I've taken, Giancarlo? What number proves I'm who you think I am?"

He heard her voice break slightly as she asked the question, and a kind of ripple went through her lush body. He felt it. This time when she urged him into her, he went, slick and hard and even better than before, making him mutter a curse and press his forehead to hers. And he didn't have the slightest idea if this was his form of an apology, or hers.

"I don't care one way or the other," he lied, and he didn't want to talk about this any longer. He didn't want to revisit all those images he'd tortured himself with over the years. Because his sad little secret was that he'd never imagined her in prison, the way he'd told her he had. He'd imagined her wrapped around some other man exactly like this and he'd periodically searched the internet to see if he could find any evidence that she was out there somewhere, doing it with all that same joy and grace that had undone him.

And it had killed him, every time. It still killed him.

So he took it out on her instead, in the best way possible. He set a hard pace, throwing them headfirst into that raging thing that consumed them both, and he laughed against the side of her neck when she couldn't do anything but moan out her surrender.

He held on, building that perfect wildness all over again, making her thrash and keen, and when he thought he couldn't take it any longer he reached between them and pressed hard against the center of her need, making her shatter all around him.

And he rode her until he could throw himself into that shattering, too. Until he could forget the truth he'd heard in her voice when she'd told him there hadn't been anyone since him, because he couldn't handle that—or what he'd seen on her face that he refused to believe. *He refused.*

He rode her until he could forget everything but this. Everything but her. Everything they built between them in this marvelous fire.

Until he lost himself all over again.

"Violet is asking for you," Giancarlo said.

Paige had heard him coming from a long way off. First the Jeep, the engine announcing itself high on the hill and only getting louder as it wound its way down toward her cottage. Then the slam of the driver's door. The thud of the cottage's front door, and then, some minutes later, the slide of the glass doors that led out to where she sat, curled up beneath a graceful old oak tree with her book in her lap.

"That sounds like an accusation," she said mildly, putting her book aside. He stood on the terrace with his hands on his lean hips, frowning at her. "Of course she's asking for me. I'm her assistant. She might be on vacation here, but I'm not."

"She needs to learn how to relax and handle her own affairs," he replied, somewhat darkly. Paige climbed to her feet, brushing at the skirt she wore, and started toward him. It was impossible not feel that hunger at the sight of him, deep inside her, making her too warm, too soft.

"Possibly," she said, trying to concentrate on something, anything but the sensual spell he seemed to weave simply by existing. "But I'm not her therapist, I'm her personal assistant. When she learns how to relax and handle her own affairs, I'm out of a job."

Her heart set up its usual clatter at his proximity, worse the closer she got to him, and she didn't understand how that could still happen. They'd been here almost a week. It should have settled down by now. She should have started to grow immune to him, surely. After all, she already knew how this would end. Badly. Unlike the last time, when she'd been so blissfully certain it would be the one thing in her life that ended well, this time she knew better. Their history was like a crystal ball, allowing her to see the future clearly.

Maybe too clearly. Not that it seemed to matter.

She stopped when she was near him but not too near him, and felt that warm thing in the vicinity of her heart when he scowled. He reached over and tugged her closer, so he could land a hard kiss on her mouth. *Like a mark of possession,* she thought, *more than an indication of desire*—but she didn't care.

It deepened, the way it always deepened. Giancarlo muttered something and angled his head, and when he finally pulled back she was wound all around him and flushed and there was that deep male satisfaction stamped all over his face.

"Later," he told her, like a promise, as if she'd been the one to start this.

And in this past week, Paige had learned that she'd take this man any way she could have him. She imagined that said any number of unflattering things about her, but she didn't care.

"I might be busy later," she told him loftily.

He smiled that hard smile of his that made her ache,

and he didn't look particularly concerned. "I will take that chance."

And she would let him, she knew. Not because he told her to. Not because he was holding anything over her head. But because she was helpless before her own need, even though she knew perfectly well it would ruin her all over again....

Later, she told herself. *I'll worry about it later.*

Because *later* was going to be all the years she got to live through on the other side of this little interlude, when he was nothing but a memory all over again. And she wasn't delusional enough to imagine that there was any possibility that when this thing with Giancarlo ended he might permit her to remain with Violet, in any capacity. He was as likely to fall to his knees and propose marriage.

She moved around him and into the house then, not wanting him to read that epic bit of silliness on her face, when that notion failed to make her laugh at herself the way it should have. When it made everything inside of her clutch hopefully instead. *You are such a fool,* she chided herself.

But then again, that wasn't news.

Paige swept up her bag and hung it over her shoulder, then followed Giancarlo out to his Jeep. He climbed in and turned the key, and she clung to the handle on her side of the vehicle as he bumped his way up the old lane and then headed toward the *castello* in the distance.

It was another beautiful summer's day, bright and perfect with the olive trees a silvery presence on either side of the lane that wound through the hills toward Violet, and Paige told herself it was enough. This was enough. It was more than she'd ever imagined could happen with Giancarlo after what she'd done, and why did she want to ruin it with thoughts of *more*?

But the sad truth was, she didn't know how to be anything but greedy when it came to this man. She wanted all of him, not the parts of himself he doled out so carefully, so sparingly. Not when she could feel he kept so much of himself apart.

She'd woken the morning after that first night to find herself in his bed. Alone. He'd left her there without so much as a note, and she'd lectured herself about the foolishness of her hurt feelings. She'd told herself she should count herself lucky he hadn't tossed her out his front door at dawn, naked.

What she told herself and what she actually went right on feeling, of course, were not quite the same thing.

Modify your expectations, girl, she'd snapped at herself on the walk down the hill to her cottage. The birds had been singing joyfully, the sun had been cheerful against her face, she was in *Italy* of all places, and Giancarlo had made love to her again and again throughout the night. He could call it whatever he wanted. She would hold it in her battered little heart and call it what it had meant to her.

Because she hadn't lied to him. She hadn't touched another man since him, and she'd grown to accept the fact she never would. At first it had hurt too much. She'd seen nothing but Giancarlo—and more important, his back, on that last morning when he'd walked away from her rather than talk about what had happened, what she'd done. Then she'd started working for Violet and it had seemed as if Giancarlo was everywhere, in pictures, in emails, in conversation. Paige had had the very acute sense that so much as going out to dinner with another man was some kind of treason—which she'd known was absurd. Beyond absurd, given the way in which she'd betrayed him. She'd made certain he hated her. He'd walked away from her without a single backward glance. Why should he care what she did?

And yet somehow, each of these ten years had crept by and he was still the only man she'd ever slept with. She'd been unable to contain the small, humming thing inside her then as that thought had kept her company on her walk. It had felt a little bit too much like a kind of silly joy she ought to have known better than to indulge.

But he'd turned up that night, his face drawn as if he'd fought a great battle with himself, and he hadn't seemed interested in talking about whether he'd lost or won. He'd led her up her stairs, thrown her on her bed, and kept them up for another night—this time, she'd noted, with the condoms they'd failed to use before.

They hadn't talked about that first night and its lack of birth control. Just like ten years ago, they hadn't talked about a thing.

And that was how it had been since her arrival, Paige thought now, as they drew closer to the *castello*. She'd never spent much time wondering what it felt like to be a rich man's *kept woman* before now. What she thought people in this part of the world might call a *mistress*. But she imagined it must be something like this past week.

Nothing but the pleasures of their flesh. No unpleasant topics, save the odd bout of teasing that never quite landed a hard punch. Nothing but sex and food and sex again, until she felt glutted on it. Replete. Able to know him at a touch, taste him when he wasn't there, scent him on any breeze.

The last time she'd felt so deeply a part of her own body, her own physical space, she'd been dancing more hours of the day than she'd slept.

She didn't tell him that, either. That she filled these golden, blue-skied days with dancing, as if the first dancing she'd done on that initial night with him had freed her. Paige hadn't understood how lost she'd been until she found herself out in the field near her cottage, dancing in great, wide circles beneath the glorious Tuscan sky with tears running down her face and her arms stretched toward the sun. She wanted nothing more than to share that with him.

But Giancarlo drove the Jeep with the same ferocity he did everything else—except in bed, where he indulged every sense and took his sweet time—and with that same hard edge of his old dark fury beneath it.

Almost as if he, too, preferred the little fairy tale they'd been living this past week, where she existed purely to please him, and did, again and again.

Paige knew better than to ask him about it. Or to tell him the things that moved in her, sharp and sweet, in this place that felt more like home every day. This was a no-talking zone. This was a place of sun and sex and silence. It was the only possible way it could work.

Like all temporary things, all stolen moments, it could only be a secret, or it would implode.

"What have you been up to all this time?" Violet asked, peering at Paige from her position on one of the *castello*'s lovely couches, her iPad in her lap and her voice no more than mildly reproving. "I thought perhaps you'd been sucked into one of the olive groves, never to be seen again."

"You should have told me you needed me!" Paige exclaimed instead of answering the question. Because she didn't want to know what Violet would think about the help touching her son. She didn't want to risk her relationship with either one of them. "I thought I was giving you some much-needed time and space to yourself!"

"My dear girl," Violet said, sounding amused, "if I

wanted time and space to myself, I would have chosen a different life altogether."

Paige was too aware of Giancarlo's dark, brooding presence on the other side of the living room then, lounging there against the massive stone fireplace, supposedly scrolling through his phone's display. She was certain he was hanging on every word. Or did she simply want to be that important to him?

There was no answer to that. Not one that came without a good dose of pain in its wake.

"I'm here now," Paige said stoutly, trying to focus on the woman who had always been good to her, without all these complications and regrets. *Not that she'd give you the time of day if she knew who you really were,* that rough voice that was so much like her mother's snarled at her.

"Then I have two questions for you," Violet replied, snapping Paige back to the present. "Can you operate a manual transmission?"

That hadn't been what Paige was expecting, but that was Violet. Paige rolled with it. "I can."

It was, in fact, one of the few things she could say her mother had taught her. Even if it had been mostly so that Paige could drive the beat-up car she owned to pick her up, drunk and belligerent, from the rough bars down near the railroad tracks.

"And do you want to drive me to Lucca?" Violet smiled serenely when Giancarlo made an irritated sort of noise from the fireplace across the room and kept her eyes trained on Paige. "If memory serves, it has wonderful shopping. And I'm in the mood for an adventure."

"An adventure with attention or without?" Paige asked without missing a beat, though she was well aware it had been a long time since Violet had gone out on one of her excursions into the public without expecting attention from the people who would see her out and about.

"Without," Giancarlo snapped, from much closer by, and Paige had to control a little jump. She hadn't heard him move.

"With, of course," Violet said, as if he hadn't spoken. "No one has fawned over me in a whole week, and I require attention the way plants require sunlight, you know. It's how I maintain my youthful facade."

She said it as if she was joking, but in that way of hers that didn't actually allow for any argument. Not that it was Paige's place to argue. Her son, however, was a different story.

"You're one of the most famous women in the world," Giancarlo pointed out, and the dark thing Paige heard in his voice was a different animal than the one he used when he spoke to her. More exasperated, perhaps. Or more formal. "It's not safe for you to simply wander the streets alone."

"I won't be alone. I'll have Paige," Violet replied.

"And what, pray, will Paige do should you find yourself surrounded? Mobbed?" Giancarlo rolled his eyes. "Hold the crowd off with a smart remark or two?"

"I wouldn't underestimate the power of a smart remark," Paige retorted, glaring at him—but his gaze was on his mother.

"That was a long time ago," Violet said softly. With a wealth of compassion that made Paige stiffen in surprise and Giancarlo jerk back as if she'd slapped him. "I was a very foolish young woman. I underestimated the kind of interest there would be—not only in me, but in you. Your father was livid." She studied her son for a moment and then rose to her feet, smiling faintly at Paige. "We were in the south of France and I thought it would be a

marvelous idea to go out and poke around the shops by
myself. Giancarlo was four. And when the crowds surrounded us, he was terrified."

"The police were called," he said, furiously, Paige
thought, though his voice was cold. "You had to be res-
cued by armed officials and you never went out without
security again—and neither did I. I hope you haven't
spent your life telling this story as if I was an overimag-
inative child who caused a fuss. It wasn't a monster in
my closet. It was a pack of shouting cameramen and a
mob of fans."

"The point is, my darling, you were four," Violet said
quietly. "You are not four any longer. And while I flatter
myself that I remain relevant, I am an old woman who
has not commanded the attention of packs of paparazzi
in a very long time. I'm perfectly capable of enjoying an
afternoon with my assistant and, if you insist, *one* driver."

"And you wonder why I refuse to have children," he
growled at her, and it took every shred of self-preservation Paige had to keep from reacting to that. To Giancarlo
and the pain she could hear beneath the steel in his voice.
"Why I would die before I'd subject another innocent to
this absurd world of yours."

"I didn't wonder," Violet replied. "I knew. But I hoped
you'd outgrow it."

"Mother—"

"I don't like being locked away in Italian castles,
Giancarlo," she said, and there was steel in the way she
said it, despite the smile she used. It was the famous star
issuing a command, not a mother. "If you cast your memory back, you'll remember that I never have."

There was a strange tension in the room then. And
though she knew better, though it would no doubt raise
the suspicions of the woman who could read anyone,

standing right there beside her, Paige found herself looking to Giancarlo as if she could soothe him somehow. As if he'd let her—

And she found that great darkness blazing in his eyes as he slowly, slowly turned his attention from Violet to her.

As if this was something she'd done, too.

Because, of course, she had. When he'd been far older than four. And what she'd done to him hadn't been an accident.

The truth of that almost knocked her sideways, and she would never know how she remained standing. She wanted to tell him everything, and who cared what Violet thought? She wanted to explain about her mother's downward spiral. The money owed, the threats from the horrible Denny, the fear and panic that she'd thought were just the way life was. Because that was how it had always been. Paige wanted him to understand—at last— that she never, ever would have sacrificed him if she hadn't believed she had no other choice. If she hadn't been trapped and terrified herself, with only hideous options on all sides.

But this wasn't the place and she knew—*she knew*— he wouldn't want to hear it anyway. He didn't want to know *why*. He only wanted her to pay.

He didn't realize that she had. That she still did. Every moment since.

And so she stood there, she said nothing the way she'd always said nothing and somehow she managed not to fall to her knees. Somehow Paige managed not to break into pieces. Somehow, she stared back at him as if she'd never broken his heart and she wished, hard and fierce and utterly pointless, that it were true.

"Don't worry," he said quietly, as if he was answering

his mother. All of that darkness in his gaze. All of the betrayal, the loss. The terrible grief. It made Paige's chest ache, so acutely that she forgot to worry that Violet would be able to sense it from a few feet away. So sharp and so deep she thought it might have been a mortal blow, and how could anyone hide that? "I remember everything."

CHAPTER SEVEN

LUCCA WAS A walled city, an old fortress turned prosperous market town, and it was enchanting. Paige dutifully followed Violet through the bustle of tiled red roofs, sloped streets and the sheer tumult of such an ancient place, and told herself there was no reason at all she should feel so unequal to the task she'd done so well and well-nigh automatically for years.

But her heart wasn't with her in the colorful city. It was back in the hills with the man she'd left there, with that look on his face and too much dark grief in his gaze.

And the longer Violet lingered—going in and out of every shop, pausing for cell phone photos every time she was recognized, settling in for a long dinner in a restaurant where the chef came racing out to serenade her and she was complimented theatrically for her few Italian phrases, all while Paige looked on and/or assisted—the more Paige wondered if the other woman was doing it deliberately. As if she knew what was going on between her son and her assistant.

But that was impossible, Paige kept telling herself.

This is called guilt, that caustic voice inside her snapped as Violet flirted outrageously with the chef. *This is why you're here. Why you work for his mother. Why you accept how he treats you. You deserve it. You earned it.*

More than that, she missed him. One afternoon knowing Giancarlo wasn't within reach, that there was no chance he'd simply appear and tumble her down onto the nearest flat surface, the way he'd done only yesterday with no advance warning, and she was a mess. If this was a preview of what her life was going to be like after this all ended, Paige thought as she handled Violet's bill and called for the car, she was screwed.

"Like that's anything new," she muttered under her breath as she climbed into the car behind Violet, nearly closing the heavy door on the still-grasping hands of the little crowd that had gathered outside the restaurant to adore her.

"Pardon?" Violet asked.

Paige summoned her smile. Her professional demeanor, which she thought she'd last seen weeks ago in Los Angeles. "Did that do? Scratch the attention itch?"

"It did." Violet sat across from her in the dark, her gaze out the window as the car started out of the city. "Giancarlo is a solitary soul. He doesn't understand that some people recharge their batteries in different ways than he does. Not everyone can storm about a lonely field and feel recharged."

Said the woman who had never passed a crowd she couldn't turn into a fan base with a few sentences and a smile. Paige blinked, amazed at her churlishness even in her own head, and found Violet's calm gaze on hers.

"You're an extrovert." Paige said evenly. "I'm sure he knows that by now. Just as he likely knows that therefore, his own needs are different from yours."

"One would think," Violet agreed in her serene, untroubled way, which shouldn't have sent a little shiver of warning down Paige's back. "But then, the most interesting men are not always in touch with what they need, are they?"

Violet didn't speak much after that, yet Paige didn't feel as if she could breathe normally until the car pulled off the country road and started along the winding drive into the estate. And she was impatient—the most impatient she'd ever been in Violet's presence, though she tried valiantly to disguise it—as she helped the older woman into the *castello* and oversaw the staff as they sorted out her purchases.

And only when she was finally in the car again and headed toward her cottage did Paige understand what had been beating at her all day, clutching at her chest and her throat and making her want to scream in the middle of ancient Italian piazzas. Guilt, yes, but that was a heavy thing, a spiked weight that hung on her. The rest of it was panic.

Because any opportunity Giancarlo had to reflect on what was happening between them—not revenge, not the comeuppance he'd obviously planned—was the beginning of the end. She knew it, deep inside. She'd seen it in his eyes this morning.

And when she got to her cottage and found not only it but the house above it dark, it confirmed her fears.

Paige stood there in the dark outside her cottage long after the driver's car disappeared into the night, staring up the hill, willing this shadow or that to separate from the rest and become Giancarlo. She was too afraid to think about what might happen if this was it. If that kiss he'd delivered in the garden was their last.

Too soon, she thought desperately, or perhaps that was the first prayer she'd dared make in years. *It's too soon.*

She stared up the side of the hill as if that would call him to her, somehow. But the only thing around her was the soft summer night, pretty and quiet. Still and empty, for miles around.

When she grew too cold and he still didn't appear, she made her way inside, feeling more punished by his absence than by anything else that had happened between them. Paige entertained visions of marching up the hill and taking what she wanted, or at least finding him and seeing for herself what had happened in her absence today, but the truth was, she didn't dare. She was still so uncertain of her welcome.

Would he throw back the covers and yank her into his arms if she appeared at his bedside? Or would he send her right back out into the night again, with a cruel word or two as her reward? Paige found she was too unsure of the answer to test it.

There were red flags everywhere, she acknowledged as she got ready for bed and crawled beneath her sheets. Red flags and dark corners, and nothing safe. But maybe what mattered was that she knew that, this time. She'd known the moment she'd decided to apply for that job with Violet. She'd always known.

She would have to learn to live with that, too.

Later that night, Paige woke with a sudden start when a lean male form crawled into her bed, hauling her into his arms.

Giancarlo. Of course.

But her heart was already crashing against her ribs as he rolled so she was beneath him. Excitement. Relief. The usual searing hunger, sharper than usual this time.

"Why didn't you come to me?" he gritted at her, temper and need and too many other dark and hungry things in his voice. Then the scrape of his teeth against the tender flesh of her neck, making her shudder.

Paige didn't want to think about the contours of her fears now, her certainty he'd finished with this. With her. Not now, while he was braced above her, his body so familiar and hot against hers, making the night blaze with the wild need that was never far beneath the surface. Never far at all.

Not even when she thought she'd lost him again.

"I thought you'd gone to bed already." *I didn't know if you'd want me to come find you,* she thought, but wisely kept to herself. "All of your lights were out."

She thought she saw a certain self-knowledge move over his face then, but it was gone so quickly she was sure she must have imagined it.

"Did you have a lovely day out with my mother?" he asked in a tone she wasn't foolish enough to imagine was friendly, his dark eyes glittering in the faint light from the rising moon outside her windows. "Filled with her admirers, exactly as she wished?"

"Of course." Paige ran her hands from his hard jaw to the steel column of his neck, as if trying to imprint the shape of him on her palms. Trying to make certain that if this was the last time, she'd remember it. That it couldn't be snatched from her, not entirely. "When Violet decrees we are to have fun, that is precisely what we have. No mere crowd would dare defy the crown jewel of the Hollywood establishment."

Giancarlo didn't laugh. He shifted his body so he was hard against her and she melted the way she always did, ready to welcome him no matter his mood or hers, no matter the strange energy that crackled from him tonight, no matter the darkness that seemed wrapped around him even as he wound himself around her.

There were other words for what she was with this man, she knew, words she hadn't heard in a long time but still remembered all too well. Words she'd dismissed as the unhealthy rantings of the worst person she'd ever known, the person who had taken everything she'd wanted from her—but it turned out dismissing them wasn't the same thing as erasing them.

Even so, the hollow, gnawing thing that had sat inside her all day and made her feel so panicked was gone, because he was here. She filled it with his scent, his touch, his bold possession.

Him. Giancarlo.

The only man she'd ever touched. The only man she'd ever loved.

And this was the only way she could tell him any of that. With her body. Paige shifted so he was flush against her entrance and hooked her legs over his hips, letting him in. Loving him in the only way she knew. In the only way he'd let her.

"Maybe that didn't always work out when you were a child," she whispered, hoping he couldn't read too much emotion in her eyes, across her face. "But my relationship with Violet is much easier. She pays, I agree, the end."

Giancarlo bent his head to press hot, open kisses along the ridge of her collarbone. Paige moved restlessly, hungrily against him, tilting her head back to give him greater access. To give him anything—everything—he wanted.

Because this won't last forever, that harsh voice that was too much an echo of her mother's reminded her. That was what today had taught her. There were no fairy tales. This situation had an expiration date, and every moment she had with him was one moment closer to the end.

"In a way," Giancarlo said, still too dark, still too rough, his mouth against her skin so Paige could feel the rumble of his words inside of her as he spoke, "that is every relationship that Violet has."

She heard that same tense grief that had been in him in the *castello* that morning and this time, no one was watching. She could soothe him, or try. She ran her fingers through his thick hair and smiled when he pressed into her touch, like a very large cat.

"I don't think it can be easy to be a great figure," Paige said after a moment, concentrating on the feel of his scalp beneath her fingertips, the drag of his thick hair as she moved her hands through it, the exquisite sensation of stroking him. "Too many expectations. Too much responsibility to something far bigger than oneself. The constant worry that it will be taken away. But it must be harder still to be that person's child."

He shifted away from her, propping himself up on his elbows, though he kept himself cradled there between her thighs, his arousal a delicious weight against her softness. A promise. The silence stretched out and his face was in shadow, so all she could see was the glitter of his dark gold eyes, and the echo of it deep inside her.

"It's not hard," he said, and she'd never heard that tone before, had she? Clipped and resigned at once. And yet somehow, that pit in her belly yawned open again as he spoke. "As long as you remember that she is always playing a role. The *grande dame* as benevolent mother. The living legend as compassionate parent. The great star whose favorite role of all is *mom*. When she was younger there were different roles threaded into the mix, but the same principle applied. You learn this as a child in a thousand painful ways and you vow, if you are at all wise, never to inflict it on another. To let it end with you."

Paige tried to imagine Giancarlo as a small boy, all stubborn chin and fathomless eyes, and ached for him, though that didn't explain her nervousness. It was something in the way he held himself apart from her, a certain danger rippling down the length of his body, as hard and as steel-hewn as he was. It was the way he watched her, too still, too focused.

"I'm sorry," she said, though she wanted to say so much more. She didn't dare. Just like before, when she'd stood outside and wanted him and had known better than to go and find him, she was too uncertain. "That can't have been easy."

"Is that sympathy for me, *cara*? Don't bother."

He wasn't quite scoffing at her. Not quite, though his face went fierce in the darkness, edging toward cruel the way he'd been in the beginning, and she found she was bracing herself—unable to open her mouth and stop him. Unable to defend herself at all. *Whatever he's about to say,* that hard voice reminded her, like another slap, *you deserve*.

"Here is what I learned from my mother, the great actress," Giancarlo said. "That she is a mystery, unknowable even to herself. That she prefers it that way. That intimacy is anathema to her because it cannot be controlled, it cannot be directed, it cannot cut to print when she is satisfied with her performance. It is one long take with no rehearsal and no do-overs, and she goes to great lengths indeed to avoid it."

Paige wasn't sure why she felt so stricken then, so stripped raw when he wasn't talking about her—but then he moved again, dropping his weight against her to whisper in her ear, hot and close and dark. So very dark.

You deserve this, she told herself. *Whatever it is.*

"I want a woman I can trust, *Paige*," he said with a ruthless inevitability. And it didn't even hurt. It was like a deep slice of a sharp blade. She knew he'd cut her and now there was only the wait for blood. For the pain that would surely follow. And he wasn't finished. "A woman I can know inside and out. A woman who carries no secrets, who does not hide herself away from me or from the world, who never plays a role. A woman who wants a partner, not an audience."

"Giancarlo." She felt torn apart even though he was holding her close. Wrecked as surely as if he'd thrown her from the roof of the towering *castello*. "Please."

But the worst part was, he knew what he was doing. She'd seen it in the cast of his sensual mouth. She'd felt it in the way he'd very nearly trembled as he'd held himself above her.

He knew he was hurting her. And he kept going.

"I want a woman I can believe when she tells me she loves me," he said, raw and fierce and she knew she deserved that, she knew she did, even though it felt a little bit like dying. And then he lifted his head to look her straight in the eyes, making it that much worse. "And that can never be you, can it? It never was. It never will be."

Later, she thought she might take that apart and live awhile in the misery he'd packed into those last two sentences. Later, she thought she might cry for days and check herself for scars, the way she'd done ten years ago. But that was later.

Tonight Paige thought the pain in him was far greater than the hurt he'd caused—that she deserved, that voice kept telling her, and she agreed no matter how it cut her up—and she couldn't bear it.

She didn't care if he still hated her, even now, after another week in his bed when he'd tasted every part of her and had to have recognized the sheer honesty in her response to him. She told herself she didn't care about that at all and some part of her believed it.

Or wanted to believe it.

But worrying about that was for later, too. Later, when she could put herself together again. Later, when she could think about something other than the man who stretched over her and broke her heart, again and again and again. Because he could.

"Giancarlo," she said again, with more force this time. "Stop talking."

And he surrendered with a groan, thrusting deep and hard inside of her where there was nothing but the two of them—that shimmering truth that was only theirs, wild and dizzying and hotter every time—and that perfect, wondrous fire that swept them both away in its glory.

And Paige did her best to make them both forget.

Two more weeks passed, slow and sweet. The Tuscan summer started to edge toward the coming fall. The air began to feel crisp in the mornings, and the sky seemed bluer. And if she'd allowed herself to think about such things, Paige might have believed that the tension between her and Giancarlo was easing, too—all that heavy grief mellowing, turning blue like the sky, gold like the fields, lighter and softer with age.

Or perhaps she'd taught them both how to forget.

Whatever it was, it worked. No more did she spend her days trapped in her isolated cottage, available only to him and only when he wanted—and she told herself she didn't miss it, all that forced proximity and breathlessness. Of course she didn't miss it.

Paige's days looked a great deal as they had back home. She met with Violet most mornings, and helped her plan out her leisure time. Violet was particularly fond of day trips to various Italian cities to soak in all the art and culture and fashion with a side helping of adulation from the locals, which she often expedited by taking Giancarlo's helicopter that left from the roof of the *castello* and kicked up such a ruckus when it returned it could be heard for miles around.

"I've always preferred a big entrance," Violet had murmured the first time, that famous smile of hers on her lips as the helicopter touched down.

But when Violet was in between her trips—which meant days of spa treatments and dedicated lounging beneath artfully placed umbrellas at the side of the *castello*'s private pool instead—Paige was left to her own devices, which usually meant she was left to Giancarlo's.

One day he stopped the Jeep the moment it was out of sight of the *castello*'s stout tower and knelt down beside the passenger door, pulling her hips to his mouth and licking his way into Paige right there—making her sob out his name into the quiet morning, so loud it startled the birds from the nearby trees. Another time he drove them out to one of the private lakes that dotted the property and they swam beneath the hot sun, then brought each other to a shuddering release in the shallow end, Giancarlo holding her to him as she took advantage of the water's buoyancy to make him groan.

Other times, they talked. He told her of his father's dreams for this land, its long history and his own plans to monetize it while conserving it, that it might last for many more generations. He showed her around the Etruscan ruins that cropped up in the oddest spots and demonstrated, as much as possible, that a man who knew the ins and outs of three thousand acres in such extraordinary detail seemed something like magical when the landscape in question was a woman's body. *Her* body.

Paige didn't know which she treasured more. His words or his body. But she held them to her like gifts, and she tried not to think about what she deserved, what she knew she had coming to her. She tried to focus on what she had in her hands, instead.

One lazy afternoon they lay together in the warm sun, the sweet breeze playing over their heated skin. Paige propped her chin against his chest and looked into his eyes and it was dizzying, the way it was always dizzying. And then he smiled at her without a single stray shadow in his gorgeous eyes, and it was as if the world slammed to a stop and then started in the other direction.

"I saw you dancing in the garden the other night," he said.

There was no reason to blush. She told herself the heat she felt move over her was the sun, the leftover fire of the way he'd torn her to pieces only moments before, and nothing more.

"I haven't danced in a long while," she said, and she wanted to tear her gaze away from his, but she didn't. Or she couldn't. He ran his hand through her hair, slow and sweet, and she was afraid of the things he could see in her. And so afraid of the things she wanted.

"Why not?"

And Paige didn't know how to answer that. How to tell him the why of it without blundering straight into all the land mines they'd spent these weeks avoiding. That they'd managed to avoid entirely after that night she'd come back late from Lucca.

I want a woman I can trust, he'd said, and she wanted him to trust her. She might not deserve his trust, but she wanted it.

"I was good," she said after a moment, because that was true enough, "but I wasn't *amazing.* And there were so many other dancers who were as good as I was, but wanted it way more than I did."

Especially after he'd left and she hadn't had the heart

for it any longer, or anything else involving the body she'd used to betray the one man she'd ever given it to. She'd auditioned for one more gig and her agent had told her they'd said it was like watching a marionette. That had been her last audition. Her last dance, period.

Because once she'd lost Giancarlo, she'd lost interest in the only other thing she'd had that'd ever had any meaning in her life. Her mother had descended even further into that abyss of hers and Paige had simply been *lost*. And when she'd run into a woman she'd met through Giancarlo on one of those Malibu weekends, who'd needed a personal assistant a few days a week and had kind of liked that Paige was a bit notorious, it had seemed like a good idea. And more, a way to escape, once and for all, the dark little world her mother lived in.

A year later, she'd been working for a longtime television star who had no idea that competent Paige Fielding was related to *that* Nicola Fielding. A few years after that, she had enough experience to sign with a very exclusive agency that catered to huge stars like Violet, and when Violet's previous assistant left her, to put herself forward as a replacement. All of those things had seemed so random back then, as they happened. But now, looking back, it seemed anything but. As if Paige's subconscious had plotted out the only course that could bring her back to Giancarlo.

But she didn't want to think about that now. Or about what she'd do when she was without him again. How would she re-create herself this time? Where would she go? It occurred to her then that she'd never really planned beyond Violet. Beyond the road she'd known would bring her back to him.

I want a partner, he'd said, and the problem was, she

was a liar. A deliberate amnesiac, desperate to keep their past at bay. That wasn't a partner. That was a problem.

Giancarlo was still smiling, as if this was an easy conversation, and Paige wished it was. For once, *just once,* she wanted something to be as easy as it should have been.

"I'm surprised," he said, and there was something very much like affection in his gaze, transforming his face until he looked like that younger version of himself again. She told herself that it didn't make her ache. That it didn't make her heart twist tight. "I would have said dancing was who you were, not something you did."

"I was twenty years old," she heard herself say, in a rueful sort of tone that suggested an amusement she didn't quite feel. "I had no idea who I was."

You're his toy, Nicola, her mother had screamed at her in those final, dark days, when Paige had believed she'd somehow navigate her way through it all unscathed— that she'd manage to keep Giancarlo, please her mother and her mother's terrible friends, and pay off all of that debt besides. *He'll play with you until he's done and then he'll leave you broken and useless when he moves on to the next dumb whore. Don't be so naive!*

Giancarlo's face changed then, and his hand froze in her hair. "I think I always forget you were so young," he said after a moment, as if remembering her age shocked him. "What the hell was I doing? You were a kid."

She laughed then. She couldn't help it.

"My life wasn't exactly pampered and easy before I came to Hollywood," she told him, knowing as she said it that she'd never talked about that part of her life. He had been so bright, so beautiful—why would she talk about dark, grim things? "And I did that about ten minutes after I graduated from high school. My mom had the car packed and waiting on the last day of classes."

She shook her head at him as her laughter faded. "I was never really much of a kid."

She hadn't had the opportunity to be a kid, which wasn't quite the same thing, but she didn't tell him that. Even though she had the strangest idea that his childhood hadn't been that different from hers, really. The trappings couldn't have been more opposite, but she'd spent her whole life tiptoeing around, trying to predict what mood her mother would be in, how much she might have drunk, and how bad she could expect it to get of an evening. She wasn't sure that was all that different from trying to gauge one of Violet's moods.

It had never occurred to her that she'd traded one demanding mother for another, far classier one—and she wasn't sure she liked the comparison. *At least Violet cares for you in return,* she told herself then. *Which is more than Arleen ever did.*

"I'm not sure that excuses me," Giancarlo was saying, but then he laughed, and everything else shot straight out of her head and disappeared into that happy sound. "But then, I never had any control where you were concerned."

"Neither did I," she said, smiling at him, and they both stilled then. Perhaps aware in the same instant that they were straying too close to the very things they couldn't let themselves talk about.

Or the words they couldn't say. Words he'd told her he wouldn't believe if she did dare speak them out loud.

But that didn't keep her from feeling them. Nothing could.

He studied her face for a long moment, until she began to feel the breeze too keenly on her exposed skin. Or maybe that was her vulnerability. Having sex was much easier, for all it stripped her bare and seemed to involve every last cell in her body. It required only feeling and action. *Doing*. It was this *talking* that was killing her, making her want too much, making her imagine too many happy endings when, God help her, she knew better.

Paige pushed away from him, not willing to ruin this with a conversation that could only lead to more hurt. Or worse, something good that would be that much harder to leave behind when the time came. She sat up and gathered her clothes to her, pulling the flirty little sundress over her head as if the light material was armor. But she only wished it was.

"Was it ever real?" he asked quietly.

Paige didn't ask him what he meant. She froze, her eyes on the rolling hills that spread out before her in the afternoon light, the glistening lake in the valley below. That stunning Tuscan sky studded with chubby white clouds, the vineyards and the flowers, and she didn't think he understood that he was holding her heart between his palms and squeezing tight. Too tight.

Maybe he wouldn't care if he did.

"It was for me," she said, and her voice was too rough. Too dark. Too much emotion in it. "It always was for me, even at the end."

She didn't know what might happen then. What Giancarlo might say. Do. She felt spread open and hung out in all the open space around them, as if she was stretched across some tightrope high in the sky, subject to the whims of any passing wind—

His hand reached out and covered hers and he squeezed. Once.

And then he pulled on his clothes and he got to his feet and he never mentioned it again.

Giancarlo watched her sleep, and he did not require the chorus of angry voices inside of him to remind him that this was a bad idea.

He didn't know what had woken him, only that he'd come alert in a rush and had turned to make sure she was still there beside him—the way he'd done for years after the photographs hit. He'd lost count long ago of the number of times he'd dreamed it all away, dreamed she'd never betrayed him, dreamed that things had been different. He'd grown uncomfortably well used to lying there in his empty bed, glaring at the ceiling and wishing her ill even as he'd wanted her back, wherever she was.

But this time, she was right here. She was curled up beside him and sound asleep, so that she didn't even murmur when he stretched out on his side, his front to her back, and held her there. The way he knew he wouldn't do if she was awake, lest it give her too many ideas...

So much for your revenge plot, he chided himself, but it all seemed so absurd when she was lying beside him, her features taking on an angelic cast in the faint light that poured in from the skylight above them, the stars themselves lighting her with that special glow.

He found himself tracing the line of her cheek with his finger, the memories of ten years ago so strong he could almost have sworn that no time had passed. That the pictures and the separation had been the bad dream. Because he might be wary of her, but every day it seemed that was only because he thought he should be, not because he truly was. And every day it seemed to make less and less sense.

She had been so young.

He didn't know how he'd forgotten that. How he'd failed to factor it in. When he'd been twenty he'd been a bona fide idiot, making an ass of himself at Stanford and enjoying every minute of it. He certainly hadn't been performing for a living, running from this audition to that gig with no guarantee he'd ever make his rent or make some money or even get cast. When Violet had been twenty years old she'd been famously divorcing the much, much older producer who had married her and made her when she'd been only seventeen. No one had called her a mercenary bitch, at least, not to her face. She'd been lauded for her powerful choices and the control she'd taken over her career.

Maybe that was why he'd spent a decade *this furious* with Paige. Because he loved his mother, he truly did, but he'd wanted something else for himself. He'd wanted a girl who wouldn't think of herself first, second, last and always. He'd wanted a girl who would put *him* first. Had he known Paige wouldn't stick with dancing? Had he assumed she would gravitate toward the life she had here in Tuscany, which was more or less arranged around pleasing him?

He'd told her he wanted a partner, but nothing he'd done supported that. Back in Malibu, he'd been jealous of the time she spent practicing and really anything else that took her away from him. This time around he was jealous of her devotion to his own mother. Did he want a partner? Or did he want her to *treat* him like a partner while he did whatever he liked?

Giancarlo didn't much care for the answers that came to him then, in the quiet night, the woman he couldn't seem to get over lying so sweetly beside him. All he knew was that he was tired of fighting this, of holding her at arm's length when he wanted her close. He was tired of the walls he put up. He hated himself more every time he hurt her—

We all must practice what we preach if we are to achieve anything in this life, his father had told him a long time ago as they'd walked the land together, plotting out the placement of vineyards the older man hadn't lived to see to completion. *The trouble is we're all much better at the preaching and not so good at the listening, even to ourselves.*

It had to stop. *He* had to stop. There was no point demanding her trust if he refused to give his own.

He shifted beside her, pulling her close and burying his face in the sweet heat of her neck.

It was time to admit what he'd known for years. She was the only woman he'd ever loved, no matter what she called herself. No matter what she'd done when she was little more than a kid. And he'd never stopped loving her.

"Come sei bella," he whispered into the dark. *How beautiful you are.* And, *"Mi manchi." I miss you.* And then, "I love you," in English, though he knew she couldn't hear him.

Giancarlo understood then, in the soft darkness, Paige snuggled close in his arms as if she'd been there all along, that he always had. He always would.

He just needed to tell her when she could hear him.

Paige woke up the next morning in her usual rush when the morning light danced over her face from the skylights above. Giancarlo was next to her, his big body wrapped around her, and she thought, *this is my favorite day.*

She thought that every day, lately. No matter what that voice in her head had to say about it.

And she continued to think it until her stomach went funny in a sudden, hideous lurch, and she had to pull away from him and race for the toilet.

"I must have eaten something strange," she said when she came out of the bathroom to find him frowning with concern, sitting on the side of his bed. She grimaced. "Your mother insisted we eat those weird sausages in Cinque Terre yesterday. One must not have agreed with me."

But Violet wasn't affected. "I have a stomach of steel, my dear girl," she proclaimed when Paige called her to check in, "which is handy when one is living off craft service carts for weeks at a time in all the corners of the earth." And it happened again the next morning. And then the morning after that.

And on the fourth morning, when Paige ran for the bathroom, Giancarlo came in after her and placed a package on the floor beside her as she knelt there, pale and sick and wishing for death. It took her a long moment to calm the wild, lurching beat of her heart. To force back the dizziness as that awful feeling in her stomach retreated again. To feel well enough to focus on what he'd put there in front of her.

Only to feel even more light-headed when she did.

It was a pregnancy test.

"Use it," Giancarlo said, his voice so clipped and stern she didn't dare look up at him to see if his expression matched. She didn't think her stomach could take it. She knew her heart couldn't. "Bring me the result. Then we'll talk."

CHAPTER EIGHT

PAIGE CLIMBED SHAKILY to her feet after his footsteps retreated. She rinsed her mouth out with a scoop of water from the sink and then she followed the directions on the package. She waited the requisite amount of time—she timed it on her phone, to the second—and when the alarm chirped at her she let herself look.

And just like that, everything was forever altered. But all she could do was stare at the little stick with its unmistakable plus sign and wish she wasn't naked.

That didn't merely say things about her character, she thought dimly. It said far more dire things about the kind of mother she'd be to the tiny little life that was somehow there inside her—

That was when it hit her. It was a tidal wave of raw *feeling,* impossible to categorize or separate or do anything but survive as it all tore through her. Terror. Joy. *Panic.* How could she be someone's mother when all she'd ever known of mothering was Arleen? How could she be someone's *mother*?

She was holding on to the sink in a death grip when it passed, tears in her eyes and her knees weak beneath her. It was hard to breathe, but Paige made herself do it. In, then out. Deep. Measured.

Then she remembered Giancarlo was waiting for her,

and worse, what he'd said before he'd gone downstairs. And Paige understood then. That this was her worst fear come to life, literally.

That this was the other shoe she'd spent all this time knowing would drop.

She dressed before she went downstairs, glad she'd worn something more substantial than a silly dress the night before. That meant she could truly wrap herself up in her clothes as if they would offer her protection from whatever was about to come. She pulled her hair back into a tight knot at the nape of her neck and she took longer than she should have, and she only went to find him when she understood that dragging this out was going to make it worse. *Was* making it worse.

This will be fine, she told herself as she walked down the wide, smooth stairs, aware that she was delivering herself to her own execution. But there was, despite everything, that teeny tiny sliver of hope deep inside of her that maybe, just maybe, she'd be wrong about this. That he'd surprise her.

We're both adults. These things happen…

Giancarlo waited for her in the open doors that led out to the loggia—which, she supposed with the faintest hint of the hysteria she fought to keep away for fear it might swamp her, was appropriate, given where this baby had likely been conceived. He didn't turn when she came up behind him, he merely held out his hand.

Demonstrating how little he trusted her, she realized, when she finally understood what he was doing and what he expected her to put in his palm. Not her hand, for comfort. The pregnancy test. For proof.

Because he expected tricks and lies from her, even now. Even about this.

She felt something topple over inside of her, some

foundation or other, but she couldn't concentrate on that now. There was only Giancarlo, scowling down at the slender stick in his hand before he bit out a curse and flung it aside.

A thousand smart responses to that moved through her, but she was still shaky from that immense emotional slap that had walloped her upstairs, and she kept them all to herself. He stood there, every muscle tight, even his jaw a hard, granite accusation, and he didn't look at her for a long time.

When he did, it was worse.

Paige waited for him to speak, even as something inside her protested that no, she did not deserve his anger here. That she hadn't done this alone. But she shoved that down, too.

"I thought you were on the pill."

She blinked at the ferocity in his tone. The bite.

"No, you didn't. You used condoms after the first night. Why would you do that if you thought I was on the pill?" He stared at her, and the truth of that rolled over her. For a moment, she couldn't breathe through it. Then she could, and it hurt. It more than hurt. Another foundation turned to dust in an instant. "Oh."

"Tell me," he said in that vicious, cruel way she hadn't heard in almost a month now, so long she'd forgotten how awful it was, how deeply it clawed into her, "what possible reason you could have for sleeping with a man without protection?"

"You did the same thing." But her tongue felt too thick and her head buzzed and she'd known this would happen. Maybe not *this*. Maybe not a pregnancy. But that look on his face. She'd always known she'd see that again. She hadn't understood, until now, how very much she'd wanted to be wrong. "You were right there with me."

"I thought you were on the pill."

She felt helpless. Terrified. Sick. "Why?"

He swore again, not in Italian this time, and she flinched. "What kind of question is that? Because you were before."

"That was different." She was too shaken to think about what she was saying, so she told him the truth without any varnishing. "My mother was terrified I'd end up pregnant at sixteen and forced to raise the baby, like she was with me, so she had me on the pill from the moment I hit puberty."

"And you stopped?" He sounded furious and disbelieving, and Paige didn't understand. How could he think she'd planned this? How could she have, even if she'd wanted to? *You knew he didn't use anything that first night. Why didn't you say something?* But she knew. She hadn't wanted him to stop. She'd wanted him more than anything. "Why the hell would you do something like that?"

"I told you."

Paige was whispering, and she'd backed up so her spine was against the far side of the open doorway as if the house might keep her from collapsing to the floor, but Giancarlo hadn't moved at all. He didn't have to move. His black fury took up all the air. It blocked out the sun.

This is what you deserve, her mother's voice said in her head, filled with a sick glee. *This is what happens to little whores like you, Nicola. You end up like me.*

"You're the only man I've slept with the past ten years," she told him, bald and unflinching. He let out a sound she couldn't interpret and so she kept going, because she was certain she could explain this to him so he would understand. He had to understand. They were going to be parents whether he liked it or not. "You're the only man I've ever slept with, Giancarlo."

"Do not try to sell me that nonsense, not now," he barked at her, as if the words were welling up from somewhere deep inside of him. "I didn't believe the story that you were a virgin then, not even when I thought I could trust you. I'll hand it to you, though. You really do remember all the tortured details of the lies you spin."

"What are you talking about?" Paige shook her head, trying to keep her panic at bay, trying to keep the tears from her voice, and not really succeeding at either. "Who lies about being a virgin at twenty?"

"I can't believe I fell for this twice," he spat, his gaze a molten fury of dark gold, his mouth grim. "I can't believe I walked straight into this. Let me guess. You've never given motherhood a moment's thought, but today, as you gazed upon the test that confirmed your pregnancy, something stirred within you that you'd never felt before." His laugh felt like acid. "Is that about right?"

"Why are you talking to me like I planned this?" she cried. "No one forced you to have sex with me! And no one forced you to do it without a condom!"

"You're good," he said, still in that horrible way that curled inside of her, oily and thick. "I'll give you that. I never saw this coming. I thought I was being too hard on you. I was falling in love with you all over again, but in the end, you're just like her. You always have been. *I'm such an idiot.*"

"For all you know I have no intention of keeping it," she threw at him, desperate to make him look at her like a person again, not like a scam with two legs. Exactly the way he had ten years ago, when he'd waved that magazine in the air outside her apartment and she'd almost wished he'd thrown it at her—because that would be better, she'd thought then, and less violent than that look on his face in that moment before he'd turned and walked away.

But the look of contempt he gave her now was not an improvement.

And his words finally penetrated. *I was falling in love with you.*

"Am I to understand that this is your threat?" he asked in that low, lethal way of his that made her shudder. That made that hollow thing inside of her grow wide and grow teeth. That made it perfectly clear any love he might have felt for her was very much past tense. "I applaud you, *Nicola*," and that name was worse than acid. If he'd hauled off and hit her, he couldn't have hurt her more. "Most women would dance around the issue. But you, as ever, go right to the heart of it."

"I'm not threatening you," she said wildly, only realizing when her cheeks felt cool in the breeze that tears were running down her face. "This wasn't planned. I don't know why you insist on thinking the worst of me—"

"Stop." It was a command, harsh and cold. "I'm not doing this with you again. I'm not pretending it matters what you say. You'll do what you like, *Nicola*. You always do. And like a cockroach I have no doubt you'll survive whatever happens and come back even stronger. Violet's protégé in more ways than I realized."

"Why would I force a child on you?" she demanded. "Why?"

"Perhaps you thought your payday last time wasn't enough," he bit out. "Perhaps you want to make certain you really will make it into Violet's will. Perhaps you're looking forward to selling as many tabloid stories as you can. It wouldn't take much effort to position yourself as one of those celebrities for no apparent reason, not with

Violet's grandchild in your clutches. To say nothing of the Alessi estate. You must know by now I'd never keep my heritage from my own child." He was nearly white with fury. "Which are only a few of the reasons I never wanted one."

"Giancarlo—"

But he straightened, his expression changed, and it was as if he disappeared, right there in front of her. As if the man she knew was simply…gone.

"If you decide to have the baby, inform my lawyers," he told her with a hideous finality that shuddered through her like an earthquake. There was none of that bright gold fury in his eyes any longer when he looked at her. There was only emptiness. A dark, cold nothing that made everything inside her twist into blackness. "I will pay whatever child support you deem necessary, and I will pay more if you honor my wish for privacy and keep my name to yourself. But I don't expect that's in your nature, is it? How can you leverage my privacy to your best advantage?"

"Please," she said, pleading with him now, unable to stop the sobs that poured out of her, worse, perhaps, because she'd always known this was coming. But not today. Not like this. She still wasn't ready. "You can't—"

"Do not attempt to contact my mother again." His voice got dangerous then. Flint and fury, and still, he was a stranger. "I will have you arrested and thrown in jail and no judge in any country would ever grant a woman with mental problems and a prison record custody of a child over me. I want you to remember that. You so much as text Violet and you'll never see that child again."

"Stop," she threw at him, in a terrible whisper. "You can't think—"

"A driver will pick you up in an hour," he told her, and

he was merciless. Pitiless. As if he was made of marble and was that soft, that bendable. "I want you gone. And I never, ever want to see you again. Not in ten minutes. Not in another ten years. Is that clear?"

Paige couldn't reply. She was shaking so hard she was afraid she'd fall over, the tears were hot and endless, and he looked at her as if she was a stranger. As if he was. Crafted of marble, but far crueler. Marble might crush her. But he'd torn her into pieces first.

"Do you understand?" he asked, even harsher than before.

"Yes," Paige managed to say. "I understand." She scrubbed her hands over her face and sucked in a breath and tried one last time. "Giancarlo—"

But he was already gone.

It was over.

The slippery December roads were treacherous but the wind outside was even worse, rattling his SUV and shaking the skeletons of the trees on either side of the New England country roads.

And inside him, Giancarlo knew, it was colder and darker still.

He had not been in a good mood to begin with when he'd left Logan International Airport in Boston more than two hours earlier on this latest quest to find Paige. It was fair to say he'd been in a black mood for the past three months.

The tiny, lonely little Maine town a hundred miles from anywhere sat under a fresh coat of snow, lights twinkling as the December evening fell sudden and fast in the middle of what other places might still consider the afternoon, and he felt the stirrings of adrenaline as he navigated through the very few streets that comprised the village to the small, white clapboard house that was his destination.

He'd hired detectives. He'd scoured half of the West Coast and a good part of the East Coast himself. This was the last place on earth he'd have thought to look for her—which was, he could admit, why it had no doubt made such a perfect hiding place.

This time, he knew she was here. He'd seen the photo on his mobile when he'd landed in Boston from Italy, taken this very morning. But he wouldn't believe it until he saw her with his own eyes.

He could admit the place held a certain desolate charm, Giancarlo thought grimly as he climbed from the car, the boots he only ever wore at ski resorts in places like Vail or St. Moritz crunching into the snow beneath him. The drive from Boston into the remote state of Maine had reminded him of the books he'd had to read while in his American high school. Lonely barns in barren fields and the low winter sky pressing down, gray and sullen. Here and there a hint of the wild, rocky Atlantic coast, lighthouses the only bit of faint cheer against the coming dark.

It felt like living inside his own bleak soul, in the great mess he'd made.

Giancarlo navigated his way over the salted sidewalk and up the old front steps to the clapboard house's front door, able to hear the faint sound of piano music from inside. DANCE LESSONS, read the sign on the door, making his chest feel tight.

He stopped there, frozen on the porch with his hand on the doorknob, because he heard her voice. For the first time since that last, ugly morning in his Tuscan cottage. Counting off the beat.

Wedging its way into his heart like one of the vicious icicles that hung from the roof above him.

He wrenched the door open and walked inside, and then she was right there in front of him after all this time. *Right there.*

She took his breath away.

Giancarlo's heart thundered in his chest and he forced himself to take stock of his surroundings. The ground floor of this house was its dance studio, an open space with only a few pillars and a class in session. And the woman he'd accused of a thousand different scams was not lounging about being fed bonbons she'd bought with his mother's money or her own infamy, she was teaching the class. To what looked like a pack of very pink-faced, very uncoordinated young girls.

He was standing in what passed for the small studio's lobby and if the glares from the women sitting in the couches and chairs along the wall were anything to go by, he'd disrupted the class with his loud entrance.

Not that Giancarlo cared about them in the slightest.

Paige, he noted as he forced himself to breathe again and not do anything rash, did not look at him at all, which was a feat indeed, given the mirrors on every available wall. She merely carried on teaching as if he was nothing to her.

But he refused to accept that. Particularly if it were true.

The class continued. And Giancarlo studied her as she moved in front of the small collection of preadolescents, calling out instructions and corrections and encouragement in equal measure. She looked as if she hadn't slept much, but only when he studied her closely. Her hair was still that inky black, darker now than he remembered, and he wondered if it was the sun that brought out its auburn hints. She moved the way she did in all his dreams, all of that grace and ease, as if she flowed rather than walked. And she was still slim, with only the faintest thickening at her belly to tell him what he hadn't known until now, what he'd been afraid to wonder about until he'd finally tracked her down in what had to be, literally, one of the farthest places she could go in the opposite direction of Bel Air. And him.

That she was keeping the baby. *His* baby.

Giancarlo didn't know what that was inside of him then. Relief. Fury. A new surge of determination. All the rest of the dark things he'd always felt for this woman, turned inside out. All mixed together until it felt new. Until he did.

She was keeping their baby.

He would have loved her anyway. He did. But he couldn't help but view her continuing pregnancy as a sign. As hope.

As far more than he deserved.

It seemed like twenty lifetimes before the class ended, and the women in the chairs collected their young. He paid them no attention as they herded their charges past him out into the already-pitch-black night; he simply waited, arms crossed and his brooding gaze on Paige.

And eventually, the last stranger left and slammed the door shut behind her small town curiosity, and it was only the two of them in the glossy, bright room. Paige and him and all their history, and she still didn't look at him.

"You decided to keep it." He didn't know why he said it like that, fierce and low, and he watched her stiffen, but it was too late to call it back.

"If you came here for an apology," she said in a low voice he hardly recognized, and then she turned to face him fully and he blinked because she hardly looked like herself, "you can shove it right up your—"

"I don't want an apology." It was temper, he realized belatedly. Pure fury that transformed her lovely face and turned her eyes nearly gray. As if she would kill him with her own hands if she crossed the wide, battered floor and got too close to him, and there was no reason that should shock him and intrigue him in equal measure. "I spent three months tracking you down, Paige."

Her eyes narrowed and if anything, grew darker.

"Are you sure that's what you want to call me?" she threw at him. "I know that historically you've had some trouble keeping my name straight."

Giancarlo felt a muscle move in his cheek and realized he was clenching his jaw.

"I know your name."

"I can't tell you how that delights me." Her temper was like a fog in the air between them, thick and impenetrable, and he thought she might even have growled at him. "The only thing that would delight me more would be if you'd turn around and go away and pretend we never met. That's what I've been doing and so far? It's been the best three months of my life."

He had that coming. He knew that. He told himself it didn't even sting.

"I understand," he began as carefully as he could, "that—"

"Don't bother," she snapped, cutting him off. He couldn't recall she'd ever done that before. In fact, there was only one person in the world who interrupted him with impunity and she'd given birth to him—and wasn't terribly thrilled with him at the moment, either. "I don't want your explanations. I don't care."

She turned away from him, but the mirrors betrayed her, showing him a hint of the Paige he knew in the way her face twisted before she wrestled it back under control. Another sliver of hope, if he was a desperate man. He was.

Giancarlo walked farther into the studio, still studying her. She was in bare feet and a pair of leggings, with a loose tunic over them that drooped down over one shoulder. She was the most beautiful thing he'd ever seen. He wanted to press his mouth to the bare skin of her shoulder, then explore that brand-new belly of hers. Then, perhaps, that molten heat of hers that he knew had only ever been his. He was primitive enough to relish that.

He'd believed her. It had taken him longer than it should have to admit that to himself. He'd believed her then, and he believed her now—but the fact she'd only ever given herself to him had meanings he'd been afraid to explore. He wasn't afraid anymore.

Giancarlo had lost her once. What was there to fear now? He'd already lived through the worst thing that could happen to him. Twice.

"How did you find this place?" he asked as he walked toward her. He meant, *how did you settle on this small, faraway, practically hidden town it took me three months to find?* "Why did you come here in the first place?"

"I can't imagine why you care." Paige shoved her things into a bag and then straightened. "I doubt that you do." She scowled at him when he kept coming, when he only stopped when he was within touching distance. "What do you want, Giancarlo?"

"I don't know." That wasn't true, but he didn't know how to express the rest of it, and not when she kept throwing him like this. He realized he'd never seen her angry before. Or anything but wild—wildly in love, wildly apologetic, wild beneath his hands. Never cold like this. Never furious. He supposed he deserved that, too. "You're so angry."

Paige actually laughed then, and it wasn't her real laugh. It was a bitter little thing that made his chest hurt.

More than it already did, than it had since that morning in Tuscany.

"You're unbelievable," she whispered. Then she shook her head. "I could be angry about any number of things, Giancarlo, but let's pick one at random, shall we? You told me you never wanted to see me again, and I happen to think that's the best plan you've had yet. So please, go back to wherever you came from. Go back to Italy and ruin someone else's life. Leave me—leave *us*—alone."

He wanted to pull her close to him. He wanted to taste her. He *wanted*. But he settled for shaking his head slightly and watching her face, instead, as if she might disappear again if he took his eyes off her.

"I'm sorry," he said into the tense quiet. "It's not that I'm not listening to you. But I've never seen you angry, ever. I didn't think it was something you knew how to do."

Paige blinked, and pulled the bag higher on her shoulder, gripping the strap with both of her hands.

"It wasn't," she said simply. "Especially around you. But it turns out, that's not a very healthy way to live a life. It ends up putting you at the mercy of terrible people because you never say no. You never tell them to stop. You never stand up for yourself until it's too late."

And when her eyes met his, they slammed into him so hard it was like a punch, and Giancarlo understood she meant him. That *he* had done those things to her. That he was one more terrible person to her. It tasted sour in his mouth, that realization. And he hated it with almost as much force as he understood, at last, that it was true. That he'd treated her horribly. That he was precisely the kind of man he'd been raised to detest. That was why he'd come after her, was it not? To face these things.

But that didn't make hearing it any easier.

"That is not the kind of life my baby is going to live, Giancarlo," Paige told him fiercely. "Not if I have anything to say about it." She tilted her chin up as if she expected him to argue. "This baby will have a *home*. This baby will be *wanted*. Loved. Celebrated. This baby is not a mistake. Or a problem. This baby will *belong* somewhere. *With me*."

As if she really had punched him, and hard, it took Giancarlo a moment to recover from all her fierceness, and more, what it told him. And when he did, it was to see her storming across the room.

Away from him. Again.

"Come have dinner with me," he began.

"No."

"Coffee then." He eyed her, remembering that tiny bump. "Or whatever you can drink."

"And again, no."

"Paige." He didn't have any idea what he was doing and he thought he hated that almost as much as the distance between them, which seemed much, much worse now that they were standing in the same room. "It's my baby, too."

She whirled back around, so fast he thought someone without her grace might have toppled over, and then she jabbed a finger in the air in a manner he imagined was meant to show him how very much she wished it was something sharp she could stick in a far more tender area.

"She is *my* baby!" And her voice grew louder with each word. "Mine. I knew I was pregnant with the baby of a man who *hated me* for *five whole minutes* before you ripped me into shreds and walked away, but believe me, Giancarlo, I heard you. You want nothing to do with me. You want nothing to do with this baby. And that is *fine*—"

"I never said I wanted nothing to do with the baby," he protested. "Quite the opposite."

"We can debate that when there's a baby, then," she hurled at him, hardly stopping to take a breath. "Which by my calculations gives me six months and then some of freedom from having to talk to you."

"But I want to talk to you." And he didn't care that he sounded more demanding than apologetic, then. She might truly want nothing to do with him, ever again, and he understood he deserved that. But he had to be sure. "I want to see how you're doing. I want to understand what happened between us in Italy."

"No, you don't."

And her face twisted again, but her eyes were still that dark gray and they still burned, and he couldn't tell what she wanted. Only that as ever, he was hurting her. The way he always did.

"You don't want to understand *me*," Paige told him. "You want me to understand *you*. And believe me, I already do. I understood you when you were the very wealthy, semifamous director who took an unexpected interest in a backup dancer. I understood you when you were the noble son standing up for his mother against the potential lunatic who had infiltrated her home behind your back. I even understood you when you were the beleaguered, betrayed ex, drawn back into an intense sexual relationship against his better judgment by the deceitful little seductress he couldn't put behind him. I *understood* myself sick."

She pulled in a breath, as if it hurt her, which was when Giancarlo realized he hadn't breathed throughout this. That he couldn't seem to draw a breath at all.

"And then," Paige continued, her voice strong and even, "once I left, I understood that you have never, ever pretended to be there for me in any way. Not ten years ago. Not now. It never crossed your mind to *ask me* why I did something like sell those pictures, just as it never occurred to you to ask me how *I* felt about finding myself pregnant. The only thing you care about is you."

"Paige."

She ignored him. "You never asked me anything at all. You've never treated me liked anything but a storm you had to weather." She shook her head. "You're the damned hurricane, Giancarlo, but you blame me for the rain." She shifted then, her hands moving to shelter that little bump, as if she needed to protect it from him, and he thought that might be the worst cut, the deepest wound. He was surprised to find he still stood. "All I want from you is what you've always given me. Your absence."

The room seemed dizzy with her words when she'd stopped speaking, as if the mirrors could hardly bear the weight of them. Or maybe that was him. Maybe he'd fallen down and he simply couldn't tell the difference.

"You said *she*."

"What?"

Giancarlo didn't know where that had come from. He hadn't known he meant to speak at all. He was too busy seeing himself through her eyes—and not liking it at all. "Before. You called the baby a *she*."

"Yes." She seemed worn-out then, in a sudden rush. As if she'd lanced a wound with a surge of adrenaline and the poison had all run out, leaving nothing behind it. "I'm having a little girl in May."

"A daughter." His voice was gentle, yet filled with something it took him a moment to identify. *Wonder.* He heard it move through the room and he saw her shudder as she pulled in a breath, and he knew, somehow, that everything wasn't lost. Not yet. Not quite yet. "We're having a daughter."

"Go away, Giancarlo," she said, but it was a whisper. Just a whisper with none of that fury behind it, and a hint of the kind of sadness he'd become all too familiar with these past few months. And he wanted nothing more than to protect her, even if it was from himself.

Perhaps especially then.

"I can do that," he said gruffly. "Tonight. But I'll keep coming back, Paige. Every day until you talk to me. I can be remarkably persuasive."

"Is that a threat?" She rubbed a hand over the back of her neck, and he thought she looked tired again, but not threatened. "This isn't your land in Italy. I'm not a prisoner here."

"I don't want to keep you prisoner," he said, which was not entirely true. He reminded himself he was a civilized man. Or the son of one anyway, little as he might have lived up to his father's standards lately. "I want to have dinner with you."

She eyed him, and he could see the uncertainty on her pretty face. "That's all?"

"Do you want me to lie to you?" he asked quietly. "It's a start. Just give me a start."

She shook her head, but her eyes seemed less gray now and more that changeable blue-green he recognized, and Giancarlo couldn't help but consider that progress.

"What if I don't want a start?" she asked after a moment. "Any start? We've had two separate starts marked by ten years of agony and now this. It's not fun."

He smiled. "Then it's dinner. Everyone needs to eat dinner. Especially pregnant women, I understand."

"But not with you," Paige said, and there was something different in her voice then. Some kind of resolve. "Not again. It's not worth it."

She turned away again and headed toward the door he could see in the back, and this time, he could tell, she was really going to leave.

And Giancarlo knew he should let her go. He knew he'd done more than enough already. The practical side of him pointed out that six months was a reasonable amount of time to win a person over, to say nothing of the following lifetime of the child they'd made. *Their daughter.* He had all the time in the world.

He'd spent three months trying to find her—what was another night? He knew he should forfeit this battle, the better to win the war. But he couldn't do it.

Giancarlo couldn't watch her walk away again.

CHAPTER NINE

LATER, PAIGE THOUGHT, she would hate herself for how difficult it was to march across the studio floor toward the door, her car beyond, and the brand-new life she was in the middle of crafting.

Later, she would despair of the kind of person she must be, that her heart had somersaulted nearly out of her chest when Giancarlo had stormed in, startling her so profoundly it had taken her a long moment to remember why that instant sense of relief she'd felt was more than a little sick. Later, she would beat herself up about how little she wanted to walk away from him, even now.

But first she had to really do it. Walk away. Mean what she said. Leave him standing—

Her first clue that he'd moved at all was a rush of air over her shoulder and then his hands were on her, gentle and implacable at once. He turned her, lifted her, and in a single smooth shift she was in his arms. Held high against his chest, so she was surrounded. By his scent. By his strength.

A scant breath away from that cruel mouth, that sensual mouth.

Much too close to everything she wanted, so desperately, to forget.

"Put me down."

Her voice was so quiet it was hardly a breath of sound—but she knew, somehow, what that dark gold fury in his gaze was now. It was a warning that this situation could get out of control quickly, with a single kiss, and Paige rather doubted she'd be able to maintain any kind of moral high ground if she let him deep inside her again.

Especially because she wanted him there. Even now.

"First of all," Giancarlo said, in that low and lethal way that still moved over her like a seduction, making her very bones feel weak, "I do not hate you. I have never hated you. I have spent years trying to convince myself that I hated you only to fail miserably at it, again and again."

"Then you only *act* as if you hate me," she grated at him, refusing to put her arm over his shoulders, holding herself tight and unyielding against him as if that might save her. From herself. "That's much better."

He stopped next to the line of old armchairs and love seats that sat against the wall and set her down in the biggest one, then shocked her to the core by kneeling down in front of her. She froze, which was why it took her a moment to notice that he'd caged her in, his hands gripping the back of the chair behind her, putting his face about as close as it could get to hers without actually touching her.

"Why did you sell those photographs?" he asked. Quietly, his dark gaze trained on her face. So there was no chance at all he didn't see the heat that flashed over her, making her cheeks warm.

"What can that possibly matter now?"

"I think you're right about a lot of things," he said, sounding somewhere between grim and determined. And something else she wasn't sure she'd ever heard before. "But especially this. I should have asked. I'm asking now."

And the trouble was, she loved him. She'd always loved him. And she'd waited a decade for him to ask. If he'd asked in Italy, she might have sugarcoated it, but things were different now. *She* was different now.

She owed it to the life inside of her to be the kind of woman she wanted her daughter to become. That strong. That unafraid. That unflinching when necessary.

"My mother was a drunk," Paige said flatly. "Her dreams of riches and fame and escape from our awful little hometown came to a screeching halt when she got pregnant with me in high school, so it worked out well that I could dance. The minute I was done with high school she took me to Los Angeles. She made me use my middle name as a stage name because she thought it was fancy, and everyone knew you had to be fancy to be famous. She decided she made an excellent stage mother, if your definition of a stage mother is that she took all the money and then yelled at me to get out there and make more."

"That is the common Hollywood definition, yes," Giancarlo said drily, but she couldn't stop now. Not even to laugh.

"A drunk Arleen was one thing," Paige told him. "But a little while before I met you, my mother met a meth dealer. His name was Denny, and let me tell you, he was *so* nice to us. A new best friend." Her mouth twisted. "A month later, she was thousands of dollars in the hole and he was a little less friendly. Two months later, she was hundreds of thousands of dollars in debt to him, there was no possible way she could get out of it and he stopped pretending. He laid it out for me." She met Giancarlo's gaze and held it. *Unflinching,* she told herself. No matter that she'd never wanted him to know the kind of dirt that clung to her. Not when his whole life was so clean, so pretty, so bathed in light. "I could work it off on my back, or I could watch him kill her. Or—and this was an afterthought—I could make some money off my rich new boyfriend instead."

"Paige." He breathed her name as if it was one of his Italian curses, or perhaps a prayer, and she didn't know when he'd dropped his hands down to take hers, only that his hands were so warm, so strong, and she was far weaker than she wanted to be if he was what made her feel strong. Wasn't she? "Why didn't you tell me this? Why didn't you let me help you?"

"Because I was ashamed," she said, and her voice cracked, but she didn't look away from him. "Your mother was *Violet Sutherlin*. My mother was a drug addict who sold herself when she ran out of money, and it still wasn't enough. Who wanted to sell *me* because until I met you, I was a virgin."

He paled slightly, and she felt his hands tighten around hers, and she pushed on.

"The first night I spent with you, she realized I'd slept with you," Paige said, aware that she sounded hollow, when still, she couldn't regret it. Not a moment of that long, perfect night. Not even knowing what came after. "And when I got home that next day, she slapped me so hard it actually made my ears ring. But not enough to block her out. I'd already ruined her life by being born, you see. The least I could have done was let her sell the one commodity she had—I mean my virginity—to the highest bidder. She'd had the whole thing planned out with some friends of Denny's."

"How did I miss this?" Giancarlo asked, his voice a hoarse scrape in the empty studio.

"Because I wanted you to miss it." Her voice was fierce. "Because you were my single rebellion. My escape. The only thing I'd ever had that was good. And all mine. And you came without any strings." She dropped her gaze then, to where their hands were clasped tight. "But she was my mother."

He muttered something in Italian.

"I think," Paige said, because she had to finish now, "that if I hadn't met you, even if I'd had a different boyfriend, I would have just slept with whoever Denny told me to sleep with. It would have been easier."

"It would have been prostitution," Giancarlo said, viciously, but she knew that this time, it wasn't directed at her.

"What difference would it have made?" she asked, and she meant that. She shrugged. "I didn't know anything else. A lot of the dancers slept around and let the men help with their rent. They didn't call it prostitution— they called it dating. With benefits. Maybe I wouldn't have minded it, if I'd started there. But I'd met you." She blew out a breath and met his dark gold gaze. "And I was twenty years old. My mother told me a thousand times a day that men like you had a million girls like me. That I'd thrown myself away on you, that you would get sick of me sooner rather than later and we'd have nothing to show for it. And she, by God, wanted something to show for all her suffering."

"How, pray, had *she* suffered?" His tone was icy, and it warmed something inside of her. As if maybe all those foundations she'd thought he'd shattered in Italy had only frozen and were coming back now as they warmed. As she did.

"It wasn't my idea," Paige said quietly, because this was the important part. "Denny insisted that sex sold.

That you were worth an outrageous amount of money. And I thought—I really thought—that I owed her something. That it was just what love looked like. Because I might have ruined her life, but she was my mother. I loved her. I owed her."

"You don't have to tell me any more," Giancarlo said, his voice a deep rumble. "I understand."

"I loved you, too," Paige whispered. "But I'd had twenty years of Arleen and only a couple months of you. I thought she was the real thing and you were just a dream. I thought if it was really a true thing between you and me, you'd try to understand why I did it. But I wasn't surprised when you didn't."

He let out a breath, as if he'd suffered a blow.

"I'm so sorry," he said quietly. So quietly she almost didn't notice the way it sneaked into her, adding fuel to that small fire that still burned for him, for them. That always would. "I wish you'd come to me. I wish I'd seen what was happening beneath my nose. I wish I'd had any idea what you were going through."

"It doesn't matter now." And she found she meant that. She kept going, because she needed to finish. To see it through. "I did it. I got half a million dollars for those pictures and I lost you. I gave the money to my mother. It was enough to pay Denny and then some. I was such an idiot—I thought that meant we'd be fine."

"How long?" he asked, and she knew what he meant.

"Another month or so and the money was gone. Then she was in debt again. And it turned out Denny was even less understanding than he'd been before, because there was no rich boyfriend any longer. There was only me. And he was pretty clear about the one thing I was good at. How could I argue? The entire world had seen me in action. I was a commodity again."

"My God."

"I don't know about God," Paige said. "It was the LAPD who busted Denny on something serious enough to put him away for fifteen years. My mother lost her supplier, which meant she lost her mind. The last time I saw her, she was on the streets and she might be there still. She might not have made it this long. I don't know." She lifted her chin to look him in the eye. "And that's what happened ten years ago."

"You can't possibly feel guilty about that." He sounded incredulous. He frowned at her. "Paige. Please. You did everything you possibly could for that woman. Literally. You can't stop people when they want to destroy themselves—you can only stop them from taking you along with them."

She shrugged again, as if that might shift the constriction in her throat. "She's still my mother. I still love…if not her, then who she was supposed to be."

Giancarlo looked at her for a long time. So long she forgot she'd been too ashamed to tell him this. So long she lost herself again, the way she always did, in that face of his, those dark eyes, that mouth.

"I'm so sorry," he said, his voice so low it seemed to move inside of her, like heat. "I wouldn't blame you if you hated me. I don't think I understand why you don't."

"Because my whole life, Giancarlo," she whispered, unable to hide anything from him, not after all this time and all the ways they'd hurt each other, not any longer, "you're the only person I've ever loved. The only one who loved me back."

He shifted back and then he reached over to brush moisture from beneath her eyes, and Paige reminded herself that she was supposed to be resisting him. Fighting him off. Standing up for herself. She couldn't understand how she could feel as if she was doing that when, clearly, she was doing the opposite.

"Violet adores you," he said then. "And despite her excursions around the Tuscan countryside purely to be recognized and adored, she does not, in fact, like more than a handful of people. She trusts far fewer."

Paige made a face. "She has no idea who I really am."

He smiled then. "Of course she does. She tells me she's known exactly who you are from the moment she met you. Why else would she let you so deep into the family?"

But Paige shook her head at that, confused. And something more than simply confused.

"Why would she do that?" she whispered.

"Because my father was a good man," Giancarlo said, his hands hard and warm and tight on hers again, "and a kind man, but a cold one. And shortly after I told her you'd left she informed me that the only time in my life when I didn't act just like him, inaccessible and aloof and insufferable—her words—" and his mouth crooked then "—was when I was with you. Ten years and three months ago."

"She knew," Paige whispered, trying to take it in. "Is that why she was so kind to me?"

"That," Giancarlo said, a certain urgency in his voice that made her shift against the chair and tell herself it was only nerves, "and the fact that no matter what you might have been taught, it is not that difficult to be kind to you."

"You've found it incredibly difficult," she pointed out, and it was getting harder by the moment to control the things shaking inside her, the things shaking loose. "Impossible, even."

"I am a selfish, arrogant ass," he said, so seriously that she laughed out loud.

"Well," she said when the laughter faded. "That's not the word I would have used. But if the shoe fits…"

"I am my mother's son," he said simply. "I was born wealthy and aristocratic and, apparently, deeply sorry for myself. It took me all of an hour to realize I'd been completely out of line that day in Italy, Paige. It wasn't about you. It was about my own childhood, about the vows I'd made that only you have ever tempted me to break—but I have no excuse." He shook his head, his mouth thinning. "I know you didn't try to trick me. I considered chasing you down at the airfield and dragging you back with me, but I thought you needed space from the madman who'd said those things to you. I took the earliest flight I could the following day, but when I got to Los Angeles, you weren't there. Your things were packed up and shipped out to storage, but you never went there in person."

"That storage facility is in Bakersfield," she said, blinking. "Did you go there?"

"I haunted it," he said, his gaze dark and steady on hers. "For weeks."

There was no denying the heat that swirled in her then, too much like hope, like light, when she knew better than to—

But he was here. He was kneeling down in front of her even after she'd told him the kind of person she'd been at twenty. The kind of life she'd have led, if not for him. The kind of world she'd been raised in. He was *trying,* clearly.

And Paige didn't want to be right. She wanted to be happy. Just once, she wanted to be *happy.*

"I was going to ship it wherever I settled," she told him, letting that revolutionary thought settle into her bones. "There was no point carting it all around with me when I didn't know where I was going."

"What 'all' are you talking about?" he asked, his tone

dry. "It is perhaps three boxes, I am informed, after bribing the unscrupulous owner of that facility a shockingly small amount of money to see for myself." His expression dared her to protest that, but she didn't. If anything, she had to bite back a smile. "My mother requires more baggage for a long afternoon in Santa Monica."

Paige shook her head, realizing she was drinking in his nearness instead of standing up for herself and the little life inside of her. That she owed both of them more than that. That the fact she felt lighter than she had in years was nice, but it didn't change anything. That wasn't happiness, that was chemistry, and she'd already seen where that led, hadn't she? She needed more.

Paige might not be certain what *she* deserved, but her daughter deserved everything. *Everything.* She would use Arleen as her base and do the exact opposite. That meant many things, among them, not settling for a man—even if it was Giancarlo Alessi—simply because he was in front of her. Paige had watched that dynamic in action again and again and again. Her baby would not.

"How did you find me?" she asked, keeping all of her brand-new hopes, all of her wishes and all of her realizations out of her voice. Or she tried. "And more importantly, why?"

"The how is simple. I remembered you said you wanted to see the fall leaves change color in Vermont."

"I did?"

"When we first met. It was autumn in Los Angeles, hot and bright, and you told me you wanted to see real seasons. You also said you wanted to live near the sea and see the snow." He shrugged. "I decided that all those things pointed to New England. After that, I utilized the fact that I am a very wealthy, very motivated, very determined man to hunt you down."

"Giancarlo—"

"And the why is this." He reached into his pocket and pulled out a small box, and smiled slightly when she jerked back.

"No." It was automatic. And loud.

Giancarlo didn't seem at all fazed.

"This was my grandmother's diamond," he said. He cracked open the box and held it out, and she remembered, then, that first night with him in Italy, when he'd stood with his hand out and she'd thought he could stand like that forever, if he had to. His dark gaze met hers, and held. "I had the ring made for you ten years ago."

Paige felt her eyes flood then, and she let them, covering her mouth with her hands, unable to speak. So he did.

"Everything you said about me is true," he told her. "I can't deny any of it. But I want to understand you, Paige. I want to dedicate the next ten years to learning every single thing that makes you *you*. I don't simply want a partner, I want to be one. I want to be yours. I want you to yell at me and put me in my place and I want to help you teach our daughter never to surrender herself to terrible men like her father." His voice was scratchy then. "Not ever."

"Stop," she said, and she didn't mean to reach over to him. She didn't mean to slide her hand along his perfect, lean cheek. "I never gave you anything I didn't want to give. You must know that. It was only that I knew it would end."

"This won't," he whispered. "It hasn't in ten years. It won't in ten more, or ten after that, or ever." He leaned forward, sliding his hand over her belly to cup that small, unmistakable swell, and the smile that moved over that mouth of his broke her heart and made it leap at once. Then he made it far worse, leaning in to press a reverent kiss there. "I love you, Paige. Please. Let me show you."

"I love you, too," she whispered, because what was the point in pretending otherwise? They'd already lost so much time. "But trust is a whole lot more than a pretty ring. I'll always be the woman who sold you out."

"And I'll always be the man who greeted the news of his daughter's impending arrival like a pig," he retorted. "Based on the wild fears of the four-year-old boy I haven't been in decades."

"That sounds like a recipe for disaster."

"I know." He shifted then, pulling the ring from its box and slipping it onto her finger. It fit perfectly, and Paige couldn't seem to breathe. And his eyes were so bright, and she felt three times the size of her skin, and she didn't want to let him go this time. She didn't want to sacrifice him, ever again. "Believe me, I know, but it's not. It only means we've tested each other and we're still here."

He picked up her hand with its sparkling diamond and carried it to his lips. "Wear this and we'll work on it," he murmured, his eyes on her and the words seeming to thud straight into her heart, her flesh, her bones. "Every day. I promise I won't rest until you're happy enough to burst."

"Until we both are," she corrected him.

And then he leaned in close, and he wrapped himself around her and he kissed her. Again and again. Until she was dizzy with longing and love. Until neither one of them could breathe.

And Giancarlo gave her a detailed demonstration of his commitment to the cause, right there on one of the sofas in that bright, big room.

CHAPTER TEN

She made him work for it. And she made him wait.

And Giancarlo had no one to blame but himself for either.

"How do I know that you want to marry me and not simply to claim the baby in some appalling display of machismo?" she had asked him that first night, naked and astride him, when his intentions toward her, personally, could not have been more obvious.

"Set me any test," he'd told her then. "I'll pass it."

She'd considered him for a long moment, her inky hair in that tangle he loved and her eyes that brilliant green. And the way she fit him. *God, the fit.*

"Don't ask me again," she said, her tone very serious, her green gaze alight. "I'll let you know when I'm ready."

"Take your time," he'd told her with all the patience of a desperate man. "I want you to trust me."

"I want to trust you, too," she'd whispered in return.

But the truth was they learned to trust each other.

He flew back and forth from Italy as needed, and didn't argue when sometimes, she refused to go with him. He shared her tiny studio apartment with her in her snowy New England town, a hundred miles or more from anywhere, and he didn't complain. He shoveled snow. He salted paths. He made certain her car was well-maintained and he never pressured her to move.

She told him more about her childhood with that terrible woman. He told her about his childhood with a woman less terrible perhaps, but deeply complicated all the same. And they held each other. They soothed each other.

They came to know each other in all the ways they hadn't had time to get to know each other ten years ago. Layer on top of layer.

Until he came back from another trip to Italy one snowy March weekend and Paige said that maybe, if he had a better place in mind for them to live, she'd consider it.

"I don't know anything about homes," she told him, her attention perhaps *too* focused on the book she held in her lap. "But you seem to have quite a few."

"You make every house I have a home, *il mio amore,*" he told her. "Without you, they are but adventures in architecture."

And he had them back in his house in Malibu by the following afternoon, as if they'd never left it ten years ago. The sea in front of him, the mountains behind him and his woman at his side.

Giancarlo had never been happier. Except for one small thing.

"Why haven't you married her yet?" Violet demanded every time she saw him, particularly when Paige was with him. He could only raise his brows at this woman he loved more than he'd imagined it was possible to love anyone, and wait for her to answer.

Which she was happy to do.

"I'm not sure I'll have him, Violet," Paige would reply airily. She would pat her ever-larger belly and smile blandly, and Giancarlo thought that they'd both transitioned from a working relationship to family rather easily. Almost as if Violet had planned it. "I'm considering all my options."

"I don't blame you," Violet would say with a sniff. "He was horrible. I'd tell you he gets that sort of inexcusable behavior from his father but, alas, Count Alessi was the most polite and well-mannered man I ever met. It's all me."

"I don't think anyone thought otherwise," Giancarlo would say then, and everyone would laugh.

But he never asked Paige again. He kept his promise.

"And if a single photograph or unauthorized mention of my daughter appears anywhere, for any reason, in a manner which benefits you without my express, written consent," he told the great screen legend Violet Sutherlin one pretty afternoon, in her office in front of her new assistant so there could be no mistake that he meant business, "you will never see her again. Until she is at least thirty. Do you understand me, Mother? I am no longer that four-year-old. My daughter never will be."

Violet had gazed at him for a long time. She hadn't showed him that smile of hers. She hadn't said anything witty. In the end, she'd only nodded, once. Sharp and jerky.

But he knew she understood that he'd meant it.

Five months and three weeks after the night he'd turned up in Maine, when Paige was big and round and had to walk in a kind of waddle to get down the makeshift aisle, she married him at last in a tiny ceremony on Violet's terrace. Violet presided. The bride and the officiant wept.

Giancarlo smiled with the greatest satisfaction he'd known in his life. And kissed his bride. *His wife.*

"Don't ever torture me like that again," he growled

against her lips when they were in the car and headed home, finally married, the way they should have been more than ten years before.

"Surely you knew I'd marry you," Paige said, laughing. "I've been pretty open about how much I love you."

"I'm not at all certain I deserve you," he said, and was startled when that made great tears well up in her lovely changeable eyes, then roll down her cheeks. "But I've taken that on as a lifelong project."

She smiled at him, the whole world in that smile, the way it had been that long ago day on that set when they'd locked eyes for the first time. And Giancarlo knew without the slightest shred of doubt that this was merely a particularly good day on the long road toward forever. And that they'd walk the whole of it together, just like this.

And then her expression altered, and she grabbed his arm.

"We're going to have a lot of lifelong projects," Paige said, sounding fierce and awed at once. His beautiful wife. "I think my water just broke."

They named their daughter Violetta Grace, after her famous grandmother, who'd insisted, and the less famous one, who'd died before Paige was born and Arleen had gone completely off the rails, and she was perfect.

Extraordinary.

Theirs.

And they spent the rest of their lives teaching her, in a thousand little ways and few great big ones, what it meant to be as happy as they were the moment they met her.

* * * * *

Zafir slid his hands over hers.

Fern tried to look away, but he was tall and very close. He smelled good. Earthy and sweaty, but not overpowering. Masculine and intriguing. She'd never met a man with such an air of command—Zafir was in his prime: not just healthy, but radiating supremacy.

In the back of her mind she knew she was behaving like a rock band super-fan—speechless in the presence of a man with star quality, unable to move—but he was so incredible. She found herself staring into his eyes for too long. She knew it was too long, but she couldn't look away from those crystal blue-green depths. They quested, delving into hers, demanding something she didn't even understand.

Say something, she thought, and let her tongue wet her lips.

His gaze lowered to her mouth.

Her breath evaporated.

She found her own gaze dropping to *his* mouth, wondered how it would feel to have those smooth lips rubbing against hers. Her heart was fluttering like a trapped bird...her pulse was pounding in her ears.

He lifted his hand to hover hotly next to her cheek, scorching her. His brows jerked in some type of struggle.

Was he going to kiss her?

SEVEN SEXY SINS

The *true* taste of temptation!

From greed to gluttony, lust to envy,
these fabulous stories explore what seven sexy sins
mean in the twenty-first century!

Whether pride goes before a fall, or wrath leads to
a passion that consumes entirely, one thing is certain:
the road to true love has never been more enticing!

So you decide:

How can it be a sin when it feels so good?

Sloth—Cathy Williams

Lust—Dani Collins

Pride—Kim Lawrence

Gluttony—Maggie Cox

Greed—Sara Craven

Wrath—Maya Blake

Envy—Annie West

Seven titles by some of
Mills & Boon® Modern™ Romance's
most treasured and exciting authors!

THE SHEIKH'S SINFUL SEDUCTION

BY
DANI COLLINS

Published in Great Britain 2015
by Mills & Boon, an imprint of Harlequin (UK) Limited,
Eton House, 18-24 Paradise Road, Richmond, Surrey, TW9 1SR

© 2015 Dani Collins

ISBN: 978-0-263-25053-4

Printed and bound in Spain
by CPI, Barcelona

Canadian **Dani Collins** knew in high school that she wanted to write romance for a living. Twenty-five years later, after marrying her high school sweetheart, having two kids with him, working several generic office jobs and submitting countless manuscripts, she got 'The Call'. Her first Mills & Boon® Modern™ Romance won the Reviewers' Choice Award for Best First In Series from *RT Book Reviews*. She now works in her own office, writing romance.

Books by Dani Collins

The 21st Century Gentleman's Club

The Ultimate Seduction

One Night With Consequences

Proof of Their Sin

The Russian's Acquisition
An Heir to Bind Them
A Debt Paid in Passion
More than a Convenient Marriage?
No Longer Forbidden?

**Visit the author profile page at
www.millsandboon.co.uk for more titles**

With a theme like lust—well, *duh*.
Of *course* this one's dedicated to my husband, Doug.

Friends, and even strangers,
love to waggle their brows and lower their tone
to a suggestive level and ask romance writers,
"How do you research your love scenes?" Here I'd like
to officially give my husband the credit he deserves.
He's always been extremely patient when I bring the
laptop to bed so I can take notes. Thanks, honey.

CHAPTER ONE

ARRIVING AT THE oasis brought Fern Davenport back to life in a way she'd never experienced. The two-day camel trek through the dunes that she had anticipated with such excitement had been exactly what her employer and friend, Amineh, had warned it would be: a test of endurance.

But worth it. Exactly as promised.

After nothing but shades of blinding white and bleached yellow and dull red, the glimpse of greenery had Fern sitting taller, bringing her nose up the same way her camel did, searching for the scent of water. As they entered the farthest reach of the underground spring, where the palms were stunted and the grass sparse, she felt like a giant looking down on the tops of trees. The sun was already behind the canyon wall and blessedly cool air began to slither beneath the flapping edges of her abaya to caress her bare legs.

The tension of fearing for her survival began to ease. She wanted to release a laugh of relieved joy.

Outbursts of any kind weren't her thing, though. She preferred to be as invisible as possible. Fern considered herself an observer of life, not so much a participant, but for the first time she experienced something like what a frisky lamb or a cocky adolescent must feel. It was a strange awareness of being alive. Her blood cells took on new energy and her pulse returned to vigorous beats.

She wanted to throw off the weight of her clothes, expose her hot skin to the verdant air, kick up her heels and soak life through her pores. She wanted to be one with nature.

Awash in this state of renewal, she looked ahead to the clearing where the caravan would unload and saw *him*.

Just a man in a *thobe* and *gutra*. He could have been one of the camel keepers for all she knew, but a deep, feminine part of her recognized the kind of male that called to any woman. A leader. One whom other men looked to for direction and approval. Confident. A man of strength whose muscles strained the white tunic that draped his shoulders. He wore sandals and his feet were dusty, but he planted them firmly. With ownership.

She forced herself to lift her gaze to his face, barely able to withstand the impact of such handsomeness. How could a man be so beautiful yet so rugged? He was a product of the desert, she supposed, cheeks hollow and roughened by stubble, skin deeply tanned by the sun, mouth somber yet sculpted and…how did she even sense this? *Sexual*. A hawkish nose and brows as straight and firm as the horizon and then…

Green eyes. As startling and revitalizing as this oasis.

His sheer magnificence took her breath.

"Uncle!" the girls cried and the man's severe expression flashed with a smile that made wistfulness bloom in Fern's chest.

Men were such puzzling creatures to her, having mostly been passing ships in her life. She'd attended an all-girls school where even the principal was female. The library trustees, her mother's doctor and the few teenaged boys she'd occasionally met through Miss Ivy's club were the only males she really knew. She often found herself watching men like birders watched finches, studying their behavior and trying to make sense of them. She was always startled to discover they were quite human. The ones that were able to be tender with a child were especially fascinating to her. They made her wonder what it would be like to be close enough to truly understand one.

Not that she expected to get close to this one!

She had worked out that he was Zafir, Amineh's brother. Amineh's husband, Ra'id, *hupped* at his camel so it would drop to its knees. He dismounted and the men clasped hands and bent their heads together as they embraced with easy warmth.

Definitely *not* a camel keeper, Fern chided herself. Her students' Uncle Zafir was formally known as Sheikh abu Tariq Zafir ibn Ahmad al-Rakin Iram. He was leader of Q'Amara, the country bordering Ra'id's.

She must have sensed who he was and his stature impacted her, she reasoned. That's why she was suffering this flare of heightened interest. The significance of arriving and meeting such an important man was turning her inside out in a way that was both familiar yet amplified. She was not only shy by nature, but also a redhead with the overactive blushing response that often came with it. She had flushed uncontrollably the first time Ra'id had spoken to her—she'd been so self-conscious under the attention of such a strong personality. A domineering, angry mother had made her sensitive to all authority figures. Anxious to please. It was completely understandable that she'd have an attack of nerves when faced with meeting another sheikh.

She'd never felt blistered from the inside like this, though. Never electrified yet stimulated. It was very disconcerting.

Other men came forward. These ones were camel keepers and camp attendants, but she was aware of only one man now. Not that he noticed her, which was a relief. And why would he? She was buried under a niqab and sunglasses, well-protected against the harsh glare of the sun and the bite of blowing sand. He was busy carrying on two separate conversations with his nieces as they occupied each of his arms.

The girls wriggled to the ground when a boy arrived, crying the name Fern had heard several times since this caravan into the desert had been proposed. "Tariq!"

Their cousin, ten years old, she'd been informed with great awe by her much younger students, wore a long tunic like his father's and challenged the girls to race him up the path to the colorful tents being erected upstream, offering them a head start.

Ra'id helped his wife once her camel was down. Amineh threw off her niqab to hug her brother with all the affection she radiated when talking about him. They all spoke in Arabic, a beautiful language Fern wasn't even close to mastering—

"Oh!" Fern cried as her camel pitched forward.

Remember to lean back, Amineh had cautioned her a million times, but Fern had been so caught up in watching Zafir smile at his sister she hadn't noticed her camel was dropping to its knees. She scrambled to hang on, but was already sliding off by the time the animal hit the ground with a jarring thump.

Her dismount became the clumsiest in Arab history. She barely caught herself from crumpling into a heap. It was witnessed by everyone. So mortifying.

"Are you all right, Fern?" Amineh called. "You seemed to have the trick of it at the last stop. I should have asked Ra'id to help you."

"I'm fine. Just distracted. It's so pretty here," she babbled, trying to cover up her interest in Zafir. A giant magnifying glass might as well be narrowing its beam on her, she was in such a searing, uncomfortable spotlight. She overheard Ra'id say something in Arabic that she did understand, calling her "The English teacher."

"She is," Amineh confirmed. "Come over and meet Fern. Oh, thank you, Nudara," she added as her maid came forward with a canvas bag. Amineh peeled off her abaya and threw it into the bag then motioned for Fern to discard her dusty robe into it as well. "She'll shake the sand out of them so they're ready when the nomads arrive."

Before taking this job, the closest Fern had come to having servants was watching the *Downton Abbey* collection on her laptop. All her life, her mother had been too tired from cleaning other people's houses to do much of it at home, but she'd liked things shipshape. Fern had kept their small flat neat as a pin. In the final months, Fern had provided all-out hospice care, doing everything from bathing her mother to mounting the assistance bar next to the toilet. She still hadn't adjusted to leaving tasks like laundry and cooking to others. It felt presumptuous, even though Nudara took no offense.

Maybe if Fern had been on Amineh's level, making requests of servants wouldn't have bothered her, but she was in that strange limbo between being a servant and being one of the family.

Honestly, she thought with a wry, inward sigh, when had she not been the odd duck set apart from the rest of the group?

This moment was no better. Despite only having adopted the head coverings since taking her position as English tutor to Bashira and Jumanah, Fern felt terribly bold as she removed her dark glasses, unpinned her veil and tugged away both scarf and under cap in one go. It was the hair. Her abundant corkscrews of carrot-orange made everyone in this country do a double take.

She kept her hair long because it was that or resemble a

pot scrubber. It probably looked like it had been run through the food processor as it was. She'd been two days without more than a damp facecloth for a bath, but the enormous relief of cool air hitting her sweat-dampened scalp made her prickle with delight. Stripping her abaya, she revealed her sleeveless shirt with its forget-me-not print and lace collar then shook her cornflower-blue skirt from clinging to her legs, self-conscious that it only went to her shins.

"Is this too racy?" she asked Amineh in an undertone. "I didn't know we'd be taking off our abayas in the open like this."

"No, it's fine here," Amineh assured her absently as she stepped away to speak to a servant.

Fern looked to the sheikh for confirmation.

His aqua gaze was traveling over her like tropical seawater, leaving tickling trails down her limbs and making her toes curl in reaction.

Men never looked at her for longer than it took to ask the time or directions. People in general failed to notice her. She dressed conservatively and was fairly plain, didn't wear makeup and spoke softly. Skinny, freckled ginger-haired girls were as common as milk in the village she'd grown up in near the Scottish border.

In this part of the world she stood out, though. Few of the servants back at Ra'id's palace were white and no one was as white as she was. Not that she ran around showing off her arms and legs there. No, the wearing of coverings worked for her. She liked being invisible.

Fat chance right now, though. The sheikh seemed to see through the damp cotton adhered to her skin, cataloguing her every flaw and projecting what she sensed was disapproval. Her heart sank. She hated making missteps, hated being judged and hated it even more when not given a chance to prove herself first.

"Welcome to the oasis," he said.

His husky baritone wafted over her like a hot breeze, spreading a ripple of disconcerting awareness through her. Similar to Amineh's English, his accent held an intriguing mix of exotic Middle East and cool, upper-class Brit. Zafir was all man.

A widower, according to Amineh. His wife had died of cancer three years ago. *It hit him hard. He doesn't talk about her much. When he does, it's always with great admiration*, Amineh had said.

That meant she ought to be feeling sympathy toward him, Fern thought, but experienced a rush of defensive animosity. She didn't like it. For the most part, she avoided conflict of any kind. If she was cornered, she was perfectly capable of lashing out with vicious sarcasm, but she hated being that person so she tried not to let it happen.

But he was looking at her as though he knew something about her. Like whatever assumption he reached made him cynical and dismayed.

His continued study made her hyperaware of herself. Reflexively, she started doing Miss Ivy's bolstering exercises, reminding herself of all her good qualities. She was smart and kind, good at crafts if she had a pattern to follow…

Distantly, she realized this was a hugely protective reaction. He was a stranger and Miss Ivy always urged patience and not leaping to conclusions about what a new acquaintance might think.

But along with an irrational, panicked certainty that he had taken an instant dislike to her, she *felt* his rebuff in a way that was surprisingly devastating. She wasn't a snob, not even an intellectual one, didn't put on airs despite knowing the Dewey decimal system inside and out… Why on earth would she feel a near irresistible urge to tell him that? She wasn't here to impress him and *wouldn't* with statements like that.

But she was intimidated by the kind of man he was. So imperious. When had she ever come into the sphere of anyone like him? The natural instincts of the weak wanted someone this powerful to be on her side. She recognized that, but there was something else going on inside her, something she'd never really experienced before. She feared it might be attraction. Not a passing "oh, he's nice-looking," but something far more elemental. *Please consider me.*

That involuntary yearning was deeply confusing and beyond inappropriate.

A blush began to climb from her tight chest into her closing throat and across her face until her ears felt like they were on fire. She hated herself then. Hated her body and its over-the-top reaction. She was embarrassed by her own embarrassment and wanted to die.

Zafir watched a million freckles disappear in a bath of red and felt an unexpected urge to laugh.

Not nice, he realized, glancing away to hide the amusement brimming his eyes. He didn't want to soften toward this English teacher, who was drowning in her own blush of sexual attraction. He was experienced enough to know that's what was happening to her and man enough to like it.

But *English*.

Despite knowing how inappropriate she was for him, the prowling tomcat within him kept his tail standing at attention. His eyes traveled back to her of their own accord, counting the freckles that dotted her arms like cocoa sprinkled onto foamed milk. They were all over her, even the tops of her feet. The full effect naked would be an incredible sight.

One he would not make any attempts to see, he cautioned his libido, no matter how amenable she might seem.

He lifted his gaze from her disaster of a skirt, to shoulders covered in that Milky Way of freckles barely visible against the pink of her extensive blush, to liquid eyes locked on his face. He recognized the look, which was somewhere between nervous bunny and dazzled groupie.

Being a duke's grandson had entitled him to more than an academic education. Alongside economics and diplomacy, he'd learned that Western women could be incredibly accommodating to a man's basest needs. If he wanted her, he could have her.

That's why he began fantasizing about setting his mouth against her shoulder, feeling the heat under her skin and tasting that smooth, pale flesh. That's why his palm tingled to push into the folds of her skirt, to discover the shape of her backside and lock her hips into his own.

But tanned blondes were his preference. American or Scandinavian and only while traveling. He had enough power struggles with the conservatives in his country without having affairs inside his borders. He dismissed her with an arrogant blink, deliberately letting her see his rejection.

She swallowed, face blazing and lashes dropping. The corners of her lips pulled into the tortured bite of her teeth.

He had a near irresistible urge to cover her pursed doll's mouth with his own, to lightly torture her until her lips were swollen and open. He could practically feel that wild hair tangled around his fingers as he held her under him, her clasp on him tight as he thrust deep and watched her eyes fog with ecstasy.

English, he reminded with a mild curse at his own weakness. Was it genetic that he could be blindsided by lust for one, so much so that he couldn't smile, let alone speak?

He was only responding to her because he hadn't been with any woman in over two months, he reasoned. It had nothing to do with a tainted streak in his makeup. He wasn't like his father, who had fallen so hard for the wrong woman he'd gotten himself killed for it, leaving his bastard half-blood son to clean up the mess.

"Fern, this is my brother, Zafir. She may call you that while we're here, yes?" Amineh turned back and clasped his arm, then leaned her weight on him in a familiar way that yanked him back into awareness. "Be nice to her. She's shy."

Fern. It was oddly suitable. His country favored names inspired by nature and something in her buttoned-down demeanor reminded him of those tightly curled fiddle-heads he used to spy when tramping through his grandfather's estate, searching for signs of spring and the end of the semester, when he could return to the warmth of home.

"Of course," he managed to respond, fine with the level of stiffness in his tone. He was in the throes of a very wrong-time, wrong-place reaction. The feeling annoyed him enough to reflect in his voice. Still, he heard himself say, "If I may call you Fern." He would regardless, but he willed permission from her all the same. Cooperation. Capitulation.

Damn. He really shouldn't want her so badly that he was already finding ways to stake a claim. Like it was a given that he would have her. This was lust. Garden-variety. He was on vacation, relaxed. Horny. Of course he responded to an available woman. That's all this was and he could resist it.

Her lashes quivered and she nodded shakily, fingers playing together restlessly.

Her discomfiture left him grimly pleased. He was vital

and sexual and alpha. Asserting himself was second nature, but there was more at play here. Amineh might see only a blush, but Fern's reaction was carnal and that held a special allure for him.

"We're very informal here," Amineh chattered on. "We'll cover up again when the Bedouins come through, but for now the oasis is ours. That's why I love it. Oh, I've been looking forward to this." She squeezed his arm again, then gave him a frown. "But you look grumpy. Why? We're going to have fun. Act like kids again. Come on, Fern. Let's walk up to the camp and get settled."

Fern began to gather her bags onto her shoulder.

Zafir bit back an urging for her to leave them for the servants, but she was Ra'id's employee, he reminded himself. Not an ambassador's daughter. She knew her place better than he did.

She packed like an ambassador's daughter, he noted with a grimace, as he watched her try to heft a third bag onto her shoulder.

He moved to take it.

"I can come back for it," she insisted, but he brushed past her attempts to keep it and reached to remove one of the others already bending her slender spine. His thumb grazed skin like duck down, punching a shot of hot need into his gut.

What the hell? From barely touching her?

The hair on his scalp stood on end with both alarm and excitement.

She dipped her head, making it impossible for him to decipher whether she had reacted as intensely. But if he wasn't mistaken, her nipples were standing up in sharp points. It couldn't be from a chill in this heat.

Which should not make his belly tighten with anticipation, but it did.

Amineh was halfway up the path with Ra'id, leaving him to accompany Fern. He forced himself to find a neutral topic of conversation.

"The oasis is roughly seventeen square kilometers. My father designated this as a nature reserve when we were children. We have one tribe allowed to camp here without a permit as they follow bird migrations. We anticipate they'll come through while we're here, but otherwise access is strictly limited."

"I read about it before we came." Her quick statement seemed to say "thanks, but I know all I need to." She hurried along.

Let it go, he told himself. Let *her* go. If she had received the message that he wasn't welcome to a come-on, that was a good thing.

But his longer legs easily kept up to the scurrying pace that kept the color high in her cheeks. And he couldn't take his eyes off the way her remarkable hair bounced and her small, firm breasts barely moved.

And all the while, she looked straight ahead as though trying to ignore him.

"How long have you been teaching the girls?" he asked.

"Three months." She flashed a look up at him that was vaguely defensive. "I feel a bit of a fraud, to be honest. Amineh, I mean, umm, Bashira…"

"It's fine," he said. "As she said, we're casual here. No need to use her title."

"Right. Thank you. What I was going to say is that her English is perfect and the girls are already switching back and forth very easily. Aside from correcting their grammar and spelling, I'm not sure they really need me. It's just such a remarkable opportunity to experience another culture and…" She cleared her throat and her gaze flickered over him like a searchlight picking out the best parts.

"The girls are lovely," she murmured faintly. "I feel very fortunate to be here. Well, there. *And* here."

Another blush. She was really in the throes of sexual interest. How utterly captivating. The hormones that told a man to pursue a woman seared his veins like adrenaline.

"I'm sure she's delighted to have you in the household," he said, his voice as tight as his skin, brain somehow maintaining a grasp on the conversation. "My sister and I prefer our father's world, but we often feel homesick for England." He closed his mouth, not sure why he had said it like that. It wasn't real homesickness, just that all his life he'd wished he could live in both places at the same time.

Which felt like a traitorous admission, as though he wasn't wholly committed to the country he ruled, but he was. Willing to make deep sacrifices for it even. He frowned.

Beside him, Fern halted abruptly and cast a jerky glance up and down the beach. It was a scene of controlled chaos: tents going up, pillows spilling from baskets and silk rugs unrolled. "I, um, don't know where I'm going. Do I sleep with the children?"

"No, they have their own tent." He pointed to where his son was hanging the partition between his side and the girls' in the undersized tent they used.

The servants were settling near the water pump at the far end of the beach, where the cooking fire would be laid. A large tent was going up not far from the children's, for Amineh and Ra'id. His own tent was already standing at the end of a small bench of sand facing the water. Security would place their small tents at strategic places at the perimeter of the oasis.

Deductive reasoning allowed him to single out the only unclaimed lodging. Halfway between the two ends of the camp, tucked beneath an overhang of palms where a small footprint of sand pushed into the tall grass, sat a bundled tent.

Apparently Fern was expected to know how to erect the tent herself.

"That one," he said, as he grazed light fingers on her upper arm to catch her attention then pointed.

Yes, he was that weak. Unable to resist touching her.

Her breath caught and he experienced a surprisingly strong pulse of satisfaction that she responded so sharply to his barely there caress.

This was going to be a difficult two weeks.

Fern wished Zafir would take a hike so she could figure out what was going on.

Obviously she found him attractive. Who wouldn't? He was gorgeous. And he'd noticed, *obviously*, because she was useless at disguising her thoughts and feelings. That's why she preferred to hide behind books and library desks and had taken a job a million miles from home so she'd only have two students and hardly see any men at all.

Men made her nervous. Not outright afraid. They'd have to notice her for her to feel threatened, but she'd learned the hardest way possible not to beg for approval. As much as she might have a curiosity about dating and mating, she was highly reluctant to put her hard-won confidence on the line. It had been far easier over the years to stay home and *not* rile her mother by going out with men. Instead, she had excelled at her studies and worked hard to help pay rent and, yes, had even taken a martyr's pride in being the dutiful daughter. She'd told herself she was too busy for romance, but really, she'd been too cowardly.

Or perhaps, hadn't met a man exciting enough to provoke her past her reservations. The fact that something had been awakened in her today, made her want to be noticed and appreciated and found worthy, made her anxious. Emotionally vulnerable.

And disturbingly aware of herself physically. She'd never responded to a man in such an animal way. Her knowledge about sex was mostly gleaned from the deliciously graphic passages in romance novels. They always gave her a nice flush of pleasure, but thinking about doing those sorts of things in real life, wondering what Zafir liked to do to women and what it might feel like to have his hands and mouth on her naked body, made sharp sensations pierce her nipples and between her thighs. Heat that was both embarrassment and excitement throbbed painfully in her, making her feel all the more defenseless and exposed.

It was *so* unnerving.

This was why her mother had always said sex was dangerous. Fern had wondered why so many people did it if it was so bad, but until today she'd never had a man touch her. Not really. Not so she felt it like a lightning bolt into her belly. *That* was why people did it. The sensations were compelling enough to overcome logic and common sense.

She desperately wanted to move away from him and take time to examine exactly what was happening to her, label it, then put it in storage forever. Especially because some primal part of her felt like he… But no. She was making it up. Fretting because that's what she did best. She was misinterpreting basic courtesy as…

She didn't even know the words for what she thought she sensed, only that she felt like she was trapped in a tiger's cage and he was pacing around her, curious enough to sniff, but not genuinely hungry. Bored maybe. Looking for something to play with.

He walked across to drop her bags by a red bundle.

Oh, dear. Was that her tent? Well, she wasn't above

reading directions. She tried to retrieve the card from its plastic pocket.

"I'll do it," he said, looking disgruntled as he picked up the bundle, opened the drawstring and shook the contents onto the sand. He discarded the nylon outer bag.

"I'm sure I can work it out." She picked up the empty bag and turned it over to see the card was covered in foreign cursive.

"Do you read Arabic?" he asked dryly, then handed her a corner of the tent and backed away to shake out the large square.

"Not yet," she answered, moving to extend the other corner. As she did, she picked up the bag of pegs so they wouldn't be caught underneath. "Is there really no English? Because this doesn't look like traditional Bedouin accommodation."

"No, these modern designs are too lightweight and practical to ignore for the sake of custom." He snagged the small mallet she drew from the bag of pegs. "Even the nomads have moved to lighter fabrics than woven camel hair, but you'll see more authentic tents when they come through." He held out his hand for a peg.

"I can manage. I'll ask one of the other men if I can't. I don't want to inconvenience you." There. She had an assertive side. It was very polite and obliging, but it got the job done when she needed it.

He flicked his sharp gaze around the camp as though looking for one of these men she might enlist when really, she'd probably ask Amineh's maid for help before she'd find the courage to approach a stranger and beg a favor.

When his gaze came back to hers, he seemed disapproving and vaguely challenging. "I'll do it," he stated.

She locked her teeth, having learned long ago to pick her battles.

At least she was able to hurry the process. She willed her fingers to be nimble as she followed him down the side and across the back of the tent, struggling all the loops onto the pegs as he hammered them into the sand. The feeling of having her every action scrutinized was her own baggage, she reminded herself as she moved toward the front. He wasn't watching her. He was having some kind of manly back-to-nature moment, indulging his instinct to prove his superiority over nature.

Nevertheless, as she straightened from making the last attachment, the tension was killing her. She glanced at him and his green eyes were waiting, snagging her like a hook, with a pierce and a tug.

She caught her breath, limbs paralyzed with shock.

He calmly continued what he was doing. and lengthened a pole in increments with a smooth stroke of his hand and a light twist of his wrist, eyes staying on her like they'd been there a while.

He lifted the opening of the tent and slid the pole inside.

It was…

She blushed. God help her, she blushed hard.

A noise escaped him. Might have been a snort of amusement or a *tsk* of impatience. She wasn't sure because he bent to take up another shortened pole and began to extend it. When his gaze came back to hers, his was fierce and almost scolding.

His rebuke burned. She knew her reaction was obvious. Her ability to demure was nil. Worse, she knew she didn't inspire male desire. She wasn't particularly curvy on her chest or bottom. She wouldn't know how to apply eye shadow if she'd ever had the spare notes to buy it. Between the braces to fix terribly crooked teeth, the secondhand clothes, the extra studies to win a scholarship and then maintaining her position at the library while she earned her degree, she'd been the most easily overlooked nerd her entire life.

Maybe he was one of those jocks who occasionally noticed she was an easy mark and was having his fun teasing her. Maybe he was silently taunting her, sending a pithy "as if."

She usually walked away when feeling picked on, but despite the seventeen square kilometers around her, she didn't have anywhere to go. The only place she could hide from Zafir was her own quarters, so she ducked into them. She bendt under the light weight of the silky red fabric to pick up the pole from the ground and worked her way to the center, where a grommet awaited on the roof and the floor.

Of course it wasn't as easy as it looked. She got the top one hooked in, but even though the tent wasn't heavy, the tension in the fabric was resistant to her attempts to align the bottom of the pole into the floor.

"You spaced the pegs too far away," she told him, hearing her mother's voice and cringing.

"I've pitched more tents than you have, Fern," he drawled and she narrowed her eyes at him even though they couldn't see each other.

Another pole made a zipping noise as he slid it into the pocket that would form one of the corners. "Let me finish this part then I'll help you."

Oh, great. I'll just stand here looking stupid then.

The tent shifted on her hair, making it crackle with static. She debated crawling out, but couldn't make herself go out there and face him.

Another *zip, zip, zip* and he had the back and walls stabilized.

Leave when he comes in, she thought, but he lifted the front of the tent and took up all the space, bringing the middle of the tent pole so it slid through her light grip and the roof climbed as he neared her. Then he was standing before her, the narrow pole between them, his tanned face tinged by the translucent red of the fabric, his gaze fixed on hers.

He slid his hands over her limp ones and guided the bottom end of the pole into place.

She tried to look away, but he was tall and very close. He smelled good. Earthy and sweaty, but not overpowering. Masculine and intriguing. Aside from her mother's specialist, she'd never met a man with such an air of command and that physician had been white-haired and potbellied. Zafir was in his prime, not just healthy, but radiating supremacy.

In the back of her mind, she knew she was behaving like some kind of rock-band superfan, speechless in the presence of a man with star quality, unable to move, but he was so incredible. She found herself staring into his eyes for too long. She knew it was too long, but she couldn't look away from those crystal blue-green depths. They quested, delving into hers, demanding something she didn't even understand.

Say something, she thought, and let her tongue wet her lips.

His gaze lowered to her mouth.

Her breath evaporated.

She found her own gaze dropping to his mouth, wondering how it would feel to have those smooth lips rubbing against hers. Her heart was fluttering like a trapped bird, her pulse pounding in her ears.

He lifted his hand to hover hotly next to her cheek, scorching her. His brows jerked in some type of struggle. *Was he going to kiss her?*

It was remarkable yet terrifying. Did she really want to do this? It was so wrong, but he was *right there*.

"Miss Davenport, are you in there?" Bashira called from outside.

Fern's heart went into free fall. Her conscience gave her a hard shake and she jerked back, shocked.

"I am," she stammered, discovering her hand was still trapped under Zafir's on the pole.

His grip tightened briefly before he released her with a flare of his fingers. He lifted away his touch as though she'd burned him. A muscle ticked in his cheek. He looked very displeased. Accusatory, but also confused.

She surreptitiously touched her mouth, and avoided looking at him as she edged around him to open the flap of the tent.

The rush of fresh air, dry and hot as it was, made her realize how stifling it had been inside, where things had been sultry and musky. Her heart was still pounding hard and loud. It took everything she had to muster a smile for the children as they approached.

"Mama said these are for you." Bashira struggled with Jumanah to drag a basket across the sand toward her. Tariq followed, staggering under the weight of a bedroll on his shoulder.

"Have you met my son?" Zafir asked as he emerged beside her. He didn't stand so close as to be improper, but the air crackled with energy that bounced back and forth between them.

Fern stepped forward to escape the field of it. "Not yet."

What had just happened in there? Was he messing with her? She hadn't known what to expect from Amineh's brother, but cruelty wasn't on the list. The thought that he would toy with her for his own amusement was not only painful, but also opened the gap of deep vulnerability in her even wider. She wouldn't be able to avoid him here.

He moved forward to take the bedroll off his son, introduced the boy then disappeared inside the tent to lay it out.

Far too intimate a thing to do. How was she supposed to sleep on something he had touched?

"Your cousins speak very highly of you, Tariq," she said shakily. "I'm looking forward to getting to know you."

The boy regarded her with a very serious expression. Not his father's eyes, thank goodness. His were like black coffee, but they held the same intelligence and confidence.

"They speak well of you, too, but may I say with all proper respect that I no longer have need of a nanny. I have a guard." He quarter turned to indicate a man observing from a position near the children's tent. "To protect me from outside threats. I am allowed to make my own mistakes and learn from them."

Pleasantly diverted by that statement, Fern nodded. "I can see you're mature enough to do so. But I'm not a nanny. I tutor the girls in English."

"I'm on vacation," Tariq stated promptly. "My English is excellent."

Abundant self-assurance was obviously a genetic trait. Her lips were still fiery and buzzing from having Zafir stare at them. Now they twitched with amusement.

"I hope you'll join us for our field lessons anyway," Fern said. "I'm excited to explore the oasis. I brought a microscope, some tracking books and sketching supplies. Perhaps you could teach me some things about your country and its wildlife."

"Oh, yes, I could do that," he stated with generosity. "My father is also very knowledgeable," he said as Zafir emerged again to stand at her side. "He finds an animal even when it's trying to hide."

Fern outright refused to look at Zafir with that remark hovering like a balloon ready to burst. She was not interested in being laughed at even more.

"That would be a treat," she murmured, throat tightening with indignation. "But he's already gone out of his way on my behalf. I don't want to impose."

"You would do it for my cousins, wouldn't you, Baba?" Tariq said, neck craned to look up at his father.

"Of course," Zafir promised with a hand clasping warmly to Tariq's shoulder. "That's why we are here. To spend time with our family. You'll show our guest where to find everything? I can't put off confirming that everyone has arrived safely as scheduled." Turning to her, Zafir explained, "Rescues are difficult and time sensitive, so we have very low criteria for setting them off. Any delay of a message will do it. Excuse me."

As if nothing had happened between them, he nodded and walked away.

Of course, nothing *had* happened, she reminded herself. Maybe she'd imagined that whole thing.

Except her cheek still burned where he'd almost touched her.

She forced her gaze not to linger on his back, but she couldn't help wondering what that back would look like naked. Tanned and strong. When had she ever, ever fantasized about running light fingers down a man's spine? Or sprawling naked upon one?

This place was supernatural, casting a spell of some kind over her.

Distressed, she forced her attention to the children. They showed her where to find boiled water for drinking and pointed out the latrine and gave her a short broom to use to sweep out scorpions—really?—if they wandered into her tent. Then they left her to unpack as they scampered off in search of wild dates.

Fern entered the privacy of her tent and let out a long, anxious breath. Amineh had talked about the oasis like it was a place of freedom, but Fern had a sense of being kidnapped—into luxury, sure. The tent was bigger than the tiny bedroom she'd grown up in. The bedding and pillows the children had brought her were silky and colorful, while the pallet Zafir had unrolled was wide enough for two.

Stop it.

How had she even wound up here at the end of the earth? She'd grown up expecting she would take a position in a village day school, perhaps going home to a tidy flat where she'd have a cat named Fabio. Her only aspiration had been to provide the same ray of hope Miss Ivy had instilled in her—to help withdrawn, unhappy students discover their own hidden potential.

Hers had apparently been the ability to become an international teacher.

She hadn't even considered an overseas position while her mother had been alive, but after her mother had passed away, Fern had needed a fresh start. On a whim, she'd applied to a placement agency and expected to wind up in a missionary school, but had found herself in the running for this job.

It still felt like a miracle that she'd won it, but her quiet nature seemed to fit with a culture that valued modesty. She and Amineh had got on immediately, which surprised Fern. At first she had thought it was only because Amineh appreciated Fern's genuine affection for the girls and her earnest desire to act in their best interests. Now she knew Amineh better, she recognized a like soul in the sense that they'd both struggled to find their place in the jungle of female cliques during their school years.

Amineh and Zafir, Fern had learned, were the product of a rather notorious affair between an Arab sheikh and an English duke's daughter. They'd ping-ponged back and forth between their parents, not quite fitting fully into either culture. Amineh had found stability by marrying her brother's best friend, Ra'id, and living permanently in his country.

Zafir still fought for the right to rule their father's homeland, Q'Amara. He'd married the daughter of a sheikh, trying to ease resistance at having a man with such heavy Western influences governing their country.

Somehow she couldn't picture him wearing the same sad frown Amineh wore when she talked about their difficult early years. He seemed too fiercely proud to allow prejudice to reach his heart. It was hard to imagine a man that dynamic and confident struggling with anything.

Peeking out of her tent, she saw him down at the water, shin-deep in the spring where the children had told her bathing was allowed. He stood with his sharp profile angled upward to the top of the worn canyon on the far side of the water. Then he crouched, not taking any heed that his robe was soaked through. He scooped his hands into the water and splashed his face, then lifted his *gutra* to wet the back of his neck.

She swallowed, going weak as she watched him. He was so comfortable in his skin, so self-assured and compelling.

It dawned on her that this was a crush. She was suffering a full-blown case of unfounded infatuation, behaving exactly like her adolescent schoolmates used to. She stood here spying on a boy, acting geeky and awkward and keyed up, entertaining uncharacteristic fantasies of kissing the back of his neck. How puerile. If only his wife was alive to deter her.

Look away, she told herself, but she couldn't make herself do it. Why did he have to be out there acting all brooding and sexy anyway?

He stood and turned to stare directly at her tent. His

shoulders were set at what seemed a tense angle, his demeanor projecting dissatisfaction.

She couldn't tell if he saw her, but she retreated to the back wall.

This was going to be an interminable two weeks.

CHAPTER TWO

FERN USED THE excuse of ferreting out her supplies and setting up her mock classroom to avoid everyone for the rest of the day. She usually ate alone so when she smelled the evening meal, she found Nudara, who fetched her a bowl of spicy stew and flatbread with some kind of yogurt dolloped on top.

Taking it back to her tent, Fern told herself the peacefulness was nice. The bustle of the camp settled as everyone sat to eat. The children's laughter rang out often, along with Amineh's and the occasional rich male chuckle—one of which made Fern listen harder and feel...

She sighed and shook her head at herself. The light breeze whispered through the palm leaves above her, snickering. An unknown bird tittered at her.

It grew dark quickly, but the nearly full moon rose shortly after. The trip had been organized around the fattest moon as that was the likeliest time for the Bedouins to visit the oasis. The waxing orb's glow turned the landscape a pale blue and a velvety breeze caressed her cheek as she walked her dishes back to the outdoor kitchen.

Later, after she had brushed her teeth, she put herself to bed early. She'd had a long, active couple of days, she told herself, even though she could hear the children laughing over music from a stringed instrument. No one else was turning in yet. They were visiting and having fun.

Sociology classes had taught her this sort of camp built the relationships between members of a tribe. The servants were certainly in good spirits, teasing one another and making jokes. Zafir's coming together with his neighbor, Ra'id, had strengthened relations between their two countries in ancient ways, even if they only traded gossip. Corporations called something like this a "team-building exercise" and paid small fortunes for their employees to attend.

Fern was the luckiest person in the world to be able to experience this.

She told herself.

As she held her eyes closed against an inexplicable sting.

She had absolutely no reason to feel lonely in this wide bed. Miss Ivy would enjoy hearing about all of this when Fern had an online connection again.

Make some notes, she cajoled herself, but didn't move. Instead she mentally wrote something entirely different, something that belonged in an erotic novel. It was a scene where Zafir came to her tent and touched a lot more than her cheek.

It was the worst night of her life. She tossed and turned, unable to shut off her mind from conjuring fantasies of making love with Zafir.

She didn't even know how it was properly done! Obviously she knew the mechanics, but she'd been firmly sheltered from any sort of expressions of sexual passion. Her mother hadn't allowed her to go to sexy movies or watch any of those daytime serials on television. The romance novels at the library had been read from an angle under the desk. Guilt always assailed her for enjoying those stories and more than one academic friend had shamed her for picking them up, but Fern couldn't help wondering why was it so bad to like stories about love and happily-ever-after?

Because of the sex, her mother's voice said in her head. Heaven help any woman who gave in to her hormones. That only brought heartache and disappointment.

Fern being the disappointment in question, she had long ago surmised.

Yet here she was, indulging her own hormones with imaginary banquets of kisses and caresses. It wasn't the first time she'd lain in bed and imagined she wasn't alone, but she'd never been quite so explicit with her fantasies or had a particular man in mind.

It had to stop.

Throwing off her light sheet, she quietly unzipped her tent and stepped into the cool of predawn. The camp was silent, the stillness only broken by the relentless pound-ing of her pulse.

Dressed in her knee-length cotton nightgown, she walked down to the beach and sighed as her feet found the damp sand at the water's edge. The burning inside her began to ease. This was what she'd needed. A cold shower.

Was that why Zafir had come to the water yesterday?

No. No more daydreams that he fancied her. He'd only been washing off travel grime.

Still, she found herself tracking to the place where he'd stood in the water. It felt deliciously cool as it closed over her feet and climbed to the backs of her knees.

Drawn forward, she sucked in a breath as the pool deep-ened quickly, soaking through to weigh the fabric of her nightgown. Chilly water hit her loins, then her navel. She sucked in her stomach, got as far as her breasts and held her breath.

She dipped until the cold water closed over her and

stayed under a moment, nose plugged, letting the chill seep to her bones. Then she titled back her head and rose, baptized into a creature of this foreign yet intoxicating world.

The thought made her smile naturally for the first time since arriving here. Oh, she felt a million times better!

Which was silly. One little plunge into a spring couldn't wash away a lifetime of baggage and misgivings, but she wished it could be that easy. Her mother's shaking finger always seemed to follow her, though, undermining her ability to enjoy the simplest sensual experience. She would no doubt criticize her for... Well, everything. Her mother wouldn't approve of anything Fern had done since the service. Ever in her life, really.

At least she wasn't burning with desire for a man beyond her reach anymore. She thought she could sleep now and escape all her disturbing ruminations about Zafir.

Turning, she marveled at how clear the water was, completely entranced by its perfection, feeling mammalian and part of the universe as she watched her feet. Not all creatures were herd animals, she reminded herself. Many lived alone most of their lives, only seeking another of their kind to mate—

Bare, tanned feet stood on the beach before her.

Her heart stalled and her soggy nightgown clung like a skin of dread. Her feet halted and her knees locked in denial.

How? No one else was up.

Her gaze climbed athletic shins to where unbleached linen board shorts ended at his knees.

Leave it to him to wear drawstring shorts that were still the epitome of class, tailored to hang low across his brown hips in the most disreputable yet erotic way. He wasn't wearing a shirt and he was a perfect specimen of the human male. His tense, flat abs were bisected by a line of hair that flared across his brown chest. The pattern accentuated his broad shoulders and the relaxed muscles of his upper arms.

His mouth was set in a grim line, the stubble on his jaw dark making him look even more piratical and dangerous than the first glimpse she'd had of him. He had black hair, she noted. Trimmed close to keep it tight against his scalp.

His brows stayed heavy over those remarkable, glittering eyes as he opened a towel with a flick. She hadn't noticed he was holding one. He beckoned her with two bent fingers, then hissed a word in Arabic that she'd heard Amineh use to hurry the girls.

"Now," he said in a stern whisper. "The guards don't need to see you like that."

Like what?

She glanced down to see her nightgown was plastered to her front, her nipples standing out from the high curves of her breasts like traffic cones. Her lack of underwear was flagrantly obvious.

The light was coming up fast with the sun. She couldn't approach him looking like this!

Her tent looked miles away from here, however, and… *Oh, help me.* He didn't wait. He waded into the water and snapped the towel around her back, barely giving her a chance to lift her arms out of the way before he closed it across her chest and tucked it tight.

She grabbed at it to finish the job herself, then brushed his hands away and glared up at him, even though she was the idiot who'd gotten herself into this mortifying position.

"I didn't think anyone else was awake," she hissed.

"The guards patrol around the clock."

She scowled at the surrounding area, right up to the top of the jagged wall of the canyon, seeing no one. "Well, I wasn't planning to swim when I came out."

"Good thing I was." He nodded at the towel, matching her whisper, but still managing to sound patronizing.

"I wasn't trying to insult anyone," she explained, upset that she'd made a cultural gaffe.

He snorted. "That was the least of my reasons for covering you."

Again he used the tone that suggested she was a bit of a half-wit. She glared up at him, but the eye contact only sent a current of electricity through her that stayed active and hummed in her veins so her breaths stumbled unevenly. A shiver chased over her even as the burn that had kept her awake through the night rekindled.

She forced herself to look toward her tent. Told her feet to carry her in that direction, but all the illicit fantasies she'd had in there loomed large in her mind. The blood she'd cooled with her swim heated and moved with a sensual slither through her veins, creating a simmering warmth in her belly and lower. Very personal muscles clenched in anticipation.

The return to a state of receptiveness was so primeval and quick, her breath hitched in a helpless catch. How did he do this to her by only standing near? It was unsettling to have no control over her reactions.

She didn't want to know if he knew, hoped he didn't, but her gaze tracked to his to see.

He was waiting for her. Something fierce flashed in his eyes. This time when he stepped close and lowered his head, as proprietary as a man could get, she didn't feel any alarm. No sense of self-preservation. Just anticipation. *Please.*

His lips burned on contact against her cool ones, sliding easily against the dampness left from her swim.

Her eyes closed and her senses came alive to the feel of his firm mouth settling purposefully onto hers. He parted her lips with a lick of his tongue, causing heat to flow into them so fast it stung. Her whole body came alive with a jolt of powerful excitement so intense she shuddered.

And she returned the pressure of his mouth instinctively, moving hers in a type of hungry greed, Her heart pounded with excitement and fear-spiked awareness that she wanted things from him he could never give her. This was futile, but irresistible.

And so exquisite. When his tongue dashed deeper against her inner lips, both daring and deliciously stimulating, she touched her own to his. He tasted smoky and spicy, not like cigarettes, but like open fires and exotic foods. He was remarkable. The sensations he provoked in her were so sweet she wanted to moan aloud. She was drowning—

It hit her that they were still standing in the pool where anyone could see them.

Stricken, she jerked back with a splashing step.

He steadied her, mouth tightening to a harsh line as he scanned over her head. When his searing green gaze came back to hers, his eyes were brimming with frustration.

"Let's take this to my tent," he said in a graveled undertone.

Her heart exploded inside her chest like an overinflated balloon, bursting into ragged pieces. Hookups were just that easy? Women were, she supposed. For him. He obviously thought she was.

"Just like that?" she asked breathily, anguished that she'd dropped herself so low in his estimation.

He cocked his head, expression cynical. "You don't want to?"

His tone was full of the knowledge that she'd kissed him back, making it doubly hard to claim she didn't want to. Her chest was still rising jaggedly and her vision was full of a naked chest she longed to touch. She swallowed.

"I happen to like my job," she said, hating herself for not being able to honestly say she wasn't even tempted. She was. Deeply.

"They don't have to know," he said, flatly brushing that away.

"Look." She must be glowing redder than the sky at the horizon. "I can do the math. You don't have many options here." She used her chin to indicate the camp. "I suppose it's a good offer, that I should feel flattered, but I'm not in your league."

It was a detail she'd been using in her head to counter her longing and it didn't seem to sway him any better than it did her.

His expression hardened with derision. "We'll be on exactly the same level once we're horizontal."

Nice, she mentally scoffed, taking that remark like a sword in the gut, while the thought of being horizontal, with him atop her, shorted out her brain.

She startled at the way his hand gentled on her arm as it moved in a light caress that raised prickling sensations across her shoulders and up the back of her neck. He was making no effort to temper his sexuality and was quite overwhelming. Everything about him made her heart race with both apprehension and excitement. His touch was so possessive and strong that every little caress of his thumb against her skin would stay with her for the rest of her life.

"You really want me to believe you don't want to?" he chided.

"Of course I want to," she admitted painfully. There was no point in denying it. She was lousy at dissembling. Stronger people walked all over her because she had few natural defenses. It made her great with children and hopeless when it came to a captivating man like him.

So she realized what a chance she was taking in revealing how attracted she was to him. If he took it into his head to pursue her, she'd have no way of stopping him.

"Then let it happen." His reassuring caress became something more, something drugging and inducing. "I'm not going to hurt you, Fern."

"I've been given to believe differently," she protested with the caustic sarcasm she hated resorting to, but her back was to the wall. "Apparently it does hurt. The first time."

So there, she told him with a pointed look into stunned aqua eyes. Her face ached. *Yes*, she mentally transmitted. No one had ever wanted her enough to take her virginity. It was lowering and painful, but it was true.

Now her feet found the ability to propel her away to somewhere dark and small. Chest aching, she let her shaky legs carry her back to her tent.

Her plan was to shamelessly use the children as deflective shields if Zafir approached her, but he didn't.

Which was unconscionably disappointing.

But what did she think? That she was irresistible? With this bedhead?

She'd woken from a deep sleep that had been an escape from a desire to cry. If an unfamiliar towel hadn't been lying in a heap next to her still damp nightgown, she might have thought she'd dreamed the whole thing.

Sadly she hadn't. And now Zafir knew she was a virgin. One who was inordinately hot for him.

Funny how Mother was always right. Lust *did* make you miserable. Fern supposed she ought to be glad it hadn't also got her pregnant, kicked out of her home and abandoned by the father. She wouldn't be so busy trying to make ends meet and raising a burden alone that life would pass her by in an astringent blur.

"Excellent!" Tariq declared, making Fern look up from

kneeling next to Bashira as she helped the girl focus the microscope.

"What is?" she prompted, but a tickling shiver chased up her spine and she knew without following Tariq's gaze over her head.

"My father is coming to take us for a walk."

Standing, she pivoted to face Zafir, taking a breath to argue, but he stole her ability to speak simply by arriving and casting a respectful eye over her overturned wicker basket and tablet, which showed pictures of water bugs.

The girls leaped up to fetch proper shoes.

"Why…?" she asked, feeling persecuted.

"You're safe, Fern," he assured her, one hand lifting to calm her as he held his distance.

She didn't feel safe! Not when his sweeping gaze seemed to visualize her nude beneath a soaked gown. She crossed her arms, hiding that her nipples prickled into points and trying to protect the fragile ego squirming like a wisp of smoke behind her breastbone.

"I shouldn't have presumed this morning." A mixture of compunction and frustration flashed in his expression. "If I frightened you, I apologize." He sounded sincere. Looked it, even though his gaze was now penetrating hers in a way that was extremely uncomfortable. "It won't happen again."

Well, that certainly told her how irresistible she was. Her eyes grew damp with a startling mixture of frustration and longing. She lowered her lashes to hide her completely misplaced disappointment.

"Lust is bad," she managed to say, stating it for her own benefit, hoping to soothe this sting of rejection by making it sound like she wouldn't go to bed with him even if he wanted her to.

His mouth twitched, the corners deepening with a pained

and secretive smile. "Says the woman who doesn't know what she's talking about." He sobered into the man she had read was a determined leader of a troubled populace. "But in this case, yes. The consequences aren't worth it."

A thick lump rose in her throat. His words cut to the bone and set her adrift. Funny how it really didn't matter that Zafir's kiss had been incidental, brought on by proximity and availability, nothing personal. She had done what females did around all alpha males: projected willingness. His reaction had been as biological as hers.

She shouldn't want him to do it again, but she did.

Lust. Hormones. Whatever it was, they were very detrimental to a woman's good sense. She ought to thank him for dismissing any possibility of giving in to it.

But she was just hurt.

He smiled and offered, "I'm only here because Tariq pled your case at lunch."

"*My* case?"

"His own," he answered with a tilt of his head. "Ra'id has asked you not to take the girls beyond the camp without him, but he has agreed with Tariq that I am an acceptable escort."

"I—" *think*, she urged herself "—don't want to impose."

"We're also facilitating for Ra'id and Amineh," he said.

"In what way?" She looked up from setting rocks on the children's sketches so they wouldn't blow away if the wind came up.

Zafir's dry lift of his brows made the wheels roll and click in her head. But he couldn't really be saying what she thought he was saying. They were having sex?

"You're like one of those chameleons that switches color between one breath and the next." His husky tone laughed at her flush.

"Well, I can't believe what you just implied! It's rather

personal, isn't it? And she's your sister. Did they actually *ask* you…?"

"*No.* And I'm not going to dwell on whether that's what they're really doing. But the girls both have birthdays about nine months after past vacations here. Ra'id has had a killer travel schedule the last few years, but he told me last night they're looking forward to a more settled life next year." He shrugged. "And he loves his girls, but his successor is his brother. He'd like a son."

"What about your son?" she asked tartly. "Also an oasis baby?"

He lost all hint of humor as his expression shuttered. "Wedding night."

Conversation closed, she heard loud and clear. It left her feeling as though she'd overstepped, but he started it.

The children returned and they headed out. Twenty minutes later, they had followed a track through tall grass that crackled like green flames around them, then they climbed to a vantage point above the spring. Zafir explained the relay station that kept them in contact with the outside world and the girls waved at the servants in the camp below.

No sign of Ra'id and Amineh. That shouldn't make her feel envious, but Fern was. Greener than the oasis.

We all have different paths, Miss Ivy would say. *Bloom where you're planted.* She was full of those sorts of sayings. Most of the time Fern appreciated that encouraging, make-the-best-of-it quality in her friend. Today she just felt…single.

Disregarded.

Unloved and unlovable.

Zafir showed the children how to use his digital camera then stepped back to watch them stalk geckos in the rocks.

Fern stood a few feet away, looking over the camp below. Her narrow waist was emphasized by the wide band of her beige skirt and her arms were covered by an equally dull-colored shirt, but his mind kept seeing her as she'd looked this morning: a water nymph sent to inflame him. She'd risen from the water, small breasts high and firm and topped by pebbled nipples he'd longed to tongue and suck. Her form was sleek, her femininity understated, but she'd been undeniably all woman when the fabric of her nightgown had painted her stomach and upper thighs, falling away into a frustrating veil that hid her most intimate flesh.

He'd already been primed for her, having spent the night recalling those confusing moments in her tent. She'd been such a curious mixture of invitation and hesitation, baffling him. Experienced women could be notorious teases, but he hadn't caught that vibe from her. More an alarmed hesitation that had stopped him as much as the knowledge that kissing her at all was reckless.

He'd been so sure she was feeling the attraction as strongly as he was, but she'd tripped away like a frightened rabbit. He didn't prey on women so her reaction had made him feel like a cad.

Her faltering made sense now that he understood how inexperienced she was, but through the night he'd pulled his own insecurities into the equation and tortured himself by wondering whether she really wanted him. The idea that she didn't, when he burned for her so strongly, had been painful. Really, truly agonizing.

And then she'd stood before him in the pool and projected all those signals of yearning again, her body on display. He'd had to know.

Her lips had latched to his as she surrendered to passion and that had been it. He couldn't remember a time when a simple kiss had ignited him so thoroughly. They were a perfect match and only the knowledge that his and Ra'id's men were watching over them had kept him from giving in to the barbarian ancestry that had raged to the fore. He'd trembled with the effort to keep from pressing her back onto the dry sand, lifting her night dress and filling her with the flesh that had thickened in powerful response to the sight of her.

Getting her into his tent and under him had been imperative.

And if she had agreed, he would have breached her maidenhead.

That still confounded him. Her reluctant "of course I want to" had been ringing in his head since she'd said it, soothing his ego. It now offered bittersweet consolation as he faced that he really couldn't seduce her. It would be the height of dishonor.

Why couldn't she be the sophisticate that most of her countrywomen were?

"Tell me about yourself, Fern," he commanded, still not fully believing what she'd revealed. "Have you never been curious?"

She flashed him a startled, slightly harassed look, then glanced at the children working out a rotation system for the camera. Tariq's guard had wandered farther up the path and beyond their hearing.

"I'm highly curious," she argued with small flags of pink on her cheekbones. "For instance, I wonder why Tariq's guard came with us but none to watch the girls. What conclusion should I draw from that?"

"My son's guard is our best snake handler," he replied with amusement, more than aware his culture was still quite sexist by Western standards, but in this case his reasons were purely practical. "I thought it wise to have him scout the area before letting the children poke around. Now stop evading my question. You know what I'm really asking. How old are you? If you were from this part of the world I wouldn't be surprised, but how does an English girl remain untouched until she's twenty-two?"

"Three," she countered with a little grimace and a defensive fold of her arms. She pushed her straw hat more firmly onto her head, no doubt trying to hide beneath its wide brim. "I had other priorities," she said. "And it's not something I want to throw away out of mere curiosity."

She sounded prudish and uptight, not like a typical product of the Western world. Male or female, most people her age were hooking up out of boredom if nothing else. He'd been a kid in a candy store at that age, having developed some skill by his early twenties and feeling the pressure to marry soon. He'd taken advantage of every opportunity while he'd had his freedom.

Good thing he had, since his married years had been dry.

"That wasn't meant to sound like a challenge," she added, sending him a look he supposed was intended as a rebuff, but as he held her gaze, her expression softened to yesterday's absorption.

She didn't realize it, but that mixed signal of defensiveness and yearning challenged him to show her what she was missing. Just touching her bare arm had filled him with excitement. Something more could be truly volatile and he was darkly tempted to discover the extent of it.

"There are other ways to find pleasure without going all the way," he pointed out, mind already several hundred meters down that road with her. "I'm having trouble believing you're so inexperienced you've never been kissed."

"I didn't say that," she retorted. "Just that I haven't—" Pain flashed across her expression and she fixed her attention on the children. "I'm no supermodel. Men don't find me interesting."

Her bruised confidence got to him. It made him soft and weak when he needed to be strong and resistant, but he understood the feeling of being spurned better than most. Her lack of self-assurance wasn't something he could ignore and allow to grow like a cancer.

"Don't underestimate yourself. Men are lazy and will pick the lowest-hanging fruit. It doesn't mean the apples higher up aren't appealing."

"Says the man who turned up his nose at the only fruit in the bowl this morning," she retorted, then went red. "Ignore that. You're right. Let's forget all of this. It makes me feel ridiculous."

Such a quick, defensive reaction suggested he'd hit a nerve. Her insecurity went deeper than he'd realized. That made him uncomfortable. He ought to let her think he had rejected her and leave it at that, but he couldn't.

"I covered you this morning because I didn't want other men seeing what I want for myself. You *have* my interest, Fern," he admitted.

His words snapped her head around, her shocked face framed in the brim of her silly hat. A vulnerable softness that was appealing and very temptingly receptive edged into her eyes.

He reached for what little control he had, which was surprisingly tenuous.

"But do you know anything about our history?" His low tone came out aggressive and rough, colored by lifelong bitterness at the hurdles put in front of him by the accident of his birth and now the addition of this…denial of something he wanted quite badly.

"My father's affair with my mother caused a huge rift in our country. He called off his arranged marriage, flaunted his half-breed son as his heir. Any hint of my Western up-bringing is seen as a flaw by my detractors. If we were in London, I would seduce you into my bed right this second, but we're not. So even though one of my favorite things in the world is finding wild strawberries in a field, for the sake of my country and quite possibly my life, you and I can't happen."

His words poured lava through her arteries. Not the part where he made it clear the consequences of sleeping with her really might be dire, but the part where he acted like he truly wanted to. That made sensuous feelings pool into her loins as a hot, heavy ache turned her into the ripe fruit he was talking about. *Reach for me. Consume me.*

She couldn't look away from him and didn't know how to hide the effect he had on her. With a kind of desperation, she searched to be sure there was no laughter or subterfuge in his expression and only saw his pupils flare.

Her heart skipped.

"What kills me is knowing *you* have options," he said in a begrudging growl, flicking a glance toward Tariq's guard. "Several."

"What?" She glanced at the man who was nudging beneath a stunted bush with a long stick. "I'm not attracted to him! Not to any of the men."

"Only me?" he challenged, but even though there was a hint of belligerence in his tone, it was a statement, one that made him nod once in satisfaction. "Good."

"No, it's not!" she said loudly enough to make the children stop and look toward them.

Fern crossed her arms, annoyed with herself, but Zafir easily excused her outburst.

"Miss Davenport is taking issue with my calling England soggy. She doesn't realize I'm speaking with the affection of a countryman." Turning back to her, he contradicted quietly, "If you began visiting other men's tents, I don't think I would react very well."

"I don't… What does that mean? You'd be…" She couldn't make herself say it. It would be reaching way beyond her grasp and she'd fall on her face.

"Jealous?" Zafir suggested through teeth set in a dangerous smile. "It's worse than that. My ego likes knowing you react only to me. It's not civilized, but only half of me is English. The other half is centuries-old barbarian. I want you, but if I can't have you, no one else can."

Her brain was doing three-sixties, stunned by his arrogance, cursing her inability to disguise her attraction, and some wicked part of her was deeply thrilled by his seeming possessiveness. It made her realize exactly how seductive it was to feel wanted by the person who intrigued you.

On the other hand… "This is ludicrous," she muttered. "No one has ever… I *am* completely English. Is this how you talk to every woman you meet?" She was blushing—of course she was—but she was indignant enough to feel her spine lock into place. "Because I can't believe you're acting as if this is…something that could really happen. *I barely know you.*"

"But the way you look at me says I can have you. I *want* to have you," he warned, looking every inch the desert warrior who stole women for his harem and kept every single one of them pleasured.

A swirl of excitement spiraled downward from her throat to sting her breasts, coil in her abdomen and end as a spark between her thighs. It was a promise of something that had eluded her all her life and she wanted to hang on to it, kindle it and watch it glow hotter.

"You could help me out," he said with a feral growl, nostrils flaring. "Tell me I'm wrong. Refuse me."

She opened her mouth, knowing she should, but he stood there so commandingly. This wasn't about her being too shy or intimidated to assert herself. It was about her being an honest person who was overwhelmed with attraction for the first time in her life. She wasn't a victim of her own urges or his aggression. She finally felt alive and wanted to embrace everything about this glorious awareness.

So not a good idea.

She lifted a hopeless hand. "I told you men don't come on to me. How much experience do you think I have with refusing one?"

He bit out an old-fashioned English curse, one she supposed was apropos, and turned away, too athletic to lurch, but his movements were jerky as he joined the children and admired the shots they'd taken so far.

Fern forced her gaze to the footprints he'd left behind, fearful that she was more like her mother than she'd ever be able to bear.

CHAPTER THREE

"THANKS FOR STAYING behind with me, Fern. This has been a nice day."

Fern couldn't help a small snort as she lifted her eyes off the book she was reading on her tablet. "We've barely done anything. I feel like I'm taking advantage, having such a lazy day."

"Oh, don't be silly. This trip isn't just about Zafir wanting to ensure he has the backing of the nomads. It's a holiday." Amineh came up on her elbow on the mat next to Fern's. "Speaking of the men, I could tell you were curious. Do you wish you'd gone with them?"

"I've never seen anyone hunt with falcons," Fern lied, hoping it was a sufficient excuse for the temptation she'd revealed when Tariq had invited her to join him, his father and Ra'id. Every cell in her body was begging to be near Zafir, but after a glance into his inscrutable expression, she'd declined and had spent the day feeling his absence. "It seemed like male-bonding time, though. And I'd probably cry if they caught something."

That made Bashira look up with a giggle from where she was building a sand castle with her sister. They all looked exactly as they did when they spent occasional afternoons beside the shaded pool at the palace. Amineh wore her bikini and Fern her one-piece. They'd waited until the sun had lowered enough to create a strip of shade for them to lie upon without needing sunscreen.

"The question is, do *you* wish you were with the men," Fern teased. "You've been glued to your husband since we arrived." It had been four days and while Fern had had the children for a few hours every morning and afternoon, the adults tended to keep their distance, as did Fern. It was the only way she could disguise her fascination with Zafir, but her attraction toward him had only increased rather than abated.

"I'm sorry, Fern—" Amineh began.

"Oh, please don't apologize. You've said before how much you miss your husband when he's traveling or tied up with other things. I'm glad you finally have time together. It's nice."

"It is nice," Amineh agreed. "Glorious," she added on a luxuriant sigh as she settled onto her back, mouth curved into a smugly reminiscent smile.

Her contentment made Fern think that Zafir was probably right about what the couple was doing in their own time. It made Fern long to ask what it was like.

She was sinfully curious to know what it would be like with Zafir. At night she practically called to him with her body, aching for him to come to her and show her everything he'd hinted at. By day she was tortured with angst, trying to fight her obsession while hoarding the little details the children inadvertently dropped about him, wishing she could find something wrong with him that would turn her off, but he seemed to be everything she admired in a person: honest and fair and smart.

The worst part was, he'd said the consequences wouldn't be worth an affair, but all she could think was that she didn't care. She would never meet another man like him. Making love with him would probably push a self-destruct button on her future, making it impossible for any other man to ever live up to the bar Zafir set, but part of her was willing to take that risk. She knew she would always regret it if she didn't.

So irresponsible.

"I should still be a better friend," Amineh said. "Especially since you haven't abandoned me for my brother, which every other female acquaintance has done at one time or another."

"I can barely hold my own with Tariq," Fern muttered, ducking her eyes to her tablet to keep from revealing how quickly she would turn her back on Amineh if Zafir crooked his finger.

"Ra'id likes that you're reserved. He had misgivings about bringing a Western woman into our household. He was afraid there'd be…" She lifted her head to glance at the children, checking to see how closely they were listening, but they were debating the position of a flag. "Politics," she announced with a significant quirk of her mouth. "So don't wish yourself to be different. We like you exactly as you are."

Fern smiled at Amineh, touched. "And that is why you are already a wonderful friend. You make me feel comfortable being who I am. Thank you."

Amineh's compliment was the counterbalance Fern needed to her silly illusions about Zafir. It reinforced that she was better off keeping a low profile and continuing to resist his pull. Her employment and her friend's respect mattered far more than scratching an itch with a man who couldn't offer her a future, she reminded herself.

Mother would be so proud, Fern mentally chided herself sourly.

An hour later, a male voice said something in Arabic that made Amineh gasp and the girls cry, "Baba! You're back! Where is Tariq?"

Fern's heart took flight as she looked for Zafir, but it was only Ra'id. She missed his response as he answered the girls while kissing their heads. The girls looked toward the trail to where the camels were kept and Ra'id added something about "Uncle" so Fern concluded Zafir and Tariq had hung back.

"Miss Davenport," Ra'id greeted with the sparest of acknowledgments before he dropped to sit next to his wife. He set one proprietary hand on Amineh's hip as he leaned in to kiss her with unapologetic thoroughness.

Fern rose to fling her sarong around her waist and begin gathering her things.

"Oh, Fern, you don't have to rush away," Amineh protested breathlessly.

"It's your family time," Fern said, trying not to look too flustered even though she was fighting a stab of envy so deep she could barely speak. "And I should prep for tomorrow's lesson." *Because I'm a spinster schoolmarm who will never have what you have.* Her heart wrenched in her chest as she acknowledged that she did want what Amineh had. Badly. So badly.

"You've embarrassed her, being all sexy like that," Amineh chided, nose-to-nose with her husband.

"Can't be helped. All I've been thinking about since we saw you from the plateau is getting down here to kiss you." He kissed her again, making Amineh release a stifled moan.

Fern walked away, deeply self-conscious, trying not to be obvious as her gaze traveled to the top of the canyon wall. What had Zafir thought when he had looked down on her? she wondered. He hadn't rushed to see her, so apparently she didn't hold the same allure.

Oh, stop it. Of course she didn't. She *had* to shake this preoccupation with him. It wasn't healthy.

She reached her tent and dropped her bag in front of it, then went to the side where she was using the wires as a clothesline. She hung her damp towel then swept her sarong from her waist and shook out the sand.

"Fern." *Zafir.*

Snapping her head up, she pressed a hand to where her heart nearly left her chest.

His shadow came around the side of the tent and his expression tightened when he saw her. He took in her swimsuit and the colorful sarong dangling from her loosened fingers.

Contradictory messages went through her. Habits of a lifetime urged her to cover herself, but a more overpowering weakness held her still for his inspection. Her body tingled under his gaze. Yearning to please stripped her naked to her soul. She was behaving shamelessly, standing here like this without making any attempt at modesty, thinking of all the ways he'd ravished her in her mind, but she did it anyway.

Did he know what she dreamed about?

She looked into his eyes and felt a delicious kick of desire right into her belly. He did. The magnetic pull she felt toward him was visceral. He grew bigger before her eyes as he drew in a hissing breath, chest expanding—

He grasped her arms, overwhelming her as he walked her backward to the tiny strip of sand behind her tent.

She pressed her hands into his chest, more for balance, alarmed by how quickly and easily he'd taken control of her, yet incredibly weak. He wasn't being rough. There was nothing forceful in his handling of her. She capitulated like her bones were sand and her muscles melted wax.

When she felt the powdery give of sand beneath her back, she had another moment of thinking *do something,* but Zafir was looking at her mouth and her lips were searing with need. She licked them and he swooped to kiss her. She responded by parting her lips and moving them against his.

A punch of pure desire went into her middle as the kiss deepened like a fall into an abyss. Her buckling arms fell away from between them. She splayed her hands on his rib cage and began lightly kneading to learn his form through the folds of his *thobe*. When his tongue flicked into her mouth, she dashed her own against his and white light flashed through her. The pressure of his mouth increased and she welcomed it, opening more for him, not able to breathe but not caring.

His hand slid up her arm to her shoulder and cupped her neck, and the weight of his thumb almost seemed to urge her to calm. Like he was reassuring her they had time. He would be here a while. They didn't have to kiss each other to death this second.

She relaxed and his mouth played with hers, nipping, sucking at her lips, feasting on her, filling her with liquid pleasure, making her arch up to his big body, seeking more contact.

He made a growling noise and his knee came between hers and parted her legs in a way that was so shockingly proprietary she opened her eyes. He lifted his head and watched as he peeled the strap of her suit off her shoulder until her small, pale breast was revealed.

Oh, please, she thought, when she really should have been thinking and acting far more sensibly, but the avid light in his gaze made her feel pretty and wanted. Her nipple prickled, anticipating his touch. Aching for it. This was everything she'd been fantasizing about. More.

He traced light fingers over her skin, watching as he tickled the swell, grazed the underside then settled his hand in a light cup. Hot. His hand was so hot on her cool, damp skin. When he drew his finger and thumb together in a delicate pinch of her nipple, the sensation was so sharp and exquisite, she could only open her mouth in a silent scream.

He bent again, this time capturing her nipple with his masterful lips, burning her like a brand and making her twist in confusion at how flagrant this was. Daylight. Barely hidden from view. It was a familiarity she'd dreamed of, but hadn't realized that it would make her belly knot with pulses of pleasure. Heat flooded into her loins, creating an ache that made her want to beg. Her fingers went into his hair under his *gutra*, but the feel of it was so sensual and spiky and masculine, she could only massage his scalp in encouragement, pushing the headdress off, wanting this to last forever.

His hand scalded the top of her thigh, slid low and pressed to open her legs wider so he could cover her mound with his burning hand.

"Zafir," she moaned, dying at how bold he was being, yet it felt incredible. Hot and *oh*… Streaks of pleasure rocketed into her thighs.

His mouth came back to hers, kissing her deeply, capturing her shaken breaths. "Shh," he breathed and licked her neck under her ear. "Lift into my hand. Show me what you like."

She couldn't. Didn't even know how. But somehow her hand went over his and she pressed and arched and dug the back of her head into the sand as sensations glittered through her. She writhed with abandon under his provocative touch, dying at how flagrantly she was behaving, but she'd been thinking about this and wanting it and it was so much better in real life.

They kissed again and again. She could feel his erection against her hip and rubbed, finding a rhythm with him that built the sensations. This was what lovemaking felt like, she distantly thought. Like heaven. Like nothing else in the world mattered except continuing to do this until they reached their nameless destination.

He shifted his hand, fingertips sliding along the edge of her bathing suit and pushing it aside so she was naked to his touch.

She gasped and turned her head into his shoulder, breaking their kiss as she dealt with the reality of knowing she was as naked and brazen as a woman could be. She looked up at him with alarm, certain she'd find judgment there.

"You're so close. Let me." His hot breath caressed her lips and his fingertip eased along her center and parted her flesh with a stunning sensation that stole any willpower she had. She let him trace back and forth and explore her in a way that was so mesmerizing she had to close her eyes, but that made the feelings all the more acute.

"Oh," she gasped softly as a particularly sharp sensation pierced her.

She felt him smile against her mouth, but her focus narrowed to only his touch, delicate and certain, pressing, circling, rubbing and rubbing, drawing her closer and tighter to the edge of reason, making her scalp tighten—

"Oh, Zafir—" He covered her mouth as the sob built in her throat, reminding her to hold it back as he slid his finger into her and made her world shatter.

She clung to him, overwhelmed by the cataclysm. Nothing in her sheltered little world had prepared her for how amazing he made her feel. Delicious convulsions of joy rocked through her, settling her in a place where nothing existed but him, his touch, his kiss.

The sensations went on and on, slowly fading and leaving her in a floaty place where she felt closer to him than she'd ever felt to another human being. A distant part of her was aware that he was still fondling her, soothing her down from the clouds in the most intimate way, but it felt natural and delicious and she wanted to stay right here luxuriating in—

"Miss Davenport? Are you in there?"

Tariq.

They jerked apart and her hands automatically scrambled her swimsuit back into place. *What had she just done?*

Zafir nudged her to rise and she flashed him a look, cut by the grim scowl he wore. He mouthed *Answer.*

"I'm, um, yes, I'm here, Tariq." She grabbed her sarong off the ground and wrapped it around herself, trying not to hang herself on the wires as she glanced back to ensure Zafir wasn't visible. "What did you need?"

"Did my father come see you?"

"Um…" Her brain blanked, unable to conjure a lie even to a child when it was critically necessary.

"To invite you to eat with us tonight?" Tariq prompted.

"Oh! Was your, um, hunt successful?"

"Just three birds, but it's enough. Are you coming swimming? Walk with me. I'll tell you about it."

"I've been swimming already. I need to rest now." Take cover. Regroup. She couldn't believe what she had just let happen.

"You should cool off in the water," he suggested. "You look hot."

She blushed harder as she thought of the reason she looked overheated.

"Good advice," she choked. "I'll think about it and join you in a minute." There. Finally a credible lie.

As Tariq ran off, Fern stood there in bewilderment. Her blood still sang and her skin felt like it was made of velvet. Forget swimming. She was so lethargic, she could barely stay on her feet, but she was gripped by mortification so intense she was terrified to move.

Glancing around the camp, she saw no one who might have seen what she'd been doing, where she'd been, or with whom. Was he still there?

Ducking into her tent, she went to the back wall and whispered, "Are you still there?"

Nothing. When she looked out the screen that formed a small window in the back wall, she saw no one. It was both a relief and a disappointment. Going back outside, she went behind the tent and kicked sand across the impression they'd left with their rolling, then scrubbed her bare foot over the man-sized sandal prints that disappeared into the forest of grass and palm trees behind her tent.

Two days ago, she'd snuck his towel into the latrine and left it on a hook. For someone who didn't know how to be deceptive, she was becoming very duplicitous.

The full impact of what she'd just done with Zafir began to hit her. Before this it had been a kiss and a conversation. Now...

She wouldn't let herself savor how it had felt. He'd had his hands on her in places she felt guilty touching herself!

She was entering the territory her mother had always warned her about. Behavior that was dangerous and had no future. She could hide the evidence, but she couldn't deny that clothing had been moot and inhibition nonexistent. He'd held her in the palm of his hand, literally. He'd driven her to a point of supreme vulnerability and helplessness and she hadn't fought him because nothing in her had wanted to.

Her mother had names for women who acted this way. Fern burned with humiliation at the thought of Zafir labeling her the same way. Where was her self-respect?

How would she ever face him again?

* * *

Zafir was suffering like a man staked on an anthill in the desert. His skin prickled, his core was on fire, he couldn't fight his way free of the situation he was in and regret sat like dust in the back of his throat because all of this was his own fault. He should have left Fern alone.

His control had been holding up well, even though he was aware of her every move in the camp. Even though her voice sometimes carried to him and he felt so drawn he shook with the effort to ignore her. When she'd looked to him as his son had invited her to spend the day in the desert with them, hunting the falcons, he had willed her to refuse.

She had, and his inner being had screamed like a hawk, angry that she had denied herself to him.

It made no sense. He barely knew her and was making every effort to remain estranged, but he'd thought of her the entire time they were hunting. He had easily imagined her inquisitive, engaging manner and pictured her freckled face turned to the sky in anticipation. He'd wanted her to see his desert and this ancient practice and be a part of his world in this elemental way.

Why?

Aside from his wife, he'd never attached himself to any woman and even that had been…

He ducked thoughts of his marriage as he always did, instead comparing Fern to some of his much more pleasant, lengthier affairs. Pretty, sensuous women who purred under his touch. But he'd never felt more than mild inconvenience when those relationships ended. If a new female in his sphere caught his eye, but turned out to be married or otherwise unavailable, he easily transferred his interest elsewhere.

So why couldn't he dismiss Fern? Was it because no other choices were open to him, as she'd accused him?

His marriage had lasted nearly five years and he'd gone without sex *that* long. A fortnight without a woman ought to be well within his endurance level.

But Fern's hold on him was unprecedented. When they'd returned to the oasis and looked down on the camp, Tariq had said Miss Davenport looked a skeleton on the sand. Ra'id had chuckled and Zafir had had to bite back a sharp remark, managing to remind his son in a measured tone that he should be more respectful.

Yes, she had been pale and leggy, but like a piece of carved ivory. Her hair had been a rope of red-gold, hanging in a plait against her back. All he'd thought about the rest of the descent was wrapping it around his fist and holding her for his kiss.

Trying to get a grip on his libido before he saw her, he'd hung back with Tariq to watch him dress the birds they'd caught. After a few moments, his son had said, "I can do it" with that hint of exasperated annoyance children had when a parent hovered. Rather than take offense, Zafir had accepted that he was being a coward. He had gone to relay Tariq's invitation to dinner, then found himself following Fern across the camp.

He should have called out sooner and spoken to her in the open, but the male animal in him had fixated on the twin cheeks that were not voluptuous, but were lovely, firm lobes that moved under the tissue-thin veil of her sarong. Her ambling walk had been lazy. The way she had craned her neck had spoken of her enjoyment in her surroundings.

That sensuous streak was his undoing. His thoughts had turned to how she would react to other physical pleasures. When he'd finally caught up to her in the relative privacy at the side of her tent, he'd already been so primed that her near nudity had devastated what little self-discipline he'd had left. He hadn't even spoken to her. It was a wonder he'd taken the time to press her out of sight before he'd fallen on her.

If only she had recoiled from his touch, but the responsiveness in her was not only a frustrating thrust of responsibility totally onto him, but also pure seduction. When she'd opened her mouth and kissed him back, he'd lost it. His one and only glimmer of sanity had been a recollection that they could be discovered at any second.

And now that he knew how reactive she was, how she melted under his touch and abandoned herself to his lovemaking, he could think of nothing but touching her again. Arousing her to that same level of wildness and thrusting into her. Making her cry her elation into his ear.

So impossible.

Especially as she sat across from him, her lashes lowered, her tongue sweeping her lips between bites of stew. The children bandied for her attention. Even Amineh was determined to engage her.

He did everything he could to avoid even looking at her.

But he noticed Fern had buttoned herself into cotton armor and was acting like she was sitting on a pin. Her hair was hidden under a scarf. Its edges fluttered around her face and she kept touching her collar and tugging her skirt to cover her shin, trying to hold her own against the breeze that had come up as the sun had gone down.

His friend Ra'id could caress his wife's cheek, but he, Zafir, could not reach across and tuck an errant strand of hair under his lover's scarf. The injustice—and the intensity of oppression he felt at being denied—confounded him.

"You've been in such owly moods this trip," his sister said with a nudge of her elbow into his side. "What's bothering you?"

Ra'id covered Amineh's hand and murmured, "Men in our position can't always talk about the concerns we shoulder."

Amineh's gaze flicked to Fern, and Fern was sharp enough to get the message that she had just been labeled an outsider. Her mouth tightened in a tiny flinch, but she quickly hid it behind a smile for Tariq.

"I must thank you again, young man. This has been such a treat. Both the delicious meal and dining with your family. I find such a lively table a bit overwhelming to be honest. It was always just my mother and I growing up. She often worked late so eating alone feels very normal to me."

I won't be insulted if you don't invite me again, her chipper remark seemed to say. *In fact, I'd prefer it.*

It tugged an unexpected pang from Zafir's heart. Ra'id wasn't a snob, but he was a realist. Fern's position in his household was well defined and it behooved all of them to remember it.

Fern started to draw back and excuse herself, but Tariq asked in his direct way, "Where was your father? Did he die?"

"No, um…" Fern widened her eyes like she'd stepped into unexpected traffic. "I mean…" She swallowed.

"Parents don't always live together," Amineh ventured, sending an empathetic look to Fern who was looking at Ra'id with deep shame, like she expected him to banish her to the edges of the earth for daring to be illegitimate in front of his daughters. Obviously she was forgetting that the girls' mother and uncle were bastards.

"Like grandmother stayed in England, rather than live here?" Bashira asked.

"Exactly," Amineh said, setting a hand on her daughter's head while she flashed a long-suffering look toward Zafir.

Being the product of an unwed union wasn't something they talked about often, and neither of them had found the best way to dig deep into the topic with their children, but it was a scar they both carried. It shouldn't matter in this day and age, but he still faced bigotry every day from certain factions in his country, for being illegitimate and half blood, making it impossible for him to forget he was not wholly a product of his own country.

And there was Fern looking like she shared the same agony at being born on the wrong side of the blanket.

You're in good company, he wanted to blurt, but she was rallying, mustering a smile. "Thank you again. I wish I could offer to make you some traditional English food, Tariq, but I think you've probably tried all of it with your grandmother."

"She won't let the chef make fish and chips. That's my favorite. Sometimes Baba and I sneak out for it."

"State secrets revealed after all," Fern murmured, then bit her lips together. Her face darkened in the glow of the candles as she rose jerkily from her cushion and bowed to take her leave.

"No, don't go," Jumanah urged.

"Listen, I hear the music starting." Fern touched her ear and pointed in the direction of the cooking area. "That means it will be your bedtime soon. But if your parents allow it, you may come to my tent and we'll see if we can identify some of the constellations from the guide on my tablet before it loses the last of its charge."

"Please, Baba?" the girls begged.

Tariq gave Zafir an excited, expectant look. For a boy who thought she looked like a skeleton and who was on vacation from school, he seemed quite taken with Miss Davenport. Genetics again, Zafir thought, wanting to shake his head at the irony.

"Of course," he said with a nod. "I have a travel unit with several charges left. You can use it to keep your tablet going through the rest of our stay."

"If it's not an imposition," Fern said, flashing him a slightly fraught glance. It was the first and only direct eye contact of the night and burned a trail through him like a comet.

"I'll get it," Tariq said, leaping to his feet.

Fern's shoulders softened with relief and she herded the children into the shadows toward her tent.

"Well, that was the height of awkward," Ra'id said in Arabic.

"Oh, don't start!" Amineh protested, throwing her weight into her husband.

He caught her close as he chided, "Be honest. Have you ever seen anyone that uncomfortable for two solid hours? It was painful. Wasn't it, Zafir?"

"You don't realize how intimidating you are! Zafir, too. And she's not a talkative person. That's why I like her. There's no gossipy 'Did you hear this or that?' She talks about real things."

"Such as?" Zafir asked, trying to keep his tone idle as he mentally castigated his son for stealing his one valid excuse to seek her out.

"The girls and their progress, mostly. But she wants to learn about our culture. We both agree the world would be a better place if women ran it," she taunted with a grin up at her husband.

"Goes without saying," Ra'id agreed, kissing her nose.

"You're not bonding over unwed parents, then," Zafir said, recognizing the nuzzling as his cue to make himself scarce.

"Okay, that *was* awkward," Amineh agreed, sitting up a little. "And no, we don't. I gather her mother was a bit of a hard case, but she doesn't go on about it or pry. She's very earnest."

"I'll give you that," Ra'id said, reaching to drain his cup of tea. "I have stacks of picture books awaiting my approval before she reads them to our children. How dangerous a political message could be hidden in a story that wishes the moon a good-night? When she started, she asked me how much of her curriculum she should devote to British history and suggested twenty-five percent because the girls are one quarter English."

Zafir didn't want to laugh at her, but he couldn't help the twitch of his lips as he considered the contradiction of the laced-up schoolmistress and the woman who had broken all the rules with him this afternoon. His ego soared with triumph at how much she had let go with him.

"Stop," Amineh insisted to Ra'id. "Or I'll tell her you want to mark all their written work yourself."

They started to snog openly so Zafir pushed to his feet and went to his tent. There he discovered that Tariq had taken his charging unit, but left all the attachments.

His mind said *don't*. His fingers gathered up the velvet bag of adaptors and weighed the package in his palm.

He managed to resist going to her until Tariq came to say good-night. The boy was riding a streak of independence these days, insisting he could scrub his own teeth and put himself to bed. As he rushed off to do so, Zafir stepped outside.

Ra'id was carrying his daughters like rolled carpets, one giggling girl under each of his arms, to where their mother waited near the children's tent.

Fern stood alone near her own, tablet in hand, face turned to the sky as she moved from beneath the canopy of palms.

As Zafir debated lame excuses to go to her, like asking if he could help her find a particular constellation, without any word to anyone, Fern made a decisive turn and headed up the path he'd taken her and the children a few days ago.

CHAPTER FOUR

FERN'S ANTENNAE PICKED up his presence before she heard or saw him. All the hairs on her body lifted and a jolt of such electric awareness shot through her, she expected her tablet to short out.

She kept walking, heartbeat picking up speed under the sense of being pursued, but she wasn't frightened. Not exactly. He wouldn't hurt her.

But when she finally heard his voice asking, "Where the hell are you going?" his stern undertone was daunting enough to make her halt with apprehension.

She hugged the tablet to her chest like a shield and turned to face him. They were still under the palms at the top of the spring so the filtered light left only a few glinting strips on his face, not enough to read his expression, but she received his message of disapproval loud and clear.

He didn't think she was looking for one of the guards, did he? They were so elusive, she wouldn't know where to find one if she needed one.

"The plateau," she replied, managing a conversational tone. "We couldn't see much of the sky from the camp. I wanted to see if it's worth asking to bring the children up tomorrow night for a proper stargaze."

"You're not allowed to leave the camp without an escort."

That took her aback. "I'm not supposed to take the children out of the camp. No one said I can't go for a walk by myself."

"I'm telling you that you can't. You could fall or get a bite, especially in the dark."

"Are you serious?"

"Completely."

She had read all the stories about stupid tourists getting themselves into sticky situations and didn't fancy becoming one, but his order seemed silly. She huffed, feeling like she was being treated like a child. "Fine. Will you take me?"

A loaded silence was his response.

"I meant—"

"I know what you meant," he growled impatiently.

What did one say to that? She hugged the tablet so tightly her fingers hurt where the edges dug in.

When he moved toward her, she pivoted to the side of the trail, making room for him to take the lead.

He stopped in front of her, hands coming to her upper arms the way they had this afternoon. His touch was light, but his voice heavy. "Come off the path with me."

"Zafir," she whispered hoarsely, but a pulse of desire expanded in her so hard her entire body hurt. She reminded herself there was no future with him, but the warning carried zero weight against her inner yearning. Even if all she had was his kisses and caresses, it was more than she'd ever imagined for herself.

She wasn't completely senseless, though. She understood one dire consequence she'd be courting if she went with him.

"I don't have anything. I'm not on the pill." The white of his *thobe* filled her blurred vision and the scent of him, dusty and spicy and heady, fogged her senses into a state of capitulation. Was she making assumptions saying that?

Looking like a fool? At this point it didn't matter. She'd already bared herself about as much as anyone could, but he needed to know how completely unprepared she was for anything like this.

"I won't make love to you like that," he assured in a voice that gently stripped her of her flimsy defenses, like sensually pulling away silky veils. "Your virginity is for the man you marry. I just want to hold you. Kiss you and touch you like I did this afternoon. You liked it, yes? It was good?"

He sounded like he really wanted to know. Like he couldn't tell? She'd shattered under his touch!

His husky whisper, the feel of his breath stirring her hair, brought it all back so she was exactly as she'd been a few hours ago: completely enthralled by him. She bit back a moan and her head felt too heavy for her neck. Her forehead fell against the hard wall of his muscled chest.

"You're so sweet, Fern. Like honey." He drew her to align with his body so she could feel his arousal through their clothes. She pushed the tablet away from between them and let it fall to the sand. His hands molded her with familiarity even as he shuffled her off the path to a place where they had a measure of privacy.

"This is bad, Zafir. You said so," she reminded.

He only braced his back on a palm trunk and opened his legs to make a space for her. She was burning alive, but she snuggled into his heat, arms encircling his neck like her body knew what it was doing even if she didn't. She angled her head and followed the pressure of his hand in her hair to mate her mouth to his.

So bad and so good. They kissed like long-lost lovers. Maybe he was using her. Maybe she was being fanciful, but this felt like reunion. His hands on her were magic, his mouth divine. The evidence of his desire for her was so mysterious and heartening, she couldn't help pressing into him with gratified joy.

When he pulled her shirt free and stroked her back, she caught back a moan and searched for his skin, but it was impossible to find. The shape of his chest and ribs were hard and wide, enthralling to her splayed fingers, but the cloth of his *thobe* was trapped by the press of their bodies.

He loosened her bra and found her breasts. His knowing hand tenderly caressed her and circled her nipple, making it feel taut and achy. She wriggled her hips into him even more. Oh, she wanted him to suckle at her again.

"Zafir," she said, breaking their kiss to gasp. "I want to feel your skin, too."

He breathed a ragged curse against her lips and set her back a step, pulling up his *thobe* from between them. When she burrowed beneath it and discovered the hot skin of his waist, her hands couldn't get enough. His chest expanded, his abdomen contracted, his chest hair was a fine, intriguing texture traveling in a line downward—

She gasped as she was realized what grazed her wrist. "You're naked under here."

"I am." He opened the button at her throat and moved to the next.

"Can I—"

"Yes."

Looking down but seeing only his sleeve as he continued opening her buttons and the bunched white cotton draping her own arms, she let her fingers hesitantly explore, blind but curious.

So amazing. His shape was steely under a layer of smooth velvet, and he quivered at her light touch. Taut and aggressive and so thick. She couldn't imagine how men and women fit together when she held the girth and weight of him in her fist.

"Am I doing it right?" she asked in an anxious whisper.

"Harder," he murmured against her lips, cupping both her breasts beneath her loosened bra and then teasing her nipples so she pinched her legs tight against a pulse of heat.

She loved this. Loved feeling him tighten in her hand, loved hearing his breath catch and feeling his tongue delve into her mouth as he kissed her and seemed excited by her touch. If she could give him what he'd given her this afternoon, she'd be overjoyed.

He drew back unexpectedly and she looked into his shadowed face, wondering if it was a trick of the light that his eyelids were so low, his mouth slack with passion.

"What's wrong?" she whispered, loosening her touch on him.

"Nothing." He sounded drugged. "Keep going. It feels good."

He gathered her skirt as he talked. The hem tickled her bare legs, sensitizing her, building anticipation so she throbbed between her thighs. He slouched lower and caught her leg to guide her knee over his muscled thigh, opening her to his touch. Her thigh was scraped by the abrasion of his and she flinched.

"What—?" Off balance, she fell into him, hand squeezing and making him grunt. "I'm sorry! I'm bad at this."

"No, Fern, you're not." He laughed softly against her mouth as he caressed her through her knickers.

Her turned to gasp and pull away a fraction before he could kiss her. "What are you doing?"

"We'll do this together." He tucked his fingers into her underpants and let the cotton trap his hand against her needy flesh.

Her body responded with a rush of liquid heat, clasping with hollow need.

"This is really bad. It has to be," she murmured, thinking, *under the shirt, down the pants*. Nothing good came of this, but it felt incredible.

"Do you want to stop?" His lips played along her jaw, enticing her mouth to catch up to his while her mind was filled with nothing but the delicate stroke of his fingers where she ached and throbbed.

"No," she admitted on a sob, pushing into his hand for a firmer touch.

"Neither do I."

Fern woke to a pleasant awareness of the flesh between her legs and a memory of holding the sun as it went supernova in her hands. Afterward, as they'd leaned there, shaking, his arm locking her to his pounding heart, he'd whispered, "It's probably best we don't go all the way, Fern. It might kill us."

She smiled into her pillow as she thought of it again. The way he'd kissed her after they'd put themselves back together had been incredibly encouraging.

"It's not bad, Fern," he'd promised her. "It's not smart," he admitted in a dry whisper, "but what we're doing isn't sinful. I won't let it go too far. You won't lose your job or get pregnant. I'll be discreet."

"You're saying you want to do this again?"

"Don't you?"

"I do," she'd breathed, massaging the muscles of his back, incredulous that she was in his arms, that he held her so close, that this was even happening. She had pushed aside reservations and worries about being the only fruit in the bowl, focusing instead on the way he kneaded her bottom and seemed reluctant to release her so they could find the things they'd dropped on the path and walk back to camp. He had kept her hand in his until the last moment.

Her mother would call this kind of sneaking around

cheap, but even if he was taking advantage of her naiveté and inexperience, he was doing it tenderly. This was
the kind of affair she'd always secretly dreamed of. She
couldn't imagine regretting it, especially if there weren't
any long-term consequences.

That word—*long-term*—made her bite her lip and lick
at the sting.

Zafir and Amineh were close, but in the way of adult
siblings who lived in two separate countries. They stayed
in touch, but didn't spend a lot of time together.

This affair, if it qualified to be called such a thing,
would be very short-lived. She had absolutely no future
with Zafir, she knew that. Still, she couldn't resist stealing this chance to be intimate with him, not because she
wanted to learn about sex, although that was definitely part
of it. She also liked feeling desirable and prized. But more
than all of that, she wanted to learn about him.

So she wouldn't worry about the future. They had today,
Fern assured herself as she pushed up from her bed, already wondering how he would find her and when.

Except the din from the camels that she had put down
to one of their cranky periods seemed to be growing and
the babble of voices speaking Arabic increased in volume.

Peeking out of her tent, she discovered they were being
invaded.

Zafir's father had loved all things Western, to the point
that he'd pushed his new ideas too hard and fast on a culture still catching up to the twentieth century and far from
ready to embrace the twenty-first. Ra'id's father had been
more conservative, which had bequeathed a host of different issues on Ra'id as a leader, but one thing they both
needed without question was the support of the Bedouin
clan that roamed their lands.

He and Ra'id had come to the oasis specifically to meet with the leader of this tribe and reaffirm their alliance with him. The tribe might stay as long as a week, but Zafir found himself wishing they would hurry themselves along.

Fern was waiting for him. Fern, with her shy touch and eagerness to please and her abandonment to passion. They were behaving like teenagers in the back of a car and it was one of the most exhilarating experiences of his life.

Yet he was back to barely acknowledging her when he glimpsed her walk past with his nieces. She wore her abaya and it had smudges of dust at the wrist, but she still managed to look prim and cute at the same time. Her glorious hair was hidden beneath a black scarf, the curled tip of the tail peeking from the hem on her back. She had pinned a veil across her face so only the freckled bridge of her nose was visible, along with her quiet gray eyes.

Her strawberry-blond lashes had dropped demurely when she'd caught his eye. He could only see that narrow band of her face, but he'd been sure she had blushed.

Because she was remembering.

The memories stoked heat through him, too, filling him with need, but there wouldn't be so much as a conversation between them while the nomads filled the oasis. The servants kept to themselves and his guards might turn a blind eye to his stealing off with her, but he couldn't afford to dent his reputation with people who already mistrusted him for his father's bold antics.

So he kept his distance while discussing where decent range land could still be found and stayed up late, nodding his head to the music and admiring the skills of the sword dancers. When asked, he agreed that yes, he was considering remarrying. No, nothing was formalized, but yes, he would search for his match within his own borders.

He kept to himself that the prospect filled him with

dread. He resented his father for seeking his own pleasure at the expense of not just his country, but his immediate family. Even the woman his father claimed to have loved beyond reason, Zafir's mother, had suffered under his father's selfish pursuit of his own happiness. Zafir refused to commit the same crime. His marriage had been difficult, but he had Tariq from the union and more stability in his country as a result. The sacrifice had been worth it. He would do it again.

But not yet. *After* he left the oasis.

Indulging himself with Fern didn't make him like his father, he reasoned, throwing an arm over his eyes as he lay in bed fighting the urge to go to her. One small dalliance with an English woman on holiday was not the same as sentencing two children—*two*—to a lifetime of conflict in their identity.

Not that he allowed that conflict to continue to rage in him anymore. He was wholly a man of the desert and did his best to prove it, hunting with the men the next day and playing a type of polo on camels the following. If he longed for the sweet yet tart taste of strawberry bursting in his mouth, no one, most especially the forbidden fruit in question, knew.

Until the next afternoon when she stunned him by calling, "Zafir!" and came running toward him across the camp.

His companion, the sheikh of this visiting Bedouin tribe, stopped beside him and swung a look of startled denunciation at Zafir. Who was this girl to act so familiar?

Zafir bristled, accosted by a sensation like his innermost desires, the things he kept most private to himself, had been turned out onto the sand. Like she was jerking back a curtain and crying "he's English, he's mine" exactly when he was needing to be seen at his most independent and Arabic.

And because of that instant sense of exposure and shame in his own weakness, he stopped her with a glare.

She halted and a startled, guarded look came into her eyes as she looked uncertainly between them.

"I mean, abu Tariq," she said, using the more formal address as she took a few hurried steps toward him. Amineh had arranged for Fern to spend time with the Bedouin women, to observe their sewing and weaving, but it really was better if Fern was seldom seen and rarely heard while the nomads were here.

"Not now," he stated flatly and started to turn his friend away, asserting that she was nothing to him.

"It can't wait," she insisted, circling into his line of vision.

He let her see his outrage. If she thought their touchy-feely little tryst entitled her to his attention on her whim, she was dead wrong.

Hurt flashed in her eyes, but even though her slim build seemed to pull tight and become even more narrow, and the little he could see of her face was pale enough to make her freckles stand out in dark spots, she kept her gaze locked with his.

"A girl is ill. Her mother isn't taking it seriously and I can't find your sister. I only have Bashira to interpret."

The man beside him demanded to know what she was saying. Zafir translated, aware exactly how much Western interference was welcomed, especially when it involved women making demands. His friend urged him to let the girl's mother be the judge. He dismissed Fern with a step toward her and a flick of his hand to shoo her away.

The action, not meant to actually strike her, still set Zafir's control on edge. Bigotry was his fatal weakness and Fern was being advised firmly of her insignificant status.

She jerked back a step, trepidation fixing her eyes on

the man as she excused, "I wouldn't do this if I wasn't worried—"

The wounded throb in her voice told Zafir she realized how completely she was being disregarded. But where he would have called her meek at any other time, she showed inordinate boldness, straightening her spine, growing a fraction taller and speaking with insistence.

"But her mother doesn't want to talk about it because she, well, the girl looks about thirteen. Her mother thinks she's starting her time. I think it's appendicitis."

"Time…?" Comprehension dawned. "She probably is," he averred. What did he know about these things?

"I've had both and you don't get a fever from puberty," she retorted hotly. "You can't ignore this. *I* can't. Come and see for yourself."

That imperative tone of hers made the other sheikh huff out a noise of impatience.

Fern looked braced for a blow, but she stood her ground and stared hard at Zafir, genuine fear in her eyes as she willed him to do as she asked.

If she was wrong, this would turn out badly.

It might anyway. When he assented with a growl and followed her, the girl's mother was appalled that Fern had brought her daughter's condition to the attention of men, most specifically ones in such exalted positions. She tried to wave them away, scolding Fern thoroughly in loud, rapid Arabic. All the women and girls in the communal tent stared, Zafir's nieces included. The girl was so embarrassed, she started to move to the back of the big lean-to.

The Bedouin sheikh pressed Zafir to come away, telling him to let the women handle things. His vile glare at Fern, sharp with censure and mistrust, didn't abate when he looked at Zafir.

Fern caught at Zafir's sleeve and tugged as the girl

failed to get her feet under her. "That is not normal," she insisted. "You have to make them realize."

"You've had your appendix out? Tell me the symptoms," he growled. He crouched to talk to the mother and girl and lifted a hand to stay his companion's arguments as he translated Fern's suspicion.

The girl started to cry and her mother wrapped her arms around her, both of them denying it could be that serious. He understood. Who wanted to need surgery when they were two days by camel to the nearest hospital?

Zafir called on one of his guards who was trained as a medic. The guard wasn't allowed to physically examine the girl, of course, but he agreed that the diagnosis could be correct. The father of the girl was found and the entire family sent by helicopter with the girl for treatment.

Fern buttoned herself into her tent—an act that poked at Zafir's conscience—but if he had just had a girl airlifted to a hospital for menstrual cramps, he was going to look worse than his father for listening to her. His attempt to hide that they had a personal relationship would be moot. An affair was already presumed. He'd be labeled as weak, ruled by the same aberrant crush that had undermined his father's ability to govern well.

An air of tension hung over the camp as they waited word via the relay station. Ra'id and Amineh returned from being in the desert with another group, concerned that they'd seen the helicopter come and go. Zafir explained and Ra'id came to Fern's defense, assuring the Bedouins she wasn't the type to stir up false drama.

Zafir couldn't have argued in her favor. It would have looked suspicious and the fact was, he didn't know her well enough to judge her as knowledgeable or trustworthy.

He only knew he never should have touched her.

* * *

"Fern." Amineh's voice woke her to the first fingers of daylight. "Are you awake?"

"Yes." She sat up, eyes gritty, and watched the zip climb on the front of her tent.

Amineh poked her head in. "You were right. It was appendicitis. She had the surgery late last night and will be okay. Can you dress and come out? Her uncle wants to thank you."

Relief lifted a huge weight off her chest. Fern took a big breath and let it out. She'd barely slept, she'd been so worried.

And hurt.

Zafir had been so dismissive, like she didn't know her place. He'd certainly made it clear how much value he placed in her opinions. Her mother was right. Men didn't respect women who were easy.

A few minutes later, after ensuring she was covered to the tips of her fingernails, only her eyes showing, she approached the group of men waiting for her near the nomad's cooking fire.

Zafir was in her periphery. She thought she felt his eyes on her, but didn't look to check. It was probably just her constant awareness of him playing up anyway.

The tribal leader, the man who had tried to convince Zafir not to listen to her, set his palm on his chest, closed his eyes and bowed his head. Through Amineh, Fern expressed her relief that the girl would survive. The nomads spent a short hour packing and were gone before anyone was hungry for lunch.

The rest of the day was quiet, even the children not talking much. The men kicked a football with Tariq and Jumanah down the beach while Bashira settled in to show Fern the clothing she'd made for her doll with the help of one of the Bedouin women. Amineh joined them and sat down next to Fern with a huge sigh.

"*Now* we can relax."

"Be honest," Fern said as Bashira ran off in search of a dress she'd forgotten in her tent. "Did I cause a political disaster?"

"It could have gone south if you'd been wrong, but you weren't. Zafir has to be so careful not to be seen as acting like our father and our father was *so* determined to not just modernize, but Westernize. He tried to settle land rights on the tribes and make them farm it. They're already losing clansmen to cities and steady jobs. Their way of life is hard enough without government eroding it. Seeing Zafir with Ra'id, whose family always respected their rights to migrate, goes a long way. That's why we make a point of meeting here like this. The Bedouins travel so much, and talk to so many different people, their opinion can be the difference between large-scale support or opposition for Zafir."

"And I nearly derailed the whole thing."

"You did the right thing. You know that. In fact, Zafir tells me you earned yourself an offer of marriage for it." Amineh nudged her shoulder into Fern's.

"*What?*" Zafir had told Amineh about them? And he wanted to—

"From the cousin of the girl you saved," Amineh continued, her grin widening. "I guess this young man heard you were learning to weave and that the children liked you. He saw you have red hair, which intrigued him. You've already had your appendix out, so that will never be an issue…" She gurgled the last words with great humor.

That was *not* where she had thought Amineh was going. Mortified by how her hopes had soared under such a wrong assumption, especially when Zafir wasn't even speaking to her, Fern could only look at the ground as an enormous blush flooded into her cheeks.

Amineh burst out laughing and called down the beach to the men, "I told you she'd turn red as a fire engine!"

Fern tried to act like she saw the humor in it, but she was achingly aware that she was secretly dreaming for more with Zafir when the hard fact was, Amineh had just outlined to her how completely wrong she was for him. Not worth the consequences, he'd said that first morning, and no doubt that had been reinforced for him by yesterday's events.

Assuring herself it was for the best, that furthering their physical intimacy would only set her up for a broken heart, she maintained her distance, ate alone and was in a surprisingly sound sleep when she woke to a hand over her mouth.

CHAPTER FIVE

"IT'S ME. DON'T SCREAM."

His whisper, scented faintly of cloves and anise, caressed her cheek.

Belated shock went through her and she jerked her limbs into reacting. Unfortunately he was half on her bedroll, pinning her sheet and keeping her reflexive movements muted. She couldn't even wriggle as he settled his weight half over her.

"Shh. Don't make any noise. I just want to talk."

Forcing herself to stillness, she tried to ignore the way her body blossomed against his, even with his *thobe*, a sheet and her nightgown between. Her breasts tingled, her thighs grew restless. Desire concentrated in her loins, anticipating his touch.

And her helplessness at her own reaction made tears burn her eyes. She turned her head away from him, dislodging his hand from her mouth.

His fingers curled under and he smoothed her cheek with his knuckle. "I know I was harsh to you," he said tightly. "This thing between us—"

"Is nothing. I know," she asserted, not wanting to hear him say it. "I'm weak, not stupid. I wasn't trying to stake a claim on you. I wasn't assuming we're friends or anything else. We don't even know each other."

His touch stalled, then his breath clouded against her ear in a drained sigh. "I know you're willing to put every-

thing on the line for the life of a girl you barely know."
His touch caressed from below her ear, along her jaw and
down. He opened his hand on her throat and aligned his
thumb along the artery throbbing with needy anticipation.
"Thank you for doing that. I couldn't sleep, knowing you
thought I was angry with you for it."

She knew she ought to say something. Forgive him. Tell
him to go. All she could think about, however, was how it
would feel if he slid his hand down to her breast.

"That's all I came for," he said, lifting his hand off her
as he started to roll away.

"Is it?" Weak, weak Fern. She closed her eyes against the
clamor inside her, the yearning that was so self-destructive
as to invite more of his dispassionate lovemaking.

His breath hissed in. He set his hand on her stomach.
"You want me to stay?"

She shouldn't. She knew that. But she slid her hand
from under the sheet, covered his and lightly drew it up
to her breast. "I know it's bad," she whispered achingly.

"I'm the one behaving badly, Fern." He took up her hand
and brought her fingers to his lips. "Your first lover should
be someone who offers more than a week of stolen rendez-
vous in the dark. I'm very conscious that I'm taking advantage of you."

She heard the confirmation that this was all they had
and it cracked a wide fissure through her. Turning her hand
in his, she traced the smooth shape of his lips, aching for
better words to come out of them.

"Apparently I have a suitor if I want marriage," she said,
smiling sadly and glad he couldn't see it. "At first I thought
you were him, here to kidnap me into the desert."

"That's not funny." His grip on her hand tightened
and he leaned over her, lips questing for hers. "I wanted
to knock his young ass into the dirt when he asked about

you. I told you before that if I can't have you, no one can."

"But you can," she told him, smoothing her fingers over the scuff of his growing beard and into his hair to explore the shape of his skull. A distant part of her already wept at the idea of losing him in a few short days, but his possessiveness healed the fracture in her chest with crooked, stinging stitches. Oh, how she wanted this. Him.

His hot mouth caressed the side of her face and she turned her mouth into his, unable to resist.

He muffled a groan and she felt his chest swell. She wondered if it meant he was feeling what she was: heart exploding into faster pounds, nerve endings snapping to life with a pulse of acute need.

She closed her fist to begin bunching his *thobe* behind his shoulders and he lifted to peel her sheet down. Then he reared back on his knees to shed his tunic. His sculpted form was barely visible in the dull purple light inside the tent, a vague silhouette that was undeniably masculine in its size. Powerful. Weakeningly beautiful.

Fern did something she never imagined herself able to do. She shimmied her nightgown up and over her head, tossing it away, then slid her own knickers off and kicked them to the floor as she opened her arms to him.

He fell on her and they kissed and clung like drowning victims. She knew it was bad to wrap her legs around him, but oh, it felt good to feel his aggressive sex rubbing against hers. He thrust his tongue into her mouth, telling her what he wanted to do to her, and she couldn't help releasing a moan of encouragement.

"Shh, *albi*. We have to be quiet." He nibbled down her neck, sending prickles of excitement through her chest, making her nipples stand taut and sensitive to the friction of his chest hair.

"I know, but it's so hard," she gasped, seeking with her hands for the shape of him. *So* hard.

He muffled a curse against her skin and slid lower, away from her reach as he captured her nipple in his mouth and teased her mercilessly.

"Zafir," she protested, knee coming up in reaction to the jab of sensation his erotic suckling drove into her center.

He only skimmed his hand along her inner thigh, his teeth sinking in lightly around her nipple as his touch slid easily against her ready flesh. She arched in blinded reaction to his caress and he deepened his exploration, pressing a finger into her.

She threw her arm across her mouth to stifle her cry of joy, so aroused she could barely stand it.

He stoked her desire with tender ruthlessness, refusing to do more than let a few light touches of his thumb pad stroke her where she ached for pressure most. He switched to her other breast, making her want to beg as he continued to tease with those light thrusts of his finger and the not-quite-there caress.

"Zafir, please," she finally pleaded, fisting her hand in his hair to make him stop.

He dragged her hand from the back of his head and bit the heel of her palm before he slid even lower and pressed her knees open. Then he gave her what she'd been anticipating, but with his tongue.

It was too much. She pushed her hand beneath her pillow and folded it across her face, releasing her sobs of ecstasy as orgasm took her. It was intense and scandalous and so powerful her eyes dampened with emotion while her body continued to tremor with aftershocks.

How could this be sinful? How?

When he rose over her and stole her pillow, she only thought, *yes*. Whatever he wanted, yes. If he pushed his length into her, she'd welcome him. Revel in his claiming of her.

He rolled her over and brought her hips up, then pinned his steely shaft between her slippery thighs, trapping her knees in place with his own on either side. Covering her the way every other species mated, he slid a hand to where they touched and pressed his shaft against flesh still tingling with postclimax sensitivity. He started to move.

She fisted her hands into her bedroll and held still for his lovemaking, wishing he was inside her. She wanted him to feel the same pleasure he'd given her and—

"Oh!" she gasped as the friction deepened and caused a sharp sensation to yank her back into arousal.

"Shh," he urged, slowing his movements, caressing her hip and breast. "Are you okay?"

"Yes," she breathed. "Don't stop." She grabbed her pillow and buried her moans into it, giving herself over to him and his needs and the excitement he was rekindling in her. She moved with him, finding the rhythm, wanting this to be the real thing, unable to believe she was almost there again, almost...

They found the crisis together, the sweetness of it so intense she forgot to breath, but maybe that was his arm locked around her rib cage. She kneeled in his fierce grip, loving the feel of his muscles twitching with contractions as she held in her scream of abandonment as her thighs quivered in ecstasy.

His heart continued to pound against her shoulder even after they'd collapsed onto their sides, spooned together. His breaths stirred her hair and he had one warm hand clasped possessively over her breast.

Fern blinked to focus in the dark, stunned by how wild that had been. Very lusty. Kind of dirty. Yet it made her feel so close to him. She resisted the urge to snuggle backward into him, but he stroked his hand down her front and tugged her tight against him, then kissed her shoulder before he relaxed with his nose in her hair.

She blinked her damp eyes, feeling cherished and safe.

"I want to see you. All of you," he whispered.

"Why?" she asked, warming at the thought.

"Because I think your freckles would be pretty."

"They're not. I look like a speckled pony. That's what my mother used to say. She didn't like them. Should you stay?" she asked, partly to change the subject, partly because she wanted to prepare herself. This was really nice, but she had to remember it was temporary. "I don't want to fall asleep."

"Can you put your tablet on vibrate and set the alarm?"

As she reached through the dark to where she'd left it and clicked it on, he tilted the light to her chest.

"Don't," she murmured, lifting it away and tapping, showing him the time she set.

"That's fine," he agreed, gathering her into his naked length as she set it away again. "Why didn't she like them?" He caressed down to her belly and back up to her breast.

"Probably because I got them from my father. Maybe just because they were a part of me. She didn't like me much."

His hand stalled on her hip. "Are you being serious?"

"I shouldn't be, should I? I'll stop." She rolled into him and nuzzled her nose into the hair sprinkled against his breastbone, hands fondling between them. "Why are you still hard? I thought men, you know, relaxed after."

He'd run a towel down her belly and thighs before pulling her to the mattress with him. They'd definitely found their pleasure together.

"I'd dearly love to know how to 'relax' around you, Fern. Being hard this much hurts."

Don't laugh, she thought, pretty sure that men didn't have much of a sense of humor when it came to sexual frustration, but she was insanely flattered.

"I feel the same, like I'm some kind of sex addict, thinking about you all the time. Is it always like this?" she asked, stroking him with a light grip. "I've never felt so greedy about anything. Sometimes I might think, 'oh, that man is handsome,' or something like that, but I've never wanted to—" *Take a man with my mouth.*

She really wanted to do that. He was covering her hand, teaching her how he liked to be stroked. As she found the rhythm, she searched out his flat nipple with her mouth. It was a bold move, but that's what he'd done to her and she'd loved it. Surely he would, too?

He cupped the back of her head, then tilted her up for his kiss. She let him have the lead for a while, but he was so steely and aroused. So intriguing. All she could think about was owning him the way he had taken possession of her.

"I want to do something," she whispered as she pulled away and pressed his shoulder so he was flat on his back.

As she slid down his body, he went hard all over, like he was made of marble. "You don't have to."

"I want to. Tell me how to make it good."

"It's already good."

She laughed. "I'm not there yet."

"I know, but it's still great," he whispered, making her smile as she touched her lips to his hot, velvety shape.

Zafir had one foot in heaven, one in hell.

He counted the daylight hours until he could go to Fern, and cursed when the sun arrived, extinguishing another night with her. When he picked up the message relayed from base camp, his heart sank into the underworld.

He told Ra'id first, because it was expected that he would.

"I have to leave in the morning," Zafir said, explaining the situation with demonstrators in his home city.

"I've been thinking of leaving myself," Ra'id admitted. "Amineh wants to stay the full two weeks, and the girls would live here if I could arrange it, but I'm restless. There are things I should be looking after at home. We've had the meeting we needed. It's time."

Zafir nodded. They were both high-energy men, used to demanding days and schedules that took them around the world in a week. As children they'd been neighbors and acquaintances. At boarding school, they'd gravitated to each other, Ra'id for Zafir's mastery of English and Zafir for Ra'id's understanding and sharing of his Arab blood. As adults they were as close as brothers and never tired of each other's company, but they also knew and respected the responsibilities each had. Idleness was not a natural state for either of them, so leaving made sense.

But Zafir wasn't ready.

"You look genuinely worried. Is this demonstration worse than the others?" Ra'id asked.

"No," Zafir said, consciously clearing his scowl, but unable to stop thinking about what he would be giving up. "It's the same group that rabble-rouses every time I'm away. Things will settle the minute I'm in residence so I'll go home and make that happen." He wouldn't ignore these small uprisings as his father had done, allowing them to escalate into riots and bloodshed.

"This man who keeps causing unrest. Abu Gadiel? I thought you were going to marry his daughter and quiet him for good?"

Zafir gave a tight smile at the running joke. "That suggestion is looking less outlandish and more practical every day." His mouth twisted on the words. He was not quite ready to face what could be inevitable.

Ra'id snorted, then sobered as he saw the gravity in Zafir's expression. "You're really considering it."

"She's nineteen. Young, educated traditionally, but she's continuing her schooling, planning to be a doctor."

"So she's smart, but perhaps not as interested in playing politics as she is in helping all people," Ra'id suggested.

"Exactly." Not a bad match at all.

"Pretty?"

Zafir cut him a does-it-matter? look.

Ra'id only shrugged. "It helps."

"I never did give you that herd of goats for taking my ugly sister off my hands," Zafir drawled, making Ra'id's mouth twitch with humor. Ra'id had begun drooling over Amineh before they'd left third form. If he could have, he would have married her before she'd finished school. Their father had been gone by then and it had been up to Zafir to insist his sister pass her A levels before she could marry.

She had, and not only had she been able to marry, but she'd also married for love. Zafir knew she believed he'd come to love Tariq's mother, but it was not an emotion he'd ever aspired to. It had been his father's weakness. The driver of actions that had been his undoing.

Love, for him, was a luxury he couldn't afford. Another arranged marriage for the sake of peace was his lot.

"You'll let me know if there's anything I can do to assist," Ra'id said.

"Appreciated," Zafir said, slapping his friend on the shoulder as he moved away. "I'll let the children know." It was an excuse to see Fern. They did their best to avoid each other during the day, which made him feel a heel, but what option did he have? He'd promised her he wouldn't cost her her job.

"Promise them you'll send Tariq to us for a few weeks. I'll find a pocket in my schedule after my cousin's wedding. It will soften the blow," Ra'id said.

Fine for Tariq and the girls, but how would he soften the blow to himself?

Amineh was sitting in on Fern's lesson today, lending her excellent art skills to sketches of "my favorite animal spotted in the oasis." When Zafir arrived to say everyone would be leaving in the morning, her tiny class erupted into disorder. Amineh was most vocal of all.

"You know I can't ignore these things," Zafir told his sister testily.

Fern was afraid to look at him, certain she'd betray her distress. This was it. The end of her nights with strong arms around her, the scent of a man on her skin, his lips whispering praise and compliments into her soul. It wasn't just the pleasure he gave her that she'd miss, but the illusion of closeness. She was sure he laughed with all the women in his bed, told them all they were pretty and tasted like honey and smelled like wildflowers, but this was her first experience with pillow talk and she loved it.

As he walked away, she couldn't help a yearning look at his back, wishing life wasn't so unfair—

He moved out of sight and her gaze came back to the group and Amineh's alert, probing stare.

The burn of a hard flush swelled up from Fern's throat, choking her and making her cheeks ache. She was such an *idiot*.

Somehow she managed to say, "Didn't you tell me all your friends suffer the effect? He's…" She lifted a helpless, hopeless palm. There weren't words to describe how compelling he was or why she'd fallen under his spell. She just had.

Amineh's shoulders fell and she smiled with amused sympathy. "They do. And you shouldn't take it personally that he's completely oblivious. Oh, Fern."

Fern waved away the compassion, glad Amineh assumed her crush was platonic, not one fueled by midnight encounters of the most licentious kind. But the prospect of losing those trysts sat like a knife in her chest.

Fortunately the news they were leaving cast a pall over the whole camp. Her long face was one of many. The children were querulous, distracting the adults from Fern's morose mood, and when Tariq invited her to join them for the final meal, she had a valid excuse to maintain her privacy and keep her misery from being noticed.

"I really do have a lot to gather up and pack. I'm sorry."

"I'll miss you," he told her, making her want to hug him, which was odd for her. She had worked with children his age as part of her certification, had enjoyed them immensely, but being affectionate with students wasn't encouraged and she wasn't naturally effusive. Perhaps Zafir had unlocked something in her. She finally felt like she had warmth to offer.

"I'll miss you, too. You're a remarkable young man. But I'll see you in a few months, when you visit your cousins."

She wouldn't see his father, but what she had with Zafir was already stolen property, not something she could keep.

She took her time memorizing every aspect of him when she held him that night. He seemed to be doing the same. They'd taken to drawing out their caresses these last few nights, letting the sensations build upon themselves, learning to hold each other at the height of passion so every sensation was played out to its greatest degree.

He sat with his back against pillows pushed up against her stack of packed bags and baskets. She kneeled on either side of his thighs, both of them naked and damp, trembling with arousal. Her mouth couldn't stop feasting on his and his hands were firm and thorough, like he intended to imprint his touch on her skin forever.

Rising onto her knees under the urge of his hand on her bottom, she offered her breast for his loving attention. They had perfected silent communication, keeping talking to a minimum for fear of discovery, making love blind in the dark.

He tugged at her nipple, tender and bruised by the sweet, nightly torture of his insatiable appetite. It hurt and felt so good. She let her head fall back as she fought groaning aloud at the acute sensations. How would she survive without him? Without this? She'd never felt so free as she did when she was with him. He was magic and fantasy and perfection.

Folding her arms around his head, she kissed his hair and drank in his dark scent, her eyes burning with an emotion she feared was far deeper and more permanent than infatuation.

He pulled back and drew her down to kiss her hard, to stake his claim on her mouth in a fierce way that threw her heart into flight. She pressed herself to him and writhed in desperation, wanting to crawl inside him and stay with him forever.

Her movements slid her throbbing loins against his rampant erection, so firm and ready. She felt like her hands knew that part of him better than she knew her own body. She moved herself against him, wet and aching, aware that abandoning herself this way aroused him nearly to the breaking point.

The carnality of it thrilled her, made her yearn. Rubbing and sliding against him took her very close to drawing him into her. She slowed, savoring every millimeter of his shape against her sensitive core. Pressure threatened as she found his tip and slid away again. Oh that was wickedly tempting, making her entrance weep with desire, strumming her to unbelievably desperate levels.

Barely realizing what she was doing, she grew more deliberate with her movements, pressing harder, liking the piercing intensity and stretch against her aching center. She did it again, pressing for that hot thickness to sink deeper into her.

"Fern," he gasped as he pulled back, his hands hard on her hips.

"I want it to be you, Zafir," she sobbed in defeat, scraping her nails across his shoulders as she buried her mouth in his neck. Intense sexual hunger nearly shattered her into weeping. "I don't want another man to be my first. I want it to be you."

He was *right there*. Her body needed his so badly.

"I don't want to hurt you." His words were barely audible and he held himself in such tight control, he trembled.

"You won't," she assured him, rocking and catching him into her, feeling him press to the deepest point yet.

His breath rushed out and his arms slid to lock around her.

"Don't stop me," she begged.

"Gently," he said, shaking hands moving up her back to her shoulders. "Go slow—" He bit off a curse as she sank down a little more.

It did hurt. A lot. But she was so aroused it happened easily and she was so happy to feel him filling her. So dazzled by the unique sensation of sitting on his lap this way, nose-to-nose, lips-to-lips, tender flesh burning as she accommodated his thickness, bodies locked in this ancient way.

She smiled as she kissed him and settled fully onto

him, taking all of him, possessing him as much as he possessed her.

He ran his hands over her, nipping at her mouth with tender, inciting kisses as he whispered soft words in Arabic that sounded sweet and grateful and loving.

He played with her breasts, teased her nipples and made her react with a tight clasp around him. Intense excitement shot stars behind her eyelids. She wriggled with ecstasy, discovering the deliciousness grew the more she rocked.

"Careful. You're driving me mad," he said with a hard hand on her hip. "I'm so close I'm going to lose it if you keep doing that."

She ignored him as she arched and writhed, moving with all the skill she'd learned from him. She gloried in grinding herself tight against him, then pulling away until she could feel the tension in his fingers as he urged her not to let his flesh leave hers. Her entire existence narrowed to the place where they joined, where her flesh was taut and sensitized and quivered in joy.

And every time she clasped herself tight on him, a deeper pleasure crept closer, like waves lapping at her, climbing, swelling, threatening to engulf her.

"I'm there, Zafir," she breathed in his ear, feeling the tidal wave rising inside her. "Come with me. It's so good. So good." She sank onto him, clinging as the crisis arrived, expanding a white light through her that was pure elation. Exaltation.

Her body clenched around his shape, stunning her with the intensity of it, the tremendous heightening of their connection. He held her so tightly, she could barely breathe, but she needed his arms to hold her together as she shook and her abdomen contracted in ecstatic catches of bliss.

In the middle of it all, she fell, flying, plummeting and landing on her back on a bed of silken sheets. His big body covered hers and his hips moved in sharp, possessive thrusts, stinging her tight flesh, but escalating her orgasm into a new realm. He muffled her cries of joy with a hard kiss and bucked, filling her as his body convulsed in release.

She locked her knees at his waist, embracing him. Her ankles hooked in the small of his back, trying to keep him in her forever.

And when his weight settled fully onto her, she let her breath release with gratitude, utterly at peace. Happier than she'd ever been in her life.

In love, hopelessly and irrevocably in love, but that's how a woman should feel with her first, right?

Zafir forced himself to gather his strength and roll away.

Leaving Fern was like stripping his body from his soul, but that part of him would be consigned to hell for this anyway.

It was as dark in her tent as it was every night that he stole in here, but he threw his arm over his eyes anyway, trying to block out reality.

He had meant to pull out.

He had never intended to fully possess her at all, but she'd tempted him beyond bearing, her desire for him the juiciest forbidden fruit to a man going mad with thirst.

And she'd been exquisite. Despite his best efforts to retain his sanity, he'd lost himself to the moment. To her erotic movements. Her heat and the pound of her heart against his own and the fire raging in his blood.

He didn't even remember how she'd wound up under him, had only come back to real awareness of where he was and how wrong this was when the crisis had been peaked. The most all-encompassing satisfaction had filled him.

Until awareness had crept in with the slowing of his

heart rate. Her tight, wet fit around him. Her soft sigh of repletion.

This should *not* have happened.

"Zafir—" she began in a whisper.

"Shh." He came up on his elbow and touched her lips with his finger, listening.

Across the camp, he heard one of the girls sobbing and Amineh's comforting voice going to her.

The small action of caressing Fern's tender mouth and catching her scent rising warmly off her body made him stir with renewed excitement. He couldn't trust himself if he stayed here. He'd have her again and now they weren't the only ones awake in the camp.

"I have to go," he whispered as he leaned close. "Before we're caught."

Her lips tightened under his touch in a flinch. "Okay."

Her acceptance of his loving and leaving made him disgusted with himself. He wanted to ask about timing, but if he stayed any longer, he'd kiss her, fist his hand in her hair and make love to her all over again. Letting her go and rising from her bed was the hardest thing he'd ever done, but he made himself do it. He left her without saying goodbye, because he was afraid he'd fail to do it at all if he didn't do it fast and quiet.

Later that morning, he ensured his caravan was ready first. He hugged his sister and kissed his nieces and learned from their father that Jumanah had been crying in the night because she didn't want to leave.

He could relate.

He wouldn't let himself dwell on the silky hold of Fern's body, though, or the clinging limbs that had clawed with passion for his.

"Goodbye, Miss Davenport," he managed to say when Fern brought one of her bags to the camel keepers. He wanted to ask where she was in her cycle, but they weren't alone.

She wore sunglasses and her mouth pouted sexily— from sadness? Or his insatiable kisses last night?

"Thank you, abu Tariq," she said. Their use of more formal names reset their relationship to where it ought to be. Her pale face colored with a pretty shade of pink as she added, "For making it possible for me to visit such a remarkable place." Her voice wavered and color came up in her cheeks like a thermometer in the sun.

His heart twisted. It had been extraordinary for him, too.

"Bissalama" was all he said. *Have a safe journey.* It made him feel small until she replied in her quiet voice.

"You, too. Always."

He took a breath that he wished could knock the weight off his heart, nodded and moved to take the reins of his camel.

CHAPTER SIX

FERN MIGHT HAVE pined away her life if she hadn't been so distracted, but within a few weeks of returning to the palace, the entire family was packed up to attend a wedding of Ra'id's cousin in the south.

Ra'id's country was quite conservative, but this new state was even more so. Fern had to relinquish her passport at the airport and was given a room in a modern-day harem. The annexed compound was a collection of bungalows around a courtyard with an opulent pool, fountains and bronze statues. One passageway led to the main palace.

Her rooms were very nice, but few people bothered to speak to her—just the other foreigners, one a Malaysian nanny and another the wife of a pastry chef flown in from Paris. The rest of the women were family from both sides of the wedding party and came and went, keeping to themselves.

Fern didn't mind. She was slipping quietly into a state of terror as she awaited proof she and Zafir hadn't cashed in on the gamble they'd taken that last night. Unfortunately, her cycle grew later by the hour, making her certain they had.

Impossible, she thought. They'd only made love the once. Loads of women took years of active trying to get pregnant. How could she wind up pregnant after one time?

She wrung her hands as she waited for Amineh to collect the girls one afternoon. The girls had another dress-fitting today, but Amineh was adamant that they keep as much to routine as possible. Jumanah was mixing up the direction of her letters, which wasn't uncommon at this age, but Amineh wanted Fern to stay on top of it to ensure it wasn't a more serious concern.

"I kept putting off starting Bashira's schooling because we had so many other commitments and now she's six and will fall behind her peers if I don't make their education a priority," Amineh had said when asking Fern to accompany them on this trip. "I know it won't be ideal, but will you come?"

Fern hadn't been able to say no. Teaching the girls was what she was contracted to do. Plus, she enjoyed the distraction of learning every nuance and aspect of this culture she was immersed in. Welcomed it.

Her mind kept screaming, *it was* one *time*. Completely the wrong time in her cycle, too. She didn't understand it.

But what was there to understand? Sex made babies. She had had sex.

She and Zafir had made—

No.

But as the days wore on and the tenderness in her breasts became nearly unbearable and her churning stomach couldn't be blamed solely on worry, she accepted that she was as bad as—quite possibly worse than—her mother. Fern, at least, had had the benefit of her mother's lectures. She should have *known* better.

The final straw was a pronouncement by Amineh. When she arrived for the girls, she looked as washed out as Fern felt. The girls ran to their quarters to change while Amineh huffed out an exhausted breath.

"Ra'id told me Zafir was talking about arranging another marriage for himself, to the daughter of one of his challengers. Brilliant, I said. I want peace in Q'Amara as much as he does, but if he thinks I'm putting myself through another wedding before this baby comes out— Oh, I've shocked you." Amineh's hand came onto her arm. "I thought you might have guessed after I nearly fainted on you this morning. You sounded so sympathetic, like you knew what I was going through in this heat."

"Oh, no, I—" Fern was dumbfounded. Part of her went into cardiac arrest at what else she might have betrayed by being "sympathetic," the rest was screaming in agony at what Amineh had just told her. She did her best to shake it all off. "No, I honestly didn't realize," she said. She'd been too obsessed with the possibility she was pregnant herself. "That's wonderful. Congratulations."

She hugged Amineh and couldn't help the tears that came into her eyes. Expecting with her friend was so perfect, yet such a disaster.

"Oh, Fern, you really are the sweetest person, crying for me. Honestly, I feel like crying myself. I'm so tired, and look! Barely six weeks and I feel like I'm beginning to show. Nothing fits right. Ra'id is being a gem, making my excuses and promising me that after this, we're home for a year, but we have another two *weeks* of this nonsense."

Fern could only offer a shaky smile, wishing the father of *her* baby would be a gem and look after *her*, but he had an entire country to worry about.

And he was getting married.

That night she cried until her throat burned and woke to such a violent bout of morning sickness, she knew she could be found out. As much as she wanted to tell Zafir, she couldn't. Not like this, from a country where her condition, especially as an unmarried woman, could be seen as a crime. What if someone found out? What if he didn't care?

Staring at her ravaged face the next morning, she knew

what she had to do. She was a terrible liar, but at least her emotions were on such a seesaw, her anxiety so very real, that when she requested a meeting with Ra'id, she looked convincingly distraught.

"I've had some bad news from home. A dear friend. She's like a mother to me." Miss Ivy was perfectly fine, as far as Fern knew, but as Fern considered the way she'd derailed this wonderful career she'd been given, fresh tears came into her eyes. "I'm so sorry. I need to return to England immediately."

Amineh was out with the girls and other women from the wedding party. Fern had planned it that way, unable to speak her bald-faced lies directly to someone she considered a true friend. Especially when she'd betrayed that friendship by sleeping with Amineh's brother.

It was far easier to let Ra'id recoil from her display of feminine emotions, snap into making arrangements and put her on a plane within the hour. She promised she would be in touch about her return, claiming it shouldn't be more than a week or two.

Her first order of business after checking in to her London hotel half a day later was a pregnancy test. Her life changed completely in the one minute it took to watch the blue positive sign appear. She had known, but now she *knew*.

Sitting on the edge of the bathtub, she saw her dream job dissolve into a blur, just like her pale reflection in the mirror across from her. She couldn't face Amineh after this. Couldn't face Zafir after being so stupid as to let it happen. She couldn't put him in a position of choosing between his country and her. Not when she knew something of the anguish he and his sister had grown up in, feeling torn between two worlds. She couldn't do that to her child.

She was having a baby!

Unable to process that reality, she went through the motions of what had to be done. She wrote her resignation letter with hands that shook so badly she could barely type. Then she made arrangements for the agency to forward it on her behalf. Her apologies were profuse, her regret profound, but she was unable to return. The circumstances here at home made it impossible, she said, and wished the girls well in their studies.

After cutting those final ties, the day after her arrival in London, she put herself on a train to the north and took a cab from the station to Miss Ivy's flat.

"Fern!" her friend gasped when she opened the door. "I wasn't expecting you!"

Fern dropped her cases. "I am. Expecting." Now came the tears as the magnitude of it all finally hit her. "Oh, Miss Ivy! What am I going to *do*?"

Six months later

Zafir was preparing for a very private, very delicate meeting. Abu Gadiel had agreed to let Zafir introduce himself to his daughter. They, with her mother and two brothers, were arriving at any minute. The air in his expansive office was already thick with tension and he was the only one in it.

Zafir silently went over his reasons for seeking a union with her, how it would strengthen confidence in his ruling of the country while giving her father a voice near his ear. It would benefit the country they all cared about. He already knew her only reservation: whether she would be allowed to continue her ambitions to become a doctor.

He would encourage her, of course. Offer a long engagement, wait until she'd finished her degree even. It would press him into celibacy, but he would need time to work up the desire to bed her anyway. Sexual hunger tortured him every hour of every day, but he only thought of one woman.

This obsession had to stop. He would *not* become his father, keeping a mistress in England. That way led to the madness of falling in love, having a family as though they were a proper couple with a future. Q'Amara needed stability. That came from a man with a clear mind, not one tortured by passionate emotions like love.

So he would ignore the fact that Fern had gone back to England, even though the knowledge had sent a rush of excitement roaring through him. The imperative to go and stamp and ensconce had been pacing like an angry lion inside him since Tariq had come home with the news of her departure from Ra'id's palace. A widowed Mrs. Heath was in residence as Fern's replacement. She was nice enough, but didn't make jokes or let them wander off topic. Photos had shown a woman of later years, white hair and a plump body.

"Why did she leave?" Zafir had questioned Tariq, experiencing a pierce that should have been fear, but was too anticipatory.

"Her friend was sick. Auntie said it sounded like what my mother had."

Zafir's mind had sheared off the thought that had barely formed, that Fern had had another reason for leaving, and he'd focused on reminding Tariq that rules were relaxed at the oasis. *An understatement.* Miss Davenport might also have been strict if she'd been in her proper classroom, he'd said, so Tariq shouldn't be too hard on the new Mrs. Heath.

Tariq hadn't agreed, insisting Miss Davenport was superior in every way, but they'd moved on to other things.

And Zafir had spent weeks imagining where he would buy her a flat in London, even going so far as to look at real estate listings. He didn't even know what she might like.

They hadn't talked much, always too busy quietly eating each other alive. Obviously she'd always lived modestly. He'd gathered that she'd taken care of her mother through a terminal illness. Surely she would appreciate not having to work or worry about meeting her basic needs anymore.

His desire to continue their affair was a type of insanity. An obsession. It had to stop. He tilted his head back, fighting yet again the memory of having her under him, lissome and smelling like heaven, hot and writhing with abandon. Had he known he *would* have her, he would have taken her from the beginning. All the way, every night.

The knock on his door was like an axe hitting the chopping block. No more thoughts of her after today. His life was moving in a different direction. A necessary one.

But when he called permission to enter, his guest was Ra'id.

Zafir frowned. His brother-in-law never arrived unannounced and never looked so grim. Zafir's mind instantly whirled into terrible possibilities. He rejected each frightening concern as quickly as it came. Please not his sweet nieces. Let Amineh be well. She was pregnant. Was something wrong with the baby?

"What's happened?" he demanded as Ra'id closed the door behind himself.

Ra'id lifted a staying hand. "Your sister and the children are fine. But she has insisted I come see you, since she's too far along to travel and confront you herself."

Ra'id looked more severe than Zafir had ever seen him, as if an angry black cloud surrounded him. The accusation narrowing his friend's eyes suggested he pinned some sort of blame on Zafir.

That took him aback. He tried to think of what Tariq might have possibly done during his stay three months ago. He'd talked of one of Ra'id's prized horses...

Folding his arms, Ra'id stated belligerently, "My wife and I have been arguing for months. I knew she was keeping something from me, which is not like her at all." The couched fury in Ra'id's voice put Zafir on high alert. "And when she finally told me her suspicions, I assured her she was so wrong that this would go down in our marriage as the most unfounded disagreement we have ever had."

"She cannot be accusing you of an affair?" Zafir said with disbelief. His friend had been married to Amineh long before the formal ceremony had taken place. If Ra'id had had any other lover but his wife, Zafir would be shocked dead.

"Not me, no," Ra'id said, adopting the full superiority of his station. "You."

Zafir's breath stalled. His lifetime of being attacked with denigrations served him well. He deflected this one with a neutral expression and only elevated one eyebrow as he blithely responded, "I'm not married."

"Miss Davenport left our household rather abruptly some months ago. Amineh is convinced you are the reason."

"This *will* go down in history as a ridiculous fight if you've come all this way to involve me in your domestic employment issues," Zafir intoned.

"It has turned into a contest of which one of us knows you better. She thinks you quite capable of an affair with her friend, while I have assured her you have more honor and sense."

And so they were found out. Zafir's ears rang as he met his friend's eyes. It wasn't comfortable to let Ra'id see that he would not go home crowing about being right. Zafir did, indeed, have less honor and sense than his best friend had credited him.

Ra'id's face tightened. "Because it was obvious to anyone with eyes that Miss Davenport was not the type to engage in affairs, I said. As much of a hound that your brother can be, he indulges himself elsewhere with sophisticated women who know what they're getting into. The kind who accept jewelry, but don't expect a diamond ring. He would never prey on a virgin dormouse and take advantage of her."

Self-disgust rose like a cloud of grit inside Zafir. He couldn't hide it.

"You had an affair with my children's teacher," Ra'id persisted as Zafir failed to deny the implications. Ra'id's voice rose with genuine fury. "Do you realize they have just now stopped crying for her? She was under my protection, Zafir!"

"You slept with my sister before you married her. In my *house*," he snarled back.

"I wanted to marry her," Ra'id retorted. "I *loved* her."

And there was the slap of truth that made Zafir look away. He had told himself Fern was English. English girls had affairs. His actions weren't that dishonorable. *She had wanted it to be him.*

"It was not my best hour," he acknowledged. "I'll admit that." But he wouldn't try to explain it. There was no explaining it. Sexual infatuation had got the better of him. He couldn't offer excuses because there were none.

"So Amineh's intuition strikes where my conviction, my certainty that I knew you better, fails."

"Yes," Zafir said with a tight smile. "I'm sorry that you must now go home and tell your wife you were wrong. A fate worse than death for any man. Are we finished? Because that tap on the door means my guests have arrived."

"No," Ra'id said with false pleasantry. "Because if she's right about your sleeping with her, she might be right about something else. You see, the piece that has been really bothering her is the way Miss Davenport has cut off all communication."

For a moment that made Zafir wonder. Worry. Was she ill? Then he remembered... "She's nursing a sick friend. People insulate themselves in that situation." He had, when his wife had been dying. You tired of singing the sad song, giving details that were the furthest thing from optimistic, looking into pitying eyes and facing the inevitability of your own mortality.

"Is she?" Ra'id asked, tucking his hands behind his back and rocking onto his heels. The edges of his *gutra* swayed around his supercilious expression. "I certainly thought that's why she was leaving, when she came to me so distressed I couldn't put her on an airplane fast enough. But Amineh has tracked this friend online and there's no indication she's suffering anything but impatience with a wet winter. Miss Davenport has let her own accounts go stale while her friend is cheerfully stating that she has begun a training regime for a half marathon and recently posted photos of her mountain trek in Portugal."

Zafir didn't know what to make of that, but he sensed the walls closing in on him.

"Miss Davenport appears to have lied to Amineh. Why would she do that, Zafir? What possible reason could she have to leave so abruptly and fail to return any of Amineh's emails? Shall I tell you the theory your sister, the amateur detective, has formulated?"

Please don't. But they both knew what the most logical conclusion was.

"She would have told me," Zafir muttered as a refutation, wanting to believe it. Because the alternative, that Fern was pregnant with his child and hadn't told him, was too much to face. The reasons behind choosing *not* to tell him were too ugly to absorb.

"Another type of woman would have tried to trap you," Ra'id said. "She would have told you and extorted a lifetime of support. Marriage even. Did this woman even have the sense to use birth control? Did *you*?"

Zafir's skin was dark enough to be Arab, but his green eyes were windows into his impure soul. All of him burned in the fire of culpability as he stood there, a man as close as a brother judging him for his reprehensible behavior. He had abandoned any sense of consequence. He was no better than the father who had condemned him to this half life of never belonging.

He had no defense for his actions.

"Ya gazma," Ra'id spat. *You shoe.* Zafir felt lower than a shoe.

"She would have told me," Zafir insisted. Had she been too embarrassed? Or was it shame?

"She quit because she feared running into you again?" Ra'id queried. "Given how sensitive and conscientious she seemed, I could believe that. But you better find out if that's all it was before you proceed with what you've started here." Ra'id jerked his chin toward the door and the place where Zafir's proposed fiancée waited.

Zafir's heart sank like a stone in quicksand, slow and inevitable and irretrievable. He had ruined everything. He was a disgrace.

He ran a hand down his burning face, trying to think.

"What will you do if she's pregnant?" There was the voice of his friend. Anger had abated and troubled understanding clouded Ra'id's eyes. He knew what a terrible position Zafir could be in.

Somehow this reaction was worse. Zafir would rather be reviled than consoled.

Why had he allowed something so superficial to go so far? Was it in his blood to be this careless?

He shut down the rage of helplessness. It was done. He had to find out if Fern was pregnant.

"I don't know," he responded truthfully, voice as bleak as the rest of him.

"I had time to think on the way here," Ra'id said. "I have a suggestion."

CHAPTER SEVEN

FERN HURRIED FROM the bus stop with the collar of her rain-coat clutched tightly closed against her throat. With her other hand, she grasped the umbrella in a firm grip against the midday gusts trying to yank it away. The rushed walk made her breathless, partly due to the extra weight, she supposed. Possibly because she needed more iron.

Pregnancy was a lot of work, she had discovered with a small pang of understanding for her mother's beleaguered outlook. It was disconcerting to feel as though your body wasn't yours anymore, but she didn't resent the process, *Mother*. She didn't blame this baby growing inside her for the anxiety she felt about their future.

She blamed herself.

Tramping quickly through the puddles in her boots, she felt icy splashes strike her knees through her tights, urging her even faster toward the sanctuary of Miss Ivy's little flat. Not a whole house. Not even a proper two-bedroom. Fern was on the sofa bed at Miss Ivy's insistence, saving the nest egg she had squirrelled away during her teaching contract with Amineh. She was even bringing in a few extra pounds with some adult tutoring. She hoped to take over a flat two blocks away when it came avail-able in a few months.

None of this was ideal. In fact, it was the kind of repeti-tion of history she hated to own up to, but she would manage. And her baby would not carry the burden of fault that had been hers most of her life.

As she reached the steps to the converted row house that held Miss Ivy's flat, the self-satisfied lambent green town car at the curb caught her attention. Its tinted windows and details of chrome where out of place in this village. The driver's side door opened, startling her into halting.

Zafir straightened and slammed the door with a firmness that made her flinch. As he came around the bonnet, seemingly unaware of the rain that pattered onto his uncovered head, she told herself to run, but could only stand there and stare.

No tunic or headdress, but he was as exotic and resplendent as always, even in a bespoke English suit of cast-iron-gray with a sharp white shirt and a silver tie. His beard was shaved to a narrow line that edged his set jaw and cut a goatee around the uncompromising firmness of his mouth.

His remarkable green eyes were as flat as frosted glass as they traveled to the billow of her overcoat. He flinched, but it wasn't with surprise. More like, *okay then*.

The way he moved was smooth and unhurried, but his approach still felt like a blast of hurricane-force wind. He covered her hand on the umbrella and lifted it high enough so he could stand under it with her. Her hearing dulled and became more acute at the same time. Damp, earthy, male scents of aftershave and coffee, wool and warm, masculine skin, clouded into the little space and overwhelmed her senses.

She swallowed, falling into lust all over again.

Pathetic. She was in the middle of her third trimester, about as sexy as a cow ready to calf, but she wanted to lie with him. Naked and joined.

"Let's get out of this mess," he said in the voice that

had been raising the hairs on her scalp since the first time she'd heard it.

Out of the rain? Or the situation?

Her heart kicked into gear as he nudged her into movement. His free hand grazed her elbow and he pointed her in the direction of the steps. She began to tremble as the enormity of his being here hit.

Did he know? Of course he did *now*. She wasn't the size of a house, but her coat was tented over her bump like a tarp over the bow of a boat. That radiation of umbrage from him was unmistakable. She'd grown up with those sorts of vibes directed at her. She knew all too well this sense of disapproval jabbing into her like the point of a sword.

But had he known? Had he come to see her? Or because he'd learned of the baby? How?

As they stepped into the small space beneath the overhang of the stoop, he stole the umbrella from her nerveless grip, lowered and shook it, then followed her through the door that her numb fingers could barely unlock. He dropped the umbrella into its stand and paced his footsteps into hers as they climbed the two narrow flights to Miss Ivy's door.

Her mind raced, but she couldn't seem to catch a solid thought. Bring him into the flat? Take him somewhere else? Where? Why was he here? What was he going to say?

How much did he hate her for this?

"Fern?" Miss Ivy called from the tiny alcove of the kitchen as they entered. "A woman called for you. She didn't leave her name, but I told her you'd be back about now so I expect—"

Miss Ivy trailed off as she emerged with a glass and a tea towel in hand. "Hello," she said with a lilt of curiosity in her tone, eyes going sharp as she looked into Fern's face—which had to be ghostly pale. Her brows pulled together with concern.

"That was my assistant," Zafir explained. "You must be Ivy McGill? Thank you for saving me the trouble of waiting in the rain any longer than I had to. You're well? Our family was given to understand you were quite ill."

His tone dripped sarcasm. Fern tried to ignore it.

"Miss Ivy, this is Sheikh abu Tariq Zafir ibn Ahmad al-Rakin Iram. Or you might be more familiar with him as, um, Mr. Zafir Cavendish, grandson of the Duke of Sommerton, who sits in the House of Lords. I did—" she cleared her throat "—give the impression that you were in need of care when I cut short my teaching contract with his sister's children."

"I see." No doubt Miss Ivy saw very well. No one had ever accused her of lacking math skills.

"Let me take your coat, Fern," Zafir said, stepping behind her so her heart nearly leaped out her mouth.

You don't live here. It's not your job to take my coat, she wanted to protest. *Don't stay. Don't talk to me. Don't even look at me.*

Then she felt the brush of his fingertips against her shoulders and the sensuous memory of his stripping her clothing from her body came back to her like sunshine breaking its warmth across her face. She suppressed a shiver of mixed longing and mortification.

He stepped away to hang the dripping coat on the hooks over the rubber mat. Fern balanced a hand on the wall and unzipped her boots, taking extraordinary care with placing them so the insides wouldn't be filled by the rivulets off her coat, afraid to turn and face him.

"Why don't you make us some tea," Zafir suggested behind her, but Fern suspected he was looking at her, not Miss Ivy. He was willing her to face him and own up to what she'd done. "Fern and I need to talk."

Hugging herself, as if that could disguise this huge evidence of her carelessness that stretched the knit of her oversized jumper, Fern forced herself around.

Miss Ivy looked worried. She had pressed Fern many times to tell her who the father was and now there was such anxiety in her small dark eyes.

Fern managed a tight smile. "It's fine," she assured her.

Miss Ivy nodded jerkily and slipped into the alcove, where she'd be able to hear the murmur of their voices while she filled the kettle and brought out her good china.

Fern dared a glance at Zafir and saw a puzzling mixture of emotions on his face. He aimed his hard stare at her belly. Something fierce yet angry gripped him. Not dangerously threatening, but deeply primal.

She swallowed and edged toward the sofa, where she lowered to perch on the edge of the cushion, facing him, facing up to all of this that she'd mostly been denying. Visiting a doctor and reading ads for flats was only the tip of the iceberg as far as fully accepting her pregnancy went.

A rush of despondency hit as the biggest part that she'd been avoiding—the fact her baby had a father—confronted her with ominous silence.

"I didn't mean for this to happen, Zafir." Her voice was husky with self-castigation.

"It's mine," he said, more statement than question, but the demand for confirmation made her choke out a shocked laugh.

"Who else?" she asked, askance.

"I needed to hear it." He looked away, his profile carved sharply from granite. His hand fisted at his side and his jaw worked, but the news didn't seem to please him.

"Are you surprised?" she asked as she realized how much easier it would be for him if she'd been promiscuous. And even as her mind told her to change her answer— make things easy so maybe he wouldn't hate her—

she blurted, "Sorry I'm not a slut with a list of possible fathers—"

He swung his gaze back. The hardness in his aqua eyes buttoned her lip.

She felt enough of a slut as it was, whether he wanted to call her one or not. She clenched her pale fingers together, rather wishing for the warmth of a blush to take away this bone-deep chill.

"Why didn't you tell me?" he asked, his tone so tight with fury she flinched.

"I didn't think you would want to know," she answered, hating how thin her voice had gone.

Again with the glare that encased her in ice.

"Was there something in the way I treat Tariq that suggested to you I would take no interest in my child?"

"No." She bowed her head under his stark condemnation. His relationship with his son had actually tempted her to tell him, *But I didn't want you to think I did this on purpose. We both know this is...* She couldn't bring herself to call her baby a mistake, but the situation was far from ideal. "You're not happy, Zafir. You're barely holding on to a civil tone." She squirmed her fingers together. "It seemed better not to tell you."

"And do what instead?"

"What do you mean?"

"Are you keeping it?"

"Obviously." She waved at the size of her belly.

"I mean, are you thinking to give it up for adoption or something?"

"No!" The suggestion astonished her, never once occurring to her as a realistic possibility.

He looked away again, not giving her a chance to read his eyes, but some of his animosity seemed to ease as he said with a husk of emotion, "So you want this baby."

"Yes! Why would you imagine anything else?"

"You tried to keep my child out of my life, Fern. It follows that you might want to purge it from your own." He swung his attention back to her and the force of his gaze kicked her low and hard.

Maybe that was the baby, scolding her. She had worried, for about ten minutes, that she would begrudge her child for coming along when she'd finally been free of family obligation. But it wasn't as if she had had high career plans or wanted to live fast. While her mother had felt cheated as a single parent and had made sure to let Fern know it, Fern viewed raising a child alone as a challenge, yes, but a fairly common one. Many women managed this. Yes, she worried about her future, but because her baby would depend on her. Taking care of another life was a responsibility she wanted to get right. She didn't want to mess it up.

But while she'd glossed very quickly past any thoughts of not keeping the baby, Zafir had obviously convinced himself she wouldn't.

"I knew almost from the moment I realized I was pregnant that I'd keep it," she told him quietly. "But when I looked at all the factors…" She frowned at her twisting fingers, still unable to bring all the dangling threads together into anything less than a messy, painful knot. "It seemed like putting you in this position of acknowledging your child was more unfair than keeping you ignorant of it."

"You were offering me plausible deniability? How kind." His voice peeled a layer off her, astringent as paint thinner.

She jerked her gaze up, not liking the acerbic response when she'd honestly been trying to put his needs ahead of her own. "I won't pretend to be an expert on your country's politics, but I know this is the last thing you need. I'm doing what I can to keep the baby secret—"

"Obviously," he said with a bite. "But I'm not here to pay you off. I'm here to claim my child. I want him or her in my life."

Her heart shook in her chest, quaking with both intimidation and the ferocity of a mother whose child was threatened. "Did you miss what I just said? I have no intention of giving it up. Not even to its own father!"

"Then you'll marry me," he stated, like it was as easy as snapping fingers.

And her nerves twanged, mind skewing in a thousand directions because in all her scenarios of what could possibly happen if he learned of this baby, none of them had included his proposing. Even as coldly and flatly as that.

"I…" Her heart, already taxed with stress and emotion, pounded extra hard. The feeling was nearly painful, making tears spring to her eyes. Live the rest of her life under that baleful glare? After the first twenty years of her life had been blistered by the same? No thanks. "I can't. Or do you mean just to make it legitimate? And I'd stay in England while you—"

"No," he interrupted, adamant. "You'd live with me and Tariq, in our palace."

Which sounded like a fairy tale except for the part where she'd be treated like a troll.

She realized she was biting her lips together and forced them to relax, soothing them with her tongue. But he made her so nervous, standing there like a—well, like a damned sultan who could demand she give him a baby. She'd seen this uncompromising side of him at the oasis, when he'd taken control and insisted on treatment for the Bedouin girl. It wasn't a level of command she wanted to pit herself against.

Especially not when he was demanding to be part of his child's life. Her own father hadn't even bothered sticking around to find out if she was a boy or a girl. There was a huge part of her that melted beneath Zafir's show of fatherly interest.

But what about her?

Now she began to understand her mother's sense of lost entitlement. Sure her baby would force her to make certain compromises, but for the most part, alone as a single parent, she controlled their fate. With Zafir in the picture, she faced huge concessions.

See, Mum? You were actually lucky not to have this dilemma.

"Marriage isn't on my radar," she murmured.

"Put it there."

She shook her head.

"Why the hell not?"

Had he listened when she had introduced him? "Think about who you are—"

His head snapped back like she'd struck him.

"That wasn't—" *What she'd meant...*

Miss Ivy clattered her tray into the room, killing Fern's chance to explain.

A hoar frost coated the room as Miss Ivy set everything out and poured. Into the condemning silence, she said, "Shall I take mine into my room?"

"Please," Fern said through a tight throat. She needed privacy to straighten out Zafir's wrong impression.

Fern's roommate was the homeliest woman Zafir had ever seen. Small and hunched, she had dull brown hair streaked in gray, definitely a home cut, teeth like an old cemetery and beady brown eyes that were deeply set.

But as she left, she touched Fern's shoulder with a maternal hand. Fern covered the woman's gnarled knuckles and the glance the two exchanged was complex. Sheepish and forgiving and reassuring. The kind of unspoken communication women had when they were very close.

As one of the two doors off the main room closed, Zafir swung his gaze around the flat. It was charming, he supposed, in the way of modest, dated rooms kept tidy and warm. There was an odd collection of photos showing young men and women in graduation caps and gowns, accepting awards, waving from the window of a pilot's seat and standing at a podium.

"Who is she?" he asked, still reeling from Fern's gross insult, not ready to deal with how deeply she had cut him.

"A teacher. She made me a member of her Shyness Club when I was nine." Her freckled face tinted. "Zafir, that's not what I meant. About you being who you are…"

Her voice trailed off as she twisted her fingers. It would be a wonder if the digits remained attached at the rate she was torturing them.

He wouldn't ask what she *had* meant. Wouldn't wheedle to understand. He didn't even want to face her, there was such an agony of rejection coursing through him, but his gaze snagged on the bump of their child swelling her middle. It continued to stun him. His wife had kept to herself in hundreds of ways, including an almost complete retreat when she became heavily pregnant. If she had been in his presence, she had draped herself in oversized garments that hadn't really let him see evidence of the child she was giving him.

The heir she had hidden like something unwanted and merely endured because her husband was something unwanted and endured. Lower than her. Not good enough.

Still deeply scarred by that disdain, he focused instead on the way Fern let her bump sit so prominently in her lap. He itched to set his hands on her. All of her. She was fuller everywhere, from her cheeks to her breasts to her bottom. It suited her.

Her hair was longer, drying and starting to spring out from its catch at the back of her neck. Her skin was as much a display of cinnamon and cream as ever. She was tempting and as sweet as almonds and honey, he'd thought when he'd stood under the umbrella with her outside. Her scent had mingled with the rain and wind of English storms and struck him as oddly familiar. Heartening.

Everything about her was the same and more, especially her ability to enthrall him.

But she hadn't told him about the baby because of who he was. Didn't she mean *what* he was?

Funny how dozens of women had overlooked his birth and half-caste status, wishing to marry his money and blue blood, but the two females he'd actually proposed to had been unable to get past it.

Misery lined Fern's expression. "I meant that a man in your position could have anyone." Her bottom lip disappeared as she pulled it between her teeth, while her brows crooked and trembled.

"Anyone except you," he challenged, fighting the tightness that gripped him.

Couched hope glimmered in the gray depths of her gaze, but dimmed as he returned her look with one that refused to give anything away.

Obviously struggling to hold on to her composure, she looked away, her voice scraped raw. "You didn't come here for me."

"No," he agreed, aware it was cruel to be so bald, but what did she expect? Declarations of love? They'd had an affair. That was all. He still couldn't believe how many times he'd thought about her. How he'd wanted to set her up in London.

But as he watched her flinch and nod, absorbing his slight, he realized that the woman who had welcomed him each night to her tent was not the sophisticated mistress he had let her become in his mind. The one confident in her allure and ability to drive him mad. No, Fern didn't seem to have any idea the hold she still had on him. The depth of want he felt even more intensely now, when she was within reach. His desire, his ability to rationalize making her his, was greater than ever.

And she made no effort to draw him back. The slump of her shoulders spoke of hopelessness.

He supposed her ignorance was a relief, but it seemed to open a huge gap in the small room, one he didn't know how to bridge.

"How is Amineh?" she asked.

The sudden change of topic threw him.

"Fine," he replied. "According to Ra'id. That was a few days ago. You?" he asked, as it belatedly occurred to him. "Everything is normal with the baby?"

She gave an absent nod. "The supplements make me feel a bit off and I can't stand the smell of sausage or bacon, but we're both healthy and fat." Her doll's mouth pursed in a self-deprecating smile. "That's what the midwife said."

"When are you due?"

She told him.

It was strange to imagine himself a father again and so soon, but as he mentally counted down the handful of weeks, a rush of eagerness to get there and see his son or daughter unexpectedly slid through him. A girl? With kinky red hair and a pert little mouth like her mother? What would Tariq think?

He skimmed a hand over his damp hair. He hadn't even told his son, being totally focused on confronting Fern and discovering if there was a baby on the way. The minute he'd seen her, he'd needed to know it was his. Had needed to claim it.

He wanted to claim her, lies to the contrary and discomfort with the truth notwithstanding. His mind was exploding with the simplicity of it. Of course he would marry her and bring her back to Q'Amara. His personal ethics would accept nothing else.

But she didn't want to marry him. She wasn't looking at him and he couldn't look away from her. Heat climbed in him, some of it embarrassment at his partiality for her, so wrong for him, but a fresh emotion brimmed inside him as he took in her fertile figure: determination. She *would* marry him. She *would* live in his house with his child. They *would* make this work.

He hoped they could make it work. A stealthy fear snaked through him that he was repeating history on more than one front, but he would not turn his back on his child.

"Fern, marriage is the only—"

"No it's not," interrupted. "*You* know it's not."

"I won't be my father," he insisted, growing annoyed as she vehemently shook her head. "This baby might not be heir and successor to Q'Amara, but I won't have an illegitimate child. People would look at Tariq as my 'real' son and say this one is something less. No. We *must* marry."

"You'll hate me," she stated. Then, with the quiet ferocity she'd used when demanding medical attention for the Bedouin girl, she added, "I won't live like that again. I *won't*."

Anguish tortured her expression before she looked away, tears standing on her wide, unblinking eyes. She set her jaw, though, so obviously ready to hold her ground, he had to take her seriously.

"Again?" he prompted, disbelief scuffing his tone. Aside from this current streak of obstinacy, she was fairly compliant. Not someone difficult to get along with. He was furious with her, but couldn't imagine anyone actively disliking her. "What do you mean by that? Who else hated you?"

"My mother," she said in a small voice, looking at her wringing hands. Her pale brows crushed together and the corners of her mouth went down. Bright red lit her cheekbones while the rest of her was so pale her freckles stood out like stress cracks that warned she was on the brink of crumbling. "She got pregnant with me when she was seventeen. Her parents threw her out. My father disappeared. She barely scraped by trying to support me."

"And she blamed you for that?" His heart took a sharp swerve. He distantly remembered her saying something like *she didn't like me much*. He'd been distracted with making love to her, but now the hackles of his parenting instincts rose at the idea of a mother denigrating her child. His own had made a ton of mistakes, but nothing like that.

"She blamed me for all of it," Fern said with equal parts incredulity and despondency. "As an adult, I can see it wasn't really my fault, but this baby *is*." She covered her bump with protective palms, turning up a face that was so anguished his gut clenched as though he'd been kicked. "She told me so many times that lust was bad and I slept with you anyway. I don't blame you for hating me, but I can't live with the glares and the snide remarks, Zafir. I won't bring my child up in that. There has to be another way."

The ground seemed to shift under him. *Wasn't really my fault, but this baby is…*

"Fern…" He could hardly believe what she was saying. "Is *that* the reason you didn't tell me about the baby? You thought I'd blame you for it?"

"Don't you? You're obviously furious." Her hand came up as she choked out a helpless noise.

"Because you hid this from me!"

She jerked at the sharpness of his tone, but only pinched her mouth into a mutinous purse. "I shouldn't have let it happen. I knew what I was doing was bad."

She was ashamed to have slept with him, but not in the way he'd feared.

It struck him that all this time, while he'd been remembering the way she'd kissed him with abandon and taken him greedily into her, he'd been forgetting something far more important. *Men don't come on to me. How much experience do you think I have with refusing one?*

Moving forward on feet weighted with self-reproach, he took a seat on the wingback chair that faced her. As he leaned his elbows on his knees, he resisted the urge to tuck the loose tendrils of hair that fell against her cheek behind her ear. He didn't trust himself to let it end there.

And she had no idea.

"Fern, how many people were in that tent that night?" he asked quietly.

She lifted a baleful glance. "I know what I did, Zafir. I remember exactly who instigated this conception."

Her skin radiated with color all the way down her neck. He would bet it went well into that belly and even into the thighs that had clamped around his hips with determination to draw his hard sex deeper into her welcoming depths. Not just offering, but begging. Insisting. She dropped her face into her hands as if she couldn't bear to recall.

While it was all he thought about. Heaven had opened its gates and pulled him inside. He hadn't even tried to resist. Not really.

"I meant to pull out," he stated baldly. "I knew the chance we were taking before I let it go as far as it did." As much as he would love to let her carry all the blame, he remembered precisely the moment when he'd stilled her hips and tried to maintain his sanity. Then she'd said, *I want it to be you.*

He had wanted it to be him. The thought of any man following where he was being invited had been unthinkable. She belonged to him. He remembered the way the word *mine* had echoed in his head as he had breached and possessed and imprinted himself so indelibly onto her body that they were now tied together for the rest of their lives.

"You might have been at your best fighting weight that night, but I could have pushed you away. I'm not a victim."

She shook her head, keeping her face covered. "I knew better. I was reckless and this is the consequence."

"My baby is a punishment?" he asked testily.

She flinched and scowled at him over her fingers. "No. I just mean that I'm no victim, either. I knew what I was doing."

The hell she had.

He rubbed the tops of his thighs, hearing Ra'id's condemnation of him. Accepting it. He never should have touched her.

But he had.

"Maybe we're both casualties of a divine sense of humor, doomed to repeat our parents' ill-conceived actions." He let his brow quirk at his own bad joke. "We made that baby together, Fern. Literally."

She lowered her hands, face red as a beacon, but a light of earnestness glinted in her wet eyes. "Do you really see it that way? Because I'm not blind. I know what a mess this is."

"It is," he agreed. "I'm not going to sugarcoat that part. Right here, the two of us working out what to do, this is the easy part. When we take it out there, it will get ugly. I know that and I'm angry that I'm in this situation, but with myself, not you. If that's the reason you're trying to keep your distance from me, because you think I'll blame you, then stop. Coming here to take responsibility for my child means *taking responsibility*."

She seemed to let that sink in, her body seemingly braced, shoulders set with wary tension.

"Is that all you feel?" she challenged in a way that punched his heart. Vulnerability widened her eyes as she hurried to add, "I mean toward the baby." Her lashes dropped in a way that left claw marks down his insides.

He wished he could offer her love. He was starting to realize she'd probably never known it in any form.

"Because if you just feel a sense of duty..." she continued.

"No, that's not all I feel," he assured her, hitching forward on the cushion, willing to lay himself bare because on this topic, he felt no shame and he thought it might reassure her. Win her over. "The first time I held Tariq, I experienced such a rush of emotion. Something I'd never felt before." He clenched his fist, experiencing again the knock of his heart punching the inside wall of his chest, extending itself outward to try forming a shield around the baby. It reached across the space between them now, trying to take in this new one. "I felt so protective and proud it was laughable, but terrified and overwhelmed, too."

The intense vulnerability had been foreign and unnerving to a man who took for granted his health and strength and power, but he'd grown to accept this feeling as a part of parenting.

"He was mine and I knew I'd stop at nothing to keep him alive and well. There's no word to describe that emotion except fatherhood. I already feel that toward this baby."

Her jaw softened and her expression went misty and soft. "Really?"

"Really. You have to marry me, Fern."

She brushed impatiently at the tears that brimmed at her eyelids. "But I feel so guilty. Mum warned me so many times not to have sex, not to get carried away, and I just let it happen. I couldn't face telling you. I was so certain you'd look at me like she would have. Like I was so *stupid*."

He wondered if she remembered why they'd let it happen.

She sat there, a ball of misery, not exactly encouraging him to believe she looked back fondly on their time at the oasis the way he did.

Which was neither here nor there, he told himself. Marriage was his priority. The rest could be addressed later. Maybe that was a shortsighted attitude given the hurdles they'd face, but he *would* marry her.

"You should pack. If we don't leave soon, we'll be driving in the dark."

"Pack?" Fern was still absorbing the fact that he wasn't pinning all the blame for this pregnancy on her when he made a suggestion that was more of a politely worded order. Her brain emptied all over again.

He smiled faintly. "We'll stay with my grandfather until you're cleared to travel. If that means waiting until the baby comes…" He shrugged.

She felt her world dissolving and pressed her lips together, trying to keep herself in control of her own destiny. "But…" There were too many arguments rising in her to find them and put them in order of importance.

"As comfortable as this flat looks, it's not very secure. Do you even have a real bed here? Or are you pulling a mattress out of that thing?" He pointed at the sofa she perched upon.

She glanced at the blankets she folded each morning and set on the hassock before putting her bed back under these cushions. "Miss Ivy and I do it together," she murmured. "It's spring-loaded, not heavy. Just awkward."

"Well, I don't want you tripping around, rearranging furniture."

"But I have work here. Students who are counting on me."

"You left one teaching job without notice. Surely someone can step in?"

Fern had already talked to a few students about helping them over email or webcam, especially after the baby was born. The library had a modern setup and Zafir was right. Miss Ivy was retired, but she could take over until other arrangements were made.

"I'm not ready to change my whole life," she protested.

"Your whole life has already changed," he reminded her with a patronizing smile.

He was right, but she still scowled anxiously toward the small bureau where she kept her clothes. Her own photo stood upon it, showing her accepting her teaching diploma. That's who she was supposed to be: a middle grade teacher in a quiet village here in the north of England.

"I don't think you know what you're doing," she told him. Had he heard the bit about how she was illegitimate? She knew nothing about her father.

"My first marriage was arranged and we were even less acquainted than you and I. I'm already a father. I grew up the son of a sheikh and an Englishwoman. There won't be many surprises for me in any of this."

Right. His first marriage to a woman he always spoke about with reverence, according to Amineh. Did that mean he was capable of loving a spouse he acquired through an arrangement based on logic? Could he come to have feelings for her?

Worrying her lip, she glanced up to see him watching her and licked where her teeth had made her bottom lip raw, then swallowed as forbidden thoughts crept into the corners of her mind. Would they…?

The consequences of giving in to lust were bad. She was being slapped in the face with them right now.

Come on, Fern, a voice chided in her head. *How much more pregnant could you get?*

But even if he wasn't angry with her, it didn't follow that he *liked* her. While she was in love with him. What sort of future did that set up? Her pulse started to trip into a racing flight and clammy sweat broke out all over her skin. She'd never imagined she would marry anyone, especially a catch like him. This was surreal. He was going to wake up tomorrow and scream loud and long at what he'd proposed today.

He stood and glanced around. "Is there a case somewhere that I can fetch?"

"Can I…" Oh, he looked very tall and dapper and unreachable, standing over her that way. They were the worst match ever. She'd have to make him realize that before things went too far. "Can I just say that I'll come with you and we'll talk more about the marriage idea later?"

"If you want to say that, go ahead," he said dryly. "But we're marrying, Fern. As soon as I can arrange it."

"I really do think you'll regret it, when you've had time to realize what you're suggesting," she insisted.

"Your concern for me is cute. If I had an ounce of chivalry in me, I'd extend the same consideration toward you. Give you more time to talk both of us out of it. But even though I don't blame you, neither of us is going to hide from this. We made a baby. We're going to marry. Then we're going to live in Q'Amara and raise it together."

Fern ruminated in the car, aware that she was being a pushover. Did you call a woman *easy* when she couldn't seem to say no to marriage?

His already having regard for their child had moved her,

she couldn't deny it, but she was letting him take complete control of her life and she knew that was wrong.

Part of her was relieved, of course. His plan would lift some huge worries off her shoulders, like where would the money come from? But she was a fairly independent person. She'd had to be. Emotionally and financially. And the fact was, she might have got to know what he liked between the sheets, she might be certain she was in love, but in many ways, they were still strangers.

"You're sighing a lot," he remarked, gearing down to take the off ramp.

He drove with smooth confidence, not like he had anything to prove, but owning the road regardless. Late winter rain battered the roof and swished under the tires. The wipers slapped at full speed. There was no use trying to listen to music so they'd been sitting in silence since she'd made him stop to let her use the loo at a fast-food place.

"How well did you know your first wife when you married her?" she asked.

There was a pause of surprise, then in a cautious and very neutral tone, he said, "Not well."

If she wasn't mistaken, a thin, transparent, bullet-proof wall had just slid up between them. It was disconcerting and certainly didn't reassure her. It made her think she should leave things at that, but as much as she liked to avoid confrontations, this marriage idea of his needed more discussion before she could get behind it.

"How did you come to choose her? Or…how did it all work?"

He kept his gaze on the road, movements still steady and economical, but a hint of stiffness shaded his voice. "Given the situation with my parents, I knew when I took over that I would have to prove I was more Arab than English." His mouth twisted in dismay.

"The expectation that I would reject my mother and the Western half of my life did not sit well with me," he admitted with a sidelong glance. "We have our differences, but my mother is as much my family as my father. However, I knew that marrying a woman from Q'Amara, *proving* I was not given to blind passion for all things English—" another glance, this one filled with dry significance "—was necessary. Sadira was from an excellent family. Her father was known for his traditional values. Politically, the match allayed many fears that I would try to force change at the pace my father had. The fact that I thinned the foreign blood in my successor helps my approval rating and eases their acceptance of Tariq as my successor."

A small "oh" of apprehension escaped her as she computed that his second child might not be viewed so charitably.

He covered her hand and squeezed with warm strength, pressing reassurance, but also a streak of sexual awareness, through her blood.

"We'll make it work, Fern."

She stiffened in surprise at the way his light touch flooded her with giddy warmth. Should she squeeze back? She was sure that continuing to behave like a teenager in heat would only cloud things. His people expected decorum, for heaven's sake! Not some British nymphomaniac as their First Sheikha or whatever she'd be called.

"I don't see how," she protested, voice made husky by the weight of his hand on hers. "Did you have a happy marriage with your first wife even though you were strangers? Is that why you're so confident we can prevail?"

He removed his touch and draped his hand on the stick, but didn't change gears.

"She knew what was at stake," he said in a level tone. "We both went into the marriage willing to make compromises for the sake of maintaining peace within the palace and beyond it."

"See, Zafir? I can't offer you that! I'm a guarantee of conflict for you."

"My mother never once came to Q'Amara. My father didn't think it safe, but from remarks I've heard over time, her actions were taken as a snub. I am hopeful that your willingness to live there, your acceptance of our culture, will go a long way to smoothing rough edges."

"Yes, well, you have to know it's one thing to take a contract in a foreign country, quite another to adopt one as your home. Especially one so patriarchal."

"We visit my mother two or three times a year. You won't be held hostage there," he said with a twitch of impatience around his mouth. Then, somewhat defensively, he stated, "I know we're behind with women's rights, but change doesn't happen overnight. I have learned from my father's experience to take things one step at a time. And I can't be everywhere, doing all things," he added tiredly, then perked up. "But look at the work Amineh does. You could take up those same causes in Q'Amara," he urged, warming to the topic. "You're bright. A natural educator. I would like that, Fern. I would like that very much."

The suggestion stunned her. She considered working with women to ensure the health of their children. It wasn't bra burning, but it was something everyone could get behind and benefit from. Within seconds, her eager mind was leaping with excitement to get started. And it meant she could be an asset to him, not a detriment.

But the way he said it, like it had only just occurred to him, made her wonder.

"Did your first wife do that sort of thing?" she asked, already sensitive to wearing the woman's shoes.

"No," he said flatly. Something flashed in his expression, but she could only see his profile and whatever it was gone before she could identify it. "She was pregnant. Tariq was young."

I'm pregnant, she almost said. And Amineh managed a work schedule around having two children.

He must have sensed her puzzlement because he added, "As I said, she was very traditional. Not complacent, but not like Amineh, who was educated here and exposed to different ideas. Sadira wasn't interested in taking a public role."

Sitting deeper into her bucket seat, Fern let that explanation sink in. "She didn't really have time, did she? Amineh said she died of cancer."

"She did." The privacy field he'd erected swelled with thick layers.

"Did you come to love her?" she worked up the courage to ask, even though her trepidation of the answer was so strong her voice shrank.

His jaw worked as he took care to gear down and follow a curve through a gate and into a tunnel of wet, overhanging tree branches down a long graveled drive.

"Love—the passionate kind found in marriage—is a Western notion. Not something that served my father well."

Zafir is more Arab than English, remember that, Fern. Her lungs shrank and hardened, squeezing her heart. *But Amineh has love*, she wanted to argue.

The boulevard of trees ended abruptly and the estate house, gloriously regal with spiking chimneys and a staid facade, struck her in the face. It perched on the highest hillock that overlooked rolling grounds, a pond and, farther in the distance, thick green woods, all of it curtained by a fey mist of rain.

The house itself was intimidating in its sense of peerage, and consisted of ancient bricks and tall windows. The north side was coated in ivy, the south held what she thought might be a solarium. The garage was its own building with seven double doors.

Zafir followed the circular drive around a fountain then parked before the wide front stairs, clicked off the engine and turned toward her while the rain pattered loudly on the roof above them.

"Sadira is Tariq's mother. I love him with everything in me. For giving him to me, I will always have the utmost regard and respect for her. You already have the same from me, Fern."

Meeting his steady stare was hard. She was afraid he'd see the shadows of wanting more in her eyes when she'd never realized how badly she *did* want more until this moment. He expected her to tie herself to him for the rest of her life, cut off any chance of meeting the man who might love her and settle for what was, quite possibly, more than she had ever expected before today.

"I'm worried you won't respect me in the long run," she admitted. "I'm not a good match for you. I don't have a strong personality. You can, quite obviously, talk me into anything," she said with a disparaging gesture at where they were. "I don't want to be a doormat and I don't want to see your contempt as I turn into one."

He frowned, deflating her.

"That puts me in a difficult position," he growled. "If I disagree with what you just said, you'll accuse me of talking you around. Let's do this. Try me, Fern. I've seen you hold your ground. I'll keep in mind that a little defiance is a lot for you and we'll see how far we get."

She snorted and said, "Okay," then rolled her eyes at the irony of capitulating. Again.

He grinned, looking so handsome he made her catch her breath. When his gaze fixed on her mouth, her heart stopped.

A flicker behind him made her nod toward the house through the drizzle-coated window.

"Someone's coming," she told him, reaching for her handbag. Had he been thinking of kissing her? She really would be a puddle of spent willpower if he did.

"Stay there," he commanded as she started to reach for her door latch.

He pushed out of his side and said something to the man who'd rushed out with an open umbrella.

Now would be the time to push back against one of his dictates, but it was no easy task to throw herself from a vehicle these days in a fit of independence. She sat there like a lump and waited for him.

A moment later, while the young man extended his arm to cover them both with the umbrella, Zafir helped her from the car, giving her an illusion of grace as he levered her bulk with a firm but gentle hand under her elbow.

With a murmur of thanks, Zafir exchanged keys for an umbrella and escorted her inside while the servant—was he called a footman?—collected her case from the boot.

Is this it? Zafir had asked when she had only that one case and an overnight bag after completing her packing.

She had a few boxes in Miss Ivy's storage compartment in the basement. "But they're just sentimental things I wasn't ready to part with after my mother passed. Nothing I really need," she'd explained. "I was starting fresh when I took the overseas contract."

He hadn't said much to that, had only carried her things to the car while she'd said her goodbyes to Miss Ivy. Fern had lingered to assure her friend that while she didn't know if she was marrying Zafir, she had to admit that he was devoted to his baby and that meant more to her than only another child rebuffed by their father could understand. She couldn't in good conscience keep him out of her baby's life.

Somewhat reassured, Miss Ivy had repeated that she was always there for Fern and now, entering what looked more like a museum than a house, Fern wondered if it was too late to change her mind and go running back to the sofa bed with the iron bar that had dug into the middle of her back every night.

A butler greeted them. At least, that was Fern's assumption of his title when introduced to Mr. Peabody, who bowed and took her coat. He glanced at the footman as the young man entered with her case. "I'll ask Mrs. Reid to prepare a room in the guest wing—"

"Miss Davenport will stay in my suite," Zafir interrupted. "I'll take her there now. Please let my mother know we're four for dinner."

"Of course." Another bow and Mr. Peabody disappeared.

Zafir guided Fern up the right wing of the curving dual staircase to the landing where they were level with the ornate chandelier over the entranceway. So much space! It was like visiting a posh opera theater, not a home.

Their footsteps made no sound on the thick ivory carpet. They passed ancient portraits and little tables and vases and candle sconces that she had enough history education to assess as Tudor and Regency and Victorian. Old, old family heirlooms.

Zafir was out of his mind, bringing her into this.

His "suite" was essentially a town house, taking up all three floors of the southeast corner of the main house.

"My mother converted it for when my father stayed with us. After he passed, she couldn't bear to be in here so she moved back into her old rooms. Tariq has the upstairs to himself. I don't bother keeping a full staff. We eat in the main house, but there's a kitchen below along with laundry and the rest."

The rest being...an indoor pool? A bowling alley?

"And you make do with this," she murmured, pacing the lounge that could fit a dozen of Miss Ivy's little parlor.

An archway on the left led to an expansive dining room with a balcony that overlooked the *outdoor* pool, covered at the moment. The fading light through those windows was the only natural light into the lounge because, she quickly realized, the front of the apartment was dominated by the master bedroom. Peeking through *one* of the sets of French doors into his private space, she noted that he liked earth tones and modern art and tons of room to stretch. The view of fields and woods beyond the tall windows was breathtaking.

The footman left her case at the bottom of the stairs. His curious eyes glanced off her belly before he offered a quick smile. "Will that be all?"

"Thank you, James," Zafir said.

With a bow, the young man started off, pulling a buzzing mobile phone from his pocket as he went. Glancing at it as he reached the door, he turned and said, "Excuse me, sir. I'm to let you know that Ms. Calloway has arrived. Mrs. Reid will bring her up. She wants to check that the guest room is in order. Also, your mother would like to speak with you."

"Leave the door open for Vivienne, tell Mrs. Reid we're not using the guest room and please inform my mother that I'll be tied up until dinner."

James nodded and hurried off, leaving the door open.

Fern stared hard at Zafir's stony expression. Had he heard her at all in the car five minutes ago? Her nerves pulled taut with anxiety at having a confrontation, and part of her was so hot for him, she didn't even want to fight him on this, but…

"Is this a test? You just told a stranger that I'm sleeping with you without asking me first." She didn't even know if she was allowed to have sex!

He blinked as though her complaint surprised him. "It's a little late to pretend we haven't shared a bed."

"And a little early to start doing it again!"

"What do you…? It's a big bed," he said, going a little darker beneath his deeply tanned skin. "I realize we might have to wait until the baby comes, but where you sleep is not negotiable. We can't make this marriage work if you're haunting another side of the house."

Haunting. Interesting choice of words, but hardly the most pertinent factor here. "But you are expecting this to be a real marriage. With, um, sex and everything." Oh, she hated herself for blushing with anticipatory heat.

He tucked his chin and lifted his brows. "You said you weren't a good match for me, but when it comes to bed, we're inflammable."

She'd love to think that would be enough, but… "There's no guarantee that sort of thing sustains," she argued, crossing her arms. "What if it wears off?"

"Shall we see if it's still there now?" He took a step toward her.

"No." She retreated and hugged herself, trying to contain the bloom of excitement that expanded in her. She could barely think when the prospect of sex with him filled her mind.

He stopped, rooted and still, his posture aggressive, and scowled as he narrowed his sharp gaze into some kind of tractor beam that willed her toward him.

"This is what I mean, Zafir! I don't have any defenses against you, especially physically. Marriage is the biggest decision a person makes. Look where giving in to my hormones has got me so far. Do I really want the rest of my life to be decided by the simple fact that you turn me on?"

"So you don't want to sleep with me?" he demanded.

"I'd like a chance to think about it!" she cried as she finally identified which door led to the powder room and moved through it.

It was as much an escape as to use it for its intended purpose, but she didn't come to any firm conclusions until she emerged to find him talking to an attractive brunette. The woman was smiling and nodding and blinking her thick, darkened lashes with flirty awe at him.

A green monster, warty and equipped with dangerously sharp teeth, rose inside Fern. He's *mine*, she thought, and knew in that second that she was sunk. The idea of him sleeping with any other woman was abhorrent. He had said to her at the oasis that if he couldn't have her, no one else would. Well, if she *didn't* accept him, someone else would. The only way she could ensure he wasn't making love to other women would be to lie with him herself.

Such a chore, she chided herself. But there was an insecure part of her that wondered if they really were still as volatile as they'd been. She wasn't the pristine virgin he'd had eight months ago.

"Here we go," Zafir said, indicating Fern so the supermodel pivoted on her high heels and gave Fern a once-over with a sharp, critical gaze. "Fern, this is Vivienne Calloway, Amineh's stylist."

"I'm delighted to work with you. Please call me Vivienne," she said as she came forward and shook Fern's hand. Her stomach was concave and her hips were the width of a soda straw. Her shiny hair slithered with silky, shampoo-ad brilliance. Her perfect teeth practically dinged as she smiled. "May I call you Fern? Amineh and I are on first-name terms and she has instructed me to pull out all the stops for you."

"Amineh?" Fern repeated, glancing warily toward Zafir.

"I spoke with her while I was loading your things into the car."

Fern's knees weakened. Her hand was still in Vivienne's warm grip and turned into cooked asparagus. "What did she say…?"

"That you would need something to wear tonight," Zafir answered blithely. "We dress for dinner."

"She suggested the blue dress from her own wardrobe and I agree, now that I've seen you. The color will bring out your eyes. Let's try it on, see if it needs adjustment."

Minutes later, Fern was in a silver slip with a powder-blue lace sheathe over it. The sleeves were a demur three-quarter length, the collar scalloped across her plump breasts. Shoes were another matter, but Vivienne brought a bag filled with a variety of sizes and styles from her car.

"Maternity wear is so tricky, but if you feel comfortable in those, they'll do," she said about a pair of low silver pumps. "We'll have more choices when we're not worrying about swollen ankles. Now lie down and rest while I tailor that dress and set up to do your hair and makeup."

Fern did as she was told, partly out of genuine exhaustion, partly to escape what was happening to her. This morning she'd woken in Miss Ivy's flat, gone to work for a few hours, caught her regular bus and wondered if there was enough of last night's chicken to make a sandwich for lunch. In the last few hours, her entire life had spun into chaos and she needed to be still for a few minutes to let the pieces settle.

She didn't expect to sleep, but crashed hard and woke to the click of the lamp.

Vivienne smiled. "I let you sleep as long as I could. Rest is the ultimate beauty enhancer. But it's time to dress."

Fern submitted to makeup and hairpins and a fitting for a new bra, one in ice-blue lace with matching bottoms that she was thankfully allowed to change into privately. When she looked at the final result, she blinked at the stranger in the mirror.

Her eyes popped like freshly minted shillings from a face where her freckles had been downplayed with a layer of light powder. Her mouth was coated in a shiny nude gloss and her hair was gathered like an Edwardian maiden's with a pearlescent blue ribbon woven through it. She looked as modest as she usually did, but sweetly maternal and, she had to be honest, quite pretty.

When she moved into the lounge, she was both anxious and excited to see Zafir's reaction.

He wore black pants and a white shirt closed at the throat with a black bow tie, and he shrugged on a white dinner jacket as she emerged. He looked her over as he buttoned his jacket, his gaze incredibly thorough, but dispassionate and assessing.

"No?" she prompted uneasily. Behind her, Vivienne was zipping and clipping things back into bags and cases. She'd taken such care and shown such enthusiasm for the result, but maybe Fern was a lost cause.

"Honestly?" he asked.

Bracing herself, she nodded. "Yes."

"Don't cover your freckles. And I prefer your hair loose. But you look very lovely." He moved close to brush his lips against her cheek. Something flashed in his eyes as he drew back. Pride or possessiveness. Maybe both. When he showed her what he was holding, his expression shifted from a hard stubborn set to something less implacable. Appeal. "Will you wear this? Please?"

A ring.

"Oh," she breathed.

"It was my English grandmother's. My first wife wore one that belonged to my father's mother."

Another heirloom from some yesteryear when jewelers were romantic enough to set a blue sapphire in white gold and encircle it with diamonds like petals on a flower. A pair of green stones off either side played the part of leaves.

It was elegant and priceless. Fern could only stare.

"In my country, wedding rings are worn on the right. Do you mind?" He held up his palm, inviting her to place her hand in his.

"Zafir, are you sure...?"

He picked up her hand himself, but just held it as he said, "I can't see into the future any better than you can, Fern. But right now, yes, I'm sure this is what I want. I'm sure *you* are what I want. Do you want me?"

She couldn't lie. Deception wasn't ever easy for her and right now, with him standing so close and looking at her like she meant something to him, she couldn't be anything but completely honest.

"I do," she whispered, and reinforced her agreement with a shaky nod.

His breath came out in a light caress on her knuckles and he smiled with arrogant satisfaction, but what looked like relief, too. Like she'd made him happy.

His touch as he threaded the ring onto her finger and kissed her knuckle sent a thrill of joy through her. Maybe he was right. Maybe they could make it work.

CHAPTER EIGHT

ZAFIR WASN'T USED to feeling anything less than wholly confident. He wanted to take heart from Fern's willingness to accept his ring, but the way she'd talked about not having any defenses, especially physically... Did she think he would force her? Not in a million years! He hadn't pressed his first wife—

But then, he hadn't felt a need for her like he did for Fern. Was he above seducing her? Clearly not.

Her balking at agreeing to sleep with him bothered him. Not in an arrogant, entitled way. In a deeply disturbing way. Even before he'd found her and confirmed her pregnancy, he'd been unable to shake the near irresistible urge to fetch her back into his life. Sleep together. Make love to her one more time.

A storm he'd barely acknowledged had been crashing inside him for months as he fought those urges, only settling when he'd had her in the car beside him. Now a fresh turbulence kicked up, despite the flash of his grandmother's ring from the hand that gripped his arm as she steadied herself on the shiny oak floor.

She had reservations about resuming intimacy with him and he supposed he couldn't blame her. He'd promised he wouldn't cause her to lose her job or get pregnant and that vow had been thoroughly shattered. If she'd rather have a platonic marriage while she learned to trust him again, he should be prepared to accept it, but he found it wasn't something he could face easily.

Glancing pensively at her, he saw only a bundle of cascading red curls held in a blue ribbon.

"Chin up," he said, refusing to let her hang her head before his family. "Neither of us will be apologists for making a baby out of wedlock."

"More like poster children," she commented under her breath, surprising him with her levity. "I was looking at the pattern in the parquet. This house is beyond words."

It was a country cottage compared to the palace in Q'Amara, not that he said so aloud. The staff would put rat poison in his dinner if they overheard such a remark. But she did make him see things with new eyes.

"I think you'll be good for me, Fern," he told her as they arrived at the music room door. "You remind me not to take things that I value for granted." He held her gaze with a significant look.

Whether that reassured her at all, he wasn't given an opportunity to judge. Peabody opened the door to exit the room with an empty tray and stepped back as he saw them, allowing Zafir to enter with Fern.

Her grip on him tightened, betraying her nerves. Soft greens and old gold leaped at him. He took in antique furniture and silk area rugs that he did take for granted, along with the cheery fire beneath the white mantel and the green-and-gold drapes that closed out the blustery night. This was, in many ways, the happiest place of his childhood since it was where his family had been whole.

The two people waiting in tight-lipped silence weren't happy. His bringing a woman into the house was unusual. His accommodating her in his private quarters was eyebrow-raising. Her pregnancy, well, there was a reason his mother had wanted to speak to him upon his arrival. She was always the first to smell scandal and in spite of her personal history, maybe because of it, she was always the first to try smothering any flames that threatened to disgrace the family again.

His grandfather sat in his favorite wingback chair. He wore a dark suit that set off the gold chain of his pocket watch. Zafir's mother wore a long black velvet skirt and a starched white blouse. The flouncy ribbon at her throat was the only bit of softness in her elegantly aged demeanor. She had not broken when Zafir's father died. She'd hardened like carbon placed under extreme pressure.

His grandfather betrayed no surprise at seeing either of them, even though Zafir's arrival at the house had been as unannounced as his guest's.

"What is that infamous quote by that American ballplayer?" his grandfather asked rhetorically. "Something about déjà vu all over again?"

Zafir's mother snapped a look to her father and brought it round to her son, keeping it as sharp as an ice pick. "It would be nice if I could learn certain news directly from you, rather than through the servants," she stated.

"They told you I was engaged? How did they know when Fern only accepted my proposal a few minutes ago? Grandfather, Mother—my fiancée, Fern Davenport."

Zafir provided their titles, but as his mother offered her hand for a reserved handshake, she said stiffly, "William and Patricia, please," and found her Lady-of-the-Manor smile. "I see my daughter has replied to my call with a message after all. I was told she was indisposed." Her gaze slid down the dress Fern was wearing. "I remember now where I heard the name Davenport," she added condescendingly.

"Your granddaughters spoke of me?" Fern said, pink beneath the layer of powder on her skin, but earnest, which was appealing in its particular way. "I've missed them. I hope they're well?"

His mother's expression flickered with indecision, as she tried to determine if she should soften or not. "I didn't talk to them long. I was distracted, but yes, they're quite well. Taking some sort of dance lessons."

"You know the girls?" his grandfather asked. "Forgive me for not rising. Gout."

"Fern," Zafir offered as he turned a chair from its place near the fire so she could sit.

She thanked him with a smile and lowered into it, then answered his grandfather. "Amineh hired me last year to tutor the girls in English. I lived with them for about six months."

"Really, Zafir," Patricia said in an undertone meant only for him. "The governess?"

"It's a bit late for snobbery about who we make our children with, isn't it, Mother?" Zafir replied in a conversational tone loud enough to make Fern pinch her lips together.

"Are we speaking openly then?" his mother asked, metaphorically dropping her gloves. "Because I have to wonder if you did make this one."

"Don't take offense to that, Fern," Zafir said without breaking eye contact with his mother. "It's a family tradition. My grandfather said the same thing to my father."

Fern might have gasped. His mother definitely did.

His grandfather leaned forward to admit to Fern, "It's true. I did." Ice rattled in his glass as he lifted it with a palsied hand and tilted it at Zafir's mother. "All three of my girls were highly sexed. Zafir's father wasn't her first."

"No, your solicitor was," Zafir's mother declared with a very fake, very tart smile.

"We'll have a paternity test when the baby is born if

it will set your mind at ease, but I'm quite confident it's mine," Zafir said. With false geniality aimed at his mother, he added, "You'll have another grandchild. I thought you'd be delighted."

His grandfather snorted. "Heard that one before, too. I hope you're proud of yourself," he said to his daughter, raising her ire even further.

"How is this my fault?" she demanded, elegant and composed, yet indignant. "I didn't get her pregnant."

"No, but you were after Amineh about schooling the girls in English."

"*Here*. I wanted her to put them in school here. Not hire someone—" She glared at Fern.

Fern sat very still, body language braced and watchful, hands a tight knot in her lap.

Zafir was sorry to put her through this, especially when his mother was lobbing some heavy artillery and Fern was already sensitive to being blamed, but he wouldn't have the strong personality he did possess if he hadn't grown up holding his own against the ones who'd raised him.

"She did it to please you," his grandfather pointed out before Zafir could interject, indicating Fern with his half-empty glass. "This girl never would have been under his nose if you hadn't interfered."

"That's funny," Zafir said with a snort.

"It is *not*," she retorted frostily. "And even if I do bear some responsibility for her hiring someone, you ought to know better than to let an opportunist—"

"Talk to Ra'id before you decide who took advantage of whom, Mother," Zafir interrupted, leaning a hand on the back of Fern's chair. "Fern's virtue was his responsibility while she was under his roof and he failed to preserve it. He's barely speaking to me right now."

Fern looked up at Zafir, her brows tugged into an anxious crinkle. "Really? He's not upset with me for being a terrible example for his daughters?"

"Their grandmother is a terrible example for them," he stated, enjoying it. "But no, partly he's taking advantage of the chance to get back at me for all the years I was so protective of Amineh, but he knew exactly how worldly you were. He is genuinely offended with me and remorseful toward you. Expect a sincere apology when you see him next."

"That's not necessary!" she insisted, chin crinkling as she tried to hold a wobbly smile. "I'm just glad they're not cross with me. I'd love to see Amineh and the girls again."

"She's anxious to see you, too," he assured her, moving his hand so his knuckles felt the tickle of her curls as he brushed them back from her shoulder. "I should have explained when I said that we come here a few times a year, Amineh and I try to overlap our visits. If she doesn't come to us in Q'Amara first, we'll—"

"Zafir," his mother said sharply. "You are not actually marrying her. What happened to the marriage you were arranging with that troublemaker's daughter?"

"Ra'id has suggested his cousin would be a better match for the girl," Zafir said, straightening. "As a personal favor to his family, I have stepped out of the running. My real motives will be obvious after our marriage is announced," he told Fern. "But it's a very good alliance for both sides, he's closer to her age, and it still provides the girl's father some of the influence he craves. By facilitating it, I hope to defuse some of his animosity. My hope is that it will turn out well."

"You hope!" his mother repeated. "That doesn't mean it will. That doesn't mean you should marry—I'm not being a snob," she remarked to Fern. "My sister married a male nurse, of all things, so I understand that spouses come in all vocations."

"At least she married him," Zafir's grandfather said in an aside, proving that pretentiousness came in all sizes in this household.

"Well, I couldn't marry, could I?" his mother snapped with such vehemence it took the temperature to arctic levels. "Everything we worried could happen, *did*. Do I wish I could go back and marry him? *Yes!* But we'd all be dead now if I had. So no, Zafir, you may *not* marry this English woman. You won't stir it all up again and leave me sleepless here, terrified every time the telephone rings. You'll live here, Fern," she said firmly. "I realize I've said some things that might have put you off, but you're a mother. You understand our instincts to protect our children. That doesn't go away no matter how old or pigheaded they get." She tossed that last statement at Zafir. "And you've seen how private the southeast unit is. We won't be in each other's way. I would enjoy finally having one of my grandchildren so close."

Zafir half stepped so his leg was right up against Fern's chair. He had expected resistance to his marriage because Fern didn't have a pedigree dating back to Elizabeth I. Not *this*.

"I'm not here to ask permission, Mother."

"It's denied regardless." His grandfather finished the last of his drink and set it on the table with a decisive *clack*. "Your mother will be worried sick, Zafir. How can you even consider doing that to her again? And the baby? You can't put it in harm's way. Amineh's situation is different. No. Marry this girl, I agree you should do that much, but leave her here."

"No. *Don't* marry her. It makes you a target—" Patricia said, voice rising, but Zafir spoke over her, even louder.

"You two are not keeping my wife and child away from me." His hand went to Fern's shoulder. He felt her start at his touch and firmed his grip on her, dimly aware he wasn't being reassuring but snarlingly possessive. His mother's anxiety could frighten Fern off.

"We're not keeping anyone *away* from anyone," his mother said crossly. "I wish you and your sister would stop acting like your father and I were denying each other access when it was a necessary arrangement that worked—"

"It didn't work for me!" Zafir boomed so ferociously his sharp words echoed into the silence it created.

His mother went white and she looked away, chin thrust out.

Zafir realized his body was primed for a physical altercation, blood racing, muscles twitching with readiness. It wasn't just the split in his psyche that had prompted his outburst. His broken family was an old fight, but Fern and his baby were *his*.

His grandfather hitched forward on his chair, obviously finding it a struggle, but his voice was strong. "Zafir. Your father and I didn't see eye-to-eye on much, but I never doubted his love for your mother. He wanted to take her to Q'Amara with him. It wasn't safe. He had to leave her here and he couldn't even marry her. It was too much for your people to take. He had to keep her like a damned mistress. *You* were meant to be with him when he was killed. I won't let you put us through that again. She—" he pointed at Fern "—stays *here*." Then he pointed at the floor, his tone that of a man still confident in his position of power despite his physical decline.

"Do you think I would risk my wife and child if I thought that same danger existed?" Zafir demanded aggressively, but the word *love* gave him pause. Love had made his father weak enough to take up with a woman that his country had never accepted. It had weakened him in the eyes of the people he governed and had weakened him as a man, prompting him to take ridiculous chances and make bad decisions.

What was he doing if he took Fern back to Q'Amara? Was it a wise decision? Or a selfish one? Why was he so determined? Lust? Or something else? If you cared about someone, you put their interests, their *lives*, above your own.

His mother rose to pull a tissue from a box on a side table. "Was it *so* horrible to live in two places?" she challenged in a choked voice, keeping her back to them as she dabbed at her eyes.

Tortured by his inability to grasp his own motivation, Zafir did what any child did under stress. He went to his mother. Taking hold of her shoulders, he set his chin alongside her hair, sorry he'd caused her to cry, but... "If you had thought there was a chance you could have lived together, wouldn't you have tried?"

They would have, he knew they would. They had loved each other very deeply, which had formed the trade-off for the difficult decisions they'd had to make. He wasn't prepared to make those same decisions. *He needed Fern with him.* Now that he'd seen it as possible, no other option was good enough.

"Oh, I hate when you sound like him sounding like he knows he's right," she said as she brushed his hands off her shoulders and swiped impatiently at her face.

Disturbed, feeling as though he didn't quite know himself, Zafir gave her time to compose herself by moving to help his grandfather to his feet. When he offered a hand to Fern, she kept her eyes downcast.

That shook him. If she refused to come with him, he didn't know what he would do. Seduce her? Talk her around? Demand?

Leave her here after all?

Gently tilting her chin up so she had to show him the reflective silver of her eyes, he said, "I would not take you anywhere that I thought would risk your life, Fern. I hope you trust me in that."

"Childbirth notwithstanding?" she said with an ironic quirk of a smile.

He didn't laugh. Couldn't. What *had* he done to this woman?

"That was a joke," she said.

"It was a rebuke for being careless with you and I deserved it," he said, dismayed. Furious with himself. He brooded through the entire meal.

Much to Fern's relief, Zafir ended the meal by stating they would take after-dinner coffee in his suite. The minute the door was closed behind them, she asked, "Did you do that on my behalf? Do I look as exhausted as I feel?"

"*I'm* exhausted," he countered, eyeing her pensively. "Jet lag is catching up to me. But my grandfather tires easily these days and you have had a long day." His mouth twisted with self-disgust. "I'm sorry to have put you through all that."

"I had a nap earlier," she reminded him. "I'm tired, but it's more social fatigue. I feel like I was in the longest job interview of my life. Would you mind?" she asked, showing him where the zipper of the lace sheathe closed at the top of her spine.

"My grandfather liked you," Zafir said as though trying to offer a comfort.

"Who is Esme?" The old man had accidentally called Fern that for the second time right before Zafir had cut short their post-meal chatter.

"My grandmother. You don't look anything like her. She was quite short, had black hair and eyes like mine, so

I thought for a minute he'd had one too many whiskeys, but I think it's your manner that made him think of her. She was quiet and thoughtful the way you are. The rest of us are scrappers, determined to jump in ahead of everyone else and take control. She was always an influence of calm, taking time to think about things before she reacted." He released the zip on her dress and his light touch sent a ripple of pleasure through her.

"I'm not calm, I'm terrified," she admitted.

"About coming with me to Q'Amara?" He touched her shoulder, urging her to turn to face him.

"I meant in general, but…" His mother's anxiety had been contagious. The whole time she'd been answering questions about where she grew up and who she knew through Miss Ivy and when she was due, she'd been thinking about where Zafir expected her to sleep and what her future with him might hold.

A firm kick nudged her from her absorption into a light gasp and a touch on the spot where the baby was insisting more space was needed.

"Are you okay?" Zafir frowned at her belly.

She chuckled. "As far as personalities go, I think we've created another scrapper. Quite pushy," she pronounced with rueful affection, liking what he'd said about his family and how he'd intimated she had a place in it that was notable and valued.

"Can I…?" His gaze fixed on her belly and his hands came up. He hesitated as he looked to her for permission.

Her nerves jolted like an electric shock had run through her, pushing a flood of tingling warmth into her inner thighs. He hadn't even touched her!

The strength of her anticipation startled her. Her life had been fairly devoid of human contact before he had taught her how wonderful it could be. Since then, especially in the last few months, she'd discovered some people loved touching pregnant women. Strangers asked to pat her belly. Sometimes they didn't even ask, but this was different.

This was Zafir. She had been aching for his touch since forever. And it was his baby. Emotions, already amplified by pregnancy, threatened to overwhelm her.

"I— Of course," she said huskily, quivering with tension like liquid at the rim of a cup. She lifted her hands and waited.

At first he barely grazed her with splayed fingertips, like she was a soap bubble that would burst at the least pressure. The thought made her lips twitch and she covered his hands, showing him how to press firmly enough to find the baby's shape.

"That's the bum. And this is where—oh! Did you feel that? Must be a knee, right?"

He choked a breath of laughter. "Doesn't that hurt?" He explored gently where the nudge had happened.

She shrugged. "Not really. Takes me by surprise. Keeps me awake sometimes. I honestly don't think either of us will get much sleep if I—"

"Shh." Discovery of magic played across his face. "It must be so strange," he said with quiet reverence, shifting the lace on the silk of her slip as he moved his hands around the shape of her belly. "Can you even wrap your mind around it? That's our child that we made, right there. I can feel it, but I can hardly believe it. Are you scared? About the delivery?"

"Yes," she admitted, giving him a crooked, sheepish smile. "Not that I have anything to be frightened of specifically. Just apprehensive, I guess. I've read too many books on what could go wrong and keep worrying what will happen to the baby *if*. And Miss Ivy—" Wait. Would he…? "Do you want to come into the delivery room with me?"

He stopped moving his hands, but left them resting on her. His brows tugged up in surprise. He parted his lips without speaking, like he didn't know how to respond. "It didn't occur to me— Yes, I do," he asserted firmly before a rare glimmer of uncertainty entered his eyes. He searched hers. "Do you want me to?"

"I do. Very much." So much it made her head swim. Her hands found their way onto his and held him there. "I didn't even think about it until just now and…I would feel so much better if I knew you were there to make it all go well. Please come with me."

"Of course, Fern." His smile wasn't steady, but maybe that was her eyes, blurring with relief and joy. "Of course I'll be there." A shaky laugh rattled his voice and he sidled his hands up her waist to where she was more Fern than baby, his touch possessive and tender.

This was how it was supposed to be with a man when you were having his baby. She was going to burst, she was so happy right now.

"But aren't there classes or something?" he asked. "Men are pretty much useless, I suppose. Nothing to know except how to stay out of the way, but I should learn that much, shouldn't I?"

Fern laughed. "Miss Ivy was going to them with me. But didn't you go in with your wife when she had Tariq?"

He let his hands fall away, leaving an impression of coolness where his hands had been. "No. She opted for full anesthetic and caesarian section. But her specialist is world-renowned. I'll—" He pinched his lips into a frustrated line. "I'd like to call him and ensure he can take you on, if you're cleared to travel."

It was hard for him to back off a step and not tell her what he would make happen. She probably wouldn't have been able to hide her smile over how hard that was for him if she hadn't heard the greater question in his statement. He was asking if she was coming to Q'Amara.

The mere fact that he was leaving the door open for her retreat was incredibly reassuring. She genuinely didn't think he would risk her life or that of his baby and something else was niggling at her. His wife had *opted* for surgery. She wanted to know more about that and his marriage in general.

She wanted to know Zafir better.

It was not something that could happen if she was haunting a different house in another country. And she'd seen tonight how the division in his family still affected him. She couldn't bring herself to do that to him. To their child.

She nodded. "You should call him," she agreed. "If I can travel, I think it would be good to have the baby there. So there's no question of citizenship."

He nodded slowly, with more than agreement. Pride. His smile wrapped her in a blanket of approval. Cupping the side of her face, he caressed her cheek with his thumb. "This is going to work, Fern."

She hoped so. She dearly hoped so.

Zafir was ready to find his mattress.

Last night had been painful in the best possible way. Without any further debate, Fern had slipped into his bed while he was on the phone, leaving him to find her there.

It had been like Christmas morning—a tradition his mother had insisted upon despite his father's Muslim faith. Zafir had stood for a long moment admiring the ribbon of her red hair, the polka dots of her freckles, the hidden potential in her slumbering countenance.

Eventually he'd gone in search of something to wear to bed. He went naked under most things whether it was sheets, *thobe* or tuxedo so a simple pair of boxers was a struggle to locate. Then he'd dozed beside her, too aware of her to fall into a proper sleep, mind turning over possibilities while his body ached to pull her across the desert plain of sheets into the pillar of his own.

She'd been equally restless, getting up several times.

"I'm sorry I keep waking you," she'd murmured when she'd come back at one point. "Do you want me to sleep somewhere else?"

"No. I could find another bed if I wanted to." He'd rolled toward her, cursing the expanse of the mattress. "Does your back hurt?" He'd done some reading before settling in.

"No, there's just no room in this body for anything but baby anymore." She'd yawned, and added in a drowsy whisper, "I keep getting so confused. I wake up and realize you're here and think I'm at the oasis so how can I be pregnant? But it's nice to sleep with you again. I missed you."

She'd drifted off, leaving him thinking, yes. For all the ache of desire coursing through him, it was very nice to have her beside him. He'd missed her, too.

They'd then had a busy morning of appointments and arrangements. Fern was given a complete physical before an official came in to marry them in a perfunctory ceremony witnessed by his mother and grandfather.

His mother could grouse all she wanted about a proper church wedding, but the one thing his father had got right in Q'Amara's evolution was tolerance of other faiths. Zafir was often criticized for not limiting or outright censoring online content, but his mixed parentage meant neither of the two dominant faiths in his country felt threatened that he would refute one or the other.

Which is why he'd chosen a civil union rather than favoring one religious blessing over another.

They'd followed it with photographs for the press release and he'd approved his mother's preliminary guest list for a proper reception in the summer. They'd eaten in the air on the way to Q'Amara before Fern had gone to sleep in his stateroom, leaving him answering emails between fielding conversation attempts by the obstetrics nurse he'd hired to travel with them.

He had timed the release of their marriage announcement so it hit the wires just before they landed. His country's media stations were barely out of bed and no international paparazzi were among the lenses trying to get a shot of his new wife. Well veiled in the predawn light, she didn't offer much to scoop for those who'd made it to the airport in time to catch them deplane and travel to the palace.

He ought to sleep now, he knew, before the demand for interviews became too great to ignore and he was tied up for hours.

But sleep was not the reason he wanted to find his bed.

No, after the brief research on his tablet last night, he'd lain awake with a need for confirmation burning a hole in his mind. He'd waited through Fern's exam with barely controlled impatience, was heartened to hear her pronounced in excellent health and well enough to travel with sensible precautions, and then Dr. Underhill had thankfully been ahead of him.

"And since I expect any groom in your situation would want to know, Zafir, I'll save you the trouble of asking. Fern, so long as you feel comfortable making love, it should be perfectly safe to do so."

She'd blushed crimson, of course. Zafir had deflected the conversation to boring topics about transferring her file to the specialist he'd contacted to take her in Q'Amara. He hadn't said a thing about Underhill's remark afterward.

But when they'd kissed to seal their marriage, he'd quested for a response and she'd opened as beautifully as desert flowers to rain. He had been quaking inside with wanting her ever since, like a volcano threatening to crack under the pressure of burning lava rising within it.

If he could have locked out the world and seduced her, he would have. But even though he shouldn't ignore the interview requests, there was one task, one person, he absolutely could not disregard.

"Where is she?" Tariq asked as he charged into Zafir's private apartment and looked around the empty lounge.

Zafir had left Fern here, suggesting she put her feet up while he fetched Tariq. He'd had quite the father-son chat with the boy before they'd circled back along the second-floor landing to Zafir's rooms.

The drawback to having an exceedingly mature and intelligent child, Zafir was learning, was the inability to pull any wool over the boy's sharp brown gaze, even when it meant reflecting a less than admirable light on himself.

You told me before that we were born into families of influence and should never misuse that. Did Miss Davenport know that she didn't have to be nice to you in that way, if she didn't want to be?

I believe she did know that, yes, Zafir had claimed, even while a part of him still squirmed under the knowledge that his sophistication and experience well surpassed hers. He might not have coerced her, but he'd taken brazen advantage of her artless joy in discovering passion for the first time.

And was going mad with wanting to do it again.

While she was acting very quiet. His one query, when he'd seen her turning his grandmother's ring around on her finger and asked if she was all right, had been met with a rueful smile. "As you pointed out last night, I like time to consider things and haven't really had a chance to sort through all this. Yesterday I was going to rent a flat around the corner from Miss Ivy and raise this baby alone. Not everyone operates at light speed the way you do," she'd teased lightly.

Which he didn't think had been meant as a warning that he should put the brakes on his libido, but he'd taken it as such. The guilt he was carrying over thrusting her into this new life was enough to instill some worry in him when they arrived in his rooms and she wasn't there. Amineh had been anxious to have a webcam conversation, but Fern wasn't in his adjoining office at his desk or even in the small powder room off that.

His massive bedroom, which anyone could get lost in, was empty. She wasn't behind any of the marble colonnades, wasn't in the vast canopied bed, hadn't entered the dressing room, wasn't sitting in the reading alcove and hadn't walked into his small sunken library to peruse his antique books. The sauna, not recommended in her condition, was empty, as was the bathing pool and the grotto shower with the faux waterfall. She hadn't walked out to his private balcony or followed the stairs down to the pool, either.

Disquiet began to creep into his psyche as he called for her and she didn't answer. Vaguely he was aware of Tariq calling for Miss Davenport as he ran from corner to corner, but Zafir was far more concerned about her condition than maiden names versus married.

"She probably went to her room in the harem," Tariq said with snap of his fingers, chuckling as if they should have guessed that first.

Tariq opened doors that Zafir used so seldom he'd forgotten they were there. A piece of modern art sat in the alcove before them, half blocking the ornate wooden panels, but Zafir's mother had never lived in this palace and Tariq's mother had certainly never come through them.

About once a year, Tariq grew curious enough to wander through them and staff cleaned all nooks and crannies of the palace regularly, but otherwise no one entered this wing.

Pushing through with his son, Zafir feared he had the answer to Fern's level of comfort with lovemaking if she'd taken herself into this private domain.

The passage from the sheikh's quarters was short and dim, lit only by narrow slits in the door where it terminated onto a balcony that extended in a circle around the courtyard below, not unlike the main entranceway to the palace.

Unlike the front foyer, it looked down on a communal bath sunk into the lower floor. A glass dome in the roof allowed sunlight to pour onto the tropical plants that were mostly self-sustaining, provided he kept the pool filled and the fountain running. In the four corners, antique gilded cages hung silent, awaiting exotic birds.

Doors led off the surrounding walls into luxurious accommodation reserved for the women in the ruling family: daughters, sisters, mothers. Wives.

Zafir did not find his wife in the opulent suite closest to the shortcut to his rooms, the apartment reserved for Wife Number One. She answered Tariq's call and stepped out to wave from the furthest room, the one traditionally used by the groom's mother. *She* didn't need to sleep in close proximity to the sheikh.

Sadira had chosen and modernized that distant apartment, Zafir had seen after her death, adding a computer desk and a television console along with a contemporary queen-sized bed. The other rooms still contained the sumptuous, pillow-covered mattresses and silk wall hangings that had been refurbished and replaced for their marriage party eleven years ago. Was it significant that Fern had gravitated to Sadira's room?

She didn't look at him as she came toward them. A wide smile for Tariq brightened her face.

Vivienne was not being shy about spending his money on outfitting his pregnant bride, and was doing so very prettily. Fern wore the dress in a silvery moss color that she'd flown it, but her yellow cardigan, abaya and veils were gone. Her low heels clicked on the marble and even though she wasn't as willowy as when he'd first seen her, and her bump sat high and prominent, the rest of her was so curvy his mouth watered. Her loose hair bounced and shimmied. As she moved into a beam of sunlight, it caught glints of gold and auburn, producing a halo effect, making Zafir catch his breath at how utterly stunning she was.

"Tariq! It's so nice to see you." Her genuine warmth wasn't even for him, but filled Zafir with gladness.

Tariq canted his head at her. "You look...different."

"I'm sure I do," Fern said, cutting a glance at Zafir that sent him a private message. He hadn't been aware of a desire to become one of those couples who read each other's minds, but he liked the sense they were.

"Has your father talked to you about, um, why I'm here?" she asked, one hand resting with light significance on her belly.

"Yes. And I wanted to know, do you expect me to call you *Mama*?" Tariq asked in his forthright manner. He crossed his arms and hitched his hip in a way that Zafir recognized was his own stance when he had already made up his mind about something, but had to suffer through propriety before he could get to the bottom of things.

Fern's expression blanked. "Oh. I hadn't..."

"Yes," Zafir interrupted firmly.

He had thought he'd covered everything with Tariq and leave it to his son to ferret out a fine point, but Zafir found himself loving the idea of Tariq using the title. Fern, at least, would live up to the designation. She already valued Tariq for everything he was.

Fern's expression flickered and her smile was vaguely apologetic toward Zafir before she returned her attention to Tariq.

No. A cold hand clutched around Zafir's heart and his pride began to tear down the middle as he realized Fern was going to contradict him. She would *not* reject his son.

"I would be honored to know you thought of me as your mother, Tariq," she said with quiet sincerity, and he gave himself a mental shake. Of course she wouldn't reject the boy. "If your father would like you to introduce me as your mother and call me that in public, then please do. But it would mean more to me if, in private, it was something you chose to do. If…" Fern sent another contrite glance toward him that, Zafir realized, was an apology for challenging his dictate. "If your father doesn't mind, I'd prefer that you think about it and decide on your own if you'd like to address me as Mother. Until you're certain, perhaps you could call me Fern?"

And she thought she didn't know how to get her way, Zafir thought with a quirk of private humor.

"You make a good point," Zafir allowed, so profoundly relieved it was easy to be magnanimous. He wasn't used to being gainsaid, but now was as good a time as any to demonstrate to both of them that he would always be willing to take Fern's opinions into account. "Fern it is, unless you feel differently," he said to Tariq.

"That's not what I meant," Tariq said with an exasperated roll of his eyes. "I meant do I have to say *Mama*. It's so babyish. I'd rather call you *Mother*. I can't call you by your name. That would be too confusing for my little brother or sister. And disrespectful."

"Yes, I suppose it would be," Fern said, pinching her

lips together in a poor attempt to suppress a laugh. "Then yes. I would be delighted if you'd call me Mother. If you're sure."

"I'm sure," Tariq said with offhand confidence. "I don't remember my mother and I like you quite a bit. I was very disappointed when I visited my cousins and you weren't there," he declared with a pointed look. Then he transferred his attention to Zafir. "May I call my cousins and tell them Miss Davenport is my mother now?"

"You may text your uncle and ask when would be a good time to have that conversation," he said. "Then you should get back to class."

"Will you take over my lessons?" he asked, turning back to Fern.

"I think I will be busy with the baby very soon, but I will always take an interest in your studies. Please ask your tutor if I could sit in sometimes, particularly for language or history, so I can learn, too."

Tariq nodded and started toward the wide archway of the main passage back to the palace. He checked himself and came back to give Fern's expanded waist a befuddled search, arms half-raised for an embrace.

"Oh, um—" Fern bent awkwardly, accepting Zafir's quick grasp of her hand so she didn't lose her balance. Tariq's arms went around her neck and he landed a quick kiss on her cheek. She closed her eyes, mouth pressing into a smile of deeply touched emotion.

"I'm really happy you're my mother," Tariq said, making Zafir's heart swell with pride. "My cousins will be so jealous," he added with an impish grin and raced off.

"Oh," Fern said, placing a hand over her heart. "I didn't expect that."

"The kiss or the part where he treated us like half-wits?"

She laughed, glanced at the marble floor and tucked her

hair behind her ear. "The part where he made me feel like we're a family. I never had that. It means a lot."

The glitter of happy tears on her lashes filled him with the impulse to cradle her close. Sex? Yes, he wanted to fondle and caress, push into her and know the exquisite clasp of her again and again, but this desire was more than that. He wanted to feel her against him, smell her hair, bring her into his life as much as his home.

How had she come to mean so much to him when he'd only known her a little over a week last year and not even two full days in the last forty-eight hours?

She caught his eye, read something in his face that made her bashfully turn away and move to the low wall of the balcony, where she followed the curve of the nearest staircase with her eyes, leaning to study the benches and broad-leafed plants surrounding the pool.

"This place is incredible. Can you imagine what it was like— When was it built?"

"Five hundred years ago. And yes. As a teen I stood in this empty wing more than once and fantasized about exactly how incredible it must have been." He could still manifest the pictures he'd created in his mind: the abundance of naked breasts and bottoms, the mysterious configuration of a woman's body that he'd only barely understood, yet longed for the authority to command for further study.

She giggled as though reading his thoughts.

He moved closer. "But my days of valuing quantity over quality are gone," he assured her.

She blushed and retreated toward the stairs. "Are you sure? There are an awful lot of rooms here, looking ready to be filled by women of every shape and size."

"Is that why are you're in here?" he asked, moving to descend beside her, one hand clasping her elbow in case she lost her footing on the worn, slippery steps. "Are you checking up on me? Ensuring I'm not hiding anyone?" Or scoping out a residence for herself? His muscles hardened with tension.

Culpability flashed in her eyes. "I didn't realize where I was going when I started snooping. But isn't this where I'm supposed to be? Why are *you* here? Isn't it forbidden? That's what *harem* means, doesn't it?"

"Most Westerners think the word means *brothel*." He liked the slant of her smile. If he wasn't mistaken, she was flirting with him, but very shyly. Because she had so little experience with it, he supposed. He probably volleyed back a little too hard when he stated arrogantly, "I'm the sheikh. Nothing in this palace is forbidden to me."

She blushed, no match for his suggestive tone.

"These rooms are for the children?" she asked, peering into an alcove with sleeping benches around three sides. It only had a curtain, not a door.

"The children of wives—yes, plural," he confirmed at her look, "stayed with their mothers upstairs. Girls moved into their own space as rooms became available. Boys left the harem around six or seven. I moved Tariq when his mother died, since there was only his nanny to keep him from falling in the pool in here."

"Then all these little rooms were for servants?" she asked.

"Concubines and eunuchs," he explained, thinking with affectionate amusement, *so naive.*

"Oh. Of course." Her cheeks pinkened. Her expression grew more speculative as she peered into the spare accommodations with new eyes, making her way back toward the corner below where they'd come in. "This one's quite spacious," she remarked, stepping into the biggest room on the ground floor.

"Reserved for the sultan's favorite. You'll notice that aside from the Number One Wife, she has the shortest distance to walk to be with him." He pointed to where the stairs ended near the passageway to his chamber. "And all who visited him had to pass the wife's door."

"Politics are not a modern invention, are they?" she remarked, moving deeper into the concubine's lair. "She had air-conditioning," she said with surprise, studying the window of latticed marble that stood behind a waterfall that ran in his front courtyard. Glittering light bounced off the gold plate behind him to brighten this space more than the other rooms.

"One resident of this room was so prized, the most trusted eunuch slept beside her so she wouldn't be murdered by the other women." He stalked closer to her, fully sympathetic to his ancestor's beguilement.

Something wistful passed over her face. Her lashes fluttered as she realized how close he was. She tried to make her retreat look casual, but that's what her quarter turn and step away was.

He'd been chasing her around the harem long enough.

"Fern," he said quietly, keeping her from walking out of the room altogether. "We should talk about what the doctor said. About making love."

She stopped, but didn't turn. Her hands moved to clench together and her upper arms stained with an extensive blush. "Do you want to?"

A sudden pang of juvenile fear hit him. He didn't want to admit to his feelings before she did. He might be staring down his first marriage all over again. But if trust was an issue, the only way to gain hers was by being completely honest.

"Do I want to talk? Or make love? I'm prepared to wait until after the baby, if you're not up to it, but yes. I would like to make love to you."

"Even though I'm fat?"

"You're not fat. You're beautiful," he said with sincerity that bordered on reverence, moving closer. "Is that why you're hesitating? You're feeling self-conscious?"

"Yes," she said in a small, overwrought voice. "And because feeling this way seems so brazen in my condition."

A laugh of relief started to rise in him, but was knocked back into his throat by her next words.

"And so sinful if it's just lust."

CHAPTER NINE

"NOT THAT I expect you to love me," Fern hurried to add, afraid to turn and see how he was taking what she'd accidentally blurted.

But it was hard to say those words when it might be true that she didn't *expect* his love, but she yearned for it. As she'd turned his grandmother's ring on her finger in the car on the way here, taking in the way her own life had revolved into something completely unexpected, she'd realized there was only one reason she would allow it to: *love.*

She loved him so much. It wasn't a surprise. She'd known she did, but somehow she'd convinced herself it wouldn't sustain. Like such an intense feeling could wear off. It hadn't. She was carrying his baby and had held him right in the space between her heart and their child's the entire time she'd been apart from him. Her love had grown with each passing day, just as their baby did.

"Fern."

She could hardly bear the careful way he said it, like he was treading into very delicate territory.

"It's okay," she insisted, telling herself it was. "We barely know each other. When have we had time to really talk?" They'd been too busy trying to bite back their cries of pleasure. She covered where her cheeks ached, they went so ruddy and hot. "And we're married now, so it's not really a sin to feel this animal attraction, but is it enough? Was it enough for you and your wife?"

"*You* are my wife," he said forcefully. Then his chest expanded as he drew in a long, deep inhale, his expression closing her out. He indicated the door and the stairs that began right outside them.

Fern deflated as she climbed alongside him, sorry she'd brought up his first wife when it was so obviously a sore subject. Warm feelings would never grow between them if she alienated him.

Rather than open the door to the passage to his bedroom, however, he touched her elbow to draw her into the quarters closest to it.

"This is where Sadira should have slept if not with me."

Fern had glanced in here when she began her explore. She'd been taken with the round bed and its red quilted headboard and silk canopy that reminded her of their tent in the oasis. The suite had a beautiful modern bathroom along with a sitting room of Ottoman furniture and a private balcony. It was screened even though it only looked over Zafir's private courtyard and pool. She supposed the small room off the side would have been used for a nursery.

"I said the other day that because she gave me Tariq, I would never speak a bad word about Sadira. I meant that." He glanced sideways at her while he stood in the door and looked diagonally across the harem to Sadira's old rooms.

Despite his *thobe* and *gutra* and constant air of command, she sensed a kind of despondency in him. Powerlessness.

"She allowed her father to talk her into marrying me for the good of the country. I thought she felt as I did. That it was an advantageous match and that we had enough respect and liking to form the foundation of a strong relationship."

"I feel like you and I have that," she felt compelled to say, instantly concerned. "Don't you?"

His expression flickered across to her with fierce pride. "We have a hell of a lot more than she and I did. One of those things…" His gaze fell to the floor before he turned to face her. His gaze brooked no hesitations or prevarications. "Fern, does it bother you that I'm only half-English?"

Taken aback, she could only say, "No! Of course not. I barely give it any thought." He was Zafir, so sexy and striking she walked around dumbfounded that he'd ever looked twice at her. "It's only something I worry about from the side of, you know, the politics. Those things your mother worries about. Obviously it would be nice if the whole world could get over bias and never exclude someone for skin color or other superficial reasons. I kind of wish *I* wasn't English. If I was Arab, I could help you instead of being a problem."

"Don't wish yourself something you're not," he commanded with a twitch of cynicism. "Especially when you can't change the circumstances of your birth any more than I can. I couldn't remove the English part of me and Sadira had no use for it. In fact, I have come to believe, she felt soiled by having anything to do with me."

"What? No!" Fern denied.

He cast her a look that was both disparaging of her naiveté and deeply shadowed by old hurt.

"You really think so?" she asked softly. Cautiously.

He ran a hand down his face. His reluctance to confide was plain in the time it took him to form a response.

"She refused to sleep with me. Barely spoke to me. After she gave me Tariq, she kept to her wing of the palace and, I have come to fear, left her cancer undiagnosed because she saw it as her only escape."

"That's— No! But you have divorce here. Don't you?"

"She wouldn't have asked. Divorced women are looked down on as having done something wrong. And she'd already lowered herself by marrying me."

"How could she think like that?!" Fern couldn't even comprehend such a thing.

"Because of what I was. Illegitimate with tainted blood. Birthing Tariq was her duty and she fulfilled it, but when I say she gave him to me, I mean it. It was like he had contaminated her. She didn't breastfeed him, didn't care for him. I changed him and gave him his bottles along with the nanny."

She found herself shaking her head, the new mother in her feeling the cleave in her heart at the thought of anyone rejecting a helpless infant. "Amineh said you always talk about her like you loved her—"

"Amineh has no idea. No one does," he said with a snap of impatience. "Do you think I want Tariq to know his mother felt nothing toward him? Reviled him as much as she was repulsed by me?"

Fern's heart broke for the boy and the man. "Oh, Zafir. I'll never breathe a word to him, I swear." She would, in fact, do everything in her power to be the mother Tariq should have had. "But I can't believe anyone would look down on either of you for anything, especially something you couldn't help!"

He said nothing, only stared back into the harem, jaw pulsing with tension, brooding.

"So you didn't even try for more children? You love Tariq so much. I can't imagine you not wanting more."

He choked out a laugh, following it with a pained pinch of the bridge of his nose.

"I couldn't bring myself to try. Our wedding night— It was awkward, obviously. We didn't know each other. She was a virgin. I thought she was just bashful. I did everything I could to make it nice for her. I stopped more than once, aware she wasn't responding, but she insisted…"

He dropped his hands to his sides and closed them into fists, swallowed, his mouth a line of disgust. "I thought the second time might be better, but I felt like some kind of monster. It was just wrong. I wound up leaving before we were even naked. I couldn't work out where I'd gone wrong. I carried that. I agonized for weeks. Just when I found the nerve to talk to her about it, she turned up pregnant and made it clear there was no need for me to touch her again. She delivered a boy and, aside from one night when Tariq went into hospital with a bad fever, never offered herself to me again."

"What do you mean. She actually came to you…? What did you say?"

"I asked her if she wanted another child. She said no, and I said I hoped he would be fine. He was."

"She sounds so mean," Fern breathed, hurting for him. Here were the shades of suffering she'd seen in Amineh that she'd thought Zafir too strong to feel, but of course he felt it. He was just better at hiding it.

"I don't think she was capable of sexual feelings for me. There is a lot of prejudice in this world and I was subjected to it from both sides of my life. I know what it looks like and that's what it was. She was pressured to marry me for my position and her father's political gain. She saw herself as a martyr."

"Zafir, I'm so sorry." She went across to him, setting a light hand on his arm. "I can't believe anyone would not see what a remarkable man you are and feel privileged to be near you."

His face spasmed with emotion. Hooking his arm around her, he pulled her in close, one hand crushing into her hair as he pressed his mouth to her temple for a long moment.

She closed her eyes, overcome at the poignant sweetness of his embrace, for once not sexual, but emotional. It felt healing. Loving.

But the effects of his proximity were there, too. She was aware of his torso beneath the familiar, thin fabric of his *thobe*, the scent of cotton and man, the humid air and the musical tinkle of the water below. It all pulled her into the sensual spell that was Zafir. Her blood began to heat and her skin prickled into receptiveness.

Self-conscious at her instant response, she started to draw away.

"Don't," he murmured and made her tilt her head to look up at him. "Given everything I've just told you, you must realize how important it is to me that you feel physical desire for me. Don't hide it from me. Even if all you feel is lust, Fern, I'm glad it's there."

She struggled to hold his gaze, certain her true feelings were painted all over her face. He was too astute and experienced not to see the signs.

"It's love," she whispered, feeling worse than naked. Like her soul was exposed. The agony of having no defenses left against him at all twined through her voice. "I think it happened at the oasis. That's why I was so afraid to tell you about the baby. I couldn't bear for you to hate me when you'd seemed to like me a little—"

"A lot," he amended, cupping her face in two hands. "Ah, Fern." His face spasmed with great pain. "I fell in love, too. And I couldn't admit it even to myself. Not when it made me just like my father."

"I'm s—"

He set his thumb across her lips, stilling them. "*I'm* sorry that I wasted months when we could have been together. I thought I should be able to control my feelings, especially if it was only lust, but I couldn't. I *can't*. You're everything I want, the only woman I think about."

"Oh, Zafir…" She went up on tiptoes, trying to kiss him.

He groaned, hands closing into her hair as his mouth landed on hers, rough and hot.

He gentled immediately, groaning again, but didn't release her. With a growl of apology and frustration, he tenderly ravaged her mouth.

She closed her eyes, falling apart at the sweetness of having his kiss again. His arm came around her back to haul her in. Her hands closed on his *thobe*, grasping and trying to pull him into her. She couldn't get close enough. Silly bump in the way!

He moved them deeper into the room, kicking the door shut with a slam. As he pivoted to sit on the padded love seat, he dragged her onto his lap, knees on either sides of his thighs.

"Okay?" he murmured between consuming bites of her mouth, his hands riding her skirt up her thighs and then cupping her bottom proprietarily, fingering under the lacy edges of her undies.

She braced her forearms on his shoulders, kissing and kissing him. Running fingers up the back of his neck into his hair. Knocking his *gutra* askew. Reuniting. "I'm too heavy on you," she gasped, but couldn't make herself pull away. His hands wouldn't let her.

He laughed, using his nose to nudge her chin up so he could kiss her neck. He'd done that sort of thing in the tent at the oasis, told her without words what he wanted. Her throat, her collarbone, her breast. She scraped her hair back and away, offering. She told him with the angle of her body where she wanted his nibbling kisses, and sighed when he found the exact spot that melted her into heaven.

She ignited in his arms. Absolutely burst with the thrill of feeling him, smelling him, returning to this amazing place where touching and kissing and caressing was perfect and right and necessary. Where it was an expression of more than sexual attraction. *Love*.

Trying to wriggle closer, she scraped at his back, demanding the *thobe* come off, but he was sitting on it. He tried to set her on her feet and lift her dress at the same time.

"No, I'll be too self-conscious," she protested. "The lights…I just wanted to see and kiss you…" She slid to her knees on the area rug and pushed at his *thobe*, exposing his legs, running her hands up the rough hairs on his thighs.

With a savage noise, he stood long enough to pull it off and away, then sat and tried to bring her back up onto him, but she stayed on the floor and ran her fingers to the tops of his thighs, staring.

"I've never seen you," she murmured, sending him a shy look before letting her enraptured gaze fall back onto his naked, aroused flesh. He felt so familiar in her hands yet looked darker and more imposing than she'd pictured.

He swore, but let his hand fall to the armrest. The other one gripped the backrest behind him. "Look then. But I'll want to do the same and then are we really doing this? Because I love you and I want to show you how much."

She stroked him, coming up on her knees to lean forward and breathe across his taut skin. She looked up, almost asking for permission.

His eyes narrowed, intense as the blue-green at the center of a flame.

Smiling with a woman's wicked delight at having mastery over her man, she drew him into her mouth

He hissed and threw back his head, arched to press deeper against the swirling caress of her tongue. "I won't last," he said through his teeth.

She gave him an approving hum.

He held out, though, making sounds of deep torture while he grew harder than titanium under her ministrations. Her inner being soared with confidence at knowing he liked this, but more than that, she loved knowing it meant something to him that she wanted to give him pleasure. She expressed her love this way, openly and without reserve.

"I'm watching you," he told her in a voice that tightened her skin. "I've only felt you do that in the dark, but you're loving this, aren't you?"

She let her smiling eyes meet his, allowing him to see how much she enjoyed giving him physical pleasure.

He was flushed and fierce, his possessive gaze barbaric, but his caress on her cheek was tender as he made her stop. "Are you comfortable? Kneeling there like that?"

"I…yes," she said dazedly. "I don't want to stop."

His mouth widened in a feral smile. "Good. Neither do I. Stay where you are."

He rose, but set a hand on her shoulder when she would have pushed up on her knees.

"No, keep your elbows on the cushion." He lowered behind her and ran his hands under her skirt, bunching it until it sat under her breasts. Then he slid her knickers down her thighs.

"You want… Like this?" she asked, staring with scandalized eyes at the impression he'd left on the cushion between her clenching hands. "Maybe if the lights were off—" she protested.

"Lift your knee, *ya amar*." Her underpants were whisked away. His hand stroked her naked thigh and smoothed over the curve of her buttock. "Freckles everywhere," he chuckled softly. "I feared I would never know for sure. Are you as aroused as I am?"

They both gasped as he caressed between her thighs

where she was slippery and aching. She dropped her face into the cushion, stifling her moan of yearning.

"No." He continued to stroke her while he tangled his free hand in her hair, tugging just hard enough to pick up her head. "Let me hear you. We don't have to bite our lips anymore."

"Someone will come."

"We both will," he assured her smokily.

"It's too much," she whispered, growing taut all over as her climax approached.

"I never told you how good it was that night," he said as he shifted to lean over her. His naked body brushed the exposed skin at the backs of her legs, her bottom and the small of her back. He rubbed his shaft against her sex in a way that was deliciously familiar and not enough. Not anymore. Not now she knew how it felt to have that thick pressure inside her. "You took me apart with your heat and tightness. You're so wet for me again. You make me insane with desire, Fern."

"Don't tease, Zafir," she begged. "Please."

He was shaking as he entered her, passion barely restrained.

She cried out, pressing back to make it happen faster. Deeper. She was shattering and he was barely touching her, sliding his hand around to caress her as he made gentle, shallow thrusts.

He pinned her right on the cusp of climax and held her there. She arched, letting her moans of enjoyment fill the room, clutched in a storm of such magnificence she could only shudder and release ragged cries of joy. It was intense, her orgasm so close that when he decided they were ready, it arrived, swift and powerful. She feared she wouldn't survive it, but didn't care, crying out with abandoned ecstasy.

Dimly she was aware of him holding himself tight and

deep, biting through her dress at her shoulder. His fist covered hers on the cushion and crushed her hand as he convulsed, bathing her in heat, inside and out. They were like a star exploding, so perfectly attuned they were one being melded soul to soul as the waves of climax overtook and drowned them, taking a long time to recede and let them come up for air.

His body branded her where his damp skin adhered to hers. She became aware of him braced over her, still shaking. His heart was pounding against her back. Her own pulse was trying to find a resting level along with her lungs. She remembered what they'd sounded like, how guttural his shout had been over her abundance of ragged cries.

She blushed.

He chuckled and kissed the back of her neck, then stroked her hair off the side of her face with a trembling hand. He touched his lips to the side of her face. "Okay?"

"Just trying not to die of embarrassment. That was rather…" She didn't have words.

"It was," he agreed with a nuzzle of her ear. "Worth waiting for."

She turned her hand under his, wanting to link her fingers with his, but he picked up her hand and kissed the backs of her knuckles before carefully withdrawing.

She settled onto her hip, still trembling, not sure where to look as she attempted to regain her modesty, trying to tug her dress into place and not reveal that as satisfied as she was, she was also still aroused and responsive.

He leaned back on his hand, his other wrist propped on his bent knee. He ran his gaze over her, possessive and impenitent. He was gorgeous. Sexy and comfortable in his nudity. The light gilded his skin to warm polished oak. The way his mouth relaxed in a smile of smugness and his eyelids blinked with heavy satisfaction sent a ripple of warm delight through her.

"You look like a sultan who just enjoyed his concubine," she teased, pleased that she felt confident enough to say it, even though she couldn't help primly tugging her dress into place under her bum and down her thighs.

"Someday I'll be a duke," he said, leaning forward to run his hand up her leg and under her skirt. "One who compromised the governess. I'm starting to think I'll have a harem after all, full of intriguing women who all look like you."

She leaned forward to steal a kiss, but wrinkled her nose at him. "Don't remind me. Your abundance of titles intimidates me."

"Anytime you're daunted by me or any part of this life I've dragged you into, I want you to remember what you do to me. I'm utterly at your mercy. In lust and so deeply in love…" They kissed, tenderly and lingeringly.

"And it's not sinful."

"Not in the least. We're blessed…"

EPILOGUE

Two and a half years later

ZAFIR'S STRONG ARM hooked around her and dragged her from sitting on the edge of the mattress, where she was debating between two bathing suits, to half-under his powerful body.

"What are you doing?" she scolded in a whisper, as if she didn't know. "It's broad daylight."

"Freckle inspection," he whispered back, beginning to unbutton her shirt.

She giggled and combed her fingertips against the beard scuffing his cheek, thinking of the reason he'd given her when she'd asked once why he was so entranced with her spots.

They remind me that there's no clean line between my English and my Arab halves. I'm an aggregate of both, sifted together into one man.

She'd melted, loving him all the more when he made her feel like she was the absolute most right woman for him.

As he trailed kisses between her breasts and she crooked her knee against his hip, already warming with delicious slithers of arousal, she blinked at the tent ceiling above and marveled at the life she had, wondering how she'd come to deserve it.

He lifted his head to give her a puzzled look. "Did you

go somewhere? Because making babies takes two, you know."

She smiled, always amazed at how attuned he was to her. "Just having a moment of awe that we ever met. Here of all places. We could have met in England, but no, my soul mate was in a protected reserve that only a few select people are allowed to visit."

"I like to think I would have found you no matter where you were," he said, opening her top to admire her bare breasts. "But I'm glad it was here. Do you know when I think it happened for me? When I was such an ass to you and you were only trying to help that girl. I felt like the lowest form of life. Sick with guilt. Couldn't sleep."

"So you came to my tent, you wicked sheikh." And the girl was fine. She'd just been here with the tribe for five days and they'd all left a few hours ago. Fern's challenge now was figuring out how to encourage girls her age to pursue their education rather than marrying before they were out of their teens. And carefully, because the Bedouins had been instrumental in her acceptance by the rest of Q'Amara. She didn't want to offend them.

Speaking of offended, Zafir was giving her a pointed look. She would have to think about work another time.

"You would have gone away that night, but I didn't have it in me to let you," she recalled, sidling her hand up the sleeve of his *thobe* so she could shape his bare shoulder.

He shifted to settle over her more purposefully. "I like to think I would have left, but I'm glad you didn't test me." He obeyed the urging in her touch to lower his head and kiss her properly.

She had to stifle a moan, it was so good.

"There she is," he said with heated approval, as he cupped her breast and thumbed her nipple, inciting delicious tension in her belly.

They were in perfect synchronicity now. She hooked her calf across his lower back and lifted into him—

The boys' voices approached. "Mother, are you in there?" Tariq called.

Zafir drew back with a beleaguered sigh, expression ruefully disgruntled. "Excellent timing, as always."

She snickered and sat up to quickly button her shirt, cheeks hot as she called, "Yes, we're here, Tariq. What do you need?"

"Ahmed wants you." A shadow loomed against the front of the tent and separated as their two-year-old son slid off their twelve-year-old's back. Little hands made indents on the nylon as Ahmed's stern little voice said, "Mama. Come."

"I'm coming," she assured him, wrinkling her nose at her husband as she pushed off their low bed to open the front of the tent.

"Baba!" Ahmad said as he spied Zafir, running right past Fern to scramble onto the bed and tackle his father. He looked just like Tariq except for having Zafir's green eyes and what everyone agreed was Fern's pert mouth.

"Oh, yes, I can see it was me he was anxious to see," she said, sharing a grin with Tariq. He was approaching the age where his shoulders were filling out and a light shadow stood on his upper lip, making her so proud of the man he was growing into, yet so wistful at how quickly he was growing up.

"He and Sadiq were fighting over the orange shovel again," Tariq said with a long-suffering shake of his head. "He was angry when I tried to give him the red one. Started looking for you and wasn't happy when he realized you weren't still there."

The toddler cousins gravitated to each other like puppies in a pack, but scrapped for the sake of it, Fern sometimes thought. "Do you want to leave him here?" she asked.

"No, I'll wait until he's ready to come play again." He moved to hitch his hip onto the foot of the mattress, laughing when Ahmed rose from vanquishing Zafir to growl and attack him. Tariq caught his little brother and pretended to be overcome, falling onto his back on the mattress beside Zafir.

A wrestling match ensued, one Fern stayed out of as the two boys took on their father, making Zafir laugh so hard he weakened long enough for them to nearly overpower him.

"You could help," Zafir scolded her in the middle of it, but she only shook her head, chuckling at his situation.

"I'm Switzerland. I don't take sides," she claimed, and it was true. She loved them all equally, each for the wonderful person he was.

When they tired and settled, Tariq held out his arms to his little brother. "Should we go find Sadiq?"

Ahmed nodded and Tariq sat up, offering his back. Ahmed clambered onto him, pudgy arms closing around Tariq's neck. He bounced, and urged, "Go Sadiq. Go!"

"I'm glad you're having fun with him, but you don't have to spend all your time minding him," Fern said, giving in to her mother's need to smooth Tariq's hair as he came even with her. "It's your vacation, too. I know your uncle wants to take you into the desert with the falcons."

"I know. But he told me that if you and Baba have time alone, you might think about giving me another little brother. Or maybe a sister."

Oh, good heavens. Fire climbed Fern's cheeks as she realized what Tariq—what *Ra'id*—was implying. She looked to Zafir.

He was lounging on an elbow and drawled, "Your uncle said that?"

"He asked me if I wanted more siblings. I said I would so he said I should give you time to think about it and talk about it. If Baba doesn't mind, I'd especially like it if you gave me sister," he said to Fern. "We both would, wouldn't we, Ahmed?"

"Sadiq!" the toddler insisted.

"That's not how it works, Tariq!" Fern blurted.

"I know how it works," he said with a rascal's grin, hitching his brother higher on his back before walking out. "I'm just saying."

Fern clapped her hands over her cheeks as he left, staring into Zafir's laughing eyes. "We're not fooling anyone, are we?" she asked in an askance whisper.

"Apparently not." He hooked his arm behind his head and beckoned to her like the man he was: a sheikh wanting to lie with his Number One Wife, patting the mattress where he wanted her. "So zip the tent and unbutton your shirt. Let's finish making another oasis baby."

* * * * *

MILLS & BOON®

The Chatsfield Collection!

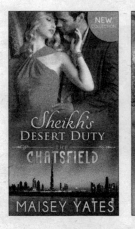

Style, spectacle, scandal...!

With the eight Chatsfield siblings happily married and settling down, it's time for a new generation of Chatsfields to shine, in this brand-new 8-book collection! The prospect of a merger with the Harrington family's boutique hotels will shape the future forever. But who will come out on top?

**Find out at
www.millsandboon.co.uk/TheChatsfield2**

CHATSFIELD_PROMO_BK

0215_INSHIP2

MILLS & BOON®

Seven Sexy Sins!

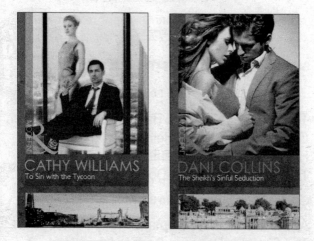

The true taste of temptation!

From greed to gluttony, lust to envy, these fabulous stories explore what seven sexy sins mean in the twenty-first century!

Whether pride goes before a fall, or wrath leads to a passion that consumes entirely, one thing is certain: the road to true love has never been more enticing.

**Collect all seven at
www.millsandboon.co.uk/SexySins**